THE DARK
WATER
GIRLS

BOOKS BY MAEGAN BEAUMONT

THE SABRINA VAUGHN SERIES

Waiting in Darkness

Carved in Darkness

The Muse

Promises to Keep

Blood of Saints

THE DARK WATER GIRLS

MAEGAN BEAUMONT

bookouture

Published by Bookouture in 2021

An imprint of Storyfire Ltd.
Carmelite House
50 Victoria Embankment
London EC4Y 0DZ

www.bookouture.com

ISBN: 978-1-80019-121-1
eBook ISBN: 978-1-80019-120-4

For Auntie Di.
I miss you.
Fly high.

PROLOGUE

GEORGIA

Angel Bay Island, Michigan

I got into Kalamazoo.

The letter came nearly two months ago, fat and large, the college's insignia—a bold, orange K—embossed in its upper left-hand corner.

Fat envelopes mean you got in.

Thin envelopes mean you didn't.

I have a drawer full of fat envelopes.

It isn't the only college I applied to. I've applied to nearly a dozen of them—some as far away as California—and so far, I'd gotten into every single one. Even though my GPA is more than decent, I know the real reason they're all saying yes.

I'm the Angel Bay Baby.

Abandoned at birth in the emergency department waiting room of the island's hospital, I'm somewhat of a local celebrity and I'm not above exploiting that celebrity to get what I want.

And what I want more than anything is to get off this island.

Every time a thick acceptance letter comes, I add it to the stack buried under a pile of socks in the top drawer of my dresser, unopened. It wasn't until I pulled the letter from the mailbox and saw Kalamazoo's insignia on the envelope that I understood what I was doing.

I've been waiting.

Because Kalamazoo is where Lincoln will be attending law school in the fall and whether I want to admit it or not, I've been holding my breath. Waiting to see if I got in because if I did, I'd take it as a sign that there's a chance for us to be together away from the prying, disapproving eyes of his parents and an island that always put me on a pedestal.

Because his parents are my foster parents.

Because they're the McNamaras—Angel Bay's answer to the Kennedys—and he's their golden boy. Has a role to fulfill. A life full of expectation to lead.

Because since I grew up belonging to no one, that somehow came to mean I belonged to everyone. I was everyone's baby.

Everyone's child.

But this is it.

A chance to show Lincoln I'm not a child. That I'm more than just the Angel Bay Baby, and he's more than the sum of everyone's expectations of him.

That's why I go looking for him, letter in hand, sneaking across the backyard, letting the gentle slope of it lead me toward the scraggly band of trees that stands sentry against the shoreline. Through their sparse branches, I catch glimpses of the dock and the boathouse Lincoln stays in when he's home from college. The lake dappled in moonlight.

He's home now.

School is over for the summer, and he's back.

I'm going to knock on his door. Show him my acceptance letter. Tell him how I feel about him. That I love him—have loved him since the moment I first saw him. I'm eighteen now and once I leave the island, there will be nothing left to stand in our way. No one to judge. To keep us apart.

We can be together.

When I hear the voices, I think it's the lake, warm and loose, lapping against the shore, but the closer I get, the easier it is to pull words from the low murmur of sound.

"... *what I'm going to do.*"

"*Shit, Jenna. Are you sure? I mean—*"

"*Are you serious? I'm* pregnant, *Linc. Of course I'm sure.*"

Pregnant.

The word stops my bare feet in their tracks.

Glues them to the ground and sucks the air from my lungs.

Pregnant.

Through the trees I can see Lincoln, standing on the dock, his broad, muscular chest bare. Dark brown hair disheveled, wearing nothing but the pair of flannel pajama pants his mother bought him for Christmas, like he'd been in bed only minutes before. "Okay." He nods at her tone, reaching up to swipe a hard, punishing hand across his mouth in a gesture I recognize well. "Okay... how long? I mean, how far along—"

"Far enough." Jenna wraps her arms around her middle like she's trying to hold herself together and shrugs. "Too far along for an abortion, if that's what you're asking."

Jenna.

Lincoln and Jenna.

Jenna, my foster sister.

Our foster sister.

She's barely sixteen,

And Lincoln turned twenty-two over Christmas break.

"I wasn't." Linc shakes his head, his forehead pinched together in a tight frown. "I mean that's not what I—" When Jenna starts to talk again, Linc holds up a hand and shakes his head at her before folding his arms over his chest. "Wait, okay? Just give me a second to—"

Suddenly Lincoln is looking at me through the trees, his gaze sharp and zeroed in on me.

As soon as he sees me, his face goes pale and his arms fall away from his body as if they've suddenly gone boneless.

And then he's moving.

Coming at me, his bare feet slapping against the dock so loudly the sound of them echoes across the water like gunshots.

I run.

Across the yard, dodging toys and bicycles, on my way back to the house.

"Georgia... Goddamnit, Georgia, wait."

I don't wait, and I'm not careful when I enter the house. I'm not sneaking. Not quiet. Not anymore. I fly up the stairs, not caring who hears me. If I wake Lincoln's parents. If I wake the whole damn house.

I can hear him behind me, his breath falling harsh and heavy against my ears.

Pregnant.

Jenna is pregnant.

There's only one reason she would sneak out to the boathouse in the middle of the night to tell Lincoln something like that.

Because he's the father.

The realization tears through me, the tilt and pitch of it making me so sick I almost gag on it as I push my way into my bedroom.

Away.

I have to get away.

Linc is only a few steps behind me now, no longer calling my name because, unlike me, he's being careful not to wake his parents. Doesn't want them to know what's happening. That he left a clandestine meeting with one of their foster girls to chase another across the yard and into the house for spying on him.

Leaving the door open so I can use the hall light as my guide, I drop the crumpled envelope in my hand onto the bed and fall to my knees at the foot of it to root around in the darkness underneath. My fingers brush against the thing I'm looking for, and I pull it out just as his shadow falls, black and heavy across my back.

Undaunted, and unwilling to look at him, I pull myself off my knees to drop the dusty, hand-sewn duffle bag on the bed. It's old and worn, given to me by his mother at a Christmas party when I was seven, along with a promise—*When you're old enough, you'll come to live here with us. Wouldn't that be wonderful, Georgia? Would you like that?*

For an Angel Bay foster kid, being selected to live with the McNamaras is like winning the lottery. They all want it. All secretly hope they'll be chosen to live in their big, fancy house on the water. Be plucked from their ordinary foster homes and given a chance at something more. Girls who are fostered by the McNamaras go to college. They get good jobs and live nice lives. They aren't throwaways anymore. They are chosen.

Richard and Alice don't foster because they need the extra money to make ends meet—they're one of the wealthiest families on the island. The McNamaras foster because they're good people.

When I was thirteen, they chose me. Opened their house to me.

Gave me a home.

A chance.

Choking back a sob, I drop the old, faded duffle on the mattress in front of me and turn toward my dresser and the doorway next to it.

Linc is still there, chest heaving like he's just run a marathon. Still watching me from the threshold like he's afraid of what he might do to me if he let himself cross it. "Georgia." He says my name carefully, like I'm a wild animal, far beyond reasoning with. "Let me explain."

"*Explain...*" The word leaves my mouth on a scoff. "Despite what you might think, I'm not a child, Linc." I say it loud enough to make him wince. Yanking open my top drawer, I scoop up a handful of socks and underwear. Under them is the scatter of fat envelopes I've collected from colleges over the last several months. Leaving them where they are, I turn away from him to dump them into my duffle. "I don't need you to *explain* anything to me."

"It's not what you think," he says as I turn toward him again. Yanking open drawer number two, I grab at my meager collection of T-shirts and toss them on top of my socks.

"So, you *didn't* get Jenna pregnant?" Turning toward him, I stop moving long enough to nail him with a hard look, my guts going cold and stiff when he winces again, this time when I say the word *pregnant*. He tosses a quick look over his shoulder, into the hallway behind him, looking for anyone who might've heard me. Like a disease, his caution catches hold. Forces me to look at the bed across the room from mine. I expect to find Rachel, my roommate, sitting up in bed, awake, and watching the drama unfold in front of her with rapt attention. Rachel is younger—only fourteen—nosy and not at all sorry about it. Where anyone else would feign sleep and listen quietly, she'd stare at us, wide eyes ping-ponging back and forth like she's front and center at a tennis match. Thinking about her, I feel a momentary pang of guilt. She'll wonder where I'm going. Why I'm leaving. Ask me to take her with me.

Instead of my roommate, when I look across the room, mouth open to deliver a hushed, *It's okay, Rach—go back to sleep*, I find an empty bed.

Rachel is gone.

Before the realization can register, Lincoln speaks.

"It's not like that, Georgia," he says, his tone thick with desperation. "Please... please just wait a min—"

Turning away from my roommate's empty bed, I glare at him, arms clenched and shaking around the few pairs of jeans I've taken from my dresser. "Then what's it like?" I demand, breath hitched on a sob when his mouth snaps shut in response. "Tell me, Lincoln," I say, my tone softening slightly. "Tell me—*please*—just tell me." I'm giving him permission to lie to me. The power to stop me. Asking him to, because whatever he says next, I'll believe.

He doesn't lie to me.

He doesn't tell me the truth.

Doesn't ask me to stay.

He just stares at me, his face pale and sick. Mouth screwed shut against whatever it is he wants to say to me, like he's already said too much.

Away.

I need to get away from here.
From him.

Turning, I jam the load of jeans in my arms into the full mouth of my duffle, packing it so tight I can feel its home-sewn stitching give a little at its seams. Not bothering with the zipper, I heft it to my shoulder and take the short trip to my nightstand to retrieve my phone. Shoving it into my back pocket, I turn toward the doorway again, my plan simple. I'll leave. Call Evie. Ask her to come get me. She will—Evie is my best friend. She'd do anything for me.

That's as far as my plan goes.

Even though my intentions are plain, Lincoln doesn't move out of the doorway. In fact, he seems to grow even larger, blocking my retreat.

Crossing the room, duffle still slung onto my shoulder, I stop in front of him, so close I can feel the brush of his chest against mine with every breath. "If you don't get out of my way, I'm going to start screaming. Your parents will come, and then I'll tell them what I saw. What I heard." Saying it makes me feel sick, but I press forward, determined to get my way. To get away from him. "Now, get out of my way."

For a second, he just glares at me, his gaze sharp and narrowed on my face, just as determined and stubborn as I am. Like he isn't going to move. Like he's willing to call my bluff, risk everything if it means keeping me from leaving.

But then he moves, slowly shifting his large frame away from the doorway to give me room to pass—his need to please his parents and keep them in the dark about who he really is winning out over everything else.

Just like I knew it would.

ONE

I've made a lot of difficult decisions in my life.

When to attack.

When to retreat.

When to relax and let nature take its course.

When to force a confrontation.

Thousands of them—not a small percentage of them holding my life and the life of others in the balance. People I cared about. People I was responsible for. People who needed me to be absolutely sure that the choice I was making was the right one.

I'm no stranger to pressure, but for some reason, this is by far the hardest decision I've ever made. At least the most difficult since I returned to Angel Bay in the first place.

"I like the blue one."

I turn my phone away from the mind-numbing array of paint sample cards on display and aim it at my face. "They're *all* blue, Evie, to varying degrees," I tell her with an eye roll. "So, I can't decide if you're actually trying to be helpful or if you're just being an asshole."

"Well, if you can't tell, I'm certainly not going to enlighten you," Evie says before throwing her head back with a loud, booming laugh that sends her dark corkscrew curls bouncing wildly around her face.

"Never mind. No need to tell me. I already know you're an—" A notification flashes across the screen, momentarily blocking out my best friend's face. A text.

Since I'm FaceTiming with Evie, there's only one other person who would be texting me. "Hold on, Eve. I think—"

"Can't," Evie says, giving me a dramatic sigh before standing up to reveal a pair of dark blue scrubs under her crisp doctor's coat, and the hospital cafeteria behind her. "Break's over—gotta go save some lives." She flashes a bright smile full of white, evenly spaced teeth at the camera—a gift in the form of braces from a particularly decent set of childhood foster parents. "Tell Deputy Dawg I said *hey.*"

Alex isn't a deputy. He's Fell County Sheriff, but before I can point that out, Evie disconnects our FaceTime session on a promise to call after her shift.

Sighing, I use my thumb to navigate my way to my text messages.

The text isn't from Alex. It's from a number I don't recognize. Frowning, I tap the notification.

I'd like to order a pizza.

It's a code.

Old code I established with some of my foster siblings when we were kids. As a foster, you move around a lot. You piss off a placement, or they suddenly decide they don't have room for you or that you're more trouble than you're worth, they call your case manager and you get bounced to the next placement. Or, in my case, you get tired of where you are and want to move on. That happened a lot. Before the McNamaras, I never wanted to be where I was. Never wanted to let people get too close, and because of who I was, I had the luxury of being able to pick up and leave whenever I wanted to because people wanted me. Wanted to be the ones to take care of the Angel Bay Baby. I was a weird status symbol in the island's fostering community. People pursued their certification just so they could have a shot at fostering me. Some would even keep their license open, refusing to take any other kids, just for the chance. They'd harbor this fantasy of being my forever family. While other fosters in the house were practically stacked on top of each other, given chores and sometimes mistreated, I almost always had my own room. Was never asked to so much as set the table or run the vacuum. Treated with kid gloves. Catered to.

I hated it.

So, I moved around a lot. Seventeen placements in fourteen years. When I was twelve, I received my first cell phone—a gift from my case manager, almost certainly given to me because of who I was, along with a promise to come and get me whenever I wanted. I used that promise plenty, but every time I left, I gave my foster siblings my number and told them the same thing: *If you need me, text me. If you're too scared to tell me what's going on, say you want to order a pizza, and I'll know you're in trouble. That's all you have to do, and I'll be there—I promise.*

The spike of adrenaline I felt only moments before breaks loose and becomes a flood, sending my heart pinballing around my chest in an instant. Fingers trembling under the adrenaline dump, I tap out a quick answer.

Where should I deliver it?

The answer comes almost immediately.

Devil's Den.

Devil's Den is an old, broken-down bar on the easternmost tip of the island that still holds a valid liquor license despite the fact it should've been condemned years ago. It's like everyone refuses to admit such an establishment would have the nerve to exist on an island like Angel Bay. It's also the unofficial clubhouse of the island's resident motorcycle club, the Disciples. That might have something to do with the island's collective blindness.

Name on the order?

The intercom overhead comes on, the loud, booming voice of the store manager announcing that *The time is now 8:50 and your Houghton HomeMart is closing in ten minutes—please make your final selections and bring them to the nearest register for purchase.*

Paint swatches forgotten, I stare at the phone squeezed tight in my grip while I scroll through the long, mental list of foster siblings I've given this number to since I've been back on the island.

Jimmy
Lilah
Andre
Rachel
Archie
Cam—

It's Jenna

Shit.
Holy shit.
Jenna.
Lincoln's Jenna.
Frowning at the screen, I feel an uncharacteristic wave of pettiness wash over me. Thumbs moving swiftly, I pound out a text.

Why are you calling me for help? Call your—

But before I can finish, another text comes through.

I'm in trouble, Georgie. Please hurry. You promised.

Shit.

The overhead lights start to snap off, a rolling wave of darkness rushing toward me from the back of the building, a visual signal designed to herd stragglers like me toward the front of the store.

"Your Houghton HomeMart will be closing in five minutes..."

Shit.

She's right. I promised.

Stay where you are. I'm on my way.

TWO

Coming over the bridge, I have the same thought I had when I made the move back home eight months ago—nothing about Angel Bay has changed. Same wide, tree-lined streets. Same postcard-perfect gas lamps illuminating businesses—antique shops and artisan bakeries; custom-made dress boutiques and art galleries—that have rolled up their awnings and gone to sleep for the night. You want a Walmart or a Starbucks, you'll have to cross the bridge to Houghton or take the ferry to Marquette, because you won't find them on Angel Bay.

Angel Bay is about community.

Small-town values you won't find anywhere else.

It says so, right in our travel brochure.

People come over the bridge from the mainland year-round, but in the summertime, they come in droves, seeking out our warm, white sandy beaches and the boardwalk lined with lakeside restaurants and clubs. The bridge is jam-packed and it's slow going, the crush of tourists turning a twenty-minute drive into a forty-five-minute crawl that has me gripping the steering wheel so tight I can feel the flex of my arms threaten to tear it out of its column.

I'm in trouble, Georgie.

Please.

You promised.

It was like this the night I left. Traffic busted down to a lethargic limp, sunburned tourists and party-hungry college kids looking for trouble, heading back across the bridge. I sat ramrod straight in the passenger seat of the car Evie liberated from her foster mom's garage, staring out the window. Dry-eyed and stiff, even though I could feel myself cracking and breaking apart with every breath I took.

Like I knew she would, Evie came for me that night.

Come get me. That's all I said to her. *Come get me* and there she was, rolling her stolen car to a stop at the foot of the McNamara's long, winding driveway, twenty minutes later. As soon as I climbed in and shut the door, she said, "Where we going?"

When I told her, she didn't argue. Didn't try to talk me out of it. Didn't tell me I was making a mistake. She just sighed and said, "Are you sure?"

"I'm sure," I told her, giving her a stiff nod before aiming my gaze out the window as she pulled away from the curb. The last thing I saw was Lincoln, standing on the front porch of his parent's house, arms crossed over his chest as he watched me drive away.

I spent the entire car ride over the bridge and onto the mainland telling myself I was glad—happy even. Happy that I was finally free of this island. Relieved that I saw Lincoln for who he really before I dug myself any deeper into him than I already had. That I was lucky. That I was getting away from him, from this place. And I swore I'd never come back.

Not ever.

Fast forward ten years, and here I am.

Back where I started.

I still can't figure out how it happened. How I ended up back here. *Why* I came back. Maybe it was Evie, the fact that she found her way home after med school and landed a job at Fell County General as its chief resident, that pulled me back. Maybe it was the house that was left to me by Elizabeth Fell, the great-great-granddaughter of Linus Fell, the island's founder. When her lawyer knocked on the door of my tiny studio apartment in Chicago, I was working freelance for a private security firm and pretty much hating every minute of it. He handed me an envelope with my name scrawled across its front in thin, spidery cursive. Inside was a note written in the same Victorian scrawl that simply said:

Georgia ∼

If you're reading this, that means I'm dead. I left you everything. All of it—from the house I died in and my seat on the island council, to that damnable rock floating in the middle of the lake. I know you're not a real Fell but real or not, you carry the name and there's no one else, so I guess that means you'll have to do.

Elizabeth

It's been almost a year now, and I decide at least once a day to sign it all over to Evie and bail. I'd do it too, if not for the fact that when she named me her sole heir, Elizabeth Fell pulled a fast one on me. The only way I'm getting off this island is if I have a kid and sign everything over to them. Or if I die.

Topping the crest of the bridge, I catch sight of what's been holding up traffic and feel myself tense in my seat. One of Fell County Sheriff's Office's infamous sobriety checkpoints, waiting for me at the foot of the bridge. Even though I'm as sober as a judge and have no reason to worry, I have to force myself to relax as the tall, uniformed figure manning the mouth of the checkpoint waves me forward with an impatient flick of his flashlight. Letting my truck coast down the slope, I push my brakes and cringe at their answering grind.

By some miracle, I manage to make an actual stop in front of the scowling deputy. Shifting into neutral without being asked, I press the brake and turn the hand crank on my window and aim a smile in his direction. "Hey, Archie." Squinting against the high-beam flashlight he has stuck in my face, I try to act like I'm not in a hurry. "How's fishing?"

"Hey, George," he says, dropping the flashlight with an answering grin that's wavering somewhere between indulgent and exasperated. "It's slow-going for a Friday night. When the hell you gonna get those brakes fixed?"

"Soon," I say, feeding him a bald-faced lie. "I've got an appointment lined up for Monday."

"Yeah? That's what you told me last week," he reminds me with a shake of his head, while he flicks his flashlight toward my dashboard to check out my odometer. "Looks like you're overdue for an oil change too."

"Aren't you supposed to be gently abusing my constitutional rights, or something? Asking me where I'm coming from? Where I'm going?" I don't have time for this. "Maybe make me get out and do some back handsprings on the side of the road, *Officer Hudson?*"

"*Alriiight.*" He draws the word out on a laugh, totally nonplussed by my sudden surge of surliness. "Where you been tonight, *Ms. Fell?*"

"HomeMart." Reaching down, I pluck my latest stack of pilfered paint samples off the bench seat next to me and flash them in his face as proof.

"Jesus, George—you *still* haven't picked a color yet?" He shakes his head and gives me another flick of his flashlight when I open my mouth to undoubtedly say something that would earn someone who *wasn't* his foster sister a trip to the drunk tank, sober or not. "Where you headed?" he asks, following the line of routine questioning he's supposed to subject everyone to.

Devil's Den.

Jenna texted me.

She's in trouble, and you're wasting my time.

"Home." The second lie comes easier than the first, and I look him right in the eye when I tell it without a whisper of guilt. "And I'd appreciate it if we could skip the handsprings—I'm in a hurry."

"No need to hurry. Sheriff Bradford's gonna be a while." Like always, when he mentions Alex or alludes to the fact that I'm involved with his boss, a faint flush creeps up his neck to disappear into his carefully clipped hairline. "Some eastern kid stole Ted Nelson's boat and took it out to the Rock." *The Rock* is short for Devil's Rock—a few acres' worth of rugged woods floating about a quarter mile off the main island's northern coast—or as Elizabeth Fell liked to call it, *that damnable rock.* If Angel Bay is the palm of a hand, then Devil's Rock is its middle finger, flipping me the bird every time I look out my kitchen window. "Dummy ran it up on one of the outcrops. Tore the bottom of it up pretty bad—Sheriff went out with Tandy and Levi to tow it in before it sinks."

"Eastern kid?" I turn away from Archie to toss my paint samples back down on the seat next to me. *Eastern kid* is what they call the kids who live on the east side of the island. The undesirables. The have-nots. "Seriously, Arch? Nelson's blaming it on an *eastern kid?* And you're buying that?"

Archie has the good grace to flush beet-red when I say it. "They cause trouble on the island, George—you know that. You're on the council. And besides, the Rock belongs to you," he reminds me, giving me a bug-eyed look that tells me just how unreasonable he thinks I'm being. "Don't you care—"

"I *know* that Ted Nelson's son is a spoiled, entitled prick and that Big Ted isn't much better," I tell him, palming my gear shift before shoving the clutch in to slam the transmission into first. "I'd bet my boots that *junior* is the one who wrecked his boat, and if there *is* an eastern kid involved, he was brought along in case they needed a scapegoat."

"Actually, it's not a *he,*" Archie informs me, giving me a scowl that says he's disappointed in me for being so shortsighted that I'd automatically assume the island's latest troublemaker is a male. "It's a she—Julie Kates."

"*Julie Kates?*" I say the name and return his scowl with one of my own while I shake my head. "Jesus, Arch—please tell me you're not really buying that load of bullshit."

"She confessed, George." Archie gives me a helpless shrug, coupled with a quick look flicked over his shoulder at the long line of cars behind me, all waiting their turn to be harassed by the local law—the price of admission if you want to party at one of our beachside clubs or just want to get home after a long day of work. When he turns to look at me again, his expression is flat and unreadable. "What do you want me to do about it? I'm not even there."

Confession or not, I don't buy it. Not for a second. All I know about Julie Kates is that she's one of the island's fosters—Rachel Alcott, my last roommate at the McNamaras', is her case manager —and she works at the shaved ice stand on the boardwalk. But I know enough about this island and the way it works to know she's innocent. "I want you to tell me you know it's bullshit, that's what I want." When all he does is continue to give me that flat-eyed glare, I lean toward him out the window and give him a glare of my own. "We were *eastern kids*, Archie. You remember that, don't you?"

When I say it, Archie's face slams shut. He's not my foster brother anymore. He's not the kid who used to trail after me, from placement to placement. The kid I taught to fold paper airplanes. Where and how to mark his shoes, so they didn't get stolen. The kid who told everyone I was his big sister *for real* and stubbornly clung to the notion even though everyone knew it was a lie and teased him mercilessly for it. In a flash, the Archie that used to follow me around is gone, and a stranger is left staring at me in his place. "No," he tells me, closing the bit of distance between us to narrow his sharp blue eyes on my face. "I *don't* remember that because you were *never* an eastern kid, Georgia—not really. You were a *Fell*, and then you were a McNamara, and then you were *gone*."

When I came back home eight months ago, the whole island went nuts. The local paper snapped pictures of me coming out of the lawyer's office and splashed them across their front page under the headline—

Fell Fortune Left to Angel Bay Baby

The McNamaras sent flowers to my hotel room with a note-card that read:

You'll always be one of our girls, Georgia.
    Come by the house for dinner sometime.

You're always welcome ~

Richard & Alice

The Fell County sheriff, Alex Bradford, showed up, hat in hand, with the offer to take me on a tour of the island *to help get me reacquainted.* A tour that turned into a dinner date. A dinner date that turned into the longest, most committed relationship of my life.

Despite the red-carpet treatment, I knew not everyone was happy to see me. That a lot of people I left behind had seen my leaving the island as desertion. That I abandoned them. A few days after my arrival, when Archie knocked on my hotel room door with a six-pack, that thousand-watt grin of his, and a *Heya, George,* I was so grateful I had to fight back tears because I thought it meant he forgave me for leaving him behind.

Looking at him now, I know I was wrong.

"At least tell me someone called Rachel and let her know what's going on," I say, because I don't know what else *to* say. It doesn't matter that it's a Friday night or that she's not on call, Rachel will want to know what's happening.

"You heard the part where I'm not there, right?" he shoots back defensively. "I don't have anything to do with it, George—but I'm sure the officers involved have a handle on the situation."

"Arch—" I say his name, unsure of what I'm going to follow it up with, but the second I open my mouth, a cacophony of engines fill the air, so close and loud the roar of them drowns out the sound of my voice. Brewing argument forgotten, I turn in my seat to watch a long line of motorcycles rip up the center of the street in front of me, single file, headed straight for us. At the last minute, they shift in unison, whipping onto the shoulder to circumvent the minivan full of wide-eyed tourists Archie's partner has stopped on the other side of the road, to breach the empty bridge that leads to the mainland. Each one of them is wearing a black leather vest with a white inverted cross stitched onto its back, a pair of black angel wings behind it, spread wide across their shoulders.

Disciples.

I count twenty of them.

That means there are roughly ten of them still squatting at their clubhouse.

That's where Jenna is.

I'm in trouble, Georgie.

Please.

As soon as they're gone, Archie turns away from the street behind him and aims his flashlight down the deserted road in front of me. "You're free to go." He says it like I'm a total stranger. "Go on home now—I'll tell Sheriff Bradford you'll be waiting for him when he's finished hauling in the Nelsons' boat."

THREE

I call Rachel and get her voicemail.

"Hey," I say into the phone while I cruise through a yellow, heading down the boulevard. "It's Georgia—I'm not sure if anyone called you yet but they've arrested Julie Kates for boat theft. I'm sure it's bogus but you might want to get down to the station and see what you can do about getting her out. Call me and let me know if I can do anything to help." Hanging up, I toss my phone onto the bench seat beside me and concentrate on the drive.

Even though the episode with Archie on the bridge took all of five minutes, I still feel like I'm late; like I let Jenna down somehow by allowing myself to get drawn into a heated debate about the island's unspoken class system instead of hurrying here like she asked me to.

Weighing the pros and cons of doing what I'm about to do without backup, I make a soft right and rumble across the cattle guard standing sentry over the ditch running parallel to the road.

The Devil's Den is on the back side of the island, perched on its easternmost tip. It sits ten yards from the shoreline, in the middle of what locals call the Wild—over a hundred acres of rough terrain and dense forest, too rocky and untamed to be developed. That's where the Den is—slump block and rusted tin roof, with

none of the usual flashing neon or roadside signs, beckoning potential patrons.

This is a place that doesn't welcome outsiders. Doesn't want to
be noticed. Squatting behind a thick line of trees in the tall marsh
grass, it knows it doesn't belong. Knows no one wants it here. But
it's too mean and stubborn to take the hint and leave.

Right now, I know exactly how it feels.

Pulling off the dirt road, I back the tail of my truck into a spot
and kill the engine. Sitting in the cab for a few seconds, I bounce
my gaze around the patchy gravel lot, cataloging potential threats—
there aren't many of them, but what I see carries weight.

The Disciples are a new addition to the island. They're what's
called a support club for the Red Reapers, a large motorcycle club
based in Detroit. By nature, support clubs are small. Vicious.
Designed for the sole purpose of carrying out the larger club's
dirtier bits of business. Hearing Archie tell it, they just showed up
one day, like a black, ugly cancer no one on the island is brave
enough to cut out. Alex and I don't fight often, but when we do, it's
about the Disciples and the seemingly free rein they have on the
island.

*"What do you want me to do, George? They're property owners,
which makes them island residents, and they haven't broken any
laws in Fell County—not that I can prove. Until they do, my hands
are tied."*

Counting eight motorcycles, I scan the rest of the lot. There's a
tight cluster of club members, all wearing the same kind of vest as
the bikers that busted through Archie's checkpoint on the other
side of the island. They're loitering to the left of the entrance,
surrounded by a cloud of thick, cloying smoke while they pass
what looks like a joint around in a haphazard circle. I count six of
them. They've noticed me, and even though they're casual about it,
they're clocking every move I make. There's an M9 pistol in my
glovebox. Another under my seat. A pump-action Benelli behind
it. Probably overkill, but where I've been, the inside of a vehicle is

considered a kill box. It's where you're preoccupied. At your most vulnerable. Especially when you're alone.

And I'm almost always alone.

Quit it, Georgia. It's Angel Bay for Christ's sake—not Fallujah. No guns.

Going into this thing armed would be the wrong move.

Better to play the part of the Angel Bay Baby. Prodigal daughter. Island celebrity. Being who I am gives me a certain amount of latitude—allows me to move unfettered from one side of the island to the other because no one knows where I came from. The surname *Fell* was added to my birth certificate because the nurse filling it out made an error. Meant to write "Fell" in the space for the county I was born in, not in the space asking for my name. From what I've been told, she was promptly fired for her mistake, but the damage was already done. I was a Fell, registered with the state of Michigan as such, and there wasn't anything anyone could do about it.

Pushing myself to make the first move, I open the door and drop my boots on the gravel and slam my truck door closed, checking to make sure it's locked before I force myself across the lot. I might regret it later—an unlocked truck makes for a faster getaway, but with the small arsenal I keep inside it, locking it is the only option.

"That you, Georgie Fell?" A voice comes at me from the loose cluster of bikers, and I use the sound of it to zero in on its source. Will Hudson, Archie's older brother, slouched against the wall near the entrance of the roadhouse. He's wearing a vest that designates him as a Disciple. When we make eye contact, he brings the joint to his pursed lips and takes a deep drag of it, his blue gaze narrowed on my face so sharp it reminds me of his brother. That's where the similarities end. While Archie has somehow managed to hang on to the open, almost boyish quality he's had since we were kids, Will is every bit the hardened criminal. His harshly angled face is framed by a mop of dark, unwashed hair. Tattoos crawl up his arms and across his neck. He did his first stint in juvie at eleven for stealing shoes from a mainland Payless. After that, Will and Archie were split up. Archie aged out of foster care here on the island while Will ended up across the bridge, bouncing from group home to juvie and back again, never quite able to hold it together long enough to get back to his little brother. I've never said it to him out loud, but losing Will saved Archie's life.

"Sure is." I answer him with a smile, forcing myself to stay loose. Keep my tone casual. "I'm looking for Jenna—you seen her?"

"Jenna..." Will takes another drag of the joint and shakes his head while he passes it off to one of his brothers. "Jenna who?" he asks on a hard expel of breath that pushes the smoke in my direction.

He knows exactly who Jenna is, but I answer him anyway because the name of the game is *Get Jenna and get out*, and I can't do that if I start a fight before I even find her. "Jenna Harri—" I catch myself. "McNamara. I'm looking for Jenna McNamara—she around?"

Reaching for the joint out of turn, Will begins to lift it to his lips again before stopping himself. "I apologize, where are my manners?" he says, holding the half-smoked joint out to me. "You want in on this?" When all I give him is a slight shake of my head, he laughs. "Come on, Georgie—live a little. You ain't a cop no more."

I was never a cop. I was with the Military Police Corps of the United States Army, and then I was a warrant officer with their criminal investigation division. There's a difference, but not one I have the time or emotional bandwidth to explain to Will Hudson. "Jenna." I look away from him and lock eyes with one of Will's companions, a twitchy little guy with an unfortunate two-toned mullet. "She inside?"

"Yeah." He gives me a quick head bob and actively avoids Will's glare. "But you can't go in—you ain't a member, and you ain't no one's old lady."

"He's right, Georgie, you ain't no one's old lady... but I can fix it for you if you want." Will again, the corner of his mouth kicked up in a lascivious grin while he drags his gaze over my frame, letting it linger a little too long on my breasts before finally making his way to my face. "Fix it for you real quick."

"*Real quick?*" I flash him a lopsided grin of my own while I reach for the door. "Yeah—I heard that about you," I say, earning myself a round of rough, howling laughter at Will's expense. They're so busy laughing they don't even try to stop me when I pull the door open and step through it. Not slowing or stopping to get my bearings, I push my way across the crowded room, letting my gaze trail the length of the bar.

I'd grossly underestimated how many bikers I'd have to contend with. Ten—I could handle ten if I needed to, but there are at least twice as many crammed into this place. Not all Disciples either. I count at least a dozen Reapers, close enough to touch. I think about the M9s I left in my truck and wish I hadn't talked myself out of bringing one with me.

Getting Jenna out of here isn't going to be easy.

I get looks. Nasty, territorial glares from the women; sly, appraising side-eye from the men. Some of them recognize me. Some are too drunk or high to recognize their own mothers. I'm a woman, so by default I don't pose a physical threat, but they know I don't belong. I'm wearing cargo pants and a drab olive T-shirt—a holdover from my military days—tucked into the waistband. My long, naturally pale blonde hair is pulled back in a tidy bun at the nape of my neck. Nearly eighteen months out and I still scream *army*. Usually, I don't think about it. Right now, I stick out like a sore thumb.

Turning slowly, I find Jenna squeezed into a booth, wedged between a pair of men who're flanked by a couple of scantily clad women wearing too much makeup. When they catch sight of me approaching, they sit up a little straighter. Scoot into the booth a little tighter. Either to claim their territory or to provide an extra layer of protection to the men next to them. Probably both.

"Georgia?" When she sees me, Jenna does her best to raise herself from her slump and pushes her limp, loosely coiled hair out of her flat, toffee-colored eyes. She's wasted. "Whaddya doing here?" she says, slurring slightly. "How'd you even get in here?" She sounds slightly alarmed, like she's been caught doing something she shouldn't.

"On these two legs," I say, giving her a flat smile. "Can I talk to you outside for a second?" I don't want to announce to everyone that she called me here. Asked me to help her. "It's about Savanna."

When I say her daughter's name, Jenna's face hardens. Her flat gaze goes flinty. Probably because Savanna isn't just Jenna's daughter. She's Lincoln's daughter too, and Lincoln is the elephant in the room neither of us wants to tackle. "What about her?" she hisses it at me, sitting back into the booth to wedge herself under the arm one of her companions has draped across its back.

"Outside." I look away from her, aiming my request at one of the men she's cozied up to. He's a Reaper, has to be because I don't recognize him from around the island. Shoulders as wide as a tank. Long black hair. A face that would be categorized as handsome if not for the deep-pitted acne scars scattered across its surface like buckshot. There is a row of patches on the left side of his vest, over his heart. The first one says PRESIDENT. The one below it says DETROIT. The one below it says KING. This isn't some two-bit lowlife Jenna is snuggled up with. This is the guy who only has to snap his fingers to get shit done. "I just need a few minutes, and then I'll go," I promise him, leaving out the part where I plan on taking Jenna with me.

The tank-sized Reaper gives me an appraising look. Not like he's sizing me up for sex but like he knows exactly who I am and what I'm capable of. Like maybe the thought of squaring off with me excites him a little. It reminds me that no one knows I'm here.

No one that'd help me, anyway.

I can feel the room behind me go still. Feel the hair on the back of my neck start to prickle. If this guy pushes a confrontation, I'm going to be in serious trouble. All I can do is hold my breath and wait.

Lifting his hand off the back of the cracked leather booth, he dips it to run a rough, calloused fingertip along the slope of Jenna's bare shoulder. "You're Georgia Fell."

"I am." It isn't a question, but I nod in answer anyway. "Five minutes," I lie to him. "Five minutes and I'm gone."

He stares at me for a few seconds, still sizing me up. Just when I think he's going to tell me to get lost, or maybe snap his fingers and set his lackeys on me like a pack of jackals, he smiles and lifts his hand off Jenna's shoulder. "Sure thing, Ms. Fell," he says with a smile, giving his head a slight tilt that sends the people wedged into the booth with him scattering like roaches. "Bring us a round on your way back, baby," he says to Jenna as she scoots across the seat to stand on wobbling legs beside me.

Giving the table a brief, polite smile over my shoulder, I wrap a loose, guiding hand around Jenna's upper arm and start to pull her away. Spotting a door at the back of the room, I push Jenna toward it, ahead of me, using her to break the crowd so I can weave a quick escape route in its direction. Hand still clamped around her upper arm, I pull Jenna outside and nearly trip over the long row of motorcycles parked just beyond our exit. These don't belong to Disciples. These belong to Reapers.

Seeing them accounts for why there were only a handful of bikes parked in front—they're all back here, out of sight. Letting my cop brain file that away for later, I keep walking. "Okay, you'll have to wait here. Will Hudson is posted up at the front entrance so, I'll have to—"

"What the *hell*, Georgia?" Jenna shouts at me, a split second before she rips her arm from my grip. "What's this about? And don't give me that *it's about Savanna* crap because you don't know shit about my daughter."

Her tone—confusion, laced with anger and resentment—stops me in my tracks. "Excuse me?" I say, turning to stare down at her. At five six, I'm not tall by anyone's standards, but Jenna is tiny—the top of her head barely grazes my nose. "You texted *me*, remember?"

"Texted you?" She laughs. "What are you talking about? Why the hell would I do that?"

"You—" Suddenly unsure of what I'm saying, I shake my head. "You texted me. You said you were in trouble. Asked me to come help you."

She scoffs, hip cocked. Like the rest of the women here, she's dressed in a pair of tight ripped jeans and a tank top cut low enough to put her ample breasts on full display. "No, I didn't."

She's an excellent liar, always has been. Standing here, looking at her, I have no idea if she's telling me the truth or not. "Well, *someone* texted me," I bite back at her, reaching into my back pocket to fish out my phone. Shoving it in her face, I show her the texts. "Someone who knew you were here. Someone who knew the code I set up when—"

She doesn't let me finish. "Well, that *someone* wasn't me," she hisses at me, slapping my hand and the phone in it out of her face. "Do I *look* like I need help?"

"Yes." I jam my cell back into my pocket and glare at her. "Yes, you do."

Her face goes pale, what little color left in it leaching out in an instant. "If I did need help, why the hell would I call you?" She closes the space between us, her flat gaze suddenly snapping fire at me. "*I wouldn't.* I wouldn't call you." She drops her glare and drags it up my frame, her lipstick-smeared mouth curling in a snarl. "Perfect little George—*Saint Georgia*—too good for what the rest of us got." Her glare, full of hatred, finally settles on my face. "If I were in trouble, I'd call Lincoln—*my husband.*"

And, just like that, the elephant in the room is charging at me.

"You think I didn't know?" Smelling blood in the water, Jenna keeps jabbing. "He told me all about your little crush. How pathetic he thought you were. We still laugh about it."

"Okay." Taking a step back, I put space between us, my hands raised in surrender. "My mistake," I say, quietly. "I'll leave you alone." Turning away from her, I aim myself toward the side of the building, intent on getting back to my truck as quickly as possible.

"You leave my daughter alone, too, while you're at it," she screams at my retreating back. "You hear me, Georgia Fell—*she's mine*. You stay away from my husband, and you stay *away from my kid*."

It's dark, most likely by design, but I push myself forward anyway. Jenna's still screaming, but I don't stop. Don't try to reason with her. Don't tell her I've never even met Savanna, and I haven't had the guts to put eyes on Lincoln, let alone talk to him, since the night he caught me spying on them down by the lake.

Vision blurry, heart hammering in my chest, I use the gentle lap of the lake against the Den's dock as a guide, the ground soft and spongy under my feet. Rounding the corner, I weave a path through hip-deep grass, along the exterior wall of the roadhouse, gaze aimed straight ahead. Just as Jenna goes quiet and I hear the back door slam closed again, signaling her return inside, I spot my truck parked about fifty yards away.

Thank God.

I'll go home, take a long hot shower and—

The toe of my boot snags on something hidden by the tall grass I'm wading through and I'm suddenly face down in it and sucking wind. Turning onto my side, I wince as I struggle to sit up. Finally managing to get a shaky arm underneath me, I turn to search the ground for the reason I'm face down in the dirt.

An arm, slim and pale, framed by a thick fringe of dark green grass, flung out and still, its palm turned toward the sky, fingers slightly curled, their hot-pink nails chipped and caked black with dirt.

A woman.

"Oh my God..." I hear myself breathe the words, feel the twinge of them in my chest as I scramble to my knees and crawl back the way I'd come to lean over her. To help her because maybe I'm wrong. Maybe she's not dead. Maybe she's just drunk or doped up and needs help—someone to call an ambulance or—

Gripping her shoulder, I try to ignore how cold it is as I roll her toward me. "Oh my God." I say it again, only this time, it doesn't come with a twinge. It comes with the force of a wrecking ball that slams into my chest and sends me reeling.

Because it's Rachel.

Miniskirt rucked up around her hips and her panties jerked down.

"Jesus, *Rachel*?" I say her name, my fingers gripping around her cold shoulder to give it a rough shake, even though I know. Can see it in her vacant, half-mast stare and the deep, ugly bruises that ring her thin, pale neck.

Giving myself a mental kick in the teeth, I force myself to let go of her. To remember my training. That I'm compromising evidence in what will become a murder investigation. Unwilling to touch her neck, I reach for the hand I tripped on and press two of my fingers against the inside of her wrist, feeling for a pulse.

Nothing.

She's dead.

FOUR

LINCOLN

My phone rings for the fourth time in nearly as many minutes. Even though it's on silent and on its charger in the kitchen, I can hear it, rattling and buzzing its way across the kitchen counter.

Determined to ignore it, I up the volume on the TV to mask the sound of it and press my shoulders into the couch. Jenna knows the rules. She knows Friday nights are for Savanna. That I close the shop early on Fridays so I can spend time with our daughter. Someone has to be here for her and it became abundantly clear, not long after she was born, that someone wasn't going to be Jenna.

The only thing Jenna cares about is Jenna.

Which is why she doesn't care what day it is or what we're doing.

Quit acting like the victim here, Linc. You knew exactly who Jenna was when you married her. Knew exactly what you were getting yourself in to, so there's no use crying about it now.

"It's her, isn't it?"

I look down at Savanna, her head tucked under my arm. Her face, a mirror image of mine, aimed up at me. I force a grin onto my face. "I dunno, Van." I give her a shrug and hope to God the grin holds. "You know the rules—no phone on Friday nights."

"It's her," Savanna sighs, her expression falling into a scowl. "You know it is." She turns her head to stare at the television, shoulders stiff and angry, pressed against my ribcage. A year ago, she would've been begging me to answer it.

Pleeeease, Dad? Please? We can pick her up and go get some ice cream or go down to the boardwalk? Please, Dad? Just one more chance...

I'm not sure when it changed. When Savanna began to realize Jenna is selfish. That I've been making excuses for her since she was old enough to notice that her mother is never around. Can't be counted on to pack a school lunch or help with homework. Can't be bothered to waste her Friday night on pepperoni pizza and movie marathons. I'm not sure when it happened but it did. One day, Savanna opened her eyes and just stopped asking.

She started to cringe whenever the phone rang. Started to disappear into her room and close the door whenever Jenna breezed in, looking for money or a safe place to crash. Stopped believing she could be a good mother if only I'd give her just one more chance.

The phone in the kitchen stops rattling, only to start again almost immediately.

Goddamn it, Jenna.

"I'm really tired," Savanna says, sitting up from her slump to stand next to the couch. She tosses a sullen look over her shoulder toward the kitchen. "I'm going to bed."

It's barely ten o'clock. She's not tired. She's just... *tired.*

Same as me.

Sighing, I reach up to swipe a rough hand over my face. "Van—"

"G'night." She feeds me back the forced smile I gave her a few minutes ago. "I'll see you in the morning," she says, turning toward the narrow staircase that leads up to her bedroom. Stopping at the foot of it, she turns to look at me. "I love you, Dad."

Feeling my shoulders sag in defeat, I sigh and click off the television. "I love you back, kiddo."

"You should answer the phone," she says, her brow crumpling slightly. "Seven times in a row is a lot, even for her."

"Okay." I give her a reassuring nod and a small smile to go with it. "I will."

As soon as she's gone the phone starts buzzing again but I don't get up to answer it. I just stare at the blank television and think of all the ways Jenna Harris has screwed up my life.

Not just her—you had a hand in it too, so quit feeling sorry for yourself.

Tossing the remote on the coffee table in front of me, I get up and make my way to the kitchen. The phone stops ringing before I can get to it but it doesn't really matter because it's going to start ringing again in *three...*

two...

one...

Like it's on a timer, the phone starts its rattle and buzz routine.

Just turn it off and go to bed. She's either high or drunk—probably both—and after what happened the last time you talked, she's looking for a fight.

I pick up the phone, intent on taking my own advice. Instead, I jab my thumb against the screen and lift it up to my ear. "It's Friday, Jenna," I bark before she can get a word out. "You know it's Friday—the one day a week I ask for *zero* bullshit from you and you don't even have the—"

Sound breaks through my tirade. Jenna sobbing uncontrollably. Someone shouting in the background—"*I need everyone to get the hell back and can one of you set up a goddamned perimeter, for Christ's sake!*"—and under all of it, a whirring, high-pitched screech that squeezes my stomach in its fist.

A siren.

Faint but getting louder fast.

"Jesus, Jen—where are you?" I bark again, turning away from the counter so fast the charge cord rips out of the wall to dangle uselessly from the bottom of my phone. "What's happening? What—"

She starts to talk again, a fast, incoherent babble, broken up by near-hysterical sobs. Closing my eyes, I take a deep breath and tell myself to stay calm. That whatever it is, it can't be that bad because Jenna is able to call and as long as I don't have to tell Savanna her mother is dead, I can handle anything. "Slow down, Jen—just tell me where you are."

She takes a deep, gulping breath and starts to spew again. Eyes still closed, I press the phone to my ear and concentrate on making sense of the words she's screaming at me.

Den.

Georgia.

Dead.

That's all I get.

All I can make out, but it's enough to tell me I was wrong.

I was wrong because this is something I can't handle.

Den.

Georgia.

Dead.

I drop the phone and run.

FIVE

GEORGIA

I call Alex.

I'm at the Den. Rachel is dead. I need you to come.

That's all I say. All I can manage before I hang up the phone.

I watch as the Reaper I had to peel Jenna away from only a few minutes ago steps through the Den's open back door. Tossing me an over-the-shoulder smirk, he climbs onto the back of a Harley Davidson Softail with a scythe airbrushed on its gas tank and rips out of the parking lot. After that, all hell breaks loose. The back door explodes open, spilling light and sound across the back lot and the motorcycles parked there. Shouts and curse words fill the air, the cacophony of voices punctuated with the roar of engines as the thirty or so bikers make a run for it rather than deal with the cavalry I just called in.

More than likely, one of them killed Rachel. They need to be detained. They need to be questioned. Photos need to be taken. Contact cards need to be filled out. Someone needs to stop them from getting away, but that someone isn't me because I'm alone here and I don't have my gun. Short of tackling one or two of them off their bikes, I don't have a chance in hell of stopping anyone.

So, I stay with Rachel. Stand sentry over her body. Wait for Alex.

"What the hell is wrong with you?"

I lift my head and turn to see Jenna, hands stacked on her hips, her small frame illuminated by the dull, dirty light reaching through the bar's open back door. Before I can answer her, she drops her arms and charges me. "Seriously, Georgia—you called the *cops*?"

"Stop, Jenna," I say, shaking my head at her, trying to find the words *Rachel is dead* and push them out of my mouth. "Just—"

"What's wrong with you?" She keeps coming, her hands bunched into fists like she's getting ready to use them on me. "First you just show up here, out of nowhere, and then you decide—"

She's on top of me now and still shouting. I can hear sirens, wailing in the distance. "*Stop*," I say it again, louder this time. Lifting an arm, I hold it out, elbow locked, to keep her from plowing straight into me. My palm plants squarely in her chest and she bounces back before going down, landing hard on her ass a few feet from where I'm standing.

"*You bitch*," she screeches at me, face screwed up and contorted with rage. "Who the hell do you think—" She stops mid-screech, her voice cutting out like someone dragged a needle across a broken record when she catches sight of what lies in the grass a few feet behind me.

"Oh my God..." She breathes it, same as I did, her face going pale. "Rach—*oh my God*." Jenna scrambles to her knees and lunges forward. "Why are you just standing there? *Help her*," she screams at me, trying to maneuver past my legs. "Jesus, George, we have to—"

I manage to catch her before she breaches the invisible barrier I've built around the body.

The body.

I feel my lungs constrict and I squeeze my eyes shut for a split second to beat back the tears prickling behind my eyes.

I can't fall apart.

I can't.

Rachel needs me.

Grabbing her by her shoulders, I haul Jenna to her feet and

give her a single, rough shake. Staring down at her, I make myself say it. "It's too late." The words catch in my throat, so heavy and thick they threaten to choke me. "We can't help her, Jenna. She's already dead."

An hour later, I'm leaning against the side of my truck, waiting. Even though I gave my statement a while ago, I was told to *wait right here—the sheriff wants to talk to you* by the deputy who questioned me.

The entire Fell County Sheriff's Department is here. All twelve of them, plus Alex, who is barking orders and assigning tasks to the deputies who are just standing around, staring at each other with no idea what to do. Murder isn't something they know how to deal with. Intoxicated drivers? Sure. Drunk and disorderlies? All day long. But this? A dead woman found strangled and sexually assaulted outside the island's dirty little secret? No, these bunch of Mayberries have no idea how to handle what happened here.

"Hour and a half ago, Archie says you were coming back over the bridge and headed for home." I look up from the toes of my boots to see Alex standing in front of me. He looks tired. More than a little pissed. "That was obviously a lie—so, you wanna tell me what the hell you're doing here?"

"Jenna texted me. Said she needed some help. Asked me to come, so I came." I tell him the truth because Rachel is dead and as the person who found her body, I'm a witness. Any lies I tell now would likely impede the investigation.

Alex turns his head slightly, casting a quick, sidelong glance behind him. Jenna's about ten feet away, clinging to an uncomfortable-looking Archie and sobbing loudly while he does his best to comfort her. Sighing, Alex turns back to look at me, his dark blue eyes unreadable. "According to her, you just showed up, uninvited, nosing in where you didn't belong. Says you dragged her out back and started a fight over her husband."

"That's not what happened," I say, crossing my arms over my chest like a shield. "I used Savanna as an excuse to get her out of the bar but she's the one who brought up Linc—" When I say his name, Alex's jaw goes tight, forcing his generous mouth into a thin, flat line that tells me he's already made up his mind about what happened between Jenna and me. Why I drove out here. Suddenly angry, I drop my arms. "*Someone* texted me," I tell him, pulling my phone from my back pocket. "Someone—"

"I know." Alex raises a hand between us, stopping me in my tracks. "I got your statement from Boggs—he confirms someone texted you, asking you to come here." He drops his hand and sighs. "What I want to know is why you did it. *Why* you thought it was a good idea to come here—*here, Georgia, of all places*—alone."

The question and the tone it's delivered in makes me angry. "Do you know where I was two years ago? Do you have any idea what I was doing?" I ask him, not really expecting an answer because of course he doesn't. No one does. There are things I don't talk about. Things I'll never talk about. My last year in the military is one of them. "I can promise you I wasn't running sobriety checkpoints and booking innocent teenage girls for boat theft." I regret saying it as soon as it comes out of my mouth. Before taking the job as Fell County Sheriff, Alex was a homicide detective with the Detroit Police Department—he's seen more than his fair share of horrible.

Alex reaches up to scrub a rough hand across his mouth like I just punched him in it. Dropping it with a sigh, he shakes his head, "Georgia, these guys are dangerous—"

"You really think a pack of lowlifes in matching outfits scares me?" I raise my voice, making sure it carries. "And for the record, I *didn't* think it was a good idea—" I shake my head. "Matter of fact, I was pretty sure coming here was a horrible idea from the start."

"And yet here we stand." He stares at me for a moment like he's having a hard time understanding me. "Why?"

Because I promised.

Instead of saying it, I aim a glare over his shoulder. Jenna is still latched on to Archie, sobbing into his uniform shirt while he looks around like he doesn't know what to do. Before I can council myself on restraint, I'm stepping around Alex and away from my truck, heading straight for her.

"*Shit*. George—" Alex reaches out to clamp a restraining hand around my forearm, but I shake him off with barely a glance and keep advancing until I'm practically standing on top of her.

Peeling Jenna off Archie's uniform shirt, I give her a hard shove, pinning her against his squad car. "How'd you know I called the cops?" I push my face within an inch of hers. It's something I've been standing here wondering for the past hour. "Who—"

A car door slams somewhere close by, pulling my attention toward the source of the sound.

Lincoln.

He's here, striding across the parking lot, barely stopping long enough to lift the bright yellow tape strung up to cordon off the crime scene. "Hey," the deputy assigned to guard the perimeter calls out with a plaintive sigh when he sees Lincoln cross the barrier. "Come on, Linc—you can't just—"

Linc stops, aiming a quick, dangerous glare at the deputy and his mouth snaps shut like a spring-loaded hinge. I watch as he scans the parking lot. He looks wrecked. His dark hair is disheveled like he's been trying to pull it out. Hazel eyes wide and a little wild as they pick through the people milling around the gravel lot, searching for something.

Someone.

He stops searching when he sees us and something passes over his face. Relief, so thick and heavy Lincoln looks like he's on the verge of collapsing under its weight.

Seeing it clamps my mouth shut, pushes me away from Jenna, and I take a guilty step back, putting space between us.

When she spots him, Jenna lets out a wail before pushing her way past me to get to her husband. Throwing her arms around him, she buries her face in his chest. Her hysterics start up again, each high-pitched sob punctuated by a round of snuffling hiccups.

"Are you done with her, Sheriff?" Lincoln asks, his voice lifted over the din while he slips an arm around Jenna's waist to keep her upright. "Can I take her home?"

"Yeah," Alex says. "And when she sobers up, you might want to have a talk with your wife about the company she keeps," he adds, shifting close enough to press the front of his shoulder against the back of mine.

Lincoln catches the move, his eyes going cold and flinty in a heartbeat as his gaze shifts between the two of us, jaw clenched so tight I can see a vein pulsing in his neck. Finally settling his glare on Alex, he cuts him a nasty smirk. "And *I* think you might want to take your own advice."

I feel Alex's shoulder go stiff against mine. "Come again?"

Lincoln jogs his glare away from the man behind me to pin it to my face. "Pretty sure you heard me just fine, Sheriff."

"Come on, Linc." Ever the peacemaker, Archie steps in and angles himself between the two of them before it can get ugly. "I'll help you get her to the car."

Pulling his gaze away from mine, Lincoln gives him a grim smile. "Thanks, Arch," he says, aiming a fast and final look in my direction before turning away from me completely.

They're halfway to Lincoln's car before I manage to turn away from them. When I do, it's to find Alex watching me.

"You should go too."

"Okay…" I have a million questions about Rachel and the investigation that's undoubtedly underway, but I know better than to ask them now. Alex won't tell me anything here—not when a good half-dozen of his deputies are within earshot. "I'll just—"

"Don't wait up. I'm most likely going to be here all night." Alex sighs while he herds me back to my truck and watches while I open its door and climb into the driver's seat. "I'll give you a call in the morning."

"Okay," I say it again, even though it's not. I don't want to go home. I want to lead the investigation into Rachel's death, not be sent to bed with a pat on my head and a half-assed promise to call.

Feeding my key into the truck's ignition, I give it a crank. "You need to talk to Jenna again. Ask her how they knew I called the police when I found Rachel. It doesn't—"

"I'll call you," Alex says again, giving me a single, stiff-jawed nod before he slams the truck door closed.

Shifting into drive, I take the long way out of the lot, passing by Lincoln's car, where he and Archie are still trying to wrestle an inconsolable Jenna into the front seat. In the back, behind the driver's seat, is a little girl. Turned away from the scene unfolding on the other side of the car, she has her forehead pressed against the window. She's the mirror image of Lincoln and she's staring right at me, watching as I drive away.

SIX

LINCOLN

Even though the Den is only a few miles from my house, it might as well be on the other side of the island. Jenna alternates between screaming and raging about Georgia *ruining everything* and crying hysterically over Rachel. I take the long way home, giving her time to scream herself hoarse before passing out.

"Sorry, kiddo," I say softly, aiming a quick look at the back seat. "I tried calling Julie to come sit with you but—"

"It's okay, Dad," Savanna answers quietly, forehead pressed against her window so she can stare through the glass. She's wrong. None of this is okay but I don't argue with her. Finally pulling into the driveway, I kill the engine and give Savanna the keys so she can open the door while I wrestle her mother out of the car.

Stepping through the front door, I look directly to my left to see Savanna already has a stack of towels pulled from the linen closet. Setting them on the coffee table, she starts lining the couch with them, spreading and tucking them across its cushions.

"That was her, wasn't it?" Savanna stops, mid-tuck, to look up from the couch she's layering with towels because the last time Jenna crashed here, she threw up all over its predecessor. "It's okay, Dad," she says, when I don't answer her. Turning back toward the couch, she shrugs. "We can talk about her. I'm not—"

"We're not talking about Georgia Fell," I say, my tone making it clear that the subject isn't up for debate. "And stop saying it's okay," I grumble, shifting a passed-out Jenna in my arms. "It's *not* okay—your mother shouldn't have said those things. She doesn't know what she's talking about."

Instead of calling me on my obvious lie, Savanna gives the towels a few final tucks before straightening to study her handy-work. "I hope she doesn't throw up," she says, watching me set her mother on the towel-covered cushions. "I like this couch."

"Me too," I say while I position Jenna on her side and send up a silent prayer she stays that way. Before tonight, waking up to find Jenna choked to death on her own vomit has pretty much been my worst nightmare.

"Think she'll be here when we wake up?"

She'll be here. She'll be wide awake in a few hours and bouncing around the house, waiting for me to wake up so she can get some money out of me. I usually make her wait. Force her to spend some sober time with Savanna before I give in and toss her some cash. As soon as she has it in her hand, she'll make Savanna a few half-assed promises about *girl time* before disappearing again.

Sighing, I straighten to stand beside her. "I don't know."

We stand quietly for a few moments, watching Jenna like she's a wild animal we have grave reservations about leaving unattended in our home. Finally, Savanna breaks the silence between us. "Is Aunt Rachel really dead?"

"Yeah." I reach out an arm and wrap it around Savanna's shoulder, tucking her into my side. She's only nine years old—she shouldn't have to deal with this kind of stuff. I wait for her to ask me how Rachel died. What happened. The inevitable speculation about how it could've been Jenna. How lucky we are that she's still alive.

But that's not what she says.

"You thought it was her, didn't you?" she asks me tentatively enough to tell me she's not talking about her mother. "You thought she was dead."

I think about it. Stopping at the front door long enough to pull my work boots back on. Being halfway out the door before I remembered Savanna upstairs in her room.

Finding my phone, I called Julie, Savanna's sitter. Heart hammering in my ears, I paced while the phone rang and rang. After a few minutes, I gave up and charged up the stairs to knock on Savanna's closed bedroom door.

Come on, kiddo—we gotta go.

The entire time, the same three words ringing through my head on a constant, terrifying loop.

Den.

Georgia.

Dead.

When I saw her standing there, I almost passed out. That's how relieved I was to see her. How thankful I was to know that whatever awful thing had happened, it hadn't happened to her.

A motorcycle cruises down the street now, its engine rumbling softly as it passes by the house, headlamp dimmed. I know who it is and I know where he's headed.

Looking down, I find Savanna still gazing up at me, waiting for her answer. Instead of giving it to her, I give her shoulder a squeeze before pulling her away from the couch. "Head on up to bed—I'll see you in the morning."

She narrows her gaze on my face and opens her mouth like she's going to argue but she closes it without saying a word. A few seconds later she's back in her room with the door shut firmly between us.

I stare at Jenna for a few seconds. Think about the havoc she'll wreak the second she wakes up. Reaching into the front pocket of my jeans, I pull out a wad of cash and toss it onto the coffee table. I don't know how much is there, but it doesn't matter—if it gets her out of the house before Savanna wakes up, it'll be money well spent.

Giving Jenna one last look, I head toward the kitchen, located in the back of the house. Outside, in the alley behind the house, the motorcycle rolls to a soft stop and its engine cuts off. Turning off the porch light, I step through the back door just in time to watch the rider kick down the bike's stand and climb off its back.

"You want to tell me what the hell happened tonight?" I ask as soon as he's through the back gate and halfway across the yard.

"I don't know, man," Will says, shaking his head as he comes to a stop at the bottom of the porch steps. "*Still* don't know—but from what I heard, Rachel is dead and Georgie's the one who found her."

I'm glad it's dark. I'm glad I remembered to turn off the porch light. Not because I don't want the neighbors to see me standing in my backyard talking to someone like Will Hudson. No, I'm glad because he mentioned Georgia and I don't need him to see how much knowing she's somehow managed to plant herself in the middle of this bullshit bothers me.

"What the hell was she doing there?" I don't have to fake the apprehension in my tone.

"Beats the hell outta me—she just showed up." Will's shoulders move upward in a shrug. "Asked for Jenna."

The one thing Georgia's done consistently since being back on the island is pretend Jenna and I don't exist. That she actively went looking for her is surprising. "And you just let her stroll on in, huh?"

Now Will laughs, a flat, one-note bark that raises my hackles. "Not sure how much you remember about Georgia Fell but no one just *lets* her do anything. When I told her she wasn't allowed into the clubhouse, she just laughed in my face and breezed on in, lookin' like *G.I. Jane* or some shit," he says with something that sounds close to admiration. "Next thing I know, Reapers are hightailing it outta there and the entire Fell County Sheriff's Office is up my ass, with our fair sheriff leading the charge." The shadows around Will's face shift and he clears his throat. "What do you want me to do?" he asks. "You want me and the boys to put a scare into her?"

Now it's my turn to wonder just how much he remembers about Georgia. Ten years ago, scaring her would've been no easy task. I'd gotten barely more than a glimpse of her up close tonight, but it was enough to know that scaring her now would be something close to impossible.

"No." I shake my head and move toward the back door, ready for this conversation to be over. "Stay away from her. If Georgia Fell starts to cause trouble, I'll take care of it myself."

SEVEN

GEORGIA

When I fell into bed, physically and emotionally exhausted, I was sure I'd sleep for a year. Instead, as usual, I'm up and dressed before the sun, dumping coffee on top of the hard, tight knot of anxiety that's been seated in my gut since I read the text from Jenna last night.

Problem is, she claims she isn't the one who sent it. That I showed up at the Den last night, unannounced and unwanted, to start a fight with her over her husband. A lie—one Alex seemed all too eager to believe. If Jenna was willing to lie about something like that, then what else is she willing to lie about? What does she know about Rachel's death that she isn't saying?

Rinsing my cup out—a dainty bone China affair with ridiculous hand-painted flowers dancing around its rim—I carefully set it in the dish drainer and stare out the kitchen window above the sink. Through the glass and a slight break in the trees, I can see the Rock, a dense, uninviting clump of rough stone and overgrown wilderness, floating off in the distance. That's where Archie said the Kates girl ran the Nelsons' boat up on an outcrop, which is weird because that's not where the kids go to party. They go to Seraphim—the smallest of the islands and the one closest to the marina. Of course, the Nelsons have their own private dock, and the Rock is directly in the sailing path of—

The trilling ring of the manor's landline pulls me out of my thoughts and away from the window. Reaching for my cell phone in response, I realize I must've left it on my nightstand. Thinking it must be Alex, I rush down the hall to duck into the alcove tucked under the stairs and pick up the phone.

"Hey—"

"Good morning, Georgia." A familiar voice reaches for me through the phone and cuts me off. "It's Kate Timmons, over at the *Herald*. I'm working on a story and I'm wondering if I could ask you a few questions?" Before I can answer, she starts rapid-firing questions at me. "Can you confirm you're the person who found Rachel Alcott's body and called the authorities?"

"What?" My grip tightens on the receiver. "Who told you that?" Thinking back, I can't remember if there was press or a news crew on the scene last night, but even if there was, Kate wouldn't have known I was the one who found Rachel's body. Not unless someone told her. Instead of answering me, she reloads and starts firing again.

"What were you doing at the Devil's Den—a place known for its alleged illegal activities?"

"I—" Because pulling Jenna into this would undoubtedly make things worse, I stop myself. "No comment."

"*Okaaay...*" Her tone tells me my refusal to cooperate is exactly what she expected. This is the same reporter who covered my return to Angel Bay. I didn't answer her questions then, either. "Can you walk me through what you were doing directly prior to discovering the body?"

Instead, I answer her question with a question of my own. "Which of the Fell County deputies are you sleeping with, Kate?"

"Excuse me?" Her brisk tone goes shrill in an instant at my accusation.

"Your questions suggest you're privy to information you shouldn't be," I remind her. "Which leads me to believe one of the deputies on the scene last night is feeding you intel—you're either paying him for it or you're screwing him. Which is it?"

As intended, my blunt assessment of the situation sends her into a tailspin. Kate sputters for a few seconds before she finally spits out, "Can you confirm the Sheriff Department's claim that there was no evidence of foul play?"

No foul play.

Now I'm the one who's spinning. My heart is suddenly pounding, my breath rushing out of my lungs in a whoosh that has me leaning against the antique telephone table so heavily, I'm sure its old, spindly legs are going to snap under my weight.

"How would I know? I'm not police, " I say, sure she's trying to bait me into giving her a juicy tidbit—something money couldn't buy her or her source wouldn't give up.

"But you used to be." Hearing apprehension in my tone, Kate attacks. "You were a homicide detective in the army. You saw the body. You know—"

Again, it's an oversimplification of what I did while I was in the military, and not exactly accurate, but I don't correct her. "Bye, Kate," I say, dropping the receiver back into its cradle while she continues to talk, seemingly nonstop.

As soon as the line is clear, I dial Alex's cell phone. It goes straight to voicemail.

"*No evidence of foul play?*" I nearly shout into the receiver. "Rachel was raped and strangled, Alex. There was bruising on her neck and clear signs of sexual assault. I'm not sure what qualifies as foul play where you come from but in my book, that's about as *foul* as it gets."

Hanging up before I can say something I might regret, I give a startled jolt when the phone under my hand rings almost immediately after I set it down. It's Kate Timmons again. I hang up as soon as her brusque tone hits my ear drum. Then I count to five and take the phone off the hook.

EIGHT

After I hang up on Kate, I feel like I have an army of fire ants marching across my bones. Thousands of them, biting and pinching. Pushing me to do something, *anything*, but sit on my ass and wait for Alex to call me back.

Telling myself I'll spend the rest of the morning scraping paint off the manor's east exterior, I pull on my boots. Checking my phone, I'm not surprised the only missed call I have is from Evie.

Nothing from Alex.

Slipping my phone into my back pocket, I head out the front door.

Twenty minutes later, I'm not teetering on top of an extension ladder, scraping old paint off the side of the manor and waiting this out like I should be. I'm walking into the Fell County Sheriff's Office because my pitifully thin supply of patience has run dry and I want answers.

Stepping up to the counter that separates the station's lobby from its bullpen, I look around. Directly to the right of Alex's closed office door is the holding area. Surrounded by a sea of Angel Bay's usual Saturday morning offering of drunk and disorderlies is a single teenage girl—Julie Kates.

She's perched on the edge of a hard, wooden bench, bare knees pressed together, toggling nervously between tugging at the hem of her sundress and defensively crossing her arms over her chest. Eyes red-rimmed from crying. This is no hardened criminal. She's scared.

"Hey, Georgia."

I force myself to look away from her and offer a smile to the deputy sitting at his desk a few feet away. "Hey, Brent—Alex around?"

"*Uhhh...*" The answering grin on his face falters for a moment, his gaze darting from me to his boss's closed office door and back again. "No." He shakes his shaggy head of blond hair at me as he stands slowly from his desk. "He hasn't been in."

"Really?" I remind myself he's just doing his job. Following orders. "His car is in the parking lot."

"Oh... well, I..." He moves out from behind his desk like he's getting ready to run interference in case I decide to charge Alex's office door, which proves he's smarter than most people give him credit for. "I mean, he's out on a call."

It's a lie.

Alex is in his office and he gave Brent orders to lie to me about it if I showed up.

I'd bet every penny Elizabeth Fell left me on it.

"Oh." I give him a little frown and hold up a large white bag, making sure the *Carlisle's* logo is visible. It's not the trendiest bakery on the island but it's the best. The kind of place locals keep secret from the tourists. "I guess he's out of luck." Setting the bag on the counter, I start to unroll the top. "Want one?" I ask, using a napkin to pull out an apple fritter. "They're still warm."

"Hell, yeah," he says, his smile returning in full force. Before he can cross the room to the counter, I go to him, lifting the bag before using my hip to push through the swinging divider between the waiting area and the bullpen. Brent throws another nervous look over his shoulder and shakes his head. Alex is definitely in his office. "On second thoughts, maybe I shouldn't. I got some—"

"Come on," I say, chiding him gently while I push the bag with the second fritter against his chest, giving him no choice but to take it. "What else do you have to do? Empty the drunk tank? Wait for a call that a bunch of kids jumped the turnstile at the ferry station?" I ask, totally ignoring the fact that last night we were both standing over the dead body of someone we know. Setting my own fritter on his desk, I head for the coffee cart set up directly across from the holding cell. "Cream and sugar?"

Giving up, Brent walks back to his desk and dumps his lanky frame into his chair. "Yeah." He nods and reaches into the bag. "Lots of both."

Back turned toward him, I take him at this word, dumping about a pound of sugar into a paper cup before topping it with coffee. Gaze aimed toward the holding cell again, I stir powdered creamer into his cup while I watch Julie Kates scoot herself to the edge of the bench and turn her knees into the wall her shoulder is pressed against. One of her cell mates—a frat boy who looks like a rumpled Gap ad with puke on his shirt—is trying to talk to her.

Sprinkling just enough powdered creamer into my coffee to lift it a shade or two, I take both cups to Brent's desk, setting his cup down in front of him before making myself at home in the empty chair next to it. Giving his coffee a testing sip, he gives me a sheepish grin over the rim of his cup. "Coffee. Carlisle's..." He gestures at me with his cup before setting it down. "I know what you're doing."

"I should hope so, Brent." I take a sip of my own coffee. It's good. Not like the stories you hear about police station coffee. "You're a cop—if you didn't know what I'm doing, I'd have serious questions about your abilities to perform your job."

"I don't know anything about the Rachel Alcott situation, Georgia." His usually smooth brow creases into a frown. "I'm the department noob—no one tells me shit."

"Someone told Kate Timmons plenty about the *situation*," I tell him, watching his face carefully for a reaction when I say her name. "She called me this morning."

"Well, it wasn't me." Sighing, Brent picks up his fritter and leans back in his chair. "She was here earlier, but I told her the same thing I'm telling you." Breaking the fritter in two, he tosses half of it back into the bag. "I don't know anything," he says, before stuffing his mouth with fried pastry—probably in an effort to keep it shut.

"I believe you," I tell him, pinching the corner off my own fritter and popping it into my mouth.

"You do?" he asks around a mouthful of pastry.

Even though I'm not entirely sure if it's the truth or not, I nod. "Yup." Taking another sip of coffee, I switch gears. "That the Kates girl?" I say, jerking my chin toward the holding cell. I can't see her from this angle but I'm sure she's still huddled against the wall, trying to ignore her vomit-covered cell mate.

"*Uhhh...*" Thrown off balance by the switch, Brent aims a look over his shoulder. "Yeah. Sheriff Bradford brought her in last night, right before you called in the dead..." He lets his words trail off, aiming a pained look my way and a muttered, "Sorry, George."

I give him a shrug, doing my best to stay calm. To stay in my seat and not jump up and scream Rachel's name. "What's she still doing here?" I ask casually, like it doesn't matter to me one way or the other.

Brent shoots a look at Alex's closed office door, probably trying to gauge how much trouble he'll get into if he answers my question. Instead of pressing, I take another drink from my coffee cup and wait. Finally, he sighs. "I reached out to her foster parents this morning, after the judge called in to set her bail—they said they won't pay it. They don't want her anymore. Rachel was her case manager and it's the weekend," he reminds me. "She doesn't have anyone."

Bail? She's a seventeen-year-old girl—an island resident accused of taking a boat on a joyride—not Al Capone. By all accounts she should have been arraigned and released on her own recognizances, case manager or not.

Instead of pointing that out, I focus on the last half of what he told me. "They don't want her anymore?" Saying it makes me angry. Like Julie Kates is an unruly dog who got dropped off at the pound. Without Rachel to protect her, she has no one.

"That's what they said," Brent tells me, giving me a half-hearted shrug. "Said she was more trouble than she's worth."

"But she's never been in trouble before." It's not a question. I make it my business to know who the island troublemakers are and I know Julie Kates isn't one of them. Brent gives me another shrug, his mouth full of fritter again. "How much is her bail?"

"Ten grand," he says, giving me a slight wince when he says it.

"Ten thousand dollars?" I hiss it at him like he's the one who set her bail. "She wrecked a boat, Brent—it's not like she knocked over a liquor store."

Looking miserable, he sets his fritter down without taking another bite. He knows, same as me, what will happen to Julie Kates if no one is willing to pay her bail. She'll sit in jail until her hearing, which given the fact that the judge who presides over Fell County only makes in-person appearances when his docket is full, could mean weeks. "Judge said he was tired of eastern kids tearing up the island, so he was setting an example."

Eastern kids.

There it is again. The island's unspoken caste system rearing its ugly head. Instead of launching into the same argument I gave Archie last night, I decide to put my unwanted inheritance to good use. "I'll pay it."

"That's all well and good, *Ms. Fell*," Brent says, a short bark of laughter following directly on its heels. "But that doesn't fix where she's gonna go once she's released—it's Saturday, remember?"

He's right. Without Rachel, Julie will get an on-call social worker who might be able to get her a bed in an emergency shelter off-island until they can find her another placement—and that's if she's lucky. Realistically, she'd be forced to spend the weekend at the island's DCFS office, bunking down on a cot in someone's cubicle and eating out of a vending machine while they shuffle her case from one desk to the next.

I can't let that happen.

I couldn't save Rachel but maybe I can do this one thing for her.

"Well, I guess that means I'm taking her home with me," I tell him, while I imagine Elizabeth Fell rolling over in her grave.

NINE

Julie Kates doesn't say a word while I lead her across the station parking lot toward my truck. She waits patiently while I unlock the passenger-side door and shoo her in.

I'm not surprised. She's a foster kid. She's used to being herded and hustled from one strange place to the next. She's used to strangers putting her in cars and vans. So used to it she goes without question. Without so much as a *where are you taking me?* It tells me she's been in the system for a long time—probably her entire life.

Slamming my truck door closed, I put the key into the ignition but don't start the engine.

"Thank you," she says quietly, clutching the clear plastic bag containing her belongings Brent gave her as soon as I signed the paperwork. "I'll pay you back, Ms. Fell—I have a job. I've been saving for college so I can make—"

"I don't want your money," I tell her, watching the rearview mirror for my prey. "I don't even want the money I have." Flicking her a quick glance, I frown. "And my name isn't *Ms. Fell*, it's Georgia. You can call me that or you can call me George," I tell her, trying my best to temper my tone because, for some reason, her gratitude bothers me.

Julie just gives me a jerky head nod in response.

"I'm sorry," I say, the words coming out rough and uneven. "About Rachel."

Her mouth starts to tremble, but only for a moment before she stretches it flat into a thin, grim line. "You knew her." It's not a question.

"Yeah." I give her a short nod. "We were in a few placements together." It's a woefully inadequate explanation for what Rachel and I were to each other but I don't have to elaborate because Julie is a foster, just like I was. She understands.

As if to prove it, her mouth twists to the side and she looks at me for a second before re-aiming her gaze out the windshield. "Then I'm sorry too."

Eager to change the subject, I sigh. "Tell me something," I say, turning toward her enough to take in her polka-dotted sundress and strappy wedge sandals. "What kind of criminal mastermind wears a dress and sandals to steal a boat?"

The question pulls her gaze from the windshield in front of her to the glare I have aimed in her direction. "I—" She swallows hard and shakes her head. "I mean, I didn't—"

"Didn't steal the Nelsons' boat," I say, finishing her sentence. Straightening in my seat again, I flick my glare toward the rearview. "Yeah, I got that."

"No." Julie shakes her head at me, the movement caught in my peripheral. "I stole the boat." Realizing I'm not buying her bullshit, she sighs and looks away. "I just didn't *plan* to do it."

"So, a kid who's never so much as boosted a lip gloss from the five and dime just randomly decides to commit a felony?" I laugh at how ridiculous her claim sounds. "Do you really expect me to believe that?"

Instead of answering me, Julie frowns. "Why are we still here?"

Before I can answer her, the reason walks out of the station and heads to his patrol car. "Don't run," I tell her before throwing my door open and hopping out of the truck. Slamming it closed, I charge across the parking lot.

"Hey," I call out, loud enough my voice carries across the sunbaked asphalt. Alex lifts his head and seeing me, stops in his tracks. "You want to explain to me why Kate from the *Herald* called me this morning?"

Shoulders slumped under his uniform, Alex looks around the lot to make sure it's empty. Even though it is, he doesn't answer me until I'm stopped and standing right in front of him. "What are you doing here?" he asks, while throwing a quick look at my truck over my shoulder. "I thought you—"

"You thought I'd just give up if you hid in your office long enough?" I finish for him. "Well, you thought wrong."

"George—"

"Don't *George* me," I say, pushing it out through clenched teeth. "I want to hear you say it."

Reaching up, he rubs wearily at the corner of his eye. "*Say what* exactly?" he asks, his tone telling me exactly what he thinks of this conversation. That it's a waste of time.

"I want you to look me in the eye and tell me Rachel *wasn't* murdered."

The tired look on his face morphs into a scowl. "Go home. I'll come over later, we can talk about it then."

"I know what I saw," I tell him, completely ignoring his attempts at shutting me down. "I know—"

"You're wrong." He cuts me off with a sharp look before letting it drift away from my face. "I know that's hard for you to believe but you're wrong. There was no evidence of foul play," he says, gaze settling on my shoulder. "Best I can figure, the subject overdosed—"

"*Rachel*," I hiss it at him, angling my face to force myself into his line of sight. "Her name is Rachel—and she didn't *overdose*." I straighten my frame and scoff like it's the most ridiculous thing I ever heard. "She didn't do drugs. I had lunch with her a few days ago and she was fine." Rachel was one of the few who welcomed me back. Was glad I came home. Didn't hate or resent me for leaving. "If she were on drugs, I would've seen it."

The scowl melts away and he lifts his face to look directly at me. "Rachel Alcott has a rap sheet as long as my arm—drug possession, petty theft, trespassing—"

"What are you talking about?" I shake my head at him like he's crazy. "Rachel was a *social worker*. She was married. She and her wife just had a baby. She wasn't some—"

"*She was*," he insists, his gaze dulled by something that looks a lot like pity. "She... struggled. Didn't always have her shit together," Alex tells me, reminding me I've been off island for over a decade. That I don't know the people I consider my family as well as I think I do. "She wasn't murdered, Georgia. I processed the scene and—"

Putting what he just told me about Rachel away for later, I focus on the fight in front of me. "You were there for less than an hour," I cut in, my tone sharp. "You didn't *process* shit."

He stops for a moment, his mouth flat. Muscle ticking in his jaw. "And while it's ultimately up to the ME, my preliminary findings are she died of a drug overdose."

"Bull*shit*." I bite the word in half and spit it at him. "It's been less than twelve hours—there's no way you got a toxicology report that fast." When he doesn't answer me, I advance. "There was bruising on her neck consistent with strangulation. I saw it. I *saw*—"

"It was dark." Alex sighs, the picture of constrained patience. "What you saw must've been a shadow or maybe dirt smudged across her neck, or maybe..."

"Or maybe *what*?"

"Or maybe you're bored." He sighs again and forces himself to look at me. "You've been back nearly a year now and you're spinning your wheels here. Maybe you're looking for something that wasn't there."

"*Bored*?" I shout at him, causing him to wince. When he reaches out to touch my arm—a silent reminder we're in public—I shove his hand away and glare at him. "You think I made up what I saw because I'm *bored*?"

Dropping his hand, Alex glares at me. "I think you came here to pick a fight and when I wasn't willing to square up, you bailed out a suspected felon and a *minor*, I might add, just to kick sand in my face."

I don't know why I bailed out Julie Kates. I don't know why she's sitting in my truck right now, getting an earful of my fight with the sheriff instead of in a holding cell, but I know I didn't do it because I'm bored. I didn't do it to get under his skin. "That's not why I bailed her out and I wasn't looking for shit, *Sheriff*—then or now." I push the last of it out through clenched teeth. "There were *bruises* on Rachel's neck," I tell him, refusing to allow him to side-track me.

"George..." He says my name carefully and I hate him for it. Hate the resigned, defeated look he's giving me. "I *looked*. Aside from a little dirt, there was nothing on her neck."

I shake my head. Try to keep arguing with him but once my mouth is open, I can't make myself say the words because I'm suddenly not sure what I saw. "Her skirt was up around her hips. Her underwear was pulled down." Despite my conviction, the words come out sounding small and unsure. "Jenna was there," I tell him, no longer trusting my own eyes. "She saw—ask her."

"I did." Alex winces again, mouth twitched slightly to the side. "According to Mrs. McNamara, patrons have been known to relieve themselves at the side of the building when the bar's only restroom is occupied. I'm thinking the sub—*Rachel* went outside to relieve herself and..." He sighs. "I'm sorry, George. I know this is hard for you to hear. I know she was your friend."

"Rachel wasn't my *friend*." I take a step back when he reaches for me. I don't expect him to understand. What it's like to move through this world alone. To cling to the tenuous ties of your child-hood because no matter how far-flung and fragile those ties are, they're all you have. Alex was raised in Grosse Pointe. His father is a lawyer. His mother fills her days with volunteer work and belonged to the PTA. They ate dinner together every night and took family vacations to Mackinac twice a year. How could he understand?

Dropping his hands, he lets them hang loose at his sides, defeated by my unwillingness to let him comfort me. "Go home, George," he tells me quietly, blue eyes narrowed and unreadable. "I'll come over after my shift, okay?"

This time when he dismisses me, I nod my head and take another step away from him before turning around and walking away.

TEN

LINCOLN

Jenna was gone when I woke up. The money I tossed on the coffee table was gone too.

She took it and left without even so much as telling Savanna goodbye.

And even though it's exactly what I'd hoped for, I resent it.

I resent a lot of things this morning.

Like I didn't sleep at all last night because I was too busy replaying the night Georgia left the island when we were kids. The way she looked at me like I was a piece of shit stuck to the bottom of her shoe, same as she did last night.

Like the fact that she's right.

Forcing myself to put it away and focus on the things I'm actually in control of, I knock on my neighbor's front door before sticking my hands into my pockets and taking a step back to wait for someone to answer while trying to look as unmenacing as possible.

No easy task.

I wasn't really worried when Julie didn't answer my call last night. It was Friday night. She knows Friday nights are my time with Savanna and even as responsible and level-headed as she is, she's a teenage girl.

But it's Saturday morning now and Julie should've been

ringing my doorbell over an hour ago, with her foster sister in tow, to sit with Savanna so I can head to the shop.

When my neighbor finally opens her door, I plaster a friendly, non-threatening smile across my face. "Morning, Tammy—is Julie around?" I ask, pretending not to notice the way she's looking at me. Like if Julie were her biological daughter and not some throwaway foster, there was no way she'd allow her anywhere near me.

"Julie's not here," she tells me, her pale, pinched face falling into a frown.

"Oh..." I nod like I understand, even though I don't. "Okay—do you know where she went or maybe why she's not answering her phone? It's Saturday," I remind her, when she just stares at me through the screen door still shut between us. "She was supposed to come over and sit with Savanna while I go—"

"I dunno." Tammy gives me a lazy shrug and sighs like I'm a religious nut she can't get rid of. "She don't live here no more."

I feel my expression slip into neutral, like I'm waiting for the punchline. When all she does is glare at me, I shake my head. "What? Since when?"

"Since last night when she stole Ted Nelson's boat and ran it up on the Rock," she informs me, managing to make it sound like somehow I'm the one to blame. "From what the sheriff says, she totaled it. No way me and Jim can afford to be held responsible for something like that."

"So, your solution is to *what*?" I scrub a rough hand over my face to try to hide the fact I'm running out of patience. "Kick her out? Just dump her off at the—"

"I ain't gotta explain myself." She looks at me the same way Georgia looked at me last night. "Especially not to someone like you."

Instead of pointing out that she and her husband deal marijuana out of their garage and only took Julie in for the eight hundred dollars a month and the free babysitting for their other fosters having her around provided, I shake my head and bite my tongue. "Where's Julie now?"

Tammy gives me a shrug while she shifts herself out of the doorway. "Probably still down at the sheriff station, waiting for someone dumb enough to bail her out," she says, making it obvious she thinks that *someone* is me. Pushing the screen door open between us, she tosses something onto the porch at my feet. A hand-stitched duffle made out of faded green fabric with yellow flowers on it. I recognize it—my mother made it. Georgia had one just like it when she was Julie's age.

They all did.

Seeing it dries my throat into sandpaper. Sends my heart racing and bouncing around my chest like it's looking for an exit.

Tammy gives me a sour look. "Give that to her when you see her—that way she don't have to come back here."

Before I can say anything else, she slams the door in my face.

"I can stay home by myself, Dad," Savanna says to the passenger-side window she's staring out of rather than look at me head-on. "I'm not a baby anymore."

"I can't leave you alone—you know that," I tell her, instead of pointing out she's not even ten yet and leaving her alone isn't something I would do, even if I could. "We're going to pick Julie up and the two of you can walk back to the house from the shop—okay?" I haven't planned past that. What I'm going to do with Julie after I get her out—or if I even *can* get her out, for that matter. All I know is she's a good kid and she doesn't deserve to be stuck in a holding cell until someone decides to give a shit about her.

When I drive past the shop, Savanna sits up a little taller in her seat and gives me a puzzled look. One that turns into one of alarm when I turn into the sheriff's station visitor lot, a half block up the road. "Julie's here?" Savanna turns in her seat completely, shoulders stiff, her face suddenly pale. "Why? What happened? Did she—"

"It's okay," I tell her, pulling into an empty parking spot before killing the engine. "Julie's fine. We're going to pick her up and the two of you can walk back to the house from the shop." I repeat the plan because it's all I've got to offer her. "It's going to be okay."

Getting out the car, I round the back of it and wait for Savanna to follow suit. As soon as she's standing next to me, she slips her hand into mine and looks up at me. "What did she do?"

"I don't know," I lie to her, pulling her across the lot toward the entrance. "All I know is she needs our help."

Giving me a nod, Savanna steps through the door when I pull it open for her. As soon as we're inside, she slips her hand into mine again, her fingers squeezed around my palm so tight I can feel the bones inside of it rub together. Instead of asking her to ease up, I squeeze back, holding on to her, just as tight.

Because the last time she was here, they took her away from me.

Stepping up to the counter, I survey the bullpen and holding cell beyond it. Brent is sitting at his desk, feet propped on top of it and leaned back in his chair, plowing his way through an apple fritter from Carlisle's and reading what looks like a romance paperback. Aside from a college kid who looks like he can't hold his liquor, the holding cell is empty.

No Julie.

Giving Savanna a reassuring smile, I aim my gaze at Brent and clear my throat. When his head pops up and he sees me standing at the counter, he gives me a bland smile. "Hey, Linc," he says, without bothering to take his feet off his desk. "Need something?"

"I'm here about Julie Kates." I give him a grim smile but don't offer him any further explanation. Julie is a pretty teenage girl and I'm an ex-con single father with an established history where *pretty teenage girls* are involved. No matter what reason I give, the fact I'm standing here asking about her is going to be cause for speculation.

When I say it, the bland smile gives way to a puzzled look "Sorry, man," he says, finally dropping his feet on the floor. "You're too late—Miss Kates is gone."

"Gone?" I should feel relief but I don't. Even if she'd been released on her own recognizances, Julie is a minor, not to mention a ward of the state. She wouldn't have just been *released* without someone to sign for her. "What does that mean?"

"It means she's *gone*." Brent inspects his fritter, looking for the bite that offers the best apple to glaze ratio. "Bailed out."

Knowing that standing here asking about Julie is inappropriate, I ask anyway. "Bailed out?" I look down at Savanna. She's wedged herself between me and the counter so she can keep an eye on Brent over the top of it, her face pinched with anxiety. "By who?"

Brent takes a bite and chews while he splits a look between me and the closed door that leads to his boss's office. But then he sighs and shrugs again. "Georgia Fell. She paid Julie's bail and took her with her when she left, not more than thirty minutes ago."

ELEVEN

GEORGIA

When it comes into view, I can tell from the soft, sudden intake of breath from the girl beside me that she's never actually seen Fell manor before.

That's not surprising.

Unlike the McNamaras, who fling open their doors to the island's foster kids, hosting Christmas parties and sponsoring charity events several times a year, the Fell family was notoriously private. The best anyone without the benefit of the last name could ever hope for was a view of Fell manor's backside from the deck of a boat while cruising Lake Superior, and even that view is obscured by the thick copse of trees that stands guard between it and the craggy shoreline.

Despite their place in Angel Bay history, the Fells were not known for their generosity.

If not for the hospital's clerical error on my birth certificate, I would've died without ever having seen it up close, much less having a key to its front door.

I drive slowly, guiding the truck along the winding cobblestone drive that cuts through the park-like grounds surrounding the house. Past gardens and fountains. The carriage house and gaze-bos. A large pond with a quaint wooden bridge arched over its placid surface, surrounded by even more gardens. Finally running out of road, I come to a stop at the top of the circular drive, in front of a set of wide, stone steps, and kill the engine.

"It's a bit much, isn't it?" Cutting the engine, I ease my foot off the clutch and turn in my seat to look at the house through Julie's window. "I've lived here for almost a year and I still haven't ventured past the second floor." The truth is, after Elizabeth Fell's attorney gave me a tour of the house and property, I never left the ground floor. I staked out the maid's quarters behind the staff kitchen as my own, which basically amounts to its own three-bedroom apartment, and called it good.

Popping my door open, I hop out of the truck. By the time I'm around the front of it, Julie is standing at the foot of the steps, waiting for me. Looking up at the house on the approach, I can't help but sigh. From this angle, you can't even see all of it—a three-story Victorian the size of a football field with stained-glass domes and turrets. Well over a hundred rooms, stuffed with priceless art and antiques. Every time I walk through the front door, I expect a museum curator to give me a tight-lipped reminder not to touch the exhibits.

Before I can shoo Julie up the stairs, I catch the unmistakable sound of a car coming up the drive. Since no one but Evie and Alex have the gate code and I know Evie is at the hospital, I turn around, expecting to see Alex's cruiser rounding the bend, mentally preparing myself for the confrontation that's about to happen.

But I'm mentally preparing myself for the wrong thing because it's not Alex making his way up my drive.

I recognize the car.

It's Lincoln's—a 1971 Dodge Demon.

He bought it the summer I came to live with the McNamaras. Spent months restoring it. Mr. McNamara hated it on sight. Told Lincoln he'd wasted his money. It's the only thing I ever remember hearing him and his father arguing over.

As soon as Julie sees his car, her eyes go wide and her mouth falls open for a moment before reaching into the clear plastic bag holding her belongings. Fishing out her cell phone, she tries to switch it on. When it proves to be dead, she jams it back into the bag and rushes forward, around the back of the truck and across the driveway to stand in front of the car as it rolls to a short stop in front of her. No sooner is the car thrown in park than the passenger door flies open and the same little girl I saw last night is diving through it to hurl herself at Julie. Lincoln moves more slowly, climbing from behind the wheel almost regrettably, like *here* is the last place he wants to be. He walks toward the two of them, careful not to look at me.

"I'm so sorry about this morning, Mr. McNamara," Julie gushes as soon as she sees him. "The sheriff took my phone after—" Somehow, she manages to go as pale as a sheet and flush bright red at the same time. "Then after everything I just forgot. I'm so sorry, I didn't mean—"

"Stop." Pulling her out of his daughter's grasp, Lincoln turns Julie to look at him, holding her at arm's length like he's taking stock of what he's seeing. Finally shooting me a quick, guarded look, Lincoln drops his hands away from her shoulders and takes a step back. "You're okay?"

Julie nods, swallowing hard against his obvious concern. "Yeah," she tells him, nodding her head before looking down at the little girl still attached to her hip. "I'm fine."

"Good." He gives me another quick look. "I... *uhhh...*" He reaches up to rub a hand across the back of his neck. "I talked to Tammy." He drops his hand and uses it to gesture toward his car. "She..." He shoots me another look. "She had your stuff packed when I went looking for you this morning. She—"

"—gave me back." It's not a question. There's no surprise when she says it. No shock. "She warned me when they took me in—any trouble and I'm gone." Julie's shoulders slump and for the first time since I put her in my truck she looks like she's going to cry. "I bet she didn't even tell the other kids where I went."

I don't know who this Tammy person is specifically but I know her type. The island is full of them—people who sign up to be fosters for the money. Approach it like a business instead of what it's supposed to be. Take older kids like Julie because they have the added benefit of providing childcare for the younger ones. Dump them when there's even so much as a whiff of trouble.

Whoever Tammy is, I pretty much hate her.

Like he knows exactly what I'm thinking, Lincoln's shoots me another look. This time it sticks. "Would it be okay with you if Savanna took Julie inside and showed her around?"

Because the question confuses me and because this is the first time Lincoln has spoken to me directly since the night I left the island, I just stand there and nod like an idiot.

"Great." Clearing his throat, he looks at his daughter and gives her a reassuring smile. "Van, grab Julie's stuff out of the back seat and take her inside—I need to talk to Georgia."

TWELVE

LINCOLN

I have no clue what I'm doing. Why I felt it was a good idea to leave the sheriff's office and drive here. Use the gate code that should've been deactivated months ago and essentially ambush her in her driveway, but here I am, looking up at her while she stares down at me from the bottom of the porch steps, light green eyes narrowed slightly. Back ramrod straight. Arms held stiffly at her sides. Pale blonde hair caught back in a tidy bun at the nape of her neck.

Despite the calm exterior, I can see it. How close she is to losing it and I'm not stupid or arrogant enough to believe it's because I'm standing here, forcing her to face me. Whatever hold I had over Georgia loosened a long time ago.

Waiting until the girls are up the porch steps and inside the house, I clear my throat and take a half-step in her direction. "How are you?" It's a stupid thing to ask. She tripped over her foster sister's body last night after having a screaming match with my wife. "I mean about Rachel. I know you must—"

Something passes over her face, softens it for a moment before it's buried. Chased away by a thousand-yard stare I remember well. "That's your daughter?"

Nodding, I clear my throat. "Yeah." I jam my hands into my

pockets and fight against the instinct to look away from her when I say it. "Her name is—"

"I know what her name is," she tells me, her head cocking slightly to the side. "What I'm wondering is what makes her qualified to give Julie a tour of my house—and how you even got past the gate while we're at it."

"I was Elizabeth Fell's mechanic," I say, telling her the truth—or at least some of it. "She kept me on retainer. I did maintenance on her cars. She was nice to Savanna. Let me bring her with me and kept her company while I worked—she could probably give guided tours of the place if you wanted to open it up to the public." Laughing a little at my own joke, I let the sound die in my throat when all she does is keep staring at me. "I had my own gate code—I gave it a try when I got here, and it worked." What I don't tell her is I'm still on retainer. That I'm still getting monthly payouts from the Fell estate to do a job I should've been fired from as soon as Georgia signed the papers on her inheritance.

She narrows her eyes at me and the tilt of her head deepens, taking it from inquisitive to dangerous in an instant. "And you felt like it was appropriate to just *give it a try* without my consent?"

As soon as she says it, I feel my hackles start to rise. "You've been avoiding me since you came home." I hate the way my voice sounds. Bitter. Resentful. I have no right to feel either—not where Georgia's concerned. Sighing, I pull a hand out of my pocket to scrub it over the back of my neck and try to temper my tone. "I knew if I'd have tried to—"

"What do you want, Lincoln?"

What do I want?

I want her to forgive me.

I want to kiss her.

I want to be able to talk to her without feeling like I'm committing some sort of crime.

Most of all, I want her to look at me like she used to.

To trust me.

Believe me.

But I can't have any of those things, so instead of telling her what I want, I tell her why I'm here. "Julie is Savanna's babysitter," I explain, dropping my hand away from my neck with a sigh. "Her foster parents are my next-door neighbors and when she didn't show up to watch Van this morning, I got worried and..." I let the story trail off because she knows the rest. "I went to the station to check on her and Brent said you posted her bail." I don't mention Alex or what Brent said about her showing up at the station to have it out with him. "I just wanted to make sure she's okay and to bring her stuff—that's it."

"Julie was supposed to sit with Savanna today?" Even though there's nothing accusatory about her tone, I still feel it. The speculation about the nature of my relationship with Julie. If she's really *just* Savanna's babysitter or if she's something more. If there's something unseemly going on between us. I wait for her to say something shitty like *wow, you still have a thing for underage orphans* or *are you going to knock this one up too?* When she doesn't, I clear my throat and nod.

"*Uhhh...* yeah." Reaching up, I swipe a hand over my face. "I used to take her to the shop with me but when Julie moved in next door..." Dropping my hand, I sigh. Stop explaining, because Georgia doesn't give a shit about how hard my life is. About what I have to do to keep Savanna safe. Make sure we stay together. "It's okay," I say, moving toward her with the intention of collecting my daughter and leaving. "I can take her with me."

Before I can take my first step, Georgia lifts her hand between us, palm flat and aimed in my direction like a traffic cop. Whether it's intentional or not, her message is clear—she doesn't want me anywhere near her. "She can stay here," she tells me, dropping her hand as soon as I stop moving. "I've got nothing planned for today."

"Oh—" I start to shake my head, to refuse the offer. "I don't think—"

"Do you need someone to watch your kid or not, Lincoln?" she asks, her tone tinged with impatience.

"What I need is irrelevant," I say, taking a testing step toward her. Like I thought she would, Georgia counters the move, angling herself away from me on the porch. I can't tell if the move was meant to put space between us or if she's instinctively readying herself for some sort of attack. If I had to guess, I'd say it was meant to do both. "I can't do that." Standing my ground, I shake my head. "I can't ask you to take care of her."

"Why?" She cocks her head again, something resembling a smile lifting the corner of her generous mouth. "Do I look like the kind of asshole who would take her personal feelings for her parents out on an innocent kid?"

"What?" The question surprises me. It shouldn't—Georgia has always been blunt. Has never been afraid to say what she's thinking. "No. I—"

"Since you were Elizabeth Fell's personal mechanic, I'm guessing you know the number for the manor's landline," she says, giving slight emphasis to the word *were*.

I know without a doubt she'll be calling her estate manager as soon as I leave and that I've seen the last of my retainer checks from the Fell estate. "Yeah, I have it."

"Then you can call the house when you're ready and I'll bring her to you," she tells me, like the matter is settled. "She can hang out here with Julie until then."

I imagine the alternative. Dragging Savanna out of the house under sullen, tween protest. Taking her to the shop and installing her in my office with a few lousy computer games and a gas station sandwich for lunch. Exposing her to rough shop talk from the ex-felons I almost exclusively employ. And she's older now. Too smart for her own good. Sees things and understands them. Which is exactly why I keep her away from the shop as much as I can.

Defeated, I sigh. "Okay."

Turning away from me, Georgia starts to move up the steps toward the house, making it clear I've been dismissed and she expects me to leave. Stung and feeling pretty ridiculous about it, I turn away from her retreating back and start to move toward my car.

"Lincoln?"

Like it always does, hearing her say my name clenches at my gut and I have to turn around slowly. Give myself time to temper my response.

"Yeah?" Despite the time and effort I give it, the word comes out gruff and uneven.

"Did Rachel use drugs?" Asking it spreads a flush across her cheeks. She's either embarrassed she'd have to ask something like that about someone she considered family or that someone like me, someone she hates and distrusts, might have known Rachel better than she did.

If I had to guess, it's a little bit of both.

"She had her problems but she put all that behind her," I answer her honestly. "Rachel'd been sober for eighteen months before..." I don't finish it. I don't have to. Something passes over Georgia's face, that same soft, wounded look she gave me earlier when I offered my condolences about Rachel's death. "I thought it was you." It comes out of my mouth before I can stop it and even though I want to slam my own head into the cobblestone drive when I hear myself say it, I keep talking. Keep making things worse. "Last night—when Jenna called, screaming and crying about someone being dead." I remember it, how absolutely terrified I was when I heard Jenna say her name. "She said your name and I thought it was you."

That soft, wounded look evaporates, her expression hardening into something guarded and wary and she does that thing again, angling her body away from me like facing me head-on is too dangerous, makes her too vulnerable, and it makes me feel like shit. Damage already done, I start to move around the front of the car, toward her, "Damn it, Georgia, I—"

She gives me a small head shake, letting me know whatever I'm about to say, she doesn't want to hear it. "Call the house when you're ready for me to bring you your kid," she says, before turning on her boot heel and walking up the porch steps, away from me, without a backward glance.

THIRTEEN

GEORGIA

My hand is cramped and my shoulders ache. My spine feels like it's slowly being fed into a meat grinder, each hard, rhythmic push of the scraper against the worn, weathered siding of the house sending curls and chips of old yellow paint flying around me like a swarm of locust.

Rachel'd been sober for eighteen months before...

Scrape.

Scrape.

Scrape.

I thought it was you.

Scrape.

Scrape.

Scrape.

On impulse, I asked Lincoln and he confirmed what Alex told me at the station—Rachel was a drug addict. That I hadn't known her as well as I wanted to believe. That things had gone dangerously awry for her in the years since I'd left.

But even if that were true, even if Rachel had been and done all the things Alex said, that didn't account for the eight months I've been back on the island. Rachel and I have seen each other plenty since then. I've been to her house. Sat at her table and had dinner with her and her wife. Held their baby during his baptism and accepted the responsibility of being his godmother.

If Rachel were on drugs, I would've known.

I'm a trained investigator. I know when someone is lying to me. And Rachel wasn't lying to me.

Whatever she'd been in the past, Rachel was clean and sober. She was a devoted wife. A proud and dutiful mother.

Jamming my scraper into my back pocket for safekeeping, I dig my phone out and dial a number.

"Hey..." Evie answers on the third ring. In the background I can hear babies crying. People talking. Someone coughing. "I called this morning as soon as I heard but you didn't answer. I meant to call back but it's a clinic day," she reminds me. I can tell by her tone she's heard about Rachel. That I was the one who found her. "How are you?"

I forgot it's Saturday. Evie volunteers at the island's free clinic on Saturdays. "I'm fine." It's a lie. I'm not fine. "Are you on shift at the hospital tomorrow?"

"Uh—" There's a pause, like she's mentally shifting through her schedule. "Yeah. Why? Do you want to—"

"They're saying Rachel died of a drug overdose," I tell her, barely able to force the words out. "They're saying she went outside to—"

"Wait—slow down." The clinic's noises fade away and then disappear completely behind the faint click of a door being shut. "Who said that?" Evie asks. "Who is *they*?"

"Kate Timmons from the *Herald*." I spit the words into the phone. "And Alex—this morning. But I know what I saw, Evie." I know I'm rambling. I'm barely making sense, but I can't help it. "He's wrong. There was bruising on her neck and signs of possible sexual assault."

"How could he miss something like that?" I hate the way she says it—not like Alex is wrong. Like maybe I am. "I mean, that's a pretty big oversight, isn't it?"

"I don't know," I tell her, because I refuse to think about it. To consider how or why the man I've been sleeping with for the past six months would or could miss something like that. "All I know is that he's wrong."

"George..." She says my name gently. Like I need to be talked off a ledge. "Maybe—"

"I was a warrant officer in the US Army military police," I remind her. "I spent the last four years of my career running a task force that investigated SHARP cases—I know what I saw, Evie."

"Okay..." Evie lets out a long sigh. "Okay, I believe you—what do you need me to do?"

"*Ms. Fell.*"

Sound, faint and muffled, reaches out and shakes me, forcing me to look down. After talking to Evie I shoved my phone into my pocket and got back to work because I needed something to keep my hands busy while my brain kept worrying and chewing on everything that's happened and everything I've learned over the last twelve hours.

That Rachel is dead.

That she'd been murdered.

That no one believes me.

That by some strange twist of fate, I took Lincoln McNamara's babysitter into my home and now his daughter is currently calling out to me.

Forcing myself to stop scraping, I look down to find Savanna at the bottom of the ladder I'm standing on, pale-yellow paint chips dotting her dark brown hair like snowflakes. Reluctantly, I pull an earbud out of my ear and let it dangle from its cord. "Yeah?"

As soon as I say it, her face falls into a frown at my brusque tone. "It's after noon."

After telling Evie what I needed her to do—examine Rachel's body; check her neck for bruising; for signs of vaginal tearing; anything that'll prove she was assaulted—and getting her to promise me she'll do it, I let her get back to work so I could get back to mine. Apparently, that was several hours ago.

"Okay," I tell her, laughing a little while trying to wrangle my earbud so I can stuff it back in my ear. "Thanks for the update."

"It's after noon and *we're hungry*," she clarifies, her face slipping further into its frown.

I give her a shrug while I finally manage to get my hands on my escaped earbud. "So eat."

"We tried." She looks up at me, her disapproval of my living conditions palpable. "You don't have any food."

"Okay," I say, conceding she's right. Aside from a loaf of bread, coffee, and a few takeout boxes with questionable contents in my fridge, the kitchen is empty of anything resembling food. "So, order pizza."

When I say the word *pizza*, her face scrunches up. "I had pizza last night."

"Alright." I laugh again, this time for real. "Order whatever you want." Before she can start peppering me with more questions, I give some clarification of my own. "I don't care from where—it doesn't matter. Just tell them to deliver it and buzz them in when they get here." Looking past her, I find Julie standing a few feet away, listening quietly to the exchange. I know without a doubt if it'd been just Julie here, she'd have eaten stale bread sprinkled with coffee grounds rather than ask me to feed her. "There's plenty of cash in the phone table drawer under the stairs."

"You're not afraid I'll steal it?" Julie says, reminding me I just bailed her out of jail for committing felony theft only a few hours ago.

"You?" I laugh at the thought. "Not a chance." Re-aiming my gaze downward, I catch sight of Savanna staring up at me, an odd look on her face. "Come get me when the food is here," I say to her, before finally stuffing my earbud back in and getting back to work.

FOURTEEN

When I finally decide I've had enough punishment for the day, I climb down my ladder and make my way back into the house, brushing off paint chips as I go.

Mounting the porch steps, I dig my phone out of my pocket to make another phone call.

"This is Mark." The smooth, professional tones of the Fell family attorney and estate manager reach out to greet me.

He also happens to be my next-door neighbor.

Stopping at the top of the steps, I turn to aim my gaze across the rolling green lawn that disappears into the thick line of trees that protects the house from the shoreline. I haven't had a decent view of the lake since I moved in. "Hi, Mark—it's Georgia."

"Hey, Georgia." Although Mark and I never really knew each other growing up, his family being from the wealthier part of the island, we've formed what feels like a friendship since he found me in Chicago and dragged me back to Angel Bay. "What's up?"

"Nothing, I just have a quick question."

He gives me a frustrated laugh. "Does it have to do with the legality of your bailing out of jail and sheltering a ward of the state without her guardian's consent?"

Her guardian is dead.

"Seriously?" Instead of saying it out loud, I shake my head and frown. "It's only been a few hours. How in the hell—"

"This is Angel Bay, Georgia," he reminds me. "I'd bet half the island knew what you were doing before you even decided to do it." He sighs. "I might be able to buy you a couple days but you can't shelter her indefinitely. Eventually, you'll have to turn Miss Kates over to DCFS."

Even though turning Julie over to child services is the last thing I want to do, I don't argue because that's not why I called him. "I appreciate that, but it's not why I called."

"No?" He sounds confused. "Okay... well, what can I do for you?"

"Why wasn't I told Lincoln McNamara was on the Fell family payroll?"

"Because when I tried to sit you down to discuss financials before you signed the paperwork, assuming stewardship of the estate, you told me in no uncertain terms you didn't care where the money went—matter of fact, your exact words were, *I don't give a shit where the money goes, Mark.* I just assumed—"

"And I *still* don't care," I assure him, making no attempt to hide my agitation. "What I care about, and should've been told about, is who has their very own security code for my front gate and can come and go as they please on my property."

"What?" The exasperated playfulness leaches out of his tone in a heartbeat, replaced by something that sounds like trepidation.

"Lincoln McNamara." That's all I say but it's enough.

Mark barks out a curse. "Damn it, I warned Elizabeth not to hire him," he tells me. "She could be unfailingly stubborn when she wanted something and for some reason, she wanted Lincoln on the payroll. I should've told you he was a past tenant on the property. At least given you the—"

"Wait." I feel the hairs on the back of my neck stand up. "Lincoln *lived* here?"

"*Uhhh...*" He must be at his desk because I can hear papers shuffling. The muted squeak of his office chair as he straightens himself in it. "Well—yes," he says, his confusion almost palpable.

"He and his daughter resided in the carriage house. For nearly two years—I thought that's why you were calling." When I don't answer him, he sighs. "I'm sorry, Georgia—you're right, of course. I should've told you, especially given Lincoln's criminal record. You should've been made aware of—"

"Criminal record?" I say it carefully, wanting to make sure I understood him perfectly. "What criminal record?"

"Well, the initial charges were felony home invasion, aggravated robbery, and attempted murder but he eventually took a plea deal for a single charge of attempted murder." He tells me like he doesn't *want* to tell me. "He served seven years on a ten-year sentence in Marquette before he was paroled."

Attempted murder?

"Who?" I hear myself ask. "Who did he—"

"His father—Richard McNamara... you don't know *any* of this?" Mark asks, sounding skeptical. "You're still tight with the family—they never mentioned it?"

"We don't talk about Lincoln," I tell him, my voice sounding faint and far-off. I knew he'd had some legal trouble when he was younger but I didn't know it was that serious. Certainly not that he tried to kill his own father or it'd resulted in a stint in a maximum-security prison. "When did Elizabeth hire him?"

"Right after he got out of prison," Mark tells me. "Actually, it was the job working for the estate that tipped the parole board in his favor. If not for Elizabeth's intervention I'm sure he would've served the full bid and I highly doubt he would've regained custody of his daughter—certainly not as quickly as he did."

"Custody?" For some reason, saying it out loud makes me sick to my stomach. "Savanna was in foster care?"

"Yes." Mark's tone softens with something that sounds like regret. "From the time she was about a year old until she was nearly eight."

"What about Jen—her mother?" I ask, stopping myself from saying Jenna's name out loud. "Even if Lincoln was in prison, her mother would still have custody."

"Even as a convicted felon, Lincoln McNamara's record is nothing compared to his wife's," Mark tells me. "She's been arrested and convicted on multiple misdemeanor and felony charges—drug possession with intent. Stolen property. Prostitution." Running out of steam, he sighs. "Look, I'm sorry, Georgia," he says again, sounding miserable. "I should've—"

"It's fine," I tell him, not because it actually is but because I don't want to listen to him apologize to me for the next fifteen minutes. "You're a lawyer, not a security expert. You couldn't have known."

"No, it was thoughtless of me," Mark says, unwilling to let it go. "I'll call him. Tell him his services are no longer required, right after I call the security company and revoke his—"

"He's still on the payroll?"

More paper shuffling. "Well—yeah."

"How much am I paying him?"

Mark sighs. "The retainer is two thousand a month, paid directly to—"

"So, I'm paying Lincoln McNamara two thousand *dollars* a month for nothing." The amount seems outrageous to me but I imagine to Elizabeth Fell it was barely more than pocket change.

"Well, if he hasn't been servicing your cars then yes, you're paying him for nothing." He sighs again. "But, like I said, I'll call him right now and tell him—"

"Double it."

My request is met with silence.

"Excuse me?" Mark says, completely confused by my one-eighty. That makes two of us.

"I said double it," I tell him, irritation bleeding into my tone.

"Okay, just so we're clear—you *don't* want me to fire him?" he says carefully, making sure he understands me. "In fact, you want me to *double* his monthly retainer."

"Yes." I have no idea what I'm doing. Even though I know firing Lincoln is the smart thing to do, I can't seem to make myself do it. "That's what I'm saying."

"Okay," Mark says, like he wants to argue with me but knows better. "If that's the case, you'll have to tell me where you'd like the additional two thousand to be sent."

"I just told you." I feel my brow furrow. "I—"

"The initial two thousand is sent directly to Angel Bay Prep to cover Savanna McNamara's tuition," Mark informs me, referencing the island's tony private school. "Where should I send the remaining funds?"

"I don't know," I say, with a small shrug. "To him, I guess—if he's an estate employee, you must have his address on file."

"I'm sure I can dig it up," he assures me. "If that's what you want me to do."

"It is," I say, preparing to hang up. "Wait—Mark?"

"Yes?"

"Why did Lincoln try to kill his dad?" None of this makes sense but that's the part I can't wrap my head around. Lincoln worshipped his father. Lived his entire life just to make him proud. I imagine what happened with Jenna made their relationship difficult, but I can't believe it'd strained it to the point that he'd lash out and physically harm his own father.

"No one really knows for sure—both parties were pretty tight-lipped about what happened but the general consensus was the attack was drug-related." Again, I get the feeling he's telling me something he doesn't really want to tell me.

"I see," I tell him, even though I don't see at all. "Thank you, Mark."

Hanging up, I drop the phone away from my ear, still trying to process everything he just told me.

Lincoln went to prison for trying to kill his own father. He's a drug addict, or at the very least had had issues with drugs in the past, and lost custody of his daughter.

And he works for me.

"Food's here."

Hearing her voice, I feel my shoulders shoot up to my ears and I turn around to find Savanna standing less than ten feet away. If the look she's giving me is any indication, she heard every word I said.

Before I can explain or make a lame excuse as to why she just overheard me interrogate my lawyer about her father's past, Savanna turns on her heel and walks away.

FIFTEEN

When I walk in, it's to find Julie and Savanna sitting at the sturdy kitchen table in the center of the room. Julie's changed out of her dress and sandals and into a pair of jeans and a T-shirt with the logo for the shaved ice stand she works at on the boardwalk. She looks like she's been crying, listlessly picking her way through a carton of orange chicken while Savanna plows her way through an Everest-sized mountain of eggrolls, jabbering a mile-a-minute between bites.

"Mildred Fell—*Millie*—was best friends with Sarah Winchester."

Crunch.

"They grew up together in Connecticut. When Sarah's husband died of tuberculosis—"

Crunch.

"—she moved to California and started building that crazy house of hers and Millie and her husband moved here and started the orphanage."

Crunch.

"They closed the orphanage in the seventies when the state decided it was better for kids to live with real families. That's why we have so many foster homes here."

Three out of five.

Three homes out of five on the island are licensed by Fell County as a foster home. It's a dumping ground for garbage kids no one wants. Kids whose parents' rights were severed but are considered unfit for adoption for one reason or another. They get dropped here and forgotten about while they wait for their eighteenth birthday.

That's what happened to me.

I'd bet that's what happened to Julie, too.

Washing my hands, I pick a carton at random and grab a pair of chopsticks from a bag full of napkins and utensils before taking a seat. Pinching the flaps of my box open, I dig in without paying much attention to what I'm eating.

Looking at me, Savanna stops her Fell manor history lesson and quirks her mouth. "I wasn't sure what you'd like so I just ordered everything," she tells me, shooting a quick glance in my direction before focusing on her pile of eggrolls. She expects me to yell at her for sneaking up on me. Maybe reprimand her for eavesdropping on my conversation with Mark about her father.

"I like everything," I tell her, giving her a shrug of my own. "Can't afford to be picky in the military."

Savanna makes a noise in the back of her throat and nods. "You were a police officer in the army?" she asks, repeating one of the things I'm sure she's heard about me around the island.

"Started out as an MP," I tell her, digging my chopsticks into my carton. "Ended as a warrant officer with the CID—criminal investigation division."

"Where you investigated sharp cases?"

The question picks my head up. "Where did you hear that?" She might've heard plenty about me on the island, but she's never heard that.

"You said it on the phone earlier." Savanna gives me a shrug when all I do is stare at her. "I'm nine—eavesdropping is the only way I ever learn anything useful."

Because I remember what it was like to be nine and feeling like everything happening to you and around you is out of your control, I laugh. "Yeah—that's where I investigated SHARP cases."

"What are they?"

"SHARP stands for *Sexual Harassment Assault Response Prevention,*" I tell her, mentally preparing myself for all the questions that will likely follow.

"Is that what you think happened to Aunt Rachel?" Her brow lowers over her warm hazel eyes like the thought of it upsets her, while Julie stops pretending to eat and sits up a little straighter in her seat. "Do you think someone—"

Whatever I expected her to ask me, that wasn't it. "I think I'm not in the army anymore and I think we should let the sheriff handle it," I tell her, mixing truth with lie. If she listened in on my conversation with Evie then she knows what I asked her to do, but that doesn't mean I'm going to willingly talk to her about it.

"The sheriff, your *boyfriend*?" I'm not sure why but something about the way she says it sounds angry.

"Yup—the sheriff, my boyfriend." Shoveling another bite of lo Mein into my mouth, I narrow my gaze on the top of her head and chew. Instead of reprimanding her or blaming her for things she has no way of controlling, I decide to meet the issue head-on. "Do we need to talk about anything else you overheard?" I ask her as soon as my mouth is clear. "Maybe what you heard me say on the porch? About your dad."

"No." She shakes her head, her jaw held at a defiant angle that makes her look like her mother. "I know what people think about my dad." The way she says *people* makes it clear she considers me one of them. Makes me wonder how much she knows about my relationship with her father. "What they say about him and my mom." Under the defiance, I can hear it—uncertainty. Whether she knows it or not, she's worried those people are right. That he did the things they say he did and worse. That her father isn't a good man.

Looking at Julie, I jerk my chin at her. "Where are your parents?"

"I don't know..." Julie's mouth twitches to the side while she gives me a shrug. "My dad was never around much. I don't really remember him and they took me from my mom when I was four—drugs." Her mouth quirks again, pushed out of place by the one-word answer that explains how she ended up in foster care. "She showed for a few court dates before she gave up. Haven't heard from her since. State severed her rights when I was six."

Taking another bite of lo Mein, I give her a nod while I chew. "My umbilical cord was still attached when they found me—I never knew either one of my parents. Couldn't pick them out of a line-up if someone put a gun to my head." Looking at Savanna, I toss my half-empty carton of lo Mein onto the table between us. "Your dad fought for you. He didn't walk away. Didn't stop showing up. That's the only thing that matters, so *people* can eat shit." Feeling exposed, I stand up before dividing a look between the two girls staring up at me from the kitchen table. Looking at my watch so I don't have to look at them, I nod. "Lincoln should be calling soon—make sure you either eat all this food or put it away before he does," I say, aiming my directive at Julie. "You're working tonight?"

Looking down at her shirt, Julie shrugs. "Yeah." Giving up on pretending to eat she pushes her carton across the table. "My shift starts in an hour."

"Do you have a driver's license?"

"Yeah." She gives me a sullen nod. "But—"

"Excellent." Shifting my gaze to Savanna, I offer her a flat smile. "You know where they keep the car keys in this place." Even though it's more of a statement than an actual question, Savanna nods. "Great—show her where they are and how to get to the garage so she can drive herself to work." Looking at Julie again, I give her a shrug. "I'm sorry to have to tell you this, but I trust you. I think you're a good kid. You're not going to steal from me and I'd bet my life you didn't steal that boat—if I had to guess, you're covering for whoever it is you've been crying over." I don't say the rest. That whoever would let her take the rap for committing a felony isn't worth her time or tears. She's seventeen—nearly the same age I was when I finally saw Lincoln for what he really is. If someone had tried to sit me down and tell me that he wasn't who I thought he was, I'd have spit in their face and called them a liar rather than see the truth.

Letting it go, I push my chair under the table. "I'm staying in the servants' quarters," I tell Savanna, pointing at the pocket door that's half hidden by the refrigerator. "Come get me when your dad calls."

"I can drop her off at the garage on my way to work," Julie offers when I'm halfway to the door, and even though it'd be the smart thing to do, I shake my head.

"No," I tell her without turning around. "Thanks, but I'll take her myself. I need to talk to Lincoln."

SIXTEEN

I pull onto the tarmac outside Lincoln's repair shop a few hours later, a sulking Savanna on the bench seat next to me. When she came to tell me her dad had texted her to say he'd be by in an hour to get her, I shoved her out the door and insisted on taking her home myself.

"He won't want you here," Savanna says from the far side of the bench seat. "He told us to wait."

The place looks like it's winding down for the day. Only one bay door is rolled open, a lone mechanic under what looks like a late model Chevy. "I'm not very good at waiting." I let the truck roll to a stop next to Lincoln's car. "And I don't really care what your dad wants."

Leaning on its kickstand on the other side of my parking spot is a motorcycle. I recognize it too. The same Harley Davidson Softail I saw parked behind the Den the night I found Rachel. This close, I can see the name "KING" stenciled over the airbrushed scythe on the gas tank.

Savanna is still frowning at me. I can see her face in the reflection of the window. "He said that—"

"I care about what he *said* even less than I do about what he wants." Killing the engine, I set the parking brake before opening my door to hop out of the truck. I start across the tarmac, heading for the open roll-up. Behind me, I hear the passenger-side door creak open and Savanna's worn sneakers scrambling across the pavement as she hurries to catch up to me.

As soon as we're inside, she breaks off, hurrying past me and down a short, dimly lit stretch of hallway, toward a closed door that leads to the back of the shop. As soon as she opens it, a cacophony of sound spills through it—the high-pitched whine of hydraulic power tools. The clank of them as they hit the concrete floor. Shouts and curses from people I can't see. Before I can piece together what I'm hearing, the door bangs closed and it's quiet again.

"Hello?" I call out to the pair of legs on a creeper, sticking out from the underside of the Chevy. My greeting is answered by the sharp metallic twang of a heavy-duty tool hitting concrete before the pair of legs digs its heels in to pull itself out from under the car.

It's Will Hudson.

"Well, if it isn't little Georgie Fell," he says, his grime-streaked face breaking into the same lascivious grin he gave me last night. "You lookin' for me?"

"Not sure," I tell him, giving him a bland smile in return. "Is that your bike?" I point out the open door, toward the motorcycle parked next to Lincoln's car, even though I know it's not.

"Why?" Standing, he pulls a shop rag from the back pocket of his jeans and starts to rub the grease off his hands while he cuts me a lewd smirk. "You want a ride?"

"Geez—is this where you promise it'll be a *quick* ride?" I say, grinning in his face in hopes of curbing my urge to punch him in it.

Will stops rubbing his hands and looks up at me. "I'm not the one who goes around making promises I don't intend to keep, now am I, Georgie?"

That was about Archie. The fact that I ran. Left him here alone.

The cacophony again, followed by another door slam.

"What are you doing here?"

Shooting my gaze past Will's uneasy smirk, I see Lincoln

standing at the mouth of the hallway, Savanna behind him, her face half hidden by his shoulder. Hidden or not, the panic plastered across it is as clear as day.

"The brakes are going out on my truck." When all I get from the two men in front of me is a whole lot of staring, I give them both an exasperated laugh. "I mean—you *do* fix cars here, right?"

"We sure do, Ms. Fell." Will's smirk shifts into an affable grin. "I got it, boss," he says over his shoulder, before lifting his hand in an attempt to usher me out of the building. "Why don't you show me—"

"No," Lincoln says, his tone sharp and heavy enough to stop Will in his tracks. "I need you to take Van home for me while I see to Ms. Fell."

"Dad—" Savanna steps into view, her face contorted into a scowl. "I can wait for you here. Uncle Will doesn't have to take me home."

"Yes, he does," he tells her, using the same sharp, heavy tone on his daughter as he did on his employee. "Go on—I'll be home as soon as I'm done here."

Savanna shoots me a quick, narrow-eyed glare before her shoulders slump in defeat. "Whatever," she grumbles, stomping past me on her way outside. Giving me a final, uneasy look, Will follows her through the roll-up, jogging a bit to catch up to her as she heads toward a primer-gray muscle car parked on the other side of the lot. I watch as he opens Savanna's door for her, closing it carefully as soon as she's inside. She stares at us through the window while Will circles the back of the car and climbs into the driver's seat. Seconds later, the car roars to life.

"I didn't know you were friends with Will Hudson," I say, watching them drive away.

"Will isn't my friend," Lincoln informs me, his tone losing some of its sharpness. "He's my employee."

"An employee you trust to take your daughter home," I point out, careful to keep my own tone neutral.

Neutral or not, he must know what I think of Will Hudson

because the sigh he lets loose is equal parts annoyed exasperation and apathetic indifference. "I told Savanna I'd come get her," he reminds me, his tone held low, like he doesn't want to be overheard. "You didn't have to bring her here."

"It's not a big deal," I tell him with a shrug, like I did him a favor, when it's obvious my being here is the last thing he wants. "Besides, my brakes really do need to be looked at and since you work for me, I figured you could do that."

When I say *work for me*, Lincoln's jawline goes tight and he looks away, a surefire sign of guilt. "You said Elizabeth Fell used to let you bring Savanna to work with you when you serviced her cars. What you failed to mention is that you and Savanna actually *lived* on the property before I moved back to the island."

The tight clench in his jaw softens and he lets out a sigh. "I'm sorry, Georgia. I wanted to tell you but—"

"But you figured if I knew you were still on the estate's payroll, I'd have you cut off and then you wouldn't be able to afford Savanna's fancy private school tuition," I say, finishing what I'm sure would've been a long-winded explanation in short order. "Again, I gotta ask—do I look like the sort of asshole who would take her feelings for the parents out on a kid?"

"No." Lincoln shakes his head at me and sighs. "But you don't seem like the sort of person who'd keep cutting checks to someone you hate, either."

I don't hate you.

I almost say it. It almost tumbles out of my mouth but I manage to keep it in. "You're in luck because it's not my money—*not really* —so I really don't care where it goes."

Lincoln's expression falls into something caught between a frown and a scowl. "Yeah—well, you should," he says, shouldering his way past me on his way out the door.

Feeling like I'm sixteen again, I scramble after him, through the doorway and out onto the tarmac. "What's that supposed to mean?"

"It means, *real* Fell or not, Elizabeth trusted you to do the right thing," he tells me while he digs his keys out of his pocket and heads toward my truck.

"I suppose you think she should've left it all to you, huh?" It's a shitty thing to say but instead of apologizing, I double down. "I mean, she *was* your benefactor, wasn't she?"

"No." Aiming a fob in its general direction, he hits a button and pops the locks on his car. "Elizabeth was my friend. For reasons I've never been able to understand, she believed me."

"Believed you about what?"

"Believed *in* me," he quickly amends, avoiding eye contact while he yanks the passenger-side door of his car open before making a motion like he's trying to shoo me into it. "She believed in me. Helped me when no one else would and, for the record, I'm the last person on the planet she should've left her money to—now get in."

"Why?" The demand, coupled with the way he's looking at me, instantly puts my back up.

"Because I'm taking you home," he tells me, his tone tight with impatience.

"I thought you were coming out here to look at my brakes."

"I don't have time right now—I have to get home, sooner rather than later, and rescue my ex-con employee from my nine-year-old daughter, so your brakes will have to wait until tomorrow." He gestures toward the open door. "I'll take you home."

"That's not necessary," I tell him, shaking my head while I reach into the pocket of my cargos for my cell phone. "I can just call Alex for a ride home."

The second I say Alex's name, Lincoln goes still. "Get in the car, Georgia."

"No." I shake my head. "He's probably on his way to the manor by now. I can just have him swing by and—"

"I don't want your cop boyfriend here," he nearly shouts at me. Letting out another heavy sigh, he swipes a rough hand over his face. "Will isn't the only ex-con I have working for me and I'd really prefer to keep my interactions with the cops *and* theirs to a minimum—so, please." He drops his hand and looks at me. "Let me take you home."

I should tell him to go to hell.

That he can't talk to me that way.

That I don't care if he has an aversion to law enforcement.

That I'm not getting into his car and he is definitely not taking me home.

But Lincoln has something I want.

So, instead, I slip my phone back into my pocket and do exactly what he says.

SEVENTEEN

LINCOLN

I was seventeen the summer my parents brought Georgia home—a senior in high school and so ready to leave for college I was doubling up on my class load and enrolled in summer school so I could graduate early.

That first night, after dinner, I saw her standing on the edge of the dock, looking at my boat tied to the end of it and out over the lake. Without even thinking about it, I rerouted myself from the boathouse where I'd been sleeping since I was fifteen to walk down to where she was standing.

"What are you doing down here?" I asked her, unable to keep the concern out of my voice. I knew who she was, of course—everyone on the island did. She was the Angel Bay Baby. The Fake Fell—but I didn't know *her*. What she was capable of. What she might be planning, out there in the dark, all by herself.

My question collapsed her face into a frown and she turned and tipped it upward to look at me. "I was thinking about stealing that boat and running away," she answered, her tone blunt and unapologetic.

"Do you know how to sail?" I asked, ignoring her confession, because unlike a lot of what I heard around here, I didn't think she said it in order to shock or upset me.

I thought she was telling me the truth.

"No." She gave me another look. "Are you going to offer to teach me?"

"Well, if you're going to steal my boat," I said, digging my hands into the front pockets of my jeans, "I'd feel better knowing you know what you're doing before you do."

Laughing quietly to herself, Georgia just shot another long, wistful look across the water before walking away. Left me standing there on the docks by myself without another word.

I liked her instantly.

I still like her.

More than like her.

That's my problem.

It always has been.

As soon as I slide into the seat next to her, Georgia turns toward me to give me the same sort of look she gave me that night on the dock. Like I'm a stranger. Not worthy of her trust.

"What?" I grumble, shoving my key into the ignition.

"There are guns in my truck," she tells me in that blunt, unapologetic tone of hers.

"Guns?" I drop my hand away from the dashboard and turn to look at her over the center console.

She nods, her chin picking itself up a bit in a defiant gesture I remember well. "They're registered," she tells me, defensively. "I have my concealed carry permit, I'm just—"

"You're just *what*?" I can't help the tone of my voice, how sharp it gets when I think about it. "Afraid me or one of my guys'll take them? Maybe go knock over a gas station?"

"No." Her dark blonde brows slam low over her narrowed eyes. "I just don't want to get you in trouble, since you're..." She lets her explanation trail off while giving me a vague hand wave. "You know."

"An ex-con?" I finish for her, my tone still sharp. It shouldn't be. I made the bed I'm lying in. She's expressing legitimate concern for me and I'm being a defensive asshole. "Don't be shy—you can say it. I mean, you've obviously been filled in on all the mistakes I made since you left."

"You tried to kill your dad—I'm not sure I'd categorize that as a *mistake*." She looks right at me when she says it, like she's daring me to deny it. Like maybe she's hoping I will.

"The only *mistake* I made was not finishing the job," I tell her, jaw so stiff it feels like she doubled up her fist and hit me in it. I know what I'm doing. I'm doing what I should've done years ago. I'm trying to scare her. Push her away.

Instead of taking the bait I'm throwing at her, Georgia turns in her seat to aim her gaze out the windshield. "I did my due diligence," she tells me with a shrug. "If you're not worried about my truck full of guns, then neither am I."

I should be worried about it. As a felon, convicted of a violent crime, I should make her clear the guns from her car and call Bradford for a pick-up. That would be the smart thing.

But when it comes to me and Georgia, *the smart thing* never stands a chance, so instead of doing the smart thing, I start the car.

Pulling out of the lot, I resolve not to say another word to her.

That lasts about thirty seconds.

"How many?" I ask without looking at her.

"Three—an M9 in the glovebox and one stashed under my seat. A Benelli pump-action behind it." Her mouth twitches and her head tilts slightly to the side. "There's also a stun gun in the map pocket and a Ka-Bar tucked into the visor."

"Jesus, Georgia," I say, shaking my head. "What the hell?"

"They make me feel better." That's it. That's all the explanation she offers me. I want to ask her why. What happened to her that she needs an arsenal to make herself feel better? But I don't because it's none of my business and if I ask her, that's exactly what she'll tell me.

"I won't let anyone else work on your truck, okay?" I tell her, trying to put her at her ease. "I'll get to it first thing in the morning so it should be done by noon or so—I'll bring it to you as soon as I'm finished with it."

"Okay. Thank you." She nods her head without looking at me, her back ramrod straight, hands resting on her thighs, and we slip into another awkward silence. Finally, she lets out a breath that slumps her shoulders a little. "Can I ask you something?"

"I guess," I answer, careful to keep my gaze trained on the road in front of me.

"Why is King's motorcycle parked at your shop?"

Shit.

Playing dumb, I let my face fall into a frown. "Who's King?"

That gaze of hers narrows into a glare before digging into the side of my face. She's not buying it but she plays along anyway. "He's the president of the Red Reapers motorcycle club—he was at the Den last night. I spoke to him about ten minutes before I found Rachel's body."

Will failed to mention that part—either because he didn't know, or because he was afraid of what I'd do if I found out Georgia put herself directly in King's crosshairs. "And?" I say it carefully, like I still don't understand.

"*And* now he's at your shop."

"No." I give my head a tight shake. "His *bike* is at my shop."

"I don't like semantics, Lincoln," she tells me in a hard tone that instantly tightens the clench of my jaw. "I never have."

"It's not semantics, Georgia—I own an auto repair shop," I remind her. "If his bike is parked in front of it, it doesn't mean he's there. It means his bike needs *repairs*—same as your truck."

"King was at the Den last night." Still not buying it, she shakes her head. "He and his buddies took off when I called Alex after I found Rachel's—"

"The guy's a biker," I say, giving her another reminder. "And not the good kind—you think he's just going to stick around and wait for your boyfriend to roll up on his clubhouse and start kicking up dirt?"

"Rachel is dead, Lincoln," she says in a tone that tells me she's not going to just let this go. That she's not going to just walk away and let Bradford do his job. "She's dead and I—"

"What do you want from me?" It comes out hard, the force of it used to mask the truth—that whatever she asks of me, I'll give her. I'll do it without a moment's hesitation.

"I need to find Jenna."

Anything but that.

"Why?"

"Because she was at the Den last night." She looks at me like it's a ridiculous question and I'm an idiot for asking it. "She might know what happened to Rachel. At least why she was there."

"Bradford already questioned her." I shake my head while I cruise through a yellow light, suddenly in a hurry to get away from her just so this conversation can be over with. "I doubt seriously she'd tell you anything she didn't already tell him."

As soon as I say it an ugly flush crawls up her neck to settle into her cheeks. "Why not?"

"Because she hates you," I tell her matter-of-factly. "She's always hated you."

"I never did anything to her," she tells me quietly, the hurt in her tone obvious enough to make me feel like an asshole for stating the obvious. "I left. When I found out about the two of you, *I left*."

As soon as she says it, my guts go loose and I can't look at her. Can't even breathe. "Georgia—"

Before I can finish, a set of revolving red and blue lights flash in my rearview and the squad car behind me turns on its siren to pull us over.

EIGHTEEN

GEORGIA

As soon as the lights flash in Lincoln's rearview, his entire demeanor changes. His mouth, open in mid-sentence, snaps shut and he sighs again, this one so long and weary, he sounds like an old man who's tired of living.

"I know you hate me," he says while he flicks another quick, tense look at the rearview mirror where the lights behind us are still flashing. "And I know you have every reason to, but I have a kid I need to get home to, so please keep your mouth shut and let me handle this." Pulling into a parking lot across the street from a row of modest, single-family homes, Lincoln rolls his car to a stop and puts it in park. "Do you think you can do that?"

"Probably not," I tell him while he turns off the engine and moves his hands into plain view on the steering wheel. This isn't the first time Lincoln's been pulled over on the island. I'd bet it isn't even the hundredth. "What about King? You think he'd be willing to help me find Jenna?"

"Jesus." He mutters it, shaking his head. "You never give up, do you?"

"Nope," I snap at him. "Are you going to help me find Jenna or not?"

His expression hardens and he looks away from me. "Not." He trains his gaze on the rearview mirror. "I'm *not* going to help you.

Let your boyfriend do his job and stay out of things that aren't your business."

Aren't my business?

Someone called me to the Den last night. Lured me there for reasons I can't explain but whatever they are, I'm positive they have to do with Rachel and why she was murdered. I can't let go. Not until I know the truth.

I want to scream it in his face.

Instead, I retreat. Let it go for now because now is not the time and this is not the place to have this conversation.

Shifting my gaze toward the rearview I watch while the officer climbs out of his vehicle and makes his way toward us, his face obscured by the flashing lights. As he walks, he reaches up and casually unsnaps the strap securing his service weapon in his gun belt.

"Does this happen a lot?"

Instead of answering me, Lincoln laughs softly while the deputy raps his knuckles on the driver's side window, a few inches from his face, the dull glint of his wedding ring flashing in the setting sun. Slowly moving his hand off the steering wheel, Lincoln rolls down the window. "Afternoon, Officer," he says, his casual, relaxed tone at total odds with his body language. "What can I do for you?"

"You can start by telling me where the hell you think you're—" The deputy bends, framing his face in Lincoln's open window perfectly. It's Levi Tate, my lawyer's younger brother. The Tates are one of the island's wealthiest families, and once upon a time, he was Lincoln's best friend. Judging by the way they're looking at each other now, I can see that's no longer the case.

When he sees me, the schoolyard-bully grin plastered across his face dulls a little. "Ms. Fell." He says it carefully, like he's not sure what else he's supposed to say to me. Snapping his gaze back to Lincoln, he smiles again, this one tight and polite, barely lifting the corners of his mouth. "You're in an awful hurry," he says, his tone matching his smile. "Where you headed?"

"Georgia dropped her truck off at my shop for repairs," Lincoln says, keeping his own tone neutral. "I'm just driving her home."

Levi makes a sound in the back of his throat like he knows the story is bogus but can't prove it. "Are you aware you ran a red light at the intersection of First and Gabriel?"

"No, I wasn't," Lincoln says, his tone matching the deputy's.

The light wasn't red, it was yellow, which means this traffic stop is complete bullshit. Instead of blurting it out, I focus on keeping my mouth shut like Lincoln asked me to.

Like he can read my mind, Levi shoots me a quick, cool smile before re-aiming his attention at Lincoln. "License, registration, and proof of insurance. Please." He tacks on the *please* before straightening himself, settling his hand on the butt of his unsnapped service weapon while Lincoln flips down his visor and retrieves a slim, bi-fold holder. "Here you go," Lincoln says, offering it to him through the open window. Levi takes it with what sounds like a quiet scoff and flips it open, barely giving its contents a cursory glance before flipping it closed again. "Go ahead and step out of the vehicle for me, Mr. McNamara," he says while taking a step back, somehow managing to make Lincoln's name sound like *you complete piece of shit.*

"No." I reach out to place a hand on Lincoln's forearm, stopping him cold. "He's not doing that."

"Georgia." Lincoln whispers my name, a quiet reminder I promised him I'd stay out of it and keep my mouth shut.

Hunkering down again, Tate nails me with a hard look. "Excuse me?"

"I said, *no—he's not doing that,*" I repeat myself, enunciating each word clearly like I'm talking to a toddler. "Not until you re-snap your holster."

Levi's gaze narrows slightly. "I'm not sure I like what you're implying, Ms. Fell."

"I'm not implying a damn thing, *Levi,*" I tell him, tightening my grip on Lincoln's arm. "I'm telling you outright—no one is getting out of this car until you secure your weapon."

Levi's gaze narrows a bit further. "Alright, Georgia." He gives me a small smirk before straightening his frame. Making a show of it, Levi re-snaps his holster before showing us his hands. "Can he get out of the car now?" he says in an overly solicitous tone that tightens my jaw.

"I can handle this." Before I can offer any sort of protest, Lincoln's out and being spun into the side of his car, his palms flat on the roof while Levi pats him down. Without thinking, I throw open my own door and scramble out after him. As soon as he sees me, Lincoln scowls.

"Goddamn it, Georgia," he growls at me while Levi secures his hands behind his back with a pair of cuffs. When he sees me, Levi scowls.

"Get back in the car, Ms. Fell," he tells me while he tightens the cuffs around Lincoln's wrists.

"Kiss my ass, Levi," I snarl back, ignoring the glare Lincoln is shooting me over the roof of the car.

"Kissing your ass is the sheriff's job, isn't it?" Levi says, flashing me another one of his smirks while he clamps a hand around Lincoln's shoulder and pulls him off the car. I watch helplessly while he marches Lincoln back to his squad car and feeds him into the back of it. When Levi climbs into the driver's seat, I'm sure he's going to drive away. Take Lincoln to the station and throw him in holding because I couldn't keep my mouth shut like he asked me to, but he doesn't. The car doesn't move and even though I can't really see or hear what's happening, I get the impression they're talking.

Just talking.

Walking down the length of Lincoln's car to get a better look, I jump like a nervous cat when my cell phone buzzes in my pocket, signaling a text. Pulling it out, I swipe at the screen to pull it up.

Where are you?

Because I have the distinct feeling Alex knows exactly where I am, I shove my phone back into my pocket without answering him.

It buzzes again almost immediately. Ignoring it, I cross my arms over my chest and focus my attention on what's happening inside Levi's squad car, trying to make out movements. Facial expressions. But the revolving red and blue lights, coupled with the glare of the setting sun bouncing off the windshield, makes it nearly impossible to see what's going on.

After a few minutes, Levi gets out and walks toward me, leaving Lincoln handcuffed in the back. "Here's what's going to happen." Mimicking my stance, he leans against the hood of his squad and crosses his arms over his chest. "Either you're going to get in my car and let me take you home or I'm going to take Lincoln to jail."

"For what?" It's a stupid question. This is Angel Bay and no matter who Lincoln used to be, his name no longer affords him the protection it once did. Levi can do whatever he wants because he has the badge and Lincoln has a criminal record.

"I'm not sure," Levi tells me with a shrug, all but confirming my suspicions. "I'll figure it out when I get to the station."

Anger swells in my gut, a black, useless surge that threatens to choke me where I stand. "You can't do that," I tell him, shaking my head. "He didn't do anything."

"I don't know about that," he says, giving me a shrug. "I'm pretty sure he took a swing at me when I attempted to detain him —or, you can just get in my car and I'll let him go," Levi tells me, his tone low and reasonable. "I'll take you home and Linc can go back to his side of the island—*to his kid*—and no one has to go to jail."

I imagine Savanna at home, waiting for her father. What might happen to her if he's arrested for attempted assault on a police officer.

"Does your brother know what a piece of shit you are?" I ask him, dropping my arms away from my chest in defeat because we both know I'm getting in the car, just like he said.

Instead of answering me, Levi just laughs while I make my way to the passenger side of his squad car and climb in.

"What are you doing?" Lincoln asks from the back, his voice tight with worry. "Geor—"

Before he can finish, his door opens and I watch in the rearview while Levi hauls him out and leans him against the squad's open doorframe to unlock his cuffs. One cuff undone, Lincoln lunges back into the car. "What are you doing?" he asks, his hand smacking against the plexi-glass partition that separates us to get my attention. When I look at him, he swears softly under his breath. "Get out of the car, Georgia—*right now*. Get out of the fuc—"

"I'll be okay," I tell him, giving him a small smile. "Go home to your daughter."

Before he can answer me, Levi hauls him back out of the car and slams the door closed between us. As soon as he gets Lincoln's cuff off, there's a short skirmish that ends with the two of them nose to nose, Lincoln's grease-stained hands buried in the crisp khaki fabric of Levi's uniform shirt. Levi's hand is wrapped around the butt of his gun.

I can't see Levi's face but I can see Lincoln's while they exchange words, too quietly for me to hear what they're saying.

Whatever Levi says, it's enough to push Lincoln back, away from the car, giving the deputy enough room to open his own door and climb into the driver's seat.

Turning in my seat, I see Lincoln through the rear window, face contorted in helpless rage, hands clenched into fists and hanging uselessly at his sides while he watches us drive away.

NINETEEN

We aren't even out of the parking lot before Levi asks: "What are you doing with Lincoln, Georgia?"

"He already told you—I dropped my truck off to have the brakes checked and he was driving me home," I tell him, repeating the explanation Lincoln gave to him less than ten minutes ago.

"You sure that's it?" He throws a quick look at oncoming traffic before he makes a right turn onto Fell Street. "When I came up on you, it looked like the two of you were fighting pretty good about something."

"Yeah, well, I'm an asshole," I tell him, shifting in my seat to aim my gaze out my window. "I fight with everyone."

He grins like he tricked me into admitting the truth somehow. "So, what were you fighting about?"

"He likes Pepsi and I like Coke." Tapping a finger on my chin, I frown. "Wait—that wasn't it. He likes the Backstreet Boys and I like 'N Sync."

Levi gives me a scoff, his jaw tight with annoyance. "That right?"

Dropping my hand, I shrug. "What can I say, I have a thing for Justin Timberlake," I tell him, falling silent as he pulls up to the intersection of Fell and Michael. Fell Street dead ends into my driveway and the manor gates loom straight ahead. "I can walk from here."

"Don't be ridiculous, Georgia. It's almost a mile to the main house and it's getting dark," he tells me as he pulls up to the deserted guard shack and rolls down his window. "Besides, the sheriff'd have my head if I let his girlfriend walk home in the dark all by herself."

It might just be my imagination, but I hear a note of amusement when he says *girlfriend*. Like he finds the whole thing absurd. Reaching an arm outside his window, Levi punches in a code. The gates to the manor swing open. Pulling his arm in, he looks at me and grins. "Police and fire have an auxiliary code for all these houses," he says, answering the question I'm sure is clearly written on my face as he pulls forward. "Just in case."

Instead of answering him, I swallow my snarky reply and stare out the window to watch the estate's park-like grounds roll by. A hundred yards in, the carriage house appears—a quaint little bungalow surrounded by a picture-perfect white picket fence.

"I bet Linc thought he won the lottery when old lady Fell made him her little pet project," Levi says, the tone of his voice pulling my gaze to his face. "He lived a pretty sweet life until you showed up and yanked the rug out from under him." He sounds sour. Like the thought of Lincoln catching a break, no matter how brief, pisses him off.

"What happened between the two of you?" I don't mean to ask but I do anyway. I shouldn't because it doesn't matter. It's none of my business, but Levi and Lincoln had been close once and I don't understand the animosity between them. "Lincoln was your best friend. The two of you—"

"Things change, Georgia. So do people," he tells me, the decisive edge in his voice telling me there's no room to push. "I'll tell you this much, though—I bet Linc kicks himself every day for knocking up the wrong eastern girl."

"What's that supposed to mean?" I ask, my entire body going stiff.

"It means, if he'd known you'd end up being the one who inherited all this, he never would've given Jenna a second look." Pulling onto the circular drive, Levi stops his squad car at its top, shifting into park behind another.

Alex is here.

I don't know why but his explanation pushes me over the edge. Like earlier, with Savanna, I feel this insane urge to defend Lincoln to someone who undoubtedly knows him and what he's capable of better than I do. "Nothing ever happened between Lincoln and me. He never touched me," I tell him, shaking my head. My entire body on fire with something that feels a lot like shame. "Not ever. Not once."

It's not true.

Not exactly.

I kissed him once—a rash, impulsive decision made late one night while we sat out on the dock, in almost the exact same place where just a few months later I overheard Jenna tell him he'd gotten her pregnant. We'd been laughing and he reached out to tuck my hair behind my ear, teasing me because as usual I forgot a hair tie and my hair was getting tossed around by the breeze rolling in off the lake. It was something he'd done a hundred times, but it suddenly felt different. It felt like more.

"Georgia..." His gaze dropped to my mouth, he whispered my name, his voice suddenly rough, the sound of it stretched so thin and tight I felt the vibrations of it in my bones. Forcing his gaze back up to meet mine, he started to drop his hand away from my face and cleared his throat like he was having trouble breathing. "It's cold. I think maybe we should—"

I kissed him.

Reached up to anchor his hand against my face as I leaned in and put my mouth on his. His lips were cold and stiff against mine. His wrist flexed tight, fingers dug into the side of my face like he was seconds from pushing me away.

What the hell, Georgia? I could practically hear him say it. See him scrambling to his feet to stand over me, his face distorted in disgusted disbelief.

Apology trembling on my lips, I'd been seconds away from giving it a voice but then the hand on my face relaxed under my grip. Slipped its fingers around the curve of my neck, pulling me closer. His mouth softened and warmed against mine, the tip of his tongue skimming along the loose seam of my lips, asking for entrance rather than pushing its way inside.

Yes.

It's the last thing I remembered thinking before I lost myself completely. The last coherent thought that flashed through my mind as I tilted my head and opened myself up to him.

Yes.

For Lincoln McNamara, the answer would always be yes.

For those few precious seconds that Linc and I were lost together, I stopped thinking. Stopped worrying. About what I was worth. About what came next. About who I was and where I came from. All I did was feel. The heat of his fingers, tight and urgent, against the back of my neck. The tease and tangle of his tongue against mine, so hot and desperate, the rest of the world melted under the heat of it. Vanished in an instant—the dizzying spin of it sending me flying inside my own skin.

And then I crashed.

Hard.

"*Shit.*" He growled it, the curse vibrating against my lips as he dragged his mouth away from mine, his fingers digging into the back of my neck to hold me in place, away from him. "*Jesus Christ.*" Another curse, this one seeming to give him the strength he needed to push me away completely.

Breath ragged in his chest, Linc scrambled to his feet, putting distance between us so fast I felt dizzy again, this time the sudden lurch of it making me feel sick to my stomach. "I'm sorry." He said it to the frigid water in front of us, shoulders stiff. Chest heaving so hard every push of it expelled a white plume against the frigid night air. "Jesus, Georgia, I'm sorry." Lincoln scratched at his jaw in agitation. "I'm sorry, okay?" He turned toward me, forced himself to look down at me, his eyes cast in shadow, making them impossible to read. "I shouldn't have done that. That was—"

"You didn't do anything," I told him, swallowing hard against the surge of desperation that his apology knocked loose in my chest. "I did. I'm the one who—"

"No." He shook his head, fast and tight, unwilling to bend. "No—*I'm* the adult here. I'm the one who should know better. I'm the one who—"

Adult?

Lincoln isn't an adult. He's... Lincoln.

My Lincoln.

The dock started to pitch and tilt beneath me as I shook my head. "Don't do that. Don't—"

"Don't do *what*? Tell the truth? I'm twenty-one, Georgia," he said slowly, hunkering down in front of me, gaze narrowed and intent on my face. I was going to listen to him, whether I wanted to or not. "I'll be *twenty-two* in a few months."

"So?" I hated the way saying it made me sound. Like a sullen child, up past her bedtime. "What does that have to do with anything?"

"So, you're *seventeen*—still a minor. My parents are your foster —" He looked sick, like he was about to throw up. "I shouldn't have kissed you like that. It was a mistake. It won't happen again. *Can't* happen again—do you understand me?"

I didn't answer him because I didn't. I *didn't* understand.

"This was a mistake." He said it again and I got the feeling that I wasn't the only one he was trying to convince. "It won't happen again."

That's the last true thing he ever said to me.

Now Levi laughs, the harsh, ugly sound of it bringing me back to the present. "I guess that makes you the lucky one then, doesn't it?"

Perfect little George—Saint Georgia—*too good for what the rest of us got.*

That's what Jenna said to me last night while we were arguing.

She'd been angry, practically enraged. At the time I thought it was about Lincoln. About the bottomless pit of misery her life had become. That she blamed and hated me for leaving. For getting out and away from this place, but now...

"What's going on, Levi?" Turning in my seat completely, I face him head on. "Not between you and Lincoln. Here—on the island. I know something isn't right and I know Rachel's—"

There's a knock on my window, inches from my ear—the sound of it so close and sudden, I jolt in my seat. It's Alex. He looks slightly exasperated, like he's been waiting for me to come home for hours now, even though I left for Lincoln's less than an hour ago and he was nowhere to be found when I did.

Looking at Levi, I open my mouth to repeat my question. To press him for information about Rachel and what she might've been doing at the Den last night that could've gotten her killed.

Before I can say a word, Levi shakes his head. "The only thing I know about Rachel is she lived a hard life and made a lot of bad choices that finally caught up with her," Levi tells me, shutting me down completely. "Stay away from Lincoln, he's not the guy you knew." Throwing a quick, nervous look at Alex over my shoulder, he reaches for the shifter to move his cruiser into drive, signaling that it's time for me to get out of his car.

Alex follows me into the house. He's wearing street clothes—a pair of jeans and a dark T-shirt—and his dark blond hair is damp from the shower. Since I wasn't gone long, he must've gotten here right after I left to take Savanna to Lincoln's shop.

"I'm sorry, okay?" he says to my back. "About this morning in the parking lot—but you *know* I can't talk to you about ongoing investigations, Georgia. You know—"

"No." I pull out a random carton and lift its flap—kung pao shrimp. Setting it on the counter, I dig around until I find another carton marked "R" for rice. "What I *know* is I'm right about what I saw last night," I tell him, dumping the contents of both cartons into a large bowl.

"We've been over this." Alex drops his well-muscled frame into a kitchen chair, long legs splayed out in front of him. Thick arms crossed over his chest. "It was dark. You were understandably upset. You'd just found your—"

"I still know what I saw, Alex—and if you'd given half a shit, you would've seen the same thing," I shout at him, shoving the bowl full of leftovers into the ancient microwave and slamming its door closed. It's something that's been bugging me. Before coming to Angel Bay, Alex was a homicide detective in Detroit. If there's one thing he's used to seeing, it's violent death. He knows what it looks like. That it can't be mistaken for anything else.

"What are you saying?" He sounds wary. "Are you accusing me of—"

"I'm not accusing you of anything," I say, even though I kind of am. I turn away from the humming microwave and lean my hips against the counter to face him. "And I don't know *what* I'm saying."

"Are you sure, Georgia..." He shakes his head at me, jaw clenched, its tendons pulsing while he stares at me. "Because I think I'm reading you loud and clear."

"Okay—Rachel was murdered." I say it plainly. "She was *murdered* and—"

"Rachel was a *drug addict*," he tells me, his tone telling me he's struggling to keep his voice down. "I know that's hard for you to hear but it's the truth."

"I know what she was." I have to force the words out. Make myself say them. "But that doesn't mean someone didn't kill her."

"No one killed her," he tells me. "You need to let it go." When all I do is stare at him, Alex shifts his blue gaze past me, mouth set in a grim, hard line. "Is that what you were doing with McNamara? You go looking for him to ask questions I already gave you the answers to?"

"Don't do that," I tell him, crossing my arms over my chest defensively. "Don't make this about him."

"Too late." Sighing, he passes a rough hand over his face. "What were you doing with him?"

"I dropped my truck off to have the brakes looked at," I tell him with a shrug. Even though it's technically the truth, unlike when I said the same thing to his deputy not more than thirty minutes ago, saying it to Alex feels like a lie. "You've been on me about it for weeks now. I figured you'd be happy I finally listened."

"Right," he says, agreeing with me while he swivels his head to pin me with a hard look. "I've been bugging you about it for weeks... so, why now?"

Instead of answering his question, I ask one of my own. "How'd you know I was with him?"

"Tate called it in when he made the stop. Anyone with a police scanner knew you were in that car with McNamara before he even rolled down his window." That tendon in his jaw jumps again. "What were you doing with him?"

"I already told you." Cocking my head to the side, I tighten the lock my arms have around my chest. "Is that why you're here? To interrogate me about some guy I knew when I was a kid?"

"No, that's not why I'm here." He gives his head a slow shake because he knows that whatever he is to me, Lincoln is a lot more than just *some guy*. "Where's your house guest?"

"Work," I tell him, giving him a shrug. "Either that or she took the ten grand in cash I keep in the telephone table drawer and the car I lent her and she's halfway to Canada by now."

Instead of laughing, Alex just sighs. "It's not funny, George," he tells me. "You have to take her back to the station, first thing tomorrow morning. We'll—"

"No, I don't." I tell him. "I paid her bail. You want her back in custody, you'll have to get a court order to have it revoked—and probably arrest me while you're at it."

"You're making a mistake," he says, giving me a tight head shake. "You start putting your nose where it doesn't belong and making a mess of my island, I *will* arrest you, Georgia. Don't think

I won't. You're not a cop anymore. Stay out of official police business."

"What official police business?" I ask in mock confusion. "According to you, Rachel died of an overdose—case closed, right?"

"Okay." Giving up, he lifts his hand, giving me a stiff-fingered wave over his shoulder. "I'll talk to you tomorrow."

"And I was never a *cop*," I call after him, right before he slams the door.

TWENTY

LINCOLN

My phone rings as soon as Levi pulls away from the curb with Georgia in the front seat of his cruiser. I don't even have to look to know who it is.

King has eyes everywhere.

Watching Georgia drive away, I swipe my thumb over my cell's screen and answer it. "What?" I bark it out, my throat tight. Free hand clenched in a fist. The answering chuckle on the other end of the line narrows my vision to a dangerous pinpoint. Washes it red and sets off a high-pitched ringing in my ears.

I haven't felt this way—been this angry—since that night with my father.

The night that changed everything.

"Wanna tell me what Georgia Fell was doing at the shop?"

"It's an auto repair shop," I tell him, trying like hell to keep my tone level. "What the hell do you think she was doing there?" It's so close to what Georgia was asking me about him not more than thirty minutes ago, it's all I can do not to bust out laughing.

"She see anything we need to worry about?"

"Not unless you count Will doing an oil change as something to worry about." It's the truth, but he'll ask Will about it just the same. "He was working the front. He stopped her before she got more than five steps inside."

He doesn't answer me but he's there. I can hear him breathing. Finally, he sighs.

"What happened to you, man?" he says in a conversational tone that is a complete and total lie. "You used to be dependable. Solid. And now..." He stops his assessment of my changes in behavior and sighs. "It's her, isn't it?"

"Her?" I say it like I have no idea who he's talking about. "Who's *her*? Jenna? I already told you, man, she's all yours. I don't give a—"

Now he laughs. "I'm not talking about Jenna and you know it," he tells me. "I'm talking about her—Georgia Fell. She waltzes back onto the island and suddenly she's got you forgetting what kind of man you really are. What you're capable of."

The way he says her name makes me wonder what he knows. Just how much Jenna told him about what happened when we were kids. It doesn't matter. I haven't forgotten who I am or what I've done. I can't forget—no matter how much Georgia makes me want to.

Instead of saying it out loud, I swallow the words like a curse and shake my head. "Georgia Fell doesn't mean a goddamned thing to me."

"That's good, Linc." The skepticism is still there, smoothed over with a thin veneer of confidence. "I'm glad to hear you've got your priorities straight, because I'd really hate to think about what'd happen if you got locked up again. You're a two-time loser. If sweet little Savanna went into the system again—"

"I get it," I snap, hand wrapped tight around the steering wheel. "You don't need to remind me."

"Oh... I'm starting to think I might."

"Georgia isn't a threat." It's the wrong thing to say. Completely contradicts everything I just told him about how I feel about her, but I can't help it. I can't stop myself, because like I said—I know how he operates. I know what comes next. "She didn't see anything. She doesn't *know* anything."

"She sure is asking a lot of questions for someone who doesn't *know anything*."

"She's protected," I remind him, grasping at straws. "She's sleeping with Bradford, for fuck's sake. You sic Will and his boys on her, you're not going to like what happens next."

"Then what do you suggest we do about her?"

"Let me talk to her." Again, the wrong thing to say. Shaking my head while I mutter a curse, I glance at the shop as I pass it on my way home. When I opened the place, it was arguably the happiest I'd been in a long time. Now looking at it makes me sick to my stomach. "I can try to—"

"You really think she's gonna listen to you? The guy who strung her along for *years* under the guise of propriety before knocking up her much younger foster sister, right under her nose? The same guy who developed a drug problem and tried to kill his own father during a home invasion gone wrong? Come on—you're not that stupid, are you? I'd be willing to bet Georgia isn't." That laugh again. Every time I hear it, I want to put his head through a wall. "No... I think it's better for everyone if we just stick to the original plan."

"Which is?" Pulling into my driveway, I slam my car into park and kill the engine. Almost immediately, the front door is thrown open and Savanna appears on the porch—a concerned-looking Will not far behind her.

"Don't worry about it, Linc," he tells me. "I have things with Ms. Fell under control."

"I think she's gonna paint it blue—not sure what shade exactly. She had *a lot* of blue paint samples," Savanna says between bites of spaghetti, carrying the dinner conversation with her usual manic, nine-year-old energy. "You know... we *could* help her, Dad."

Distracted, I make an effort to pull myself back to the present. "Help who?"

"Georgia," Savanna says, frowning at me. "She's trying to paint the manor all by herself. It's a big place. She can't—"

"Georgia doesn't want my help," I tell her, praying my tone

shuts her down before her Georgia Fell fantasies get out of hand. "She doesn't need it either."

My tone lowers Savanna's eyebrows and narrows her eyes, but she doesn't give up. "You don't know that. We could at least offer to—"

"*I said no*—the manor isn't our home anymore and Georgia isn't our friend. She isn't our *anything*. She doesn't care about us," I yell at her, using my dad voice. I hate the way it sounds. Harsh and final. I hate the way she looks at me when I use it. Like I'm the enemy. Dropping my fork, I give her a heavy sigh and shake my head. "I'm sorry, Van. I—"

"It's fine." Snatching the last piece of garlic bread from the plate, she stands. "Can I go to my room now?"

"Yeah." I nod, sitting back in my seat. "Clear your plate first."

She does what I say, dropping the plate into the sink with a sharp clatter that almost certainly means I'll be fishing through broken glass when I wash the dishes later. Instead of barking at her about it, I let her go.

As soon as I hear her bedroom door slam, I push myself away from the table. Ignoring Will, who's still sitting there, I head for the fridge. Rummaging through it, I find a beer toward the back and take it with me out onto the back porch. Sitting heavily on the steps, I twist the top off and plink it into the yard where I'll run it over with the mower next time I get around to cutting the grass.

Whatever. Right now, I'm too pissed to care.

Behind me, I hear the scrape of Will's chair as he pushes himself away from the table. The clatter of dishes while he clears it. Cleans up the mess he and Savanna made throwing dinner together. Finally, I hear him push his way through the back door, a few moments before I catch movement in the corner of my eye as he lowers himself to sit next to me on the porch steps, a beer of his own dangling from his fingertips.

"What'd she break?" I ask, raising my now lukewarm beer to my mouth to take a drink.

"A glass. Chipped a bowl, too." Will laughs. "Kid's pretty

pissed you shut her down about Georgia, huh?"

I shrug, giving him some side-eye while I take another drink. "She'll get over it," I tell him, forcing as much indifference into my tone as I can manage. "The last thing she needs is to start building fairy tales about Georgia Fell in her head." It's the last thing either of us needs. "It's Saturday night, man," I point out. "Sure you don't have some hell to raise?"

"Beer's free here," Will says, cutting me a smirk while raising his bottle to take a drink. "What? You tryin' to get rid of me?"

"Nope." I shake my head, watching him carefully. "Just tryin' to figure out if you're here because you want to be or because he told you you *had* to be." Will is a Disciple. Regardless of how he might feel about it, he'll kill me if King tells him to and King *will* tell him to if he feels like I've become a liability.

Will scoffs softly into his beer and shakes his head. "He's worried, is all," he tells me quietly, confirming my suspicions. "You've been acting weird lately. Off balance. He just wants to make sure you don't do something stupid."

"Stupid?" I snarl it at him, struggling to keep my tone low. "Like *kill Rachel Alcott outside the Den* kind of stupid or—"

"Nobody *killed* Rachel," Will reminds me carefully. "She ODed. The quicker you get that through your skull, the quicker we can all go back to business as usual."

"You were there—I guess you'd know better than me." It's a shitty thing to say. A barely disguised accusation but I can't help making it.

"I told you," Will shoots back, leaning into the space between us, "I don't know shit about what happened to her and I don't *want* to know." He sighs and looks away, a humorless chuckle rippling through him while he tips more beer into his mouth. "She shouldn't have even been there, man. Haven't seen her at the Den in ages and all of a sudden there she is—*dead*?" He shakes his head. "Just leave it alone, man. You got bigger problems on your plate right now."

He's right. I do, but I ask anyway. "Like?"

Draining his beer, Will sets his empty on the step between us. "Like, if King thinks you're making a habit out of hanging around with Georgia Fell, he's gonna send me over here to do a hell of a lot more than babysit your ass."

"He might," I tell him quietly, his warning tightening my grip on the bottle in my hand. "But I can promise you it won't go the way he thinks it will."

"Well, if you just stay the hell away from her, nobody needs to find out which one of you is right." Will gives a nervous laugh because unlike King, he knows exactly what I'm capable of. "She saw King's bike in the parking lot—was asking me all sorts of questions about it."

Shit.

Asking me is one thing. Running her mouth at Will is something else altogether.

"You tell him that too?"

The long, silent stare he aims at the yard is all the answer I need.

"She wants me to help her find Jenna." I regret telling him as soon as I say it.

Will's face drops and his eyebrows shoot up on his forehead. "What the hell for?"

"Why do you think?" I shake my head. "She wants to talk to her about Rachel."

"You're not going to actually do it, are you?" he asks, his tone telling me that he thinks I might.

"I can handle Georgia," I growl at him. "Stay the hell away from her."

My tone finally draws his attention away from the yard and he looks at me. "It ain't me," Will tells me with a slow head shake. "I'm not the one you need to worry about—I'm not the one either of you need to be worrying about."

TWENTY-ONE

GEORGIA

I wake up alone for the second morning in a row.

Trying not to think about Alex, the fight we had or who we fought over, I push the thought of him from my mind and pull myself out of bed and head for the shower.

When I get out, I have a text from Evie.

I'm heading to the hospital now. Meet me in the cafeteria in an hour.

With plans to stake out the cafeteria and wait for her there, I dress quickly, barely taking the time to comb my hair before winding it into its usual tidy bun at the nape of my neck.

After that I have nothing to do.

Even though the coffee pot in the kitchen is on a timer and surely finished brewing by now, I decide on a cup of mediocre hospital coffee instead and start to head out.

On my way out the door, I find Julie curled up on the padded bench under the stairs, still in her work clothes, her jacket wadded up and wedged under her head like a makeshift pillow. The car keys I gave her yesterday are cradled in her lax hand. Seeing them reminds me I left my truck at Lincoln's and if I want to leave, I'll have to hunt my way through the key box mounted on the wall in the butler's pantry and make my way to the expansive garage underneath the manor.

Deciding that's too much work, I reach out and lightly pluck the keys from Julie's hand.

Even though I mean to leave, I don't.

After a few moment's debate, I decide I can kill time just as effectively here as I can anywhere else. Giving her shoulder a nudge, I take a step back and wait. Like I knew she would, Julie comes up in a flash, eyes wide and fists clenched, ready to defend herself.

"You awake?" I ask, gaze narrowed as I take in her tear-stained face and rumpled clothes. When she stares up at me with flat, bleary eyes and nods, I sigh. "Coffee?" When she nods again, I jerk my head toward the back of the house and turn, retracing my steps to the kitchen. There, I snag my usual cup from the dish drainer and fill it with coffee from the pot. Turning again, I find Julie standing in the kitchen doorway, watching me. "Cream is in the fridge. Sugar's on the table," I tell her, holding the cup out for her to take.

Shoulders squared, she steps into the kitchen to take it. "Thanks," she mutters, flicking me a quick look before carrying it to the table. Sitting in the same seat she did yesterday, she takes a tentative sip while her gaze slips past me and out the window above the sink.

"You want to talk about it?"

The questions seems to jolt her back to the present. Stiffens her shoulders as she slides her gaze over to find mine. "Talk about what?"

"Whatever it is you keep crying about," I answer her plainly, shooting her a flat, over-the-shoulder smile while I grab another ridiculously flowery cup from the cabinet above the coffee pot and fill it.

"Not really." Averting her gaze, she shakes her head and takes another tentative sip of her coffee.

"Fair enough." I laugh a little as I slide the carafe back into the machine.

"What are you doing up so early?" she asks, in an obvious attempt to change the subject.

Deciding to let her, I shrug. "I've asked myself that question every morning for the past year or so," I tell her. Carrying my cup to the fridge, I pull it open to retrieve a small carton of half and half. Taking both to the table, I sit down with a sigh.

"And?"

"Habit, I guess," I say, answering her question with a shrug while I pinch the lip of the carton open and add a generous pour of cream to my coffee. "In basic, sleep deprivation was a part of our training. They'd keep you up all night doing night drills or fire watch and then expect you to muster at oh-four hundred. Somewhere along the way, you learn to sleep with one foot on the floor, ready to go at a moment's notice." Reaching for the sugar, I add two generous spoonfuls before giving it a stir. "After basic, I became an MP—Military Police—and sleep became selective." I look up from my cup to find Julie staring at me, her brow crumpled like I'm speaking a language she doesn't understand. "What?"

When I say it, her brow smooths out and she shakes her head, face flushed with embarrassment. "Nothing," she says, dropping her gaze to her own cup. "I just figured you'd drink your coffee black, like—"

"Like a psychopath?" When I say it her head comes up, her large brown eyes so wide they look like they're about to pop out of her head. Laughing, I lift my cup and take a sip. It's creamy and sweet. Just how I like it. "I was in the army, Julie. I wasn't raised by wolves."

My laughter loosens the tension in her shoulders and she relaxes a little. "I wasn't going to say *psychopath*," she tells me, giving me a small smile. "I was going to say *grown-up*." She takes a healthy swallow of her own black brew like she's proving a point. "Did you like it? Being an MP?" she quickly adds, like she's afraid I might misinterpret her question somehow.

"I liked feeling useful. I liked helping people." I give her a shrug to cover up the fact I didn't answer her question. Not really.

Julie frowns. "Then why did you leave the army?"

Even though I know the answer, I give her another shrug.

For a few moments, neither of us says anything. We just sip our coffee in a not-quite-comfortable silence. After nearly a minute slips by, Julie looks at me. "You told Savanna yesterday you investigated sexual assault cases in the army," she says quietly, her gaze aimed at my ear. "Does that kind of stuff happen a lot in the military?"

"Yes." I nod, ignoring the anger saying the word out loud brings. The anxiety that wraps itself around my chest and squeezes tight. "More than they'd like to admit."

Instead of following up with the usual barrage of morbid questions I get when people find out what I used to do, Julie gives me one I've never heard before. "Were you good at it? Finding rapists. Making sure they got punished?"

"I was very good at finding them," I tell her, giving her a smile that feels cold against my lips. "Sometimes, punishing them proved to be harder than I would've liked."

Instead of asking me why or what I mean by it, Julie stares at me. Eyes wide. Face pale. Her throat working like there's something heavy and awful stuck in it. Like whatever it is, it's choking the life out of her.

I've seen that look before.

A thousand times.

Maybe more.

It's the look of someone who has a horrible story to tell. The look of someone who knows no one will believe her and if they believe her, they probably won't care.

"Julie." I say her name gently. Whatever this is, it's not fresh. It's an old wound. Festering beneath the surface. "Is there something you—"

"Shower." She sets her cup down and stands. "I need a shower," she tells me, her fingers twisting themselves into knots in the hem of her shirt. "Can I—"

"Sure." I nod, even though I want to tell her no. Even though I want to sit her back down and force her to talk to me. "You can use my bathroom if you want," I tell her, motioning to the open doorway behind her that leads toward the rest of the servants' quarters where I live. "Everything you need is in there. Towels under the sink."

"The sheriff?" She blushes when she says it. "Is he... I mean, I didn't see his patrol car out front, but I know he—"

"Alex isn't here." I give her a reassuring smile. "Just us girls."

"Okay." She looks relieved. Gives me a too-bright smile. "Thanks." Untangles her fingers from her shirt and wipes her palms on the legs of her jeans. "For everything," she adds, flashing me another show of teeth before making her escape.

Leaving Julie a quick note trapped under the sugar bowl with my cell number, I grab the car keys I gave her yesterday and head out the door.

Parked at the bottom of the porch steps, at the top of the circular drive, is my truck. Behind it is the Mercedes I lent to Julie for work yesterday.

Pulling my phone from my back pocket, I check it for a text from Lincoln, or a missed call. Anything that would indicate he stayed up all night, working on my truck. Maybe that he decided he'd rather be officially taken off the books as a Fell manor employee and send Savanna to public school than do any sort of work for me, but there's nothing there.

I pop the lock on the truck's driver side door, immediately checking the map pocket. My stun gun is there, right where I left it. Reaching under my seat, I feel the holster I keep tucked under it. Pulling it out, I give the M9 it houses a quick check before returning it to its hiding spot. Levering the seat up, I look behind it. The shotgun is there too.

Of course it is, Georgia.

What did you think? That Lincoln was going to steal your arsenal and use it in an island-wide crime spree?

Feeling like an asshole, I climb into the driver's seat and stick my key into the ignition. When I give it a crank, the engine catches immediately and rumbles to life. Foot pressed against the clutch, I palm the gear shift and stare out the windshield for a few seconds before I finally give in.

Reaching up, I flip the visor down to check for the Ka-Bar I keep stashed there. The blade, like everything else, is exactly where I left it. Wrapped around its handle is a piece of paper. Pulling it free, I unroll it. It's a receipt from a pizza place not far from Lincoln's shop. Flipping it over, I see two words stretched across it in a haphazard scrawl.

Be careful.

TWENTY-TWO

I head for the hospital. It's a straight shot down Fell Street, which is nearly deserted on an early Sunday morning. I pull into the visitors' lot with a few minutes to spare.

Taking the elevator to the basement level, I head for the cafeteria. Aside for a few tired-looking doctors, the only other occupant is one of Alex's deputies. Her name is Tandy Shepard; the island's only female deputy and a transplant from Detroit like Alex. We don't know each other well. She's pretty—long, dark hair and wide blue eyes. I know she and Archie have gone out once or twice and I always assumed she didn't like me because of how close we are. She was at Rachel's crime scene, shooting me daggers from across the parking lot while I gave Archie my statement. She's sitting at a table by herself, scrolling through her phone. When I walk in, she looks up. Seeing me, she flashes a brief, tight smile and goes back to her phone.

Other than that, the place is empty.

No Evie.

Deciding I must be a few minutes early, I grab a tray and push it through the line. Selecting a couple of coffees and a yogurt and berry parfait that looks like something Evie would eat, I pay and carry my tray to an empty corner table to wait.

She shows up a few minutes later. Spotting me from the doorway, she hurries toward me, her soft, chocolate-brown corkscrew curls caught up on top of her head, bouncing franticly. "Sorry," she says, reaching for the coffee that's obviously meant for her in the middle of the table. "I just wanted to double-check. I needed to make sure that..." She peters out while she pops the lid off her coffee and snags a creamer cup from the pile between us. Watching her struggle to open it, I notice her hands are shaking. "And then when I did, I needed to confirm who authorized—"

"Make sure of what?" When she doesn't answer me, just continues her wrestling match with the creamer, I take it from her and rip it open and dump it into her cup. "What happened, Evie?"

I expect her to tell me I was wrong. That Alex was right. That I've been behaving like a complete lunatic for the last thirty-six hours for no reason. But that's not what she says.

"Rachel's body..." Evie whispers, giving me another nervous look while she reaches for a coffee stirrer. Dropping it into her cup, she swirls it around. "It's gone."

For a second, I just stare at her, waiting for her to deliver the punchline to what obviously has to be some sort of sick joke.

"What?" I whisper it, trying my best to match her tone. "What do you mean *it's gone*? Gone where?"

"Cremated," she tells me, reaching out to clamp her hand around my wrist to keep me from jumping out of my seat when she says it. "Last night."

"I don't understand." I shake my head and tug on my wrist. "The hospital can't just *do* that. They can't just—"

"They can when they have authorization from the deceased's next of kin." Evie lets me go, sitting back in her seat with a resigned sigh, letting her own hands drop limply into her lap. "Rachel's wife signed the paperwork yesterday morning, requesting that her remains—" She visibly pales and shakes her head. "I'm sorry. She requested the cremation be performed directly after the autopsy was completed."

Rachel's gone.

And along with her goes whatever chance I had at proving she was murdered. Refusing to accept it, I shake my head. "Did you read it?" I ask her, my gaze slipping past her to fall on Tandy. Her back is to us but I get the distinct impression she's trying to listen in on our conversation. "The autopsy report?" Jerking my gaze back to Evie's face, I pin it there, focusing on the light sprinkle of freckles that spill across the bridge of her nose and across her cheeks. "Did you read it?"

Evie nods, her mouth flat while her chocolate corkscrews bounce around her face. "Yeah."

"There's nothing there, is there?" I don't even know why I ask. Why I keep punishing myself. "The autopsy says she died of a drug overdose, doesn't it? No bruising. No signs of sexual assault."

Instead of answering me, Evie gives a casual look around the cafeteria. Satisfied no one is paying attention to us, she eases a hand into the Large kangaroo pocket sewn into the front of her scrub top and slowly pulls something out of it.

Papers.

Maybe four or five of them, stacked on top of each other, folded into a thick square and held together with a binder clip.

Covering the packet of papers with her hand, Evie slides it across the table with a sigh. "See for yourself."

TWENTY-THREE

"Georgia, wait up!"

I'm halfway to my truck when the sound of my name being called pulls my head up and slows my pace. I turn to see Tandy hurrying toward me. As soon as she's within a few feet she stops short and gives me a smile that's considerably brighter than the one she gave me in the cafeteria.

"Can I help you?" I say, my brow furrowed with confusion.

"Yeah—" She gives me another smile, this one slightly concerned. "I saw you in there, talking to the doctor, and I was just wondering if everything is okay."

"Doctor?" I pretend to be confused for a moment before I smile. "You mean Evie? She's my best friend," I tell her, giving her a relaxed shrug. "I just came by to have coffee with her and catch up before she starts her shift."

"Oh..." Her gaze strays to the side pocket of my cargos for just a second, where I stashed the photocopies of Rachel's autopsy Evie gave me, before it bounces back to my face. "That's good. I was worried maybe something had happened."

"If something *were* to happen, I'm sure you'd be one of the first to hear about it." I give her another bright smile. "Being law enforcement and all."

"I suppose that's true." She nods and smiles with me, her gaze dipping toward my pocket again while the look on her face grows sober. "Look—I know we don't know each other very well but I just wanted to tell you how sorry I am about your foster sister." She shifts uncomfortably from one foot to the other. "I can only imagine how hard it was for you to be the one who found her." When I don't say anything, she tilts her head slightly and tries again. "What I mean to say is, with Rachel's history of drugs—"

"I'm still trying to wrap my head around the fact that I didn't know Rachel as well as I thought I did," I tell her, giving my head a quick bob toward the parking spot where I left my truck. "I appreciate your concern, but I have some errands to run, so if you don't mind..."

"Oh!" Her eyes go wide and she takes a step back like it just occurred to her that she might be keeping me from something. "I'm sorry—of course," she says, making an apologetic gesture with her hand. "It was good talking to you."

Giving her another smile without returning the sentiment, I turn away from her and hurry back to my truck. Climbing into the driver's seat, I throw a quick, casual glance at the rearview while I'm fastening my seatbelt. Tandy is still standing where I left her, watching me.

Even though I'm desperate to read it, I leave Rachel's autopsy report in my pocket. I jam my key into the ignition, start my truck and drive away.

Stopping at Carlisle's for provisions, I pull into Rachel's driveway thirty minutes later, behind her ancient Toyota. It dawns on me that there should be people here. That the driveway should be full to bursting. Cars and trucks lining the street. People whispering over cold cuts and church casseroles in the front yard. Someone here to hold Jill's hand while she grieves the loss of the woman she loved.

I should've done this yesterday. Offered my condolences. White-knuckled my way through the inevitable interrogation I knew would come with being the one who found her. I don't know why I didn't. Maybe because I didn't want to face Rachel's widow without answers. Maybe because I was afraid she'd blame me somehow for what happened. If I had to guess, my reasons for not doing this sooner are all of the above. I'm not really sure—to be honest, self-reflection has never been my strong suit.

What I *do* know is that Rachel's wife authorized her cremation less than twenty-four hours after she was found dead outside of a bar under suspicious circumstances, and I want to know why.

Mounting the porch steps, I ring the doorbell before taking a step back and a look around. A patrol car turns the corner at the top of the block to creep down the street, rolling toward me. It's not unusual—I'm on the eastern side of the island and Alex prefers to concentrate his patrols on this side of Angel Bay. Matter of fact, I'm about as eastern as you can get without running into the Wild. It dawns on me that if I wanted to, I could walk to the Den from here—not more than a mile or two through the trees and I'd run right into it.

I hear a series of locks and security chains being flipped and unlatched and I turn away from the patrol car as Jill, Rachel's widow, opens the door.

"George..." When she sees me, her entire body goes limp and her hand falls away from the door. "I—"

"I'm sorry I didn't come sooner," I tell her, shaking my head. "I should've been here. I just..." I take a deep breath and let it out slowly. Keep shaking my head because I feel weak and helpless. Out of my depth and I hate it. "Can I come in?"

Jill gives me a mute nod and steps away from the door, allowing me room to slip through it and into the living room before she shuts it quietly behind me. It's a small place, furnished with repainted curb finds and thrift-store rescues. The only new furniture is a changing table and a playpen set up in the corner of the room. Usually neat, the space shows the untidiness of grief. Newspapers piled on the coffee table. A couple of wine glasses on the end table, one drained dry, the other still half full.

"Smells like Carlisle's coffee cake," Jill says softly, drawing my attention back to her.

"Guilty," I tell her, lifting the bag as proof. "I'm addicted."

"So is Rachel," she tells me with a watery smile. "She gets—I mean, she *used* to get up at the crack of dawn every Sunday and rescue one from the day-old rack. Said they always tasted better the second day—" Her voice cracks and she looks away, turning her face toward the wall for a second in an effort to compose herself. When she turns toward me again, she's managed to pull herself together. "Do you have time for coffee?" Lifting her hand, she gestures listlessly toward the playpen. "Henry's asleep, but we can talk in the kitchen."

When I give her a nod, she leads me into the kitchen. "Sorry about the mess," she says, acknowledging the sink full of dirty dishes while she gathers papers and file folders off the scarred table and into a hasty pile. "Rachel's the neat freak. She'll toss and turn all night if there's so much as a fork waiting to be—" She stands on her tiptoes and shoves the lot of it on top of the fridge. Catching herself, she drops flat on her feet and lets her arms drop bonelessly to her sides. "She's gone, George..." Her eyes flood with tears again and she shakes her head at me. "I don't understand. I don't know what happened. I don't know what to do. I don't know how I'm..."

Setting the bag on the table, I move toward her. Taking her by her shoulders, I guide her to the table and push her gently into a chair. Hunkering down in front of her, I find her hands and take them in my own. "You're going to be Henry's mother. You're going to make sure he's loved and taken care of—he's your only responsibility. The only thing you have to do—and if you need help, you're going to let me give it to you. That's what you're going to do."

"Okay." She nods at me, eyes glazed dull with tears. "Thank you..." She offers me a weak smile, her hands going limp in my grip. "Archie said you were the one who—" She swallows hard, her gaze bouncing away from mine to stare off into space. "He said you were there. That you found her."

Eight months ago, Rachel's wife was a stranger to me. She

didn't grow up on the island. Didn't grow up in foster care. But I liked her from the moment Rachel introduced us. She'd been seven months pregnant with Henry and they'd been newlyweds. Bursting with happiness and hope for their future. It's hard for me to make the switch—to stop looking at her like a friend, someone to be protected, and start looking at her like an obstacle. Someone who has something I want.

But I do it.

"I did," I tell her, confirming Archie's story. "Someone at the Den texted me last night, pretending to be Jenna. Asked me for help. When I got there, Jenna was wasted. I dragged her out the back door and we fought. After that, I left—or I tried to." I swallow hard against the dry, bitter knot lodged in my throat. "I found Rachel in the grass. What was she doing there, Jill?" It's a long shot. If Rachel *was* at the Den to score drugs, her wife would be the last person to know about it.

"I don't know." Eyes wide and slick with unshed tears, she shakes her head at me. "I didn't even know she was gone." She must see it, the skepticism on my face, because her eyes narrow slightly. "Henry's teething and he keeps us up at night. When he finally fell asleep, Rachel and I opened a bottle of wine and... I must've fallen asleep, because the next thing I remember is Archie banging on the front door."

"So, Rachel left but you don't know where she went or with who." It's not a question and I don't phrase it like one. "That doesn't make sense."

"No one else was here," she tells me, her tone defensive, tinged with confusion. "It was just us."

I sigh. "Her car is in the driveway."

Jill blinks at me.

"Rachel's car is in the driveway." I repeat myself like she didn't hear me. "If she left on her own Friday night, it would've been at the Den when I got there, and it wasn't." I remember sitting in the cab of my truck. Debating the pros and cons of walking into the Den unarmed. Scanning the parking lot. Counting the tight cluster of motorcycles near the front entrance. Assessing the potential threats they represented inside. Rachel's car wasn't there.

I know it wasn't.

"I don't understand," Jill says, giving me another stubborn head shake. "What are you saying?"

"I'm saying Rachel left with someone," I tell her, saying the words carefully. "I'm saying she didn't go to the Den alone. Someone knows what she was doing there Friday night and that *someone* is lying to me."

TWENTY-FOUR

Jenna.

She knows something.

More than she wants to admit.

What Rachel was doing at the Den Friday night.

How she got there.

What she didn't know was that Rachel was dead. I've seen fake grief. Know what it looks like. Sounds like. Jenna had been inconsolable. Nearly hysterical with it, even without the benefit of anyone but me for an audience.

No way she was faking her reaction to seeing Rachel's body.

"Who?" Jill asks, pulling me back to the present. Giving myself a mental shake, I tuck it away for later.

"I don't know," I tell her, employing my own expert-level lying skills. "There were a lot of people there that night—she could've been there to meet up with anyone." Pinning her in her seat with a look, I push harder. "Are you sure you don't know who she left with?"

"I'm sure." She narrows her gaze at me again, her forehead collapsed under the weight of a scowl. "I was asleep. I keep telling you that. I don't—"

"Is that something she would usually do?" I ask, a dog with a bone. "Just *leave* without telling you who she was with or where she was going?"

"No, not usually." Her brow smooths, the deep grooves dug into it softening slightly with grief. "But she's been different lately. Since Henry was born, she's been... off," Jill confesses quietly. "She was doing so well. Ninety meetings in ninety days. She had a sponsor. We were happy, George. Even happier after Henry was born and then—I don't know what happened. One day everything was fine and the next, she was just... different. She relapsed."

Hearing it from Rachel's wife is like a kick in the gut. "You're sure?" I ask. "You saw her use? Found drugs? Missing money? She's been neglectful of Henry? The two of you fought?"

"Well, no..." Her brow crumples again, this time more confused than sad. "But Archie said she—"

Something cold whispers against the back of my neck. "Archie said *what*?"

"He said it was a drug overdose. That Rachel went to the Den to score and she—"

"When?" Now that *something* knocks into me, dull and heavy, rocking me back on my heels. "When did Archie tell you that?"

"Friday night. He came to do the notification. He told me—" Through the baby monitor on the kitchen counter, Henry lets out a squall. "Excuse me," she says, shifting in her seat. "I need to get—"

Instead of moving out of her way so she can stand, I lean into her. "Why did you request a cremation for Rachel so quickly?"

"What?" Now Jill looks at me like she thinks I'm downright certifiable. I probably am. "I didn't *request* anything."

Henry lets out another wail.

Standing up, I move away from Jill's chair, giving her room to make her escape. A few seconds later, I hear her coo Henry's name and his wails snuffle to a stop while she comforts him.

As soon as she's gone, I move to the fridge. Reaching up, boots flat on the floor, I pull the pile of papers off its top and walk them back to the table. Dumping the lot of them onto its surface, I start rifling through them. Bills—most of them overdue. A certified letter from their landlord, threatening eviction. A few overdue pawn tickets.

"What do you think you're doing?" Jill hisses from the doorway, drawing my attention for a moment. She's glaring at me, her cheeks flushed with temper, baby Henry cradled against her chest, his face buried in his mother's neck while he drifts off to sleep again. Hanging from the end of her arm by its cutout handle is what looks like a banker's box, sealed closed with several layers of duct tape.

Barely giving her more than a cursory glance, I re-focus my attention on the pile of papers in front of me. "Trying to figure out who killed Rachel," I tell her while I shuffle through what looks like a stack of hospital bills from Henry's birth, Jill's neat and tidy signature at the bottom of each page, a broken promise to pay. They're months old now, and the hospital is threatening to send the account to collections.

"No one *killed* Rachel." Her tone dips to a whisper when she says the word *killed*, like she's afraid Henry will understand what it means. "She relapsed. It was too much—the pressure." She tips her chin at the pile of misery I'm sifting through. "My boss fired me after I had the baby and money was tight. Too tight. Rachel just fell apart. She couldn't—"

"No." I shake my head, unwilling to believe it. "Rachel didn't just *fall apart*. She didn't buckle. She wouldn't." I don't know why I'm fighting this so hard. Why I can't accept what's right in front of me and makes perfect sense. "Her skirt was yanked up, Jill. That's how I found her—with her skirt around her waist and her panties around her ankles." It's ugly. I need it to be. I need Jill to understand what I saw. What really happened to her wife. That she didn't just check out on her. That Rachel didn't choose this. That she was taken away. "There were contusions on her neck. She was strangled. Possibly sexually assaulted." Even as I say it, I hear the whispers of it. Feel it squirming. Itching against the base of my brain like a rash.

Doubt.

"What?" Jill looks at me like I slapped her. "No." She takes a step back, away from where I'm standing at the table, like I'm suddenly crowding her. "That's not what Archie said. He said—"

Archie lied to you.

It's on the tip of my tongue but I can't bring myself to believe it, much less say it out loud. Instead, I stop my shuffling and sigh. "Where's Rachel's death certificate?" It's a crazy thing to ask. She's been dead less than forty-eight hours. Death certificates take days if not weeks to finalize, but Rachel's cremation has already been performed and that wouldn't happen without an official cause of death.

That means a death certificate had to have been issued.

"Death certificate?" Jill asks like she's talking to a wild animal. Something dangerous and unstable. "Rachel's only been gone for—"

"If you signed the authorization for the cremation then you must've gotten the death certificate, Jill," I tell her, amazed at how cool and rational I sound. "That's how these things work."

"I didn't *sign* anything. I didn't *request* anything—I keep telling you that too," she fires back, her anger beginning to show. "Rachel is still in the morgue. They haven't even started her—"

"Rachel was cremated last night," I inform her matter-of-factly. Instinct pushes my hand into my pocket. Brushes my finger against the thick, folded square of papers Evie gave me at the hospital, but the same instinct that stopped me in the hospital parking lot stops me from pulling them out and showing them to her now. "And according to hospital personnel, it was performed at *your* request."

"No. I—*What?*" Jill stumbles back like I lunged at her, and the baby anchored to her chest lets out a soft bleat at his sudden loss of equilibrium. When I reach out a hand to steady her, she pushes it away, refusing my help. "That's not true." She shakes her head. "None of this is true. You're wrong."

It's so reminiscent of what Alex keeps saying, I feel my throat swell with temper. "I'm not wrong."

"Then you're *lying*," she tells me, taking another step back, away from me.

"Seriously?" Now it's my turn to feel like I've been slapped. "Why would I lie?"

"Why would *I* lie?" she hisses back. "How could I *afford* to lie? Look at those bills, Georgia. Angel Bay General is a private hospital. I owe them *thousands* for Henry's birth—they wouldn't give me a band-aid, much less cremate my wife without up-front payment."

She's right.

Before I can agree and apologize, Jill clears the doorway altogether, making an awkward gesture with the box dangling from her hand. "I want you to leave," she tells me, her tone as cold and brittle as glass. "*Now*," she says, pushing the word through clenched teeth. "*Right now* or I'll call—" She stops short when she realizes she has no one to call. No one on this island will help her—not against me. Knowing that and feeling the guilt that comes with it is what moves me. Brings me to my senses.

"Okay." Pulling my empty hand from my pocket, I nod. "I'll leave," I say, as I pass through the doorway while Jill follows me to the front door like she wants to make sure I use it. When I open it and turn back to her, she still has a sleeping Henry cradled to her chest. The box wrapped in duct tape still dangles from her hand. "Could she have walked there?"

"What?" She spits the word at me with a narrow-eyed head shake.

"Could Rachel have walked to the Den?" I look at Rachel's car, parked in the driveway. "I mean, would she have—"

"In my experience, addicts will do anything for a fix." It comes out bitter. Angry. "And Rachel was an addict."

"Maybe..." I concede with a helpless shrug. "But why would she walk? Her car is right there. Why would she—"

"It doesn't matter." Jill doesn't sound angry anymore. She sounds tired. Ground down and empty. "Rachel is gone. Take this with you." She drops the box on the floor and kicks it at me through the doorway, its trajectory pushing me onto the porch before she slams the door in my face.

TWENTY-FIVE

That couldn't have possibly gone any worse.

Taking the box like she said, I lift it off the porch. Not only is it secured with several layers of duct tape, my name is scrawled across its top in Rachel's haphazard hand. Its light, despite its bulk. Light enough that I tuck it against my hip and carry it to my truck to toss it onto the bench seat before climbing in after it.

Backing out of the drive, I flick a quick glance at the house and notice the curtains covering the living room window twitch—probably Jill watching to make sure I actually leave. Feeling like a complete asshole, I shift into first and drive away, passing another creeping patrol car on my way down the street.

Tandy Shepard.

Reminding myself she's a deputy and no matter where she was an hour ago, it's her job to patrol the island—an island that's small enough that running into the same person a few times a day has never seemed strange or out of the ordinary before—I lift my hand off the steering wheel to give her a brief, stiff-fingered wave. She doesn't look at me as we pass each other but there's no way she doesn't know it's me or where I've been.

Watching her in my rearview, I hold my breath as she drives slowly past Rachel's house, rolling to a soft stop at the end of the block before hooking a left. Driven by the same instinct that stopped me from showing Jill Rachel's autopsy report, I make my own soft stop at the opposite end of the block before making a right-hand turn onto Gabriel, intent on following her.

Because nothing feels like a small-world coincidence right now.

Because I'd bet every last penny of Elizabeth Fell's money that Tandy followed me to Rachel's from the hospital.

Looking down the next block as I pass, I catch sight of the tail end of Tandy's patrol car, heading in the same direction as I am, still on the opposite end of the block. The Wild looms in front of me, giving me no choice but to either cross the cattle guard that bridges the ditch to travel the same, narrow, hard-packed dirt road cut diagonally through the trees I took to the Den Friday night, or make another right onto 5th Avenue to cruise slowly along the Wild's nearly impenetrable tree line.

Tandy is gone.

If she were simply patrolling the neighborhood, she would've stuck with the tired but effective grid pattern, driving up and down the streets she was assigned to, looking for trouble or waiting for it to find her. Which means she'd either be driving toward me or away from me on 5th, but she'd be here.

Instead, she doubled back, heading *away* from me.

Seriously, George? First you think Tandy is following you and now you think she's running from you? Exactly how crazy are you, anyway?

I ease my truck to a stop, pulling onto the soft shoulder of the road that hugs the backside of Jill and Rachel's neighborhood. Even through the rolled-up window, I can hear children playing, laughing and yelling in backyards. Mothers shouting at them to take out the trash or to *get down from there.*

Shifting into neutral, I set the parking brake but don't kill the engine. Letting it run, I make a quick decision. Flipping down my visor, I expose the Ka-Bar I keep secured there with a wide elastic strap and pull it free. Flicking out its blade, I reach for the box, intending to slice through the duct tape and open it, right here and now, but my cell phone rings, the trill of it loud and insistent in the enclosed space of the cab. Cursing softly, I close the knife and snatch the cell out of my pocket.

"Hello?"

Nothing.

No, not nothing.

The soft, uneven breath of someone on the other end of line.

"Jenna?" I don't know how I know it's her, but I do. "Jenna, where are you?"

More breathing. The sound of the phone's handset being jostled. "Jenna, I know it's you. Just—"

"You're no fun." On the other end of the line, Jenna sighs. "Little bird says you're looking for me."

"Yes." Relief floods through me, followed closely by gratitude. Even though Lincoln said he wouldn't help me find her, he did. "I want to—"

"Yeah—I know what you want," she tells me, her tone sharp and bitter. "You want to know why Rachel was at the Den, Friday night. Well, I want something too."

Money.

I don't even have to ask.

If I want information, it's going to cost me.

"You lied to Alex," I say, my voice flat and heavy with accusation. "You know what Rachel was doing—"

She cuts me off again.

"I know more than I should," she tells me, jostling the handset again.

"Do you know how she got to the Den that night?" I ask quickly, trying to piece it all together. "I know she didn't drive. I would've seen her car in—"

"She walked—she always walked," Jenna tells me, confirming my theory. "Didn't want some nosy busybody spotting her car."

"*Always walked?*" Her explanation sits heavy in my gut. "What do you mean—"

"I'm not answering any more questions for free. You want to

know more, you'll have to pay," Jenna says, like her mind is made up. "A hundred thousand dollars."

"A hundred grand?" I scoff at her, gaze narrowed and glaring out the windshield. "Get serious, Jenna."

"What? Like you don't have it?" she claws back at me, her tone sharpening again. "You've got millions. *Hundreds* of millions."

"Use whatever brain cells you haven't wasted and *think* for a second," I say, fighting a losing battle with my temper. "It's Sunday —the bank is closed. I can't get my hands on that kind of cash on such short notice."

Jenna goes silent as she mulls over the rationality of what I just told her. "Well, that's what I want," she tells me, her tone sullen and final. "And I'm not telling you shit until I get it."

Rational or not, she's not willing to budge.

"Rachel was your sister too, you know," I remind her, making a last-ditch effort at appealing to her better angels. "She was our sister and someone killed her. Doesn't that mean anything to you? Don't you want to—"

"You were never our sister," Jenna grits out, her sullen tone giving way to anger. "You were *never* one of us and if Rachel were alive, she'd tell you the same thing, so don't pretend you care—not about her and not about me."

"Okay." I back off with a sigh. "Okay, Jenna... but that still doesn't mean I can get my hands on a hundred grand any faster than tomorrow morning."

"Then I guess neither of us is getting what we want until then," she tells me, the resolve I hear in her tone telling me our negotiations are over. "I'll call you tomorrow to set up a meet."

"Fine." I push the word through clenched teeth, moving to hang up before thinking better of it. "Tell me something," I say quickly, catching her before she can slam the receiver back into its cradle. "Does Lincoln know you're basically extorting me?"

The soft, feminine trill of Jenna's laughter reaches through the phone and shakes down my spine, pulling it stiff and straight. "Does he know?" she asks, her laughter trailing off into a sigh. "It was his idea." Bomb dropped, Jenna laughs again. "Talk to you tomorrow, Saint Georgia," she says, right before the line goes dead.

Stunned, I lower the phone from my ear, letting it and my limp hand fall to the bench seat next to me.

I reach up to brush a shaky hand across my face, disgusted with myself when it comes away wet with tears. Rubbing my palm on the leg of my pants, I make an ugly sound in the back of my throat before I grab the gearshift and slam the transmission back into gear.

With no Tandy to follow or Jenna to look for, I do the only thing I can do. I flip the truck around and point it toward home, mashing my boot against the gas pedal with enough force to make its speedometer jump, taking the truck from a quiet chug to a growling roar in a heartbeat.

I rocket down the road, trying to put a plan together. Yes, I can call Archie and have him trace the call from Jenna—but then what? Kidnap her at gunpoint? Waterboard her for information? As appealing as that sounds right now, I know it's the wrong move. Better to just go to the bank in the morning and get the money she wants and pay her for whatever information she has.

But I'm firing Lincoln.

I should've done it the second Mark let slip that he's still on the estate's payroll. Instead, I felt sorry for him. Let myself start to trust him again. Like he always does, Lincoln McNamara has shown me in spectacular fashion what an idiot I am for letting him get close enough to hurt me.

Well, I've learned my lesson. Finally and forever.

As soon as I get home, I'm calling Mark and pulling the plug. I don't care if it's Sunday. I don't care if he bills the estate triple for—

Seeing the sharp turn from 5th onto Gabriel looming ahead of me, I ease off the gas and depress the clutch while applying the brake so I can downshift into the turn.

The truck slows but not enough to make a difference.

Shit.

Heart leaping into my mouth, I give the brake pedal a heavy-booted stomp in hopes of slowing the truck enough to make the turn and feel, rather than hear, something underneath it snap.

The brake pedal beneath my boot hits the floorboard with zero resistance.

Brakes are gone.

To the right and in front of me is the Wild.

To the left, a long row of weather-beaten wood fences.

Ahead of me, a blind hairpin turn.

The best I can hope for is a rollover instead of a head-on collision with a tree or, worse, another vehicle or a backyard full of kids.

Making my decision in an instant, I jerk the steering wheel to the left as hard as I can, feeling the truck's beefy tires grip the road for just a second before they let go, losing contact with the asphalt on the driver's side as it shows its belly and starts to tip.

I catch sight of the Wild looming in front of and beside me, a dense wall of green and brown as I flip through the air, mere inches from the road, an instant before everything goes black.

TWENTY-SIX

It's still dark.

Sound is bleeding through the black.

The squeak and shuffle of thick, rubber-soled shoes.

The rustle of clothing.

Someone's deep, even breathing.

A constant, incessant beeping. Rhythmic and measured.

Threaded through the sounds are the murmur of male voices—two of them. Muffled and irritated, edging toward belligerence. Talking over each other. Arguing nearby.

Fuck you, Bradford—I'm not going anywhere.

Lincoln.

You think I won't arrest you? You think—

Alex.

You really think I give a shit?

Lincoln again.

I think both of you are gonna shut the hell up or I'll have you removed from my hospital.

Evie.

Hospital.

I'm in the hospital.

The realization crumples my brow and I struggle to open my eyes. Vision blurry, I turn my head on a neck that feels stiff and sore. The movement brings on a wave of nausea.

Lifting my arm, I see leads and tubes sticking out of it. Cuts and bruises scattered across my skin. A needle buried in the crook of my elbow.

Dropping my arm, I wheel my gaze around the room until I find the source of the breathing.

Archie.

Sitting bedside in a heavy wooden chair. Elbows braced on his khaki-clad knees. Dark head cradled in his hands.

"Hey..." The voice that says it comes out of my mouth but doesn't sound like mine. Reed-thin and weak but as soon as I say it, Archie's head snaps up like I shouted at him.

Eyes wide, he stares at me for a few seconds before his face collapses into a heap of relief. "Jesus, George." He breathes it out, his shoulders slumping under the weight of it. He stands and opens his mouth, intent on calling someone qualified—probably Evie—into the room.

"Don't." I shake my head, struggling to sit up. "Not yet..." Managing to get my arms under me, I push as hard as I can and I feel the needle in my arm shift. The tube starts to tug free. Ignoring it, I keep pushing. "Just—"

"Damn it, George," Archie swears under his breath as he lunges at me. Fitting his hands under my arms, he helps me sit up, even though the scowl on his face tells me he'd much rather push me flat and probably cuff me to the bed for good measure. As soon as I'm vertical, Arch starts stuffing pillows under my head and around my body to keep me that way. When he seems certain I'm not going to keel over he drops his hands and takes a step back. He's still scowling. "What the hell were you doing out—"

As soon as he says it, the nausea comes back, this one born of memory.

My brakes went out.

I flipped my truck.

"Did I hurt anyone?"

Archie stares at me like I'm crazy. "What?"

"When I crashed—did I hurt anyone? There were kids, I think..." It's coming back to me in pieces.

The question slumps him back into his chair and he shakes his head. "No. No one else was hurt. Just you."

I breathe a sigh of relief and close my eyes for a few seconds in an effort to chase the nausea away. It doesn't help. "Guns. I have guns in my truck. A knife and a—"

"Taser. Yeah—I found them," he says, his tone telling me he wants to ask me why the hell I turned my truck into an armory on wheels. "Everything was recovered at the scene and is at the station."

"Good. I was afraid—"

"I told you to get your brakes fixed," he growls at me, stale fear and unspent frustration ripping up his throat. "I told you, George. What the hell were you thinking?"

"I—" —did get *my brakes fixed*. Instead of saying it out loud, I pry my eyes open and turn my head to level a flat gaze in his direction. "I went to see Jill. I wanted to make sure she was okay. I don't remember anything after that." It's a lie. I remember. I remember Jill told me that Archie was the one who told her Rachel died of a drug overdose, hours before an autopsy was even performed. I remember seeing Tandy as I was backing out of Rachel's driveway. Following her through the neighborhood. Pulling over to open the box Jill shoved at me when she kicked me out.

"There was a box."

Archie frowns. "What?"

"A box." I close my eyes, pushing back against the frustration. "There was a box. Jill gave it to me. Rachel—" *Lie. You have to lie to him.* "Stuff I left at the McNamaras' when I ran away. Rachel kept it." Lie told, I open my eyes and look at him. "She wanted me to have it back."

"There was no box at the scene, George." His brow crumples over gray-blue eyes. "You're pretty banged up. Maybe you have your days mixed—"

I don't have anything mixed up.

"Did you tell Jill that Rachel died of an overdose?"

His mouth tightens. "I don't think now is the time—"

"So that's a yes." Disappointed, I nod while I beat back the prickle of tears. Blaming whatever pain meds Evie pumped into me for the sudden rush of emotion, I sigh. Aiming my gaze downward, I examine the hospital gown I'm wearing. "Where are my clothes?"

Archie stares at me like I'm crazy. "If you think I'm going to let you leave the hospital, against medical advice, you've got another think coming."

"I don't want to leave," I say, shaking my head. "I just want my pants. My phone was—"

"It's right here," he says, leaning into the space between us to open the drawer in the bedside table. Reaching in, he lifts it out. The screen is shattered, its body scuffed. "Not that it'll do you much good."

Sighing softly, I watch as he drops it back into the drawer. "What about my other stuff. My wallet. My—" I lean over and let out a soft hiss when pain shoots up my spine. Another when Archie lifts a hand and braces it against my shoulder to keep me from falling over. Quickly taking stock of the drawer's contents, I see my useless phone and the zippered leather pouch I use as a wallet. Nothing else. The square of folded papers fastened together with a binder clip I had stashed in my pocket isn't there.

Rachel's autopsy report is gone.

So is the box Jill gave me.

"Who was there?" I ask, as I let myself fall back into the pillows. "At the scene—who found me? Was it Tandy?"

"Tandy?" Archie frowns at me and shakes his head.

"Yes, *Tandy*." I can hear the insistence in my voice sharpening into hysteria and I swallow hard to dull its edge. "I saw her—before the accident. I saw her driving—"

"That can't be right, George." Archie says, sounding genuinely concerned. "Her patrol area is on the other side of the island. By the marina."

I saw her as I was pulling out of Rachel's driveway.

I followed her.

And then she disappeared.

But I *know* I saw her.

"Oh..." Even though I'd bet my life on it, I don't say it out loud. Instead, I just give my head a slight nod. "I saw her earlier, I think. Here—at the hospital. I had coffee with Evie before I headed over to see Jill," I tell him, treading as closely to the truth as I can. "I must've gotten my timeline mixed up."

The look of concern on his face smooths out and he gives me a nod of his own. "That makes sense—there was an altercation at the marina late Saturday night. She must've been at the hospital, following up—"

Something about the way he says it sets alarm bells off in my head, fuzzy and warbled by the concussion and whatever they've been pumping into my veins to beat back the pain. "What day is it? How long have I been here?"

"A while." He says it as he sits forward in his chair, ready to push me back into bed. "It's Monday evening."

"Monday *evening*?" I parrot, gaze wheeling around the room looking for some sort of sign that will tell me Archie is wrong. "I've been here for..." The math gets jumbled in my head and I let it go. "How long?"

"I don't know," Arch mumbles while he pushes me back into bed. "Linc called 911 around noon yesterday and it's after four o'clock now, so—"

"Lincoln? He was there?"

"Yeah." Standing up, he pushes his hands into his pockets and sighs. "He's the one who found you."

TWENTY-SEVEN

LINCOLN

My hands won't stop shaking.

Head bowed, forearms braced against my knees, I crank my hands into fists. Watch my knuckles turn white beneath the bloodstains.

Georgia's blood.

I thought she was dead.

Jesus.

When I found her, she'd been covered in it, hanging upside down in her seatbelt. Truck mangled and belly-up in the deep, narrow ditch dug into the ground, meant to catch runaway cars before they can wrap themselves around a tree or plow headlong into someone's yard.

I'd been coming home from the ferry station, creeping down 5th at a snail's pace, trying to think myself out of the mess I'm in. The mess I've somehow managed to get Georgia tangled up in.

Somewhere above me now I hear a sound—half snarl, half scoff, rough and buried deep in someone's throat. Raising my gaze from my hands I catch sight of Alex Bradford glaring at me from across the hall. Feeling an answering growl build itself in the well of my chest, I smother it, sitting back to toss a look down the corridor toward the nurses' station. Evie is there, talking to one of Georgia's nurses. Like she can sense the tension rising between us, she cuts us both a quick, narrow-eyed look—a reminder that if we so much as sneeze at each other, she'll make good on her promise to throw us both out on our asses.

The door to Georgia's room opens and Archie appears in the doorway. Hoping for news, even if it's not delivered to me directly, I surge to my feet. "She's awake." Archie flashes Bradford a quick, pained smile before his gaze slides back to land on my face. "And asking for you."

We all stand there for a few seconds, staring at each other, letting it sink in. When it finally does, Alex mutters a curse and stalks off down the hall, toward the elevators.

"Me?" Ignoring the sheriff, I lift a hand and poke myself in the chest. "Georgia's asking for me?"

"Yeah." Archie looks like he just swallowed a sack full of spiders. "I told her you're the one who found her. She has some questions—you know how she is."

Yeah.

I know how Georgia is—probably better than anyone.

Giving Archie a quick nod, I push past him and close the door behind me.

She's sitting up, her shoulders and torso wedged into a nest of pillows, tubes and wires sticking out of her battered arm. Face pale and bruised. A tight, guarded glare aimed right at me. Whatever she wants to see me for, I'm pretty sure it's not to thank me for saving her life.

"How are you feeling?" It's a stupid thing to ask and she lets me know she agrees with me with a quiet scoff.

"How am I feeling..." Her busted lip quirks to the side like she actually has to think about the answer. "Like the brakes went out on my truck and I flipped it into a ditch."

Knowing she thinks I'm to blame for her accident, I swallow the denial that's trying to work its way up my throat. "I'm sorry," I tell her, showing her my hands. "I should've—"

"Are you sorry because I wasn't killed or are you sorry because—"

"Excuse me?"

Her glare sharpens on my face. "You heard me."

"You think I did this?" Taking a defensive step forward, I shake my head. "You think I tried to hurt you?"

"I didn't say hurt, Lincoln—I said *killed*."

"Why would I want that?" I ask. "Why would I want you dead?"

Instead of answering me, she dismisses my question with a shrug. "Jenna called me, right before the accident."

"Jenna?" I say her name like she's not my wife. Like I have no idea who she is. "What did she want?"

"She wanted money, Lincoln—a lot of it—in exchange for telling me what Rachel was doing at the Den the night she was killed." Georgia's gaze narrows slightly, like she's trying to figure out what sort of game I'm playing. "She said it was your idea."

"She asked you for money and said it was *my* idea?" I sound stupid when I say it. Like I'm having trouble keeping up with her.

"There wasn't much *asking* involved—it was more of a demand. A hundred grand if I want information about Rachel."

I have no idea what she's talking about. I haven't spoken to Jenna since I threw her, hysterical and screaming, into the front seat of my car and took her home Friday night. Instead of telling Georgia as much, I take another step forward, and another, until I'm standing over the bed and glaring down at her. "So, which is it?" I growl at her, unable to keep my temper out of my tone. If I'd expected her to back down in the face of it, I would've been sorely mistaken.

"What?" She keeps glaring at me, head tipped back so she can keep looking me in the eye.

"Which is it?" I repeat myself, wrapping my bloodstained hands around the railing of her hospital bed. "Did I try to kill you, or did I try to extort you, Georgia? Because it can't be both," I tell her, fighting to keep my tone as calm and reasonable as possible. "Because if I were trying to get money out of you, it'd be pretty stupid of me to kill you before I got my hands on it, and if I wanted you dead, why the hell would I even bother trying to extort you in the first place?"

She shakes her head at me, light green eyes wide with confusion. "I—"

"I thought you were dead. *Again.*" I let out a long, slow breath, feeling my guts loosen a little when I think back on it. "I thought I'd—" —*lost you.*

"The brakes on my truck went out," she cuts in, saving me the embarrassment of actually saying it out loud. "Brakes I trusted *you* to fix."

I don't have an explanation for that. Not one I can give her without worrying about having to look over my shoulder for the rest of my life. Not one that won't put Savanna in danger. All I know is when I got to the shop Sunday morning to work on her truck, it was gone. I thought she'd changed her mind. That she decided she didn't trust me to fix her brakes after all and came and got her truck before I could work on it.

That's the lie I told myself, anyway.

"Look at me—I mean *really* look at me," I demand softly. Holding my hands up, I show them to her. They're covered in red, rusty stains. Still shaking. "That's your blood." I drop my hands, their palms slapping against my thighs. "I'm in love with you, Georgia," I tell her, choking on the absurd bubble of laughter that comes with the confession. "No matter how wrong it is or how much I wish I wasn't, I've been in love with you since we were kids. For as long as I can remember. Do you really believe I could do that to you? Do you really think I'm capable of hurting you like that?"

"I—" She shakes her head and looks away from me, forehead crumpled into a frown. "I had a box. In my truck, and something in my pocket. I—"

"So now I've robbed you. Is that what happened? Is that what you're accusing me of?"

Her mouth falls open and she shakes her head again, her chest expanding slightly with the sudden push of words. Before she can answer my question, there's a knock on the door, curt and loud, before it's pushed open.

"Archie says you're finally awake," Evie says from the doorway as she pushes her way inside. Letting her dark gaze skate over me she extends her arm, holding the door open. "Lincoln, do you mind stepping outside?"

Damn right, I mind.

Instead of saying it out loud, I give up.

"Sure." I croak it, the word barely making any sound at all when it leaves my mouth. Taking a step away from Georgia's bed, I spin around to push my way past Evie and out the door.

Stepping off the elevator and into the hospital's ground-floor atrium, the first person I see is Archie, standing in the center of it, talking to the last person in the world I want to see right now.

My father.

Richard McNamara.

And because this day just can't seem to stop sucking, he notices me. Offering Archie a quick handshake before dismissing him, he turns toward me expectantly, like he's waiting for me to come to him. Maybe kneel and kiss his ring.

When I give him a wide berth and keep heading for the exit instead, he calls out to me.

"Lincoln."

The warning in his tone is clear—it's the same tone he's used on me my whole life and I'm ashamed to say it still works. Still stops me in my tracks and has me falling in line.

Turning toward him with a sigh, I force myself to meet his gaze. "Dick."

He's standing a few feet in front of me, frowning at my tone and use of the nickname instead of calling him *Dad*.

"I wish you wouldn't call me that. I'm still your father—no matter what happened." He keeps frowning. Soft hands dug into the pockets of his khaki slacks. The collar of his Tommy Bahama shirt open at the throat to reveal a deep sailor's tan. His dark hair, just beginning to silver at his temples, windswept like he just stepped off a sailboat.

He probably did.

Everything about him screams casual wealth.

Unchecked privilege.

Undeserved power.

Somewhere, in the back of my brain, it registers that this is what my life was supposed to look like—*would've* looked like—if Jenna hadn't showed up on my doorstep all those years ago and knocked me off course with three little words.

I'm pregnant, Linc.

Ignoring his admonishment, I take a step forward, hackles raised like a dog guarding a bone. "What are you doing here?" I ask, doing a piss-poor job of keeping the snarl out of my tone. Because I know.

I know why he's here.

Who he came to see.

My father's brow crumples slightly at my tone. "I'm here to see Georgia," he informs me, his own tone slightly defensive. "I assume that's why you're here as well."

I let myself laugh at his formal cadence—mostly because it's either laugh or take a swing at him—and I shake my head. "I'm the one who found her truck flipped over in a ditch," I tell him, letting the irony of it sink in for the both of us. "But she's awake now and she's made it pretty clear she wants nothing to do with me, so I'm leaving." I step around him with the intention of walking away without a backward glance. Before I can make a move, he stops me, stepping in front of me to block my escape route.

"How's Savanna?" he says, pulling a hand out of his pocket to hold it up between us when it becomes clear I have every intention of walking right over him.

"Don't." My voice drops into a snarl, and my hands crank themselves into fists when he says her name.

Rather than push me, he drops his hand and sighs. "I'm not

allowed to ask about my own granddaughter?" he asks loudly, undoubtedly aware of the audience our run-in has assembled.

I laugh again, this time long and loud—long and loud enough to make it impossible for those who're pretending not to watch our little telenovela unfolding from across the lobby to *keep* pretending they don't notice us. A seemingly chance encounter between my father and me will feed the Angel Bay rumor mill for months.

Still laughing and choking on the tail end of it, I swallow the sharp, bitter taste it leaves in my mouth and look him in the eye while I shake my head. "She's not your granddaughter," I remind him.

This time, when I move around him to walk away, he lets me.

TWENTY-EIGHT

Savanna's been with Julie since Sunday morning, when I called her to come over so I could make my usual rounds at the ferry station and to make sure everything went smoothly. I was on my way home, crawling down 5th Avenue, when I saw Georgia's truck, belly up in a ditch.

I never made it.

The paramedics refused to let me ride to the hospital with her. Slammed the ambulance doors in my face and left without so much as a *you can follow behind in your own car*. I did it anyway—rode their bumper all the way there and was out of my car and running beside the gurney they had her strapped to until they slammed another door in my face and planted a bored-looking security guard in front of it to keep me out. After that, I dropped anchor in the closest waiting room and not even Bradford's threat to have me arrested could make me leave.

No one could until Georgia looked me in the eye and accused me of causing the accident. Of colluding with Jenna to extort money out of her for information about what Rachel was doing at the Den the night she died.

After that, I couldn't get away from her fast enough.

But I don't go home.

Can't go home because I'm pissed.

More than pissed.

I'm so angry I can't stop shaking.

Can't stop thinking about the way she looked—covered in blood and strapped to a gurney while the paramedics hustled her away.

And there's only one way to fix it.

Stalking across the dirt lot of the Den, I spot Will standing outside the front door. Cigarette wedged in the corner of his mouth. Gaze trained on the cell phone in his hand, beer bottle dangling from a lax grip in the other. I'm practically on top of him before he spots me. Drops the bottle and his phone, his expression going from bored sentry to *oh shit* in the blink of an eye because he wasn't paying attention. Sees me too late. Forgot what I'm capable of.

"Wait—" That's as far as he gets before I grab his grease-stained shirt and rip him away from the wall he's slouched against, just to slam him back into it so hard I knock the wind out of his lungs in a hard, fast wheeze. "Linc—"

"Was it you?" I shake him again, knocking his head into the building, but I don't yell. I snarl it, face pushed close to his because yelling will draw attention. Witnesses. Before I can stop myself, the grip I have on him moves from his shirt to his throat. Hands wrapped around it, I start to squeeze. *"Was it? Are you the one who cut her brakes?"*

"No—" He barely manages it, the word squeezing past my fingers while he gasps and gags for air. *"I swear."*

I don't believe him.

"It was you." I keep squeezing. Tighter and tighter until my fingertips disappear into the meat of his neck. "You were at my house. I had her keys. You're the only one who had access. The only one who could've done it."

"Af... ter."

Giving him a final, rough shake that smacks his head against the side of the building again, I loosen my grip and let him drop to the ground. Hunkering down in the dirt next to him, I watch while he gags and gasps some more, dragging deep, ragged gulps of air into his lungs. "Are you fuckin' crazy?" He wheezes it out between coughs, lifting a hand from the dirt to rub at the large red welts my fingers wrapped around his throat. "You almost killed me."

"Still might." The voice that says it comes out of my mouth, but it isn't mine. Hasn't been mine for a very long time. It's flat and hard. Hearing it scares me a little because I know what it means. That I'm capable of anything right now. "What do you mean, *after*?"

"I mean *after*." Will glares at me and keeps rubbing his neck. "Whatever they did to Georgie's truck, they did it after I fixed her brakes."

"You fixed her brakes." I'm still dangerous. I can feel it in my blood. Hear it in my tone and so can he. He'll tell me the truth—all of it—if he wants to keep breathing.

"Yeah." Dropping his hand, he cuts his gaze away from me and shrugs. "And I didn't need the keys to do it either," he says, reminding me that the five-year bid he served in Marquette was for grand theft auto. "It was a simple pick—truck's older than we are and so are its locks."

"Why?"

"I dunno." Will gives me a sullen shrug, his voice rough and rusty from abuse. "I didn't mean to—I went back to the shop after I left your place and I saw it sitting in the lot. It's a rough neighborhood. I figured it'd be safer if I moved it into one of the bays overnight. Next thing I know, I had it up on the lift and I was switching out its rotors—pads were ground down to the plates," he says, shaking his head in disgust. "So, yeah—I fixed her brakes but the rest of it wasn't me—I swear it wasn't. I left her truck in the bay with a note on the windshield, telling you it was done, then I locked up and went to sleep." It's a reminder that if he isn't crashing at my place or sleeping it off with some random hook-up, he usually sleeps on the couch in my office. "When I woke up, the truck was gone. I figured you saw the note, saw it was done and took it back to her."

Even though it doesn't make much sense, I believe him—but he's not off the hook entirely. "But you told King about her asking about his bike being at the shop, didn't you?" I'm trying to find a reason as to how shit went from not-so-subtle threats to bona fide murder attempts in the space of a few hours. "You opened your mouth and—"

"No." He shakes his head and holds out a hand between us. "*No*—but I told Jenna Georgie was lookin' for her. That's it. King wasn't even there. I just—" He drops his hand and sighs. "I was just tryin' to help. That's it."

"Yeah? Help *who*?" I don't give him a chance to answer me. Probably because I'm still feeling like I might want to kill him and I'm pretty sure whatever he's about to tell me will be another lie. "She in there?" I ask, jogging my glare from his face to the door behind him. When he nods at me, I make a sound in the back of my throat. "Sober?"

Now Will shrugs. "Mostly."

Right.

Sighing, I stand slowly and offer him my hand. After a moment of hesitation, he takes it, allowing me to help him up.

"Don't do anything stupid, alright?" he gripes at me, throwing my hand back at me as soon as he's on his feet. "There's a dozen Disciples in there and half as many Reapers."

"You should probably take off," I tell him, because there's stupid and then there's what I'm about to do and we both know he doesn't want any part of it.

"Come on, man—be smart." He shakes his head at me, refusing to leave me to deal with this on my own, even after I nearly choked the life out of him. "You get yourself dead, then who does Savanna have looking out for her? Me?" He scoffs as the absurdity of it. "That ain't gonna fly and you know it. They'll take her. Won't let me anywhere near her. She'll end up back in foster care."

He's right.

I have to think about Savanna.

I take a deep breath, let it out slowly. Nodding, I swipe a

rough, punishing hand over my face, trying to scrub away some of the anger. "Yeah." I nod. Drop my hand and sigh. "Yeah, you're probably right."

Will's shoulders relax and he opens his mouth—probably to tell me to take off. Go home to my kid. Let him take care of it.

Before he can say a word, I shove my way past him and step into the Devil's Den.

TWENTY-NINE

GEORGIA

"You don't have to keep shining that freakin' thing in my eyes every five seconds," I complain while I turn away from the pen light Evie has shoved in my face, squinting against the bright, headache-inducing beam it produces. "I have a concussion—I've had enough of them to know."

"Well, if you're such an expert then you know protocol dictates I have to check your orientation every few hours, regardless of whether you like it or not." Evie clicks her pen light off with a sigh and drops her hand. "What are your symptoms?"

"Sensitivity to light," I tell her pointedly, narrowing my gaze enough to make her laugh. "Nausea. Headache... some memory loss." The last one is hard for me to admit. That I don't remember what happened after the accident. How I got here. I know Lincoln found me because Archie told me he did but beyond that, nothing.

"How many concussions have you had?" Evie asks, her dark eyes clouded with concern.

"A few," I tell her with a shrug. "Enough to know what they feel like."

"What's the last thing you remember?"

"Hanging up the phone with Jenna," I tell her, the admission crumpling her usually smooth brow into a scowl. "She called me after I left Rachel's."

"Why would she call you?" Evie never liked Jenna. Could never understand why I kept trying with her.

"Because she was there Friday night." I feel the headache brought on by Evie's light settle in to stay. "She knows what happened to Rachel—or at least what she was doing there. I have to—"

Evie shoots a quick look over her shoulder to make sure the door to my room is shut and we're alone. "Didn't you read the report I gave you?"

"No, I—" I feel my own forehead collapse into a frown. "I was going to but Tandy stopped me in the hospital parking lot after we talked. I didn't get a chance."

"Tandy—*Deputy Shepard*?" Evie scrunches her nose at me. "What did she want?"

I shrug. "I don't know... I guess she saw us talking and wanted to make sure everything was okay." Saying it out loud makes me realize how strange the encounter was. We hardly know each other, and I wouldn't categorize us as friendly. "Archie said she was here because something went down at the marina Saturday night."

"I don't remember hearing about anything happening at the marina that night," she tells me with a frown. "Where did you go after that?"

"I went to see Jill," I tell her, tipping my head slightly to the side as a phantom smell hits me—butter and brown sugar. "I picked up a coffee cake from Carlisle's first." Saying it brings on the memory of Jill scowling at me in her doorway. Shoving the box at me before slamming the door in my face. "I made her mad. I was pushing about Rachel and I—"

"And you still hadn't read the report?"

"No." Even though I remember those things happened, doing them, they come to me in fragments. Like puzzle pieces I can see but can't quite fit together. "After Jill kicked me out, I got in my truck..." Another patrol car—this time it *was* Tandy. I'm sure of it, no matter what Archie says. I followed her but she disappeared. Was there one second and the next she was gone. Instead of telling

Evie that, I shrug. "I pulled over to read it." I don't mention the box Jill gave me because I already made the mistake of mentioning it to Archie and my paranoia is telling me the fewer people who know about it, the better. "That's when I got the call from Jenna." Sighing, I look away. "That's the last thing I remember."

"So, you don't know if you read the report or not?"

"I don't think I did. I think I meant to but..." I flip and maneuver the jumble of puzzle pieces in my head, trying to get them to click together. "I was upset after talking to Jenna. We fought. I just wanted to get home." I don't tell her why we fought. That Jenna wants money in exchange for information about Rachel, or that she claims Lincoln is involved. I tell myself it's because I don't have the emotional bandwidth to hear *I told you so* right now, but really, it's because I'm ashamed of myself for letting Lincoln suck me back in—even just a little bit.

"Was it about Lincoln?" she asks, her question quickly followed by a sigh. "Stupid question. Of course it was about Lincoln." She sinks slowly into the chair Archie used earlier. "He was beside himself when they brought you in. I guess they refused to let him ride in the ambo so he followed you here on his own," she tells me grudgingly. She never trusted Lincoln. Not the way I did. "Refused to leave—even after Alex threatened to arrest him for trespassing,"

Hearing her say it reminds me that Alex is here—or at least he was before I asked Archie to send Lincoln in after I woke up. Knowing it probably caused a problem I'll have to deal with later, I put it away and focus on the problem at hand. "I went through my belongings. Everything recovered from the crash—the report is gone."

Evie frowns again. "Maybe you had it out when Jenna called, and the pages flew out of the truck when you rolled. Maybe it's still at the scene."

"Maybe." Even though it's possible, I know that isn't what happened. Could I have lost a few pieces of paper in a major car accident? Yes—but that doesn't explain how an entire banker's box wrapped in shiny silver duct tape vanished from the scene. "But that doesn't help me much, does it?"

Evie keeps frowning at me, like she's trying to make up her mind about something. Finally, she sighs. "There was nothing there, George," she tells me quietly. Casts another quick look over her shoulder before sitting forward in her seat. "At least that's what the report said. No contusions noted. No signs of strangulation or recent sexual assault. No—"

"Wait." I sit forward, have to reach out a hand and brace it on the bed rail to keep myself from knocking heads with her. "Recent? No signs of *recent* sexual assault?"

Evie gives me a reluctant nod like she's disappointed I caught it. Like she was hoping I wouldn't.

"So, there was evidence of *past* sexual trauma?"

When I say it, Evie nods again. "Yeah—according to the ME it was pretty extensive. Scar tissue built up in her vaginal and rectal canals. Damage to her cervix. Healed pelvic fractures..." She visibly blanches and looks away. "The report said it looked like years of systemic abuse, starting from when she was barely pubescent until she was into her late teens." Her shoulders slump and she looks at me with a sad shake of her head. "I hate to say it but it's hardly surprising. You know how it is sometimes in foster care—it's not always a safe place." She plants her hands and pushes herself out of her chair with a sigh. "I've got other patients to harass." She gives me a tired smile while she digs her stethoscope out of her kangaroo pocket and loops it around her neck. "If Alex is still outside, I'll send him in—okay?"

"Yes. Okay." I nod. Try to smile but I can't because something bad happened to Rachel—years and years of bad.

It'd happened to her right under my nose, and I never even knew it.

THIRTY

LINCOLN

When I walk in, I get looks. A few disgruntled chin jerks. A couple of *hey Linc*s. The guy behind the bar reaches into the cooler and fishes out a longneck. Pops the top and sets it on the bar so I can snag it as I walk by with a muttered *thanks*.

I'm not one of them but my affiliation with King means I'm tolerated.

"You've got to be the dumbest sonofabitch I've ever met," Will grumbles behind me. "If you get me killed, I'm gonna be pissed."

"I told you to take off," I remind him over my shoulder, weaving my way past the pool table. "If you die, it's on you."

I get a muttered curse in response, but Will doesn't peel off and head back to the bar or outside to resume his post. He sticks with me. Follows me to the back booth, calling me every name in the book along the way.

When I get there, King is holding court in his usual booth. Wedged into the center of it, Jenna is stuck to him like glue.

Lifting the beer in my hand, I take a drink. "I'd like to talk to my wife for a few minutes," I say, forcing myself to defer to the man in front of me. Will is right—I have a kid at home who needs me. Getting into a pissing contest in the middle of a biker bar isn't a good idea.

When I say it, everyone sits up a little straighter, their expressions varying from wary to puzzled as they looks between me and the man they take orders from. They all know Jenna's my wife—they all just assumed I gave her to King when we fell into business together as a sort of offering. Truth is, I didn't *give* King my wife. Jenna is free to do whatever she wants. Beyond the fact she's been a crap mother to Savanna since the day she was born, I don't care what she does—or who she does it with.

"Oh, yeah?" King asks, the corner of his mouth kicked up in a nasty smirk while his fingertip starts drawing lazy circles on Jenna's bare shoulder. "Whatchya need to talk about?"

"Family business," I tell him, my gaze unwavering, settled on his smug, pock-marked face.

Switching tactics, King moves his hand away from Jenna's shoulder, dropping it onto the booth behind her, and gives me a smile. "How's Ms. Fell doin'?" he asks instead of either granting or denying my request. "I hear she had a nasty accident. Got all banged up and landed herself in the hospital."

Will leans in and mutters a single word behind me, so close to my ear I'm the only one who catches it.

Savanna.

Taking a deep breath, I let it out slowly before I smile and shrug. "Maybe she'll finally catch a hint and leave well enough alone," I tell him, careful to keep my tone flat and uninterested. He undoubtedly heard I've spent the last day and a half camped out at the hospital, but I play the role of apathetic bystander anyway. "My wife?"

King's smirk shifts into something resembling an actual smile and he chuckles quietly. "Sure thing, Linc." Turning, he aims his grin in Jenna's direction. "Go on, baby—see what your old man wants," he tells her, turning away from her to tip his chin at the lowlifes clustered around him like flies. As soon as he moves, they scatter, scrambling out of the booth like they can't move fast enough for him. Jenna moves slower, sliding across the cracked vinyl seat with a mutinous glare while I stand here and drink my beer. If not for King telling her to move her ass, she'd be spitting in my face and telling me to get lost.

Because she knows what this is about—or at least *who*.

As soon as she's standing next to me, I set my half-empty bottle on the table and wrap my hand around her arm. "Outside," I mutter, pulling her toward the door.

"Oh, and make sure you give Ms. Fell my best the next time you see her."

When I don't answer him, King laughs, the sound of it following me across the bar while I head for the parking lot, dragging Jenna behind me. Shoulder-barging my way through the door, I let it slam closed behind us both and keep walking. Don't stop until we're in the middle of the lot and Jenna finally digs in her heels.

"Let go," she hisses at me, trying to rip her arm out of my grip. "I'm serious, Linc. Stop—you're hurting me."

As soon as she says it, I relax my grip, letting go of her arm so I can turn to look at her. "Extortion, Jenna?" I say it quietly because I don't know who else is out here. Who could be listening. The Wild is a big place and not nearly as desolate as people think. "What the hell were you thinking?"

"I was thinking I need to get the hell off this island," she tells me, flipping a lock of lank hair over her shoulder. "And Saint Georgia's got the cash to fund my getaway."

Saint Georgia.

It's what Jenna calls her when she's feeling particularly nasty. When she needs to remind herself and the person she's talking to that *she's* the victim.

Ignoring the dig, I look at her like she's stupid. Like she's completely lost her mind. "You think King's just gonna let you go, huh?" I feel my shoulders slump under the weight of the mess she buried us under. "You think, knowing what you know, that *any* of them are going to just watch you walk away?"

"I think a hundred grand will give me wings," she tells me,

crossing her scrawny arms over her chest. "And I think I'm smarter than you give me credit for."

"Not smart enough to keep your big mouth shut around King," I shoot back, taking a step toward her before dropping my voice. "You think he just randomly decided to mess with Georgia's truck? He doesn't *do* random," I remind her, totally ignoring the fact I'm as much to blame for the danger Georgia's in—maybe even more—because he warned me. Told me to stay away from her. Keep her at arm's length, and I didn't listen. "He tried to kill her, Jenna."

"*Good.*" She pushes herself onto the balls of her feet and spits the word in my face. "I hope he *does* kill her—she deserves it."

"Why?" It's something I never really understood, why she hates Georgia so much. Maybe because I've never really wanted to. "She's in this mess because she thought you texted her. Thought it was *you* asking her for help."

"*No*—she's in this mess because even after she left, she was here. She's *always* been here," she says, indicating the space between us. The look on her face turns nasty, even though she's smiling. "Maybe I'll take my *big mouth* back inside and tell King you asked me for a divorce and she's the reason why."

I remember the last time we talked like this. She'd been like she is now, mostly sober, and I'd blurted it out because Jenna's windows of sobriety are sporadic and fast-closing and I didn't know when I'd get another chance to say what I needed to say.

This has gone on long enough. I'm filing for divorce.

"Yeah?" I reach for her again. Clamping my hand around her arm, I haul her close. "And maybe I'll tell him about how you're running around with Levi Tate behind his back." It's a calculated guess, not something I know for sure, but the expression on Jenna's face tells me I hit the nail on the head. "King isn't the kind of man who likes being made a fool of—finding out his favorite chew toy would have the audacity to run around on him—with a *cop,* no less —won't sit too well."

"*Go ahead,*" she screams at me in response. "Levi ain't afraid of King. *He* loves me. We got plans. We're getting off this shithole island but before we go, I'm gonna give Georgia *exactly* what she wants. I'm going to tell her everything."

I feel my hand tighten around her arm in response. "Shut up, Jenna," I shove the warning through clenched teeth, looking around the lot again before pushing my face to within an inch of hers. "Stop talking. For your own freakin' good, just—"

Reaching up with her free hand she grabs my face, raking her sharp nails down my cheek as she pushes me away from her. Barking out a curse, I let her go. I touch my hand against my abused cheek. It comes away bloody. *"Goddamn it—"*

"I don't need you or your *protection* anymore," she screeches at me. "You want to know what Rachel was doing here the night she died? I'll tell you—she was trying to talk me into going public about what happened to us when we were kids. She said everyone needed to know, so she could finally put a stop to it—and you know something? I've decided she was right. I'm telling your precious little Georgia the truth about you, Lincoln—I'm telling her *everything*. And not just her. I'm telling Savanna. I'm telling your mother—I might even call that bitch reporter at the *Herald* and give her sad little paper the story of the century. By the time I'm done, everyone on this island is going to know the truth."

Still ranting and screaming, Jenna spins on her heel and stalks off through the parking lot, away from the Den, spewing threats about ruining my life with the truth.

Out of options, I have no choice but to follow her.

THIRTY-ONE
GEORGIA

Alex is staring at me like he can't quite comprehend what I'm saying to him. "You can't be serious," he says, shaking his head at me.

"No." I shake my head back while fighting off another wave of nausea. "I'm not. I don't know what happened to my truck, but I don't think Lincoln is to blame."

"George..." Alex sighs and aims his tired gaze at the ceiling. "Let's look at the facts—he had access to your truck. That's means," he tells me, holding up a finger. "he was the one who was supposed to fix it in the first damn place—*that's* opportunity." He lifts finger number two. "I don't know about you, but I—"

"Where's his motive?" I ask. "I'm not saying he didn't have means or opportunity. I'm just asking why he would want to hurt me. What would he have to gain?"

I'm in love with you, Georgia. Been in love with you for as long as I can remember. Do you really believe I could do that to you? Do you really think I'm capable of hurting you like that?

The pragmatically objective investigator in me knows he probably said it to manipulate me. To use emotion to cloud my judgment and make me doubt the facts that are right in front of me.

But I also see the logic in Lincoln's reasoning. If he'd been plotting with Jenna to extort money from me in exchange for information about Rachel, then why would he have tampered with my brakes before he got his hands on it?

Alex leans back in his seat. "He has motive," he tells me, giving me a short shake of his head like even though he's pretty much told me nothing, he's already said too much.

"Great—let's hear it." I show him my palms and sigh. "Because from where I'm sitting, I can't see where—"

"He's running drugs out of his shop," Alex says without preamble, a tight scowl dug into his brow. "Best I can figure, he hooked up with the Reapers—either through Jenna or through Will Hudson's affiliation with the Disciples—about a year ago."

I think about the motorcycle I saw parked in front of Lincoln's shop Saturday afternoon. The same bike I saw King Reaper ride off on Friday night. The way Will barred me from entering too far into the shop when I was there. How eager Lincoln was to get me away from it.

"Lincoln is smuggling drugs." As soon as I say it out loud, I feel the disappointment settle in. That's how I know it's true. If he's caught, he'll lose his daughter for good. Go back to prison. This time for the rest of his life—the good parts of it, anyway.

"Yeah." Alex gives me an answering nod and sighs. "And here you come along, sticking your nose in Rachel's death, bringing the cops and a whole lot of unwanted attention to their doorstep. That's motive."

"You have proof?" I hear myself ask, still not wanting to believe it, even though every investigative instinct I have is telling me he's right. That it's true.

"Well... no." Alex shakes his head reluctantly and gives me a sigh. "I've been watching his place for a few months now—I just haven't been able to catch him or figure out how they're moving the drugs on and off the island but—"

"Boats." I sit up a little, fighting off a wave of dizziness that threatens to pull me sideways. "There's a dock behind the Den. I saw a boat there Friday night. Maybe that's what Rachel saw. Maybe she walked into their drug operation and that's why they killed her." When he doesn't tell me I'm crazy or that Rachel died of an overdose, I feel my breath go still in my lungs. "You believe me. You know Rachel was murdered and you're covering it up."

"I know the Reapers are dangerous and the Disciples are downright vicious." He sits forward in his seat, pinning me with a hard look. "I chased these guys in Detroit. They're not just a couple of biker gangs, running weed out of an old bait shop. They're slick. The Reapers cover their tracks and what they *can't* cover, they send out their attack dogs to get rid of."

"So, if you know all this, why aren't you doing something about it?" I feel like I'm on fire. Like my entire body is burning. That's how angry I am. So angry I could burn myself alive with it in this stupid fucking hospital bed. "*They killed Rachel*—why are you just letting them get away with it? Why aren't you—"

"Because if I have any hope of nailing them for good, I need proof, George. Solid proof. Not a hunch. Not a clue. *Proof.*" Alex gives me a tired head shake. "If this is anything like Detroit, they've got eyes and ears and *fingers* all over this island. They see and hear everything. Can reach anyone—if they catch wind that I suspect Rachel's death was anything more than a simple OD, then the whole thing is busted. They'll hightail it out of here and burn this island to the ground on their way out."

"So, you're covering up my sister's murder so you can make a drug bust?" I try not to sound angry when I say it, but I must've failed because Alex scowls at me.

"For now, Georgia. Just for now." Frustration softens his scowl. "Just until I can get some solid evidence against them. That's why I need you to back off. Let me do my job. Let me—"

"Why didn't you tell me any of this sooner?" I look around the room, trying to find my bearings. Find a place to put everything he just told me. Finally, I shift my gaze back to his. "We've been going back and forth about the Disciples for *months* now. How dangerous they are. How we needed to find a way to get them off the island. Why didn't you tell me what was going on then?"

"Because I didn't know if—" He stops himself short and looks away from me. "I couldn't be sure if you were—"

"You didn't trust me." The realization slams into me. Knocks something loose in my chest that comes out sounding like a laugh. "You thought I was *involved*."

"I don't trust *anyone* on this island, George—not even my own damn deputies." When all I do is stare at him, he sighs. "You're in love with Lincoln—or at least you used to be," he quickly amends, laying out the facts as he knows them. "I didn't know you. Didn't know where your loyalties lay. If I could trust you."

I think about the conversations we've had. How myopic I can be when I catch an investigative scent. How cagey and defensive he's been when I press him for information. Looking at it objectively, I can see it. How easily this whole thing got tangled. "And now that they tried to kill me, you figure I'm a safe bet."

Alex sighs, half frustrated by my blunt assessment, half relieved that I seem to understand. "Yes."

"You told Archie to tell Jill that Rachel died of a drug overdose when he did the notification, Friday night."

Wariness flashes in his eyes but he nods. "Yes—I figured the sooner I got the story circulating, the less chance of them getting spooked."

"And that's why you told Kate at the *Herald* that Rachel ODed?"

Now he looks miserable. "I did what I had to do to keep my investigation from tanking. You would've done the same thing."

He's right.

I would have.

"Did you think *I* killed Rachel?" I'm the one who found her. Called it in. Even though it's what I would've thought if I were in his shoes, it still makes me sick.

"No." He shakes his head, his answer firm and sure. "I knew you were off island. You crossed the bridge into Houghton at a quarter after six and didn't cross back until nearly ten. The ME put time of death at around then, so, I knew you couldn't have—"

He stops himself short when he realizes what he just said. What he just admitted to.

"Oh." I think about Tandy popping up in the hospital parking lot the next morning. The cruiser clocking me when I went to Rachel's to pay my respects to her widow. Tandy again, creeping past Jill's driveway when I left, even though Rachel's neighborhood is nowhere near her service area. "Am I under surveillance?" I feel dumb as soon as I ask it. Of course I am, and if I'd been in the field or still wearing a badge, I would've spotted it months ago. But I'm a civilian now. Spent the last eight months of my life trying to smother and kill the instincts that have been bred into me over the last decade of my life because I didn't want to live the rest of it feeling like I'm crazy. Just another paranoid vet, looking over her shoulder. Watching for an enemy that didn't exist anymore.

When all I get is a long, guarded look for my trouble, I flatten my mouth into a grim parody of a smile and nod my head. "And this?" I raise a hand and flip it between us. "Is this part of the surveillance package? Did you start this thing with me because you thought I was involved? Start sleeping with me to keep tabs on me —maybe a way to get information."

Alex's eyes go wide and his shoulders tense as he sits forward in his chair, mouth opening to issue an answer. Before he can, there's a knock on the door and his mouth snaps closed as we both turn to watch as it's pushed open. I expect to see Evie, coming in for another round of poking. It's not Evie this time.

It's Richard McNamara.

As soon as he sees him, Alex stands. Looks nervous. Like he's meeting my father for the first time and not someone he's spoken to on a thousand different occasions. "Mr. McNamara," he says, holding out a hand for Richard to shake.

"Sheriff." Richard gives his formality an amused smile before focusing on me. "How's my girl?" he asks, his tone filled with parental concern.

"She's fine." Putting the last ten minutes and everything Alex told me away, I give him an exasperated smile and roll my eyes.

Not at the fact that he called me his *girl*—that's par for the course. He and Alice have called those of us they took in and gave a home to their *girls* for as long as I can remember. "She wants to go home."

The amusement dies on his lips and he gives Alex a quick, concerned look before refocusing his attention on me. "What does your doctor think about that?"

"We're currently in negotiations," I tell him, and he laughs at my joke as expected but the sound of it dies quickly.

"Alex, would you mind if I had a few minutes alone with Georgia?" he says, giving Alex a tight, expectant smile.

Alex falters, but only for a moment. "Of course." He nods and turns toward me, bending over the bedrail to press a soft kiss against my temple. "I'll be back tomorrow morning," he says, giving me a long, heavy look. "You better be here." I know what he's really telling me. He trusted me. Told me things he probably shouldn't have. The last thing he wants or needs is me running around the island with a concussion, disrupting his covert investigation.

Instead of putting his worries to rest, I flip him a snappy salute and smile. "Sir, yes sir." If he or Richard can hear the sarcasm in my tone, neither of them react to it. Instead, Richard gives me a fatherly smile and nods.

"She'll be here," he says, while he eases himself into the chair Alex just vacated. "I'll make sure of it. Even if I have to sit here all night."

THIRTY-TWO

Richard brought a deck of cards.

It was something we used to do together. He'd catch me in the kitchen late at night, staring out the window above the sink, a glass clenched in my hand like I'd come down for a drink of water in the middle of the night. I didn't come downstairs for water. I was thinking about running. Staring out the window at the dock. The boat tied to the end of it. Dreaming about Canada or maybe doubling back into Wisconsin or Minnesota.

I always thought about running away. Leaving the island. Disappearing without a trace. I'd sneak downstairs and stare out the window and think about how easy it would be. Calculate in my head how far away I'd be able to get before anyone realized I was gone. How long I could survive on the crumpled bills I had hidden in the toe of one of my old shoes.

No matter how much I thought about it, I never seemed to be able to pull the trigger, thoughts of Archie and Rachel and Evie and all the others I'd be leaving behind would parade through my head. By the time I was fifteen and Richard started showing up with his cards, I wasn't staring at the boat tied to the end of the dock anymore. I was staring at the boathouse. Thinking about the boy who lived inside of it. The closer I got to freedom the closer those two fantasies began to meld. I wasn't just thinking about running away. I was thinking about running away with *him*.

Lincoln.

"Earth to Georgia?"

I look up from my hand, cards blurry in my field of vision. Blinking hard, I see Richard sitting in the same chair Alex and Archie both used when they came to see me. Not Lincoln though. Lincoln stood over me and glared. Showed me his bloodstained hands and told me he loved me. Has always loved me. That when he found me, he thought I was dead.

"Georgia." His tone isn't playful anymore. This time when Richard says my name, it's heavy with concern. When I don't answer him right away, he drops his cards on the rollaway table between us and moves to stand. "I'm going to get Dr. Jones," he tells me as he starts to push himself out of his chair. "You look—"

"Like I rolled my truck into a ditch?" I finish for him, giving him a tired smile when all he does is scowl at me. "I'm fine, Mr. McNamara," I say, pushing as much reassurance onto my face as I can. "As fine as I can be with a concussion, five staples in my head and three cracked ribs." I sigh softly. Giving up on the cards in my hand, I toss them onto the table next to his. "There's no need to go looking for her. Evie will be back, any minute now, with that damnable pen light of hers—I'm okay. I promise."

After a few more seconds of deliberation, Richard lowers himself back into his chair but he doesn't look happy about it. Instead of picking up his cards again, he just sits there and looks at me like there's something he wants to say but can't figure out how to do it. Finally, he figures it out. "I ran into Lincoln. In the lobby. He says he was here to see you."

"Yeah—I guess he's the one who found me." I don't elaborate. Don't tell him Lincoln and I spoke or what we talked about.

"I'm sorry, George." Richard's face fills with grief. "About Rachel. I know you were close. I can't imagine how hard it must've been to be the one who found her."

"Drug addiction is a disease," I tell him, sticking to the story

Alex concocted to cover the truth about what really happened to Rachel. "Not knowing she struggled with it makes it that much harder."

"I understand what you mean," he says, his tone heavy, the edge I hear in it telling me his grief isn't just about what happened to Rachel.

Instead of asking him what he means, I dive in with a question of my own. "What happened that night, between you and Lincoln? The night he tried to kill you."

Confusion plays across his familiar features for only a second or two before it's chased away by something that looks wary. Like it doesn't know where to step. "Georgia—"

"I was in love with him," I confess quietly. "I was eighteen and so stupidly in love with him that I thought for sure it meant he loved me too." I don't tell him about the time I kissed Lincoln. That he kissed me back. "But then, one night, I snuck down to the dock and I heard Jenna tell him she was pregnant and..." I give him another tired smile. "You weren't there with your deck of cards to stop me so..."

"So you left." Richard stares at me for a long time. Probably trying to work it all out in his head. That I knew about Jenna's pregnancy before he did. That I'd been in love with his son and that finding out about it was what drove me away. Finally, he gives me a short nod and sighs. "When we found out about Jenna, Alice and I were... upset." The way he says *upset* tells me it's an inadequate word choice for how they both felt. They felt the same way I had. Devastated. Betrayed. "Not only was what he did morally reprehensible, he also put our foster care license in jeopardy. The state nearly removed our other girls from our care." Slumping back in his seat, Richard swipes a hand over his face in a gesture so much like his son that watching him do it nearly breaks my heart. "So, when he told us they were getting married and going to raise the baby, Alice and I were relieved to say the least. We thought it meant he loved her. That it wasn't as unseemly and inappropriate as we'd feared. Yes, Jenna was only sixteen, but that also happens to be Michigan's age of consent and as Lincoln had barely been twenty-two at the time, everyone involved was willing to just quietly sweep it all under the rug. They got married and Alice and I were allowed to keep our foster care license, providing Lincoln was not allowed back into our home."

So far, the story Richard is telling me lines up perfectly with what Mark told me when I asked him about it a few days ago.

"We were blind to what was really happening because it couldn't be *our* son. Things like that didn't happen to people like us." He gives me a quick, guilty look, probably because he realizes how it sounds. How ridiculous and shallow it is for him to believe his wealth and standing on this island would protect him from something like that. "Before Savanna was even a year old, Jenna left. Lincoln was raising Savanna on his own. Alice and I did what we could. We gave him money. Bought a house for him and Savanna to live in, rent-free. All we asked was that he stayed away."

"But he came back." It's not a question so much as it is a prompt and when I give it, Richard gives me another nod.

"It was late. I was in bed and I heard a noise. Instead of waking Alice or calling the police, I went downstairs to investigate on my own because—"

"You run a group home for troubled teenage girls and didn't want to involve the police unless it was absolutely necessary." I remember how he'd coax me away from the window and we'd play gin rummy or spades over a plate of cookies until sunrise.

Relieved I understand his reluctance to involve the authorities, Richard sighs. "I should've called, but I could see the light on in the boathouse from the kitchen window and I knew it was Lincoln. He broke in sometimes to steal things—little things. His mother's jewelry mostly—to pawn for drug money. I never put a stop to it because Alice was so tender about the whole thing. She felt like we'd failed him and I didn't want to upset her. I didn't know what he was doing in the boathouse, what he hoped to find in there, but I knew it was him. I went out there to confront him. To tell him I was done turning a blind eye to his behavior and I was calling the police the next time something came up missing. When I got closer to the boathouse, I could hear them—crying and... other sounds." His voice breaks and he looks away. "I don't know what happened. I just—I kicked the door open and... it was Lincoln. He had Rachel on the bed. He was hurting her. Forcing himself on her."

No.

That's all I can think.

All I can say to myself when I hear him say it.

No.

Before I can give it a voice, Richard continues, lost in memory. "When I saw what he was doing, I lost it. Rachel was crying. Clothes torn, struggling underneath him. I grabbed him. Pulled him off of her. We fought. He was so strong. And angry..." He looks at me then, shame plain on his face. "I don't remember anything after that. I woke up in the hospital. I'd been badly beaten and Lincoln was in jail."

I think about what Evie told me.

That Rachel's autopsy revealed years of systematic rape and sexual abuse.

That she'd been barely pubescent when the abuse started.

She'd been thirteen when the McNamaras took her in.

The realization, coupled with Richard's account of what happened with Lincoln that night, settles in and suddenly I can't breathe. The weight of it pushes down on me—panic.

Guilt.

Grief.

Because I left Rachel there alone.

Because while I was busy building fantasies about a happily ever after with Lincoln, he was busy abusing her.

"Why didn't you tell someone?" I hear myself ask. "You caught your adult son raping a sixteen-year-old girl. Why didn't you say something? Why didn't you tell them—"

"Rachel ran away days after it happened. I was in the hospital and unable to stop her, and Alice..." Richard looks miserable now.

Like he wishes it was all just a bad dream. "I couldn't do that to either of them. Lincoln took a plea deal that ensured no one had to testify and—"

"Rachel ran away?" I never knew that. I've been back for almost a year and she never mentioned it. She never mentioned any of it.

Richard nods. "She came back a few years ago, armed with a bachelor's in social work she earned off island, and took a job with DCFS," he tells me with something that sounds like pride. "She wanted to make a difference."

Lincoln would've been out of prison by then, tucked safely under Elizabeth Fell's wing. Given a cushy job and a nice place to live. "So, he got away with it?" The question sits like a rock in my belly and I have to push it out, its sharp edges ripping and digging into my throat on its way up. "Lincoln *raped* Rachel and he just—"

"He served time, Georgia." Richard's tone hardens. "Real time. And if not for Elizabeth Fell's intervention, Lincoln would still be in prison, you have my word on that."

I stare at him, unable to put into words what I'm thinking because what I'm thinking is that Lincoln killed Rachel. Not because she stumbled onto the drug-smuggling operation he's running with the Reapers.

No.

Lincoln killed Rachel to keep her quiet about the rapes.

Maybe she threatened to tell. Maybe she was tired of living her life, watching her abuser live his, as if nothing happened. Free and unpunished for what he did to her.

"I'd always worried something had happened to make you leave," Richard tells me quietly. "That Lincoln—"

"Lincoln never touched me." I look away from him. "I'd like to sleep now. My head hurts and Evie really will be back in a few minutes to check on me."

"Of course." Richard gives me a curt nod but he doesn't move to leave. "Georgia..." He says it gently and I think I know what's coming. He's going to warn me against saying anything. To stay quiet about his son and what I know—but that's not what he says. "Julie Kates's new case manager called me this morning."

"Oh." Somehow, I'd forgotten about her. That I've been harboring an accused felon in my home for the past three days. "Whose desk did she land on?"

"Dennis Bleche—he's the agency's transitional case manager."

Nearly ten years off island and I still recognize most of the names that get dropped in conversation. I don't recognize his. "He's not island." I can't keep it out of my tone, the immediate distrust I feel. It's ridiculous. Makes me feel like one of the old biddies that sit on their porches in their house dresses, drinking their morning coffee and writing down the license plates of cars that they don't recognize that have the nerve to drive down their street.

Richard flushes. "No—he's a transplant, like Sheriff Bradford," he tells me. "But Alice and I have worked with him extensively for the last couple of years and he's a good man. He handles most of our older girls—those getting ready to transition out of the system. Helps them find housing. Vocational programs off island. Apply for college if it's a good fit. Not exactly new to the job like Rachel was, but still dedicated."

"And Alex knows him?"

Richard nods, ignoring the skepticism in my tone. "They worked together in Detroit, I believe. A happy coincidence."

I don't believe in coincidences. Making a mental note to ask Alex about him, I shrug. "Why is he coming to you?" I ask, even though I'm pretty sure I know the reason.

"Well, like I said—he's transitioned a lot of our girls, so when he was given Julie's case and couldn't make it past your lawyer to speak with you directly, he reached out to me in hopes I'd have better luck."

It's not as strange as it sounds. I was a ward of the state my entire life—there are files on me. Accountings of where I lived. What families fostered me. All this Dennis person would have to do is conduct a record search to see who my last placement was. Who might have the kind of reach he needs to get to me.

Luckily for him, Richard McNamara has very long arms.

"What does he want?" Another stupid question. I'm full of them today.

"He wanted me to talk to you about turning Julie over." He sounds guilty again. Like he knows this is the wrong place and time to talk to me about this, but he doesn't have a choice. "Given the charges she's facing, placement would be difficult, but I've talked to Alice and we're willing to shelter her until she turns eighteen in a few months."

No.

I think it again.

No.

Julie stays with me.

Swallowing hard, I force myself to nod. To accept when I've been beaten. "Okay," I tell him, letting my eyes slip closed. "I'll think about it."

THIRTY-THREE

It's Tuesday afternoon and I'm waiting outside the hospital. I can feel Evie behind the wheelchair she forced me into, looming over me and scowling so hard I can practically hear it. "I should've called Alex," she fusses behind me, watching the parking garage where Julie scurried off to only a few minutes before.

"Sheriff Bradford has more important things to do with his time than chauffeur me around the island," I remind her, tilting my head back to aim a look at her. She hadn't wanted to send me home. *I know you, George. You won't rest. You won't take it easy. You'll climb that damn ladder the second you get home and start scraping paint.* Finally, she relented, but only after I promised to stay off the ladder. Once that argument was over, we had a second, shorter argument over who I'd call to take me home. I'd insisted on calling Julie, mainly because I'm not ready to see Alex. I'm still digesting everything I've managed to piece together about Lincoln. What it means. What I think really happened to Rachel the night she died and why.

"I didn't say I should've called the sheriff," she tells me, scanning the parking lot for Julie. "I said I should've called *Alex*—your boyfriend."

"I'm a twenty-eight-year-old battle-hardened combat vet," I remind her. "I'm too old and jaded to have a *boyfriend*."

"I'm sorry, G.I. Jane—the super-hot law enforcement officer you get naked with on a regular basis," she says with a laugh. "Is that a more accurate description?"

"Better," I grumble at her, laughing a little in spite of myself. When I see Julie exit the small parking garage, I move to push myself out of the chair.

Evie reaches out and clamps a hand on my shoulder to keep me in place. "Nope," she says, her tone brisk and professional. "Not until she's here."

"You're ridiculous," I mutter under my breath, even as I allow her to push me back into my seat. Seconds later, Julie is pulling up to the curb.

When Julie throws it into park and starts to climb out to help me, Evie waves her off. "I've got her," she says as she opens the car door and feeds me into the passenger seat. "I know it's probably too much to ask, but can you please make sure she doesn't climb that stupid ladder and—"

"I hid it," Julie informs us both while she fusses with her seat-belt. When neither of us answer her, she looks up and shrugs. "What?"

"You *hid* a fifteen-foot extension ladder?" Evie asks, equal parts impressed and skeptical.

"Well, it wasn't like she was going to stay off of it on her own," Julie sniffs at us both, earning herself a loud round of laughter from Evie.

"You should adopt her," Evie tells me, only half joking. "It's about time you had a proper mother."

"That's your job, remember?" I remind her, earning myself another round of laughter in return.

"I'll call you in a few hours to make sure you're settled," she tells me, before shifting her gaze back to Julie. "You'll stay with her?" She's back to sounding skeptical.

"I won't leave her side," Julie promises while she reaches for the gearshift. A few moments later, Evie is behind us and we're on our way.

"I need to go to the crash site," I tell Julie as I stare out the car window.

"What?" Julie says, giving me a quick, nervous look that I catch from the corner of my eye. "No. Dr. Jones said—"

"It's okay—I just want to see it," I say, trying to reassure her. "I'll take it easy—promise."

The confusion on her face slides into a look of resigned suspicion but she takes a right when she hits Michael Street, putting Fell manor behind us. "You don't have to stay with me, you know," I say, watching the gates shrink in the rearview. "I know you have work and—"

"I don't actually," Julie says, careful to keep her eyes focused on the road in front of us. "I got fired."

"When?" I keep forgetting it's Tuesday. That I lost two days in the hospital.

"Saturday night." Julie gives me another one of her shrugs. I'm beginning to recognize it as a gesture she uses when she's uncomfortable. "Big Ted didn't even have the decency to do it himself." She tosses me a quick, tight-lipped smile. "He sent Teddy to do it."

That's when I remember Ted Nelson owns the shaved ice stand where Julie works, along with several other boardwalk businesses. "And that little prick actually *did* it?" I say, turning in my seat to aim a glare in her direction. "He actually *fired* you?"

"You don't understand," Julie tells me, scowl aimed out the windshield. "It's complicated."

"Not as complicated as you'd like to believe considering you're not the one who wrecked that asshole's boat in the first place," I inform her with a scoff. When all she does is scowl again, I decide to make another push. "Just tell me that much, okay? Admit you didn't steal the boat." I don't know why it matters. Why I can't leave it alone, especially when I already pretty much know what happened, but I can't, and it does.

It matters.

"Okay." She gives me another quick look and sighs. "You're right. I didn't steal the boat."

I thought I'd be satisfied with her admission but I'm not. "Teddy took you out on his father's boat. Something went wrong and Big Ted's boat ended up on the rocks and rather than own up to it, he left you holding the bag."

"What?" Julie's complexion pales and she shakes her head. "I don't—" She looks at me again, shaking her head. "How'd you know about Teddy and me?"

"I used to be a cop, remember?" I remind her, oversimplifying what I did in the army for her benefit. "There's not a lot you can hide from me—the only thing I can't figure out is what you guys were doing anywhere near the Rock in the first place."

"It's where we go to... be alone." Her face goes from white as a ghost to red as a beet in the blink of an eye. "To the old lighthouse on the back of the island. He was dropping me off so I could wait for him but he got too close to the rocks and—"

"If going to the Rock to be alone was the plan, why was he *dropping you off*?"

"Some buddies of his were stranded on Seraphim," she tells me, referring to the island closest to the marina, where the rich kids go to party. "He was going to give them a lift back to the marina." It comes out without a hiccup, so smooth no one but me would be able to hear it for what it really is.

A lie.

Giving me another look, she frowns. "For the record, I'm the one who told him to hide in the lighthouse while I called the cops. *I* told him to let me take the blame for wrecking the boat."

"Why?" I ask, even though I have a pretty good idea. "Because his father is rich and you're just an eastern girl and his future is so much more important than yours?"

Looking away from me, Julie sets her jaw and shakes her head. "You don't understand."

"Trust me, I understand perfectly." I hate the way I say it. Like I'm bitter. "You forget I grew up on this island. I know how it works."

"Teddy loves me. When he leaves for college in the fall, I'm going with him." She sounds so sure that, for just a moment, I almost believe her.

Looking at the crash site, I know I'm lucky to be alive.

If I hadn't been wearing my seatbelt, I would've been ejected from the cab. Flung into the trunk of a tree or bounced across the asphalt, tearing muscles and breaking bones along the way. At the speed I was going, there's no way I would've survived.

"What are we doing here?" Julie asks from the shoulder, leaned against the front of the car while she watches me contemplate whether or not I want to climb down the side of the ditch and scavenge through the wreckage.

"I had guns," I lie to her by telling the truth. "In my truck—I just want to make sure they didn't get left behind."

"Guns?" I can hear the apprehension in her voice. "You keep guns in your truck?"

"Yup." I chuckle a little while using the toe of my boot to kick my hubcap into the ditch. It rolls down the slope, wobbling over rocks and grass until it finally tips over and slides the rest of the way on its belly. Climbing down would be a wasted effort. The report isn't down there and neither is the box. Someone took them both in an effort to keep me from finding out the truth.

That Rachel was raped repeatedly, nearly the entire time she lived with the McNamaras—from the time she was thirteen until she ran away a few years later.

My stomach clenches and twists, wrung by invisible hands before shoving itself into my throat, trying to choke the life out of me. Taking a deep, cleansing breath, I let it out on a long exhale in an effort to beat back the rising tide of panic and guilt that threatens to knock me off my feet. How many girls passed through their home while Lincoln lived there? A dozen? More than that? How many of them did he abuse? How old was he when he became a predator?

My thoughts turn to Savanna. She's only a few years younger

than Rachel was when the abuse started. How long before Lincoln—

"Georgia?" Hearing her say my name lifts my gaze from the ditch. Aims it into the woods beyond it. Makes me realize she's never called me by my first name before. "We should go. You need—"

"Are you engaged in a sexual relationship with Lincoln McNamara?"

When she doesn't answer me, I turn to look at her. She's standing a few yards away from me, face frozen and pale. Shoulders stiff like I just punched her between them. Her head starts to shake, mouth moving like she's trying to make it work properly. "I know you have a boyfriend and you think you love him," I tell her, giving her a curt head shake of my own. "That's not what I'm asking. I'm asking if Lincoln has sex with *you*." I word the question carefully. Purposely. "If he's ever forced—"

"*No.*" She shoves the word at me like she wants to hit me with it. "No, Mr. McNamara's *never* touched me. Not like that."

I hear my own denial in her words and can see why no one believes me.

"It's not your fault," I tell her, still careful to keep my tone neutral. "Lincoln is good at what he does. He makes you feel special. Like—"

"I had a crush on him," she tells me and again, I can hear my own story in her confession. "He treats me like a real person—not just some throwaway foster—but that was a long time ago and even though I'm sure he knew how I felt, he never took advantage of it *or* me," she tells me, somehow managing to sound both haughty and contrite at the same time. "I've heard the stories. I know what everyone thinks of him and I know about the situation with Mrs. McNamara, but—"

"So, Lincoln is a great guy and he's never touched you?" As hard as I try, I can't keep the skepticism out of my tone.

"It's the truth," she tells me, her face folded into a scowl. When I don't call her an out-and-out liar, she sighs. "Can we go back now?" She asks it like she regrets her promise to Evie to stay with me. Like she'd drop me off on the curb outside the manor gates if she could.

It reminds me of what Richard told me yesterday. That Julie's case manager wants me to turn her over. Moving away from the edge of the ditch, I walk toward her. "You have a new case manager."

Her gaze goes flat and her shoulders slump. "Who is it?"

"Dennis Bleche." When I say his name, she scowls in obvious distaste. "He wants to send you to stay with Lincoln's parents."

"The McNamaras?" Something moves over her face. Something that looks a lot like fear. "You want to send me back to them?" She says *them* like they're the enemy. Like just saying it out loud puts me on the wrong side of a line I didn't even know was there—but I guess I should've. Julie's made it perfectly clear she's Team Lincoln and there's no telling what kind of lies he's told her about his parents and what happened between him and his father the night he was arrested.

"The McNamaras are good people, Julie. They took me in too. Gave me a place to live until I was ready to take care of myself." I try not to think about Rachel and Jenna. What was happening to them while I was mooning over Lincoln. What he was doing to them. "It's a safe place now. You'll—Wait..." It takes me a second to catch what she said. "What do you mean *back* to them?"

The expression on her face sharpens for a second before it's all smoothed away under a mask of careful indifference. "Nothing—I just meant back into the system. I'm almost eighteen. I hoped maybe..." She crosses her arms over her chest and gives me a sullen teenage shrug. "But it's... whatever—you're in charge, right?"

It's not what I want and I'm definitely not in charge but just as I open my mouth to tell her that, a now familiar rumble fills the silence between us. Looking over her shoulder, I watch as a long line of motorcycles roll toward us down 5th Avenue from the direction of the Alley—Angel Bay's version of a red-light district, a tight, dirty cluster of dive bars and seedy nightclubs, broken up by the occasional cheap motel and pawn shop.

On the lead cycle is the Reaper I met the night I found Rachel. No helmet, a pair of dark wraparound shades his only nod toward personal protection.

King.

He calls himself King.

I expect him to stop. Issue a veiled threat about keeping my nose out of his business. Maybe even come right out and tell me if I don't, I won't be so lucky next time.

He doesn't do any of those things.

He doesn't even look at me. None of them do. They roll right past me like I'm not even there.

Like I'm already dead.

THIRTY-FOUR

Alex is sitting on the front steps when we pull into the drive, his cruiser parked in its usual spot. As soon as Julie stops the car and kills the engine, he's down the porch steps and pulling my door open to help me out.

"I'll be inside," Julie mutters, gathering my discharge paperwork and bag full of prescriptions from the hospital pharmacy. Before I can say anything, she is gone, up the steps and into the house while I stifle a wave of frustration as Alex helps me out of the car.

"I stopped by the hospital after my shift," he says, as he closes the car door behind me. "Evie says you were discharged an hour ago." When I don't offer him an explanation for where I've been, he sighs. "Can I come in?"

I give him a tired smile. "I'm concussed, so there won't be any activities that begin with the letter F in our immediate future."

He gives me a look that says he doesn't find me very funny. "Can I come in anyway?"

Suddenly tired of fighting, I lean into him a little and press my lips against the edge of his jaw. Face aimed up at him, I pull away enough to look him in the eye, and I nod. "Yes."

His face softens with relief. "I'm sorry, George," he says,

quietly. "I should've trusted you. I should've told you about the investigation into Lincoln and I—"

"No." I shake my head. Force myself to think about it objectively. "You shouldn't have trusted me. You were right not to." The look on his face sharpens for a second like I might be trying to trick him somehow. "I'm not a cop and my ties to the island—to Lincoln —make me suspect."

"The night I came to your hotel room and asked you to dinner, when you first came back to the island, it was with the intention of checking you out," he admits, his brow creased. "I'd just started digging into Lincoln and I wasn't sure... but then I made the mistake of falling for you, George." He slips a tentative arm around my waist. "This is real, you and me. I know you don't feel the same way. I know you don't love me the way I love you but—"

"Yet," I whisper, leaning into him. "I don't love you *yet*, but I will. I can—if you're patient with me. Give me some time."

"I can do that." The relief on his face holds, softens the blue of his eyes. "I *am* sorry. I never meant to—"

"It's okay," I tell him, even though it's not. Rachel is dead. I'm pretty sure Lincoln killed her and his reason for doing it is pretty horrible, but instead of telling him that, I just shake my head. "We don't have to talk about any of it. Right now, I just want to go to sleep and forget the last few days even happened." Looking past him, at the long trail of wide, shallow steps that lead from the driveway to the manor's front porch, I sigh. Just thinking about climbing them is exhausting. "How do you feel about carrying me up these porch steps and tucking me in?"

The arm around my waist tightens as Alex dips to slip the other one behind my knees to lift me. Cradling me against his chest, he smiles down at me. "I can do that too."

It's close to midnight.

Alex is asleep and I'm attempting to sneak out of my own house like an unruly teenager. I told him all I wanted to do was sleep and forget the past several days even happened and I meant it. The problem is, every time I close my eyes, I see Rachel, laying in the tall marsh grass outside the Den. Her pale hand empty and turned toward the sky. Eyes, half closed and vacant, aimed at the water. The turn of her head exposing the deep ugly bruises that ringed her neck, so dark they seemed to glow in the moonlight.

Forgetting is impossible.

So instead of sleeping, I made a plan.

My plan is to take the ten grand in cash that's stuffed in the drawer of the telephone table and drive out to the Den to see if I can find Jenna and persuade her to tell me what she knows. Ten grand is a fraction of what she asked for but I'm betting once I start waving money in her face, her greed and impulsivity will make it difficult for her to say no.

The problem is, my truck is totaled, sitting in the impound lot, and the lock box in the pantry that's supposed to be full of keys for the fleet of cars in the garage is completely empty. Unless I want to steal Alex's cruiser or shake the Mercedes keys out of Julie, who will undoubtedly go full-tilt watchdog and call Evie to tell her I'm violating the terms of our treaty, I'm stuck.

When I exit the pantry, it's to find said watchdog standing in the kitchen doorway, a self-righteous scowl dug into her face. "I hid them in the same place I hid your extension ladder," she confesses before I can say anything. "And I'm not giving them back until Dr. Jones says you're allowed to drive."

As angry as I am, I can't help but laugh. Leaving her where she is, I cross the kitchen to the fridge and yank it open. The Chinese take-out is gone. "You hide the fried rice too?"

"No." She says it like it's a ridiculous question. "Van and I ate it." She sighs, the sound of it full of trepidation. She's not sure exactly how far she can push me, but I've already threatened to turn her over to the McNamaras, so she probably figures she doesn't have anything to lose. "I'm not going to tell you where the keys are, so you might as well go back to—"

"Not tired." Looking up from the void, I shut the fridge, empty-handed. Because it's my go-to and I've been living on hospital jello and pudding cups for the past two days, I toss a couple of slices of bread into the toaster and jam the lever down before looking at her. "Savanna was here again?"

"Mr. McNamara asked me to stay with her while he was at the hospital with you," Julie tells me in a tone that's more than a little defensive. "So, I brought her here to stay with me. I didn't think you'd mind."

"I *don't* mind," I say, carefully. "I like Savanna. She's welcome—"

"You know, I thought you were different," she hisses at me, gaze narrowed, fists clenched at her sides.

"Excuse me?" Even though I have no idea what she's talking about, I recognize the tone she's using to deliver her accusation just fine and I don't like it. "*Different?*" I repeat when all she does is glare at me. "Care to elaborate?"

Fists still clenched, she takes a step toward me. "When you were talking to Savanna the other day about the things people on this island say about him, you defended Mr. McNamara. Said he was a good dad. I thought—"

"Julie." I stifle another sigh and shake my head, keeping my tone quiet. "You don't understand. Lincoln isn't who you think. He isn't who *either of us* thought." When I say it, I realize it's true. Despite everything I know about Lincoln, there was a part of me that still believed in him. That he's a good man who made a terrible mistake and not what he really is.

A monster.

"No, *you're* the one who doesn't understand." She closes the space between us, still hissing. Blinded by infatuation or loyalty—either way, I understand her perfectly. "Mr. McNamara is exactly who I think he is. He's a good father. He loves Savanna. Anything he's done has been—"

Through the open pocket door next to the fridge, I hear the floorboards in the hallway creak. Julie hears it too and as soon as she does, her mouth snaps shut. A few seconds later, Alex appears in the doorway, wearing nothing more than a pair of low-slung track pants. Eyes squinted against the light, dark blond hair mussed from sleep, he yawns. "What's going on?" he asks, rubbing a hand over his bare chest like he's trying to orientate himself while dividing a puzzled look between Julie and me. "Everything okay?"

"Everything's fine." I give him a low-watt smile to hide my frustration at the interruption. This is the second time Julie's been on the verge of telling me something big. Telling myself it can wait—that I can talk to her in private when I take her to the McNamaras' in the morning—I set it aside. "I'm making my specialty." On cue, my bread pops out of the toaster. I rescue it and drop it on the counter, next to the butter dish. Turning back around, I catch Julie shoot Alex a quick, wary look.

"I'm going to go to bed," she says, giving Alex another look while edging her way toward the doorway. "Is it okay if I sleep upstairs?"

"Yeah." Watching her body language carefully, I notice the shift instantly. She's nervous. On the defensive. "There's thirty-something bedrooms up there—knock yourself out."

"G'night." She gives me a tight smile before looking at Alex again. "G'night, Sheriff."

"Night, Julie." A little more alert, Alex gives her a tight, guarded look of his own as he watches her scurry back the way she came. When she's gone, he looks at me and his tight expression dissolves into a slightly exasperated smile that he divides between me and my toast. "You're going to eat that in bed, aren't you?"

"That was the plan." Toast forgotten, I turn around completely. "What was that about?"

"What was what about?" Alex asks, shuffling through the doorway toward the kitchen sink.

"Julie." I say her name carefully, watching his face for a reaction. There isn't one. "She doesn't seem to like you much."

Chuckling quietly, he leans over to open the cabinet next to the sink. "She's an eastern kid, George—most of them don't like me. I'm the sheriff, remember?" Running the tap, Alex fills his glass with cold water before shutting it off. "Julie probably more than most, considering I arrested her less than a week ago."

"Oh." I feel like an idiot. I never even considered how bringing Julie home would be awkward for either of them. Turning toward the counter, I lift the lid on the butter dish and start slathering my rapidly cooling toast. "I guess you're right," I mutter, while I sprinkle a homemade concoction of brown sugar and cinnamon onto my buttered toast. Flipping one piece on top of the other to make a sandwich, I sigh. "The McNamaras offered to take her," I tell him quietly, on the off-chance Julie is still lurking around and eavesdropping. "Her new case manager reached out to them and asked Richard to talk some sense into me." Telling him reminds me of what Richard told me yesterday. "Dennis Bleche." When he doesn't react to the name, I push a little harder. "Richard mentioned he's from Detroit. He seems to think the two of you know each other."

"Dennis?" Alex nods. "Yeah, I know him. He worked juvenile probation in my district."

"Weird he ended up working here on the island, isn't it?" I ask, trying to keep my tone light.

"Not really, considering I'm the one who talked him into taking the job." Reaching past me, he picks my cinnamon sugar and butter sandwich up off the counter and takes a bite.

Not the answer or reaction I expected. "You did?"

Alex frowns at me while he chews. "Yeah, I did."

"You've never mentioned him before." I can hear it in my voice. Suspicion. What I'm suspicious of I have no idea but after years of investigative work, the reaction is second nature and hard to temper.

Tossing my sandwich back onto the counter, Alex's frown slides into a scowl. "My department works closely with DCFS, and I saw the opportunity to bring in a friendly face and I took it because this island is a minefield. I need people on it I can trust," he tells me quietly, reminding me that up until a few days ago, even though we've been sleeping together for months and,

despite my best efforts, seem to be in a serious, committed relationship, one of those people wasn't me. Brushing crumbs off his
hands, he gives a sigh. "Like I told you at the hospital, I don't
even trust all of my deputies. At first I thought it was because I'm
an outsider, a big-city cop, but I think there's something rotten
here, George, in the department and across the island. I just
don't know how rotten. So, yeah, I brought Dennis in. I brought
Tandy Shepard and Don Levitt in too, just in case you're
keeping track."

"I'm not keeping track of anything," I tell him, thinking about
those little old ladies with their notebooks full of license plate
numbers again. "I'd never heard of him before and when Richard
mentioned you knew him it surprised me, is all."

The scowl on his face melts into something softer. "Jesus, I'm
sorry, George." Reaching up, he frames my face in his hands,
brushing his thumbs along my cheekbones. "Here I am, picking a
fight, even after I promised not to."

"Contrary to popular belief, *fighting* is not my favorite F-word
activity." The quiet chuckle my quip earns me loosens the knot of
anxiety in my chest. "Julie admitted to me she didn't steal Big
Ted's boat," I tell him quietly. "Junior took it, and she took the rap."

"If that's true, why would he lie about it?" Alex gives me a
skeptical head shake. "Kid's spoiled rotten—my guess is his father
would let him take it out anytime he wanted."

"Probably," I shift closer and drop my voice, "but spoiled or
not, I don't think Big Ted would be too keen on his kid using his
boat to run drugs for our resident biker gang." It's a theory I started
to explore in the hospital, when I remembered seeing the boat
docked behind the Den—one I can't prove and is admittedly full of
holes, one of which being that I visited the Den *after* Archie told
me about the Nelsons' boat being wrecked. "What if that's what
they were doing out on the water Friday night?"

"Come on, George." Alex gives me a skeptical head shake.
"That's quite a reach."

"Think about it." My investigative brain turns over sluggishly in an effort to wake up. "Who's going to think twice about a couple of kids out on the lake on a Friday night?"

"I don't buy it." Alex's mouth flattens, his eyebrows dropping low on his forehead. "Why the hell would an Ivy League-bound rich kid want to move drugs for the Reapers? He's got a future, George—a *real* future. I can't see—"

I feel the flush of anger rushing up my neck like wildfire. "As opposed to Julie, who's just some trashy eastern girl whose best hope is aging out of the system *before* she gets knocked up?"

"That's not what I meant, and you know it," he tells me, shaking his head. "And even if it *was*, how's that any different than what you're suggesting? If Teddy Nelson *is* running drugs for the Reapers and Julie was there, that means she's involved somehow." He lets it sink in. When it finally does, he sighs. "And if they killed Rachel like we think then *that* means Julie is involved in that too," he says, his tone urging me to think rationally. "Come on, do you *really* believe that?"

"You had no problem believing she stole the boat in the first place," I remind him, fighting the frustration I can hear creeping into my own tone.

"There's a hell of a difference between taking a boat out for a joyride and international drug smuggling and murder," he says in a reasonable tone that instantly sets my teeth on edge.

"I'm not saying she's *El Chapo*," I bite back. "But she knows more than she's letting on." I don't tell him the rest. That I don't think Rachel's murder has anything to do with the drug-smuggling operation. That Lincoln killed her because she threatened to speak up about the rapes. Maybe even threatened to have Savanna taken away again. As a case manager, it would've been in her power to make it happen. "I think it's worth a look—I mean, this *is* an investigation, right? And she's a lead—so, don't you think you should follow it?"

"Okay," he says, running his hand through his hair. "If it makes you happy, we can tie her to a chair and waterboard her for information in the morning."

I narrow my eyes at him. "Are you making fun of me?"

"A little bit," he admits, before giving in on a sigh. "I'm sorry, you're right—Julie Kates might be a lead. I'll follow it."

"But?"

"*But* not tonight. It's late and you're on the injured list," he reminds me. "So, right now, you, me, and your cold toast are going back to bed."

"But you'll talk to her?"

"Yes." He sighs and rolls his eyes.

"When?"

"Tomorrow."

Tomorrow isn't soon enough.

I want now.

Right now.

I want to charge upstairs and force Julie to talk to me. Tell me the truth about why she and Teddy took the boat out Friday night and why she confessed to stealing it. I want to tear this entire house apart until I find a set of car keys. I want to drive out to the Den and drag Jenna out of it by her hair and shake her silly. Make *her* talk to me too. Make her tell me what Rachel was doing there the night she was killed. I want to confront Lincoln with everything I know. Force him to confess to raping Rachel and killing her to keep her quiet about it.

But I can't do any of those things.

Not right now.

Not tonight.

So, instead, I do the other thing I'm good at—slam a lid over the nightmares running around my head and shove them in a corner. "You sure about that, Sheriff?" I lean into him, pressing myself against him. "You hate it when I eat toast in bed."

His jaw relaxes at my playful tone. He knows it's over, that I'm letting it go—for now. "Exigent circumstances, George," he says, bending slightly to lift me into his arms again. Tilting his head, he presses a soft kiss to the corner of my bruised mouth. "Maybe if you eat the toast in bed, I'll be too annoyed by all the crumbs to think about our favorite F-word activity."

"Sounds like a long shot." I give him a grin, despite the niggling worry that's eating away at the base of my brain. I'm running out of time. I can feel it. "But we can give it a try."

I barely have a chance to grab the toast off the counter before he carries me back to bed.

THIRTY-FIVE

Ribs screaming and unable to take a deep breath, I broke down and took one of the pain meds Evie prescribed around 2 a.m. Slipping back into bed, I lay down next to Alex, teeth clenched between slow, shallow breaths, and waited for the pill I took to do its job.

The entire manor was as quiet as an old house can be, its occasional creaks and groans punctuated with the deep *bongs* and lilting chimes from the legion of grandfather clocks that the Fell family seemed to be obsessed with.

At around two thirty I vowed to drag every single one of them into the front courtyard and set them on fire.

That's the last thing I remember.

For the first time in my adult life, I wake up to the sun streaming through my bedroom curtains.

And I'm alone.

Looking for my cell phone, I fumble my hand across my nightstand for several seconds before I remember I don't have one anymore—at least not one that works.

Putting *get new phone* on my mental to-do list, I push my hair out of my face and look at the empty space where Alex is supposed to be. Dropping my hand, I run it across his share of the sheets. They're stone cold. Wherever he went, he's been gone for a while.

Pain meds worn off, I lever myself out of bed with more

caution than I'm comfortable with and totter to the bathroom like an old woman. There, stuck to the mirror, is the note I knew I'd find.

> Got an early call.
>> I'll be back to check on you around noon.
>> No toast, I'll bring lunch.

> Love you ∼ Alex

Pulling the note off the mirror, I read it again before tossing it in the trash with a sigh. Heading down the hall, I notice the pocket door leading to the kitchen is closed. Sliding it open, I expect to find Julie sitting at the table, a mug of black coffee in front of her while she goes over my aftercare instructions for the hundredth time. Instead, I find the kitchen empty. No Julie. No coffee. My hospital paperwork and the bag of prescriptions sitting on the table, save the pain meds I rescued last night, undisturbed.

"*Julie?*" I call out, instantly feeling stupid. This house is roughly the size of a Holiday Inn. If she's upstairs, sulking in one of the bedrooms, there's no way she'd hear me and even if she did, the chances of her answering me are between slim and none—not when she thinks I'm going to cart her off to the McNamaras or just want to shake a set of car keys out of her. Remembering Mark pointed out a working elevator during his initial tour, I put *find Julie* on my to-do list and bump it up to the top, directly under *ingest caffeine*.

Once I clear out the cobwebs, I'll lure Julie from her hiding spot and ask her to take me to get a replacement phone. If I know Jenna, she'll have called me—either to taunt me about the accident or make another demand for money in exchange for information about Rachel.

While I doubt I'll be able to talk Julie into a clandestine meeting with Lincoln's wife, I can at least get the ball rolling again.

Pouring myself a cup of coffee, I take a careful sip and wait for the mild jolt of energy it offers to jumpstart my brain. While I wait, I stare out the kitchen window above the sink. Across the rolling lawn that slopes gently into the trees before the thick line of them breaks against the lakeshore. The water laps against it, the manor's boat, tied to the end of the dock, bobbing softly along its surface.

The boat.

Holy shit.

I forgot about the boat—and that means there's a pretty good chance Julie did too.

Which means I don't need her. I can get to the Den by boat, and if I can get to the Den, I might be able to get to Jenna.

It's a long shot but I have to try.

Just then the deep *bong* of one of the grandfather clocks kicks off a cacophony of noise, signaling the hour. Concentrating, I count eleven of them. It's eleven o'clock. Alex said he'd be back to check on me around noon, which means I don't have much time.

Downing the rest of my coffee, I give the cup a quick rinse before heading back to my bedroom. There, I struggle into one of Alex's T-shirts and a pair of long-forgotten yoga pants with a wide elastic waistband that hugs my ribcage. Pulling it up over the ACE bandage encircling my torso, I breathe an audible sigh of relief— the pressure and support it offers my cracked ribs is enough to ease the pain of them considerably.

Afterward, I take a few half-hearted swipes at my hair with a brush, careful to avoid the neat row of staples holding my scalp together, before wrangling it into a lumpy ponytail. I slip my feet into a pair of deck shoes I bought for the boat and give myself a quick look in the mirror.

The level of sloppy I'm presented with makes my eye twitch but it's the best I can do on my own. Finding an old backpack in my closet, I carry it with me to the alcove under the stairs. The drawer under the telephone table is slightly askew, half open like someone closed it in a hurry.

Julie.

Pulling it open, I let out a sigh.

The money is gone.

In its place is a piece of paper, a single word scrawled across its face.

Sorry

Slamming the drawer closed on a curse, I drop the empty backpack and hurry as fast as I can down the hall and into the foyer. I open the front door and survey the driveway.

Like the money, the Mercedes is gone.

Behind me, the manor's landline begins to ring. Leaving the door standing open, I rush back to the phone nook and catch it before the answering service picks up. "Hello?"

"Hey." It's Alex. "I know I said I'd come back for lunch but it's not going to happen." He sounds tense. Agitated. "I've got stuff going on here I can't get away from."

"What stuff?" I ask before I can stop myself. "Does it have to do with—"

"I can't talk about it, George." It comes out harsh, almost angry. "Not here. I'll try to come over later tonight, okay?"

Remembering what he told me, that he thinks he inherited a dirty department when he took on the role of Fell County Sheriff, I swallow the rest of my questions. "Okay."

"I love you." He hangs up before I can think of what to say in response.

I drop the phone into its cradle for a second to clear the line before picking it back up and dialing.

"No, George," Archie says by way of greeting because he knows what I want. "No way. I can't—you know I can't."

"Can't what?"

"*Can't* talk to you about official police business." He sounds exasperated. Like he's talking to a toddler. "*Can't* tell you what's going on."

"Who says that's why I called?" I counter, feeling as transparent as glass. "Maybe I just called to say hi."

He laughs at me but the sound of it is strangled, like forcing it out of his mouth hurts. "You never call me just to say *hi*, George. You only call me when you want something."

He's right. The realization makes me feel horrible. Dispensing with pretenses, I sigh. "Is it Julie? Does whatever's going on involve her?" I don't know why I ask. By all accounts, my houseguest robbed me, stole my car, and jumped bail. Even if Alex knew she ran away, bail jumper or not, he doesn't think she's anything more than some harmless eastern girl who stole Big Ted's boat for the sole purpose of taking it for a joyride. He's not throwing up any roadblocks for her.

"Julie *Kates*?" Archie asks, his tone edged in confusion. "What? No—why?" When I don't answer right away, he bites back a curse. "Tell me, George—did something happen?

"I'm not sure—does running away qualify as *something*?"

Archie mutters another curse. "Are you sure she *ran* ran? Maybe she's got a boyfriend or someone she snuck off to see."

She does have a boyfriend—or at least she thinks she does. She thinks they're in love. That they're going to run away together, but I don't tell him that. "Pretty sure," I tell him on a tight, one-note chuckle. "She took my telephone table money and stole my car."

"I told you it was stupid to keep that kind of cash laying around," he grumbles at me. *Jesus, George*, he'd said when he saw the stacks of bills stuffed inside the drawer. *At least put it in a coffee can and bury it in your yard like a* normal *rich, crazy person.*

"I didn't put it there," I remind him. "Elizabeth Fell—" Squeezing my eyes shut, I shake my head. "Can we stay on topic, please?"

"Depends on what topic you want to stay on."

The topic of tell me what the hell is going on. I don't have to say it because I know Archie. I've made the ask. That's all I have to do. His resolve will eat itself and he'll cave—eventually. Pushing will only slow the process. "Can you quietly look for my car? It's the silver Mercedes coupé," I ask instead. "Maybe she's still on the island." It's a long shot but pretty much all I have.

"I suppose *quietly* means don't tell my boss?" he says, sounding more resigned than angry.

"*Quietly* means don't tell anyone."

He sighs, the sound of it telling me he's seconds away from hanging up on me. "She's been charged with a felony and out on bail. If she *did* run, that makes her a fugitive, George."

"She's just a scared kid, Arch," I tell him, even though I'm pretty sure she's a hell of a lot more than that. When my request is met with silence, I pull out the big guns. "Remember the time you ran away from the Greenburgs when you were eleven? They found you in Marquette three days later, squatting in that boarded-up video arcade." I don't mention the rest. That he'd run away because I'd been placed with the McNamaras and that meant we'd been separated again, this time for good. He'd been angry at me. Felt abandoned. Gone looking for Will, to the arcade in Marquette where they used to spend their afternoons and week-ends avoiding their alcoholic mother and her abusive boyfriend. "At least give me a chance to find her before you sound the charge."

He's quiet for a few seconds, probably lost in the memory I dragged him into. Finally, he clears his throat. "Okay—I'll call you back if I find anything."

"No." I say it quickly. Too quickly. "I don't have a cell, remember? I'll call you," I remind him in an effort to cover up my mistake.

It doesn't work.

"Then I guess it's a good thing you don't have anything better to do than sit around and wait for the landline to ring, isn't it?" When I don't answer him, Archie mutters another curse. "George..." he cautions, because he knows me just as well as I know him. "If I catch you running around this island, I'm—"

"*What?*" I ask, unable to stifle the laughter his warning bubbles up. "What are you going to do?"

"I'm going to tell the sheriff about Julie and *then* I'm going to put a BOLO out on you," he says, answering my challenge firmly. "When they find you, I'll have you detained until the paramedics come strap you to a gurney and take you to the hospital where Evie will be waiting with a horse syringe full of Thorazine."

"You wouldn't do that to me," I say with more confidence than I actually feel.

"*To* you? No. *For your own good?* You bet your ass I would." He's that Archie again. The Archie I don't really know. The man he became in my absence. "You're in no condition to go running around this island, looking for a girl who doesn't want to be found, so just stay put and let me do my job."

"What's going on?" Even though I know pushing is the wrong way to play it, I can't help it. This unfamiliar Archie is someone I don't recognize. Someone I don't understand. "I know *something* happened. Alex left without saying goodbye and he was supposed to come back but he—"

"Jenna's dead."

He says it quietly, the words hanging between us, cold and ugly.

"What?" I don't know why I'm surprised. Why I suddenly can't seem to take a full breath because this was always going to happen. Jenna was always going to wind up dead. The way she lived her life, there's no other way it could've ended. Even though I know it's true, I can't make myself believe it. "No." I shake my head. "That's not possible. She can't be dead."

"She is." His tone is distant. Rote, like he's reading off a set of cue cards. "I worked patrol overnight. A shots-fired call came in from the Eazy-8 a little after oh three hundred." Despite its name, the Eazy-8 is one of the more respectable motels on the Alley. It's full of cash-strapped vacationers looking for the island experience on a budget—not somewhere I'd expect Jenna to hole up. "Levi and I rolled to the scene and found her."

"Shots fired?" My sluggish brain is trying to catch up, make sense of what he's telling me. "Jenna was *shot*?"

"Yeah." He sighs the word, sounding more like the Archie I know. "She'd been forced into the bathtub and shot in the back of the head twice, execution-style, with a large caliber handgun..."

Archie's still talking but I can't catch hold of what he's saying. Can't make sense of it. I don't even realize I'm sinking until I land on the padded bench behind me, the force of it hard enough to jar the cracks in my ribs, rubbing them together. I barely feel it.

"There's more," he tells me, because it worked: his resolve is gone. He's my Archie again, willing to tell me everything.

The room starts to sway around me. Closing my eyes against it, I sigh. "Tell me."

"It's bad, George." He sounds lost. Like he doesn't know what to do. Doesn't want to tell me the rest of it. "Really bad."

"It's okay," I tell him, even though we both know it isn't. "It's okay—just tell me."

"There was a handgun recovered at the scene whose caliber seemed consistent with the gunshot wounds found in the back of her head," he says carefully, leaning heavily on his training. "We ran a check on the serial number. It's registered to you."

THIRTY-SIX

LINCOLN

I wake up to a text message from Julie.

I'm sorry but I can't watch Savanna today. Something came up.

Without Julie to sit with her, I'm stuck with the age-old single parent dilemma—call in sick or take Savanna to work with me. Reading Julie's text again, I notice the timestamp—2 a.m.—and feel my chest tighten in response.

Things don't just *come up* at 2 a.m. Nothing good, anyway.

Frowning, I tap out a response:

Is everything okay?

While I wait for her to answer, I shoot Will a quick text, telling him I'm not going to make it into the shop today. It's barely 8 a.m. on a Wednesday. By island summer standards, the public beach will be dead. I'll wake Savanna and let her know she's stuck with me for the day. Once the *I'm not a baby, I can stay home by myself* campaign wears out, we'll get dressed and head to Carlisle's. Grab a couple of fritters and some hot chocolate. Walk the beach and feed the gulls. Watch the old guys sweep the sand with their metal detectors and the frisbee nuts play catch with their dogs.

When we lived with Elizabeth, it was something we did all the time. Those first few months, even though she told the parole board I'd be employed full-time as her personal mechanic, she wouldn't even let me near her garage. *Right now, the only job you have is getting to know Savanna. Learning how to be her father. Everything else can wait.* When she was little, I was granted weekly, supervised visits so Savanna always knew me. Knew I was her father. But I hated it. Hated the only place I ever got to see her was the family visitation room of a maximum-security prison. Hated knowing the only way I got to hold her or play with her was with guards breathing down my neck, watching every move I made.

When I was paroled, Savanna and I were barely more than strangers and I had little to no hope of getting her back. Even though she didn't do it alone, Elizabeth changed that. Brought us back together. Made us a family.

Jenna threatened to destroy that.

Take Savanna away from me.

I'm telling your precious little Georgia the truth about you, Lincoln—I'm telling her everything. And not just her. I'm telling Savanna. I'm telling your mother—I might even call that bitch reporter at the Herald *and give her sad little paper the story of the century. By the time I'm done, everyone on this island is going to know the truth.*

My phone buzzes in my hand, bringing me back to the present. Swiping a thumb over the screen, I pull up the text. Expecting an *everything is fine* text from Julie, I find one from Will instead.

Where were you last night?

My reply is brief. *Home. Why?*

He texts back almost immediately: *Tell them I was with you.*

Something cold crawls across the back of my neck.

What the hell did you do?

Bubbles appear at the bottom of the screen, signaling Will is writing a response but before it comes through, there's a loud, pounding knock on the front door.

I recognize it for what it is, instantly.

It's the police.

Probably here to harass me about Georgia's accident.

Accuse me of causing it.

Driven by instincts honed by seven years in prison, I don't wait for Will's text to come through. Instead, I power off the phone. Lifting my mattress, I shove it underneath. If they had a search warrant, it wouldn't matter, but the fact they're knocking and not kicking my door in tells me they don't. If I'm taken in for questioning, leaving my phone behind is the smartest course of action.

Phone hidden, I exit my bedroom and push myself down the short hallway, through the kitchen toward the living room. When I get there, Savanna is standing at the foot of the stairs, still wearing her pajamas and staring wide-eyed at the front door. She looks scared. Her face a pale, miniature carbon-copy of mine.

"Dad?"

"It's okay, Van," I lie to her, reaching for the front door. "It's okay," I say again, hoping to make us both believe it. "Go get dressed."

She starts to shake her head at me, reluctant to move. Refusing to take her eyes off me for a second.

"*Now, Savanna.*" I'm stern, even though I don't want to be, hand gripped around the knob, unwilling to open the door until she's gone. "Go to your room and shut the door."

She looks like she's going to refuse again. Like she's on the verge of falling apart, but she doesn't. Chin trembling, she gives me a single, disjointed nod before she turns and flies up the steps.

As soon as I hear her door slam closed behind her, I open the front door.

It's Bradford, with Levi Tate standing on the porch a few steps behind him, his cruiser parked on the street in front of my house.

There's something on the front of his uniform shirt. Streaks and splotches soaked into the fabric. Dried stiff, turning its khaki color a dark, rusty brown.

Blood.

They aren't here to harass me about Georgia's accident.

As soon as he sees me, Levi unsnaps his holster, a barely restrained snarl rippling across his face. Neither of those actions are out of character for him but something about the way he's looking at me, coupled with the white-knuckle grip he has on the gun stuck in his belt, stiffens the back of my neck. Training my gaze on the man in front of me, I force myself to relax. "Sheriff," I say, careful to keep my tone flat. Neutral. "Something I can do for you?"

"Runnin' late for work?" Bradford asks, settling a casual hand on the butt of his service weapon. He keeps his holster snapped but his message is clear—just like Levi, he's hoping I make a move. Would love nothing better than an excuse to shoot me.

"I'm taking the day off." Behind them, the old lady who lives across the street steps out onto her porch, phone in hand, to watch the show while she gives a play by play to whoever she's talking to. "Perks of being my own boss."

Bradford smirks at that, making a noise in the back of his throat that tightens the knot between my shoulder blades.

"What can I do for you, Sheriff?" This time there's nothing flat or neutral about my tone.

"What happened to your face, Lincoln?" This from Levi, the question earning him a quick, sideways glare from his boss while I resist the urge to reach up and finger the deep rivets Jenna dug into my face the night before last.

Your girlfriend tried to claw my eyes out.

Instead of saying it out loud and getting myself gunned down on my own front porch, I ignore the question and wait for Bradford to answer mine.

Finally, he does.

"I'm here to inform you that your wife was found dead this morning and to ask you to come down to the station to answer some questions."

THIRTY-SEVEN

GEORGIA

It's registered to you.

"One of the M9s I keep in my truck." It's not a question but he answers me anyway.

"Yeah." It comes out rusty and Archie clears his throat because telling me one of my guns was used to kill Jenna wasn't the hard part. "Sheriff Bradford and Deputy Tate went to Lincoln's to make the death notification and they observed defense wounds on his face and wrists. Witnesses heard arguing coming from Jenna's room. Someone matching Linc's description, wearing a dark-colored hoodie, was seen leaving the hotel room shortly after gunshots were heard."

Someone matching Linc's description.

It's bullshit cop jargon. A loose, verbal construct used when a positive ID can't be nailed down but a suspect is in custody. Lincoln is somewhere north of six foot. Athletic build. I can name a dozen men on the island who tick those boxes, starting with Archie, and I'd bet more than half of them own a dark-colored hoodie.

"And as the first person on the scene of my accident, Lincoln had unrestricted access to my weapons." I have to force myself to say it because, even though I know what he really is and what he did, I still want to believe he's innocent. Can't seem to accept he's a monster. "He could've easily taken one of them and secured it in his car before he called 911." What I don't say, don't admit, is I'm the reason Lincoln knew I had guns in my truck in the first place. I'm the one who told him in an effort to keep him out of trouble. Trying to protect him, I gave him the means to shoot his wife in the head.

"Where's Savanna?"

"They brought her in when they brought Linc. If he's arrested, she'll be turned over to DCFS." He sighs. "You can't go down there, George," Archie warns me, reading my mind. "You can't get involved. You're—"

"Not a cop." The words taste bitter. Turn my mouth black.

"I was going to say *too close*," he says softly. "To Lincoln. To the sheriff—to the whole damn thing." I never told him about my feelings for Lincoln—I never told anyone—but I'm beginning to realize it was never a secret. Everyone knew how I felt. They all knew exactly how stupid I was. "If you go down there—"

"Don't worry," I say, trying to reassure him. "I'm stuck, remember? Julie hid all my car keys, took the coupé, and I don't have a cell phone so I couldn't order an Uber, even if I wanted to."

"I'll cruise the island and look for her, okay?" he offers, his tone caught somewhere between relief and suspicion. Archie knows me. He knows I won't just sit around and wait for him to call me, not if I can find a way out of here. "If I find Julie, I'll call."

"Okay." Thinking about the boat tied to the end of my dock, I nod. "I'll be here," I say, hanging up before I'm forced to tell him another lie.

Even though I bought a pair of deck shoes with the intention of taking the boat out, it never happened. Matter of fact, it's been years since I've even been on a boat. Not since my time at the McNamaras. Lincoln used to take me out in his, a pretty little Catalina daysailer he got when he turned fifteen, long before I claimed a seat at their dinner table.

Pushing the memory into the corner with the rest of my night-mares, I slam the lid down tight and focus on what I have to do now—the only thing left that I *can* do.

Find Julie.

It takes me longer than I like to make it down to the dock. When I get there, there are *two* boats tied up at the end of the manor's dock and neither of them is a sailboat—there's the thirty-foot cruiser I saw from the house, roughly the size of a minibus, and a much smaller square-nosed johnboat that looks like it's about to spring a leak. Undaunted, I carefully climb aboard the cruiser. A quick search turns up a set of keys attached to a small, bright blue floatation device meant to keep them afloat if they end up in the water. Having mixed feelings about the fact I opted to skip another dose of pain meds, I turn the key in the ignition. The engine roars effortlessly to life, and I make a mental note to thank whoever's listed on Mark's paperwork as my boat mechanic.

The dash is complicated—dials and switches I have no idea how to operate. I briefly consider the johnboat instead, but decide I'm in no condition to potentially have to swim to shore. Sending up a quick prayer, I cast off and focus on the instruments I recognize. Easing the throttle up as I give the steering wheel a gentle turn, I'm rewarded when the boat starts to move through the water, away from the dock.

Going slow, I guide the boat out of the small inlet dug into the shore and point the bow east. Aside from a small corner of it, carved out for the marina and yacht club, nearly the entire north side of the island is reserved for its wealthiest residents. Once upon a time, it had all belonged to the Fells, but over the years it was divided into parcels and sold. Property lines were drawn. Mansions were built. Gates were erected to keep out the riffraff.

Now there are five families sprawled across the north side of the island—the McNamaras, the Vances, the Nelsons, the Fells and the Tates. The Nelsons are my immediate neighbors to the east and that's where I'm going.

I'm not surprised to see Teddy out on his family's dock when I come around the curve of the island that hides his stretch of private beach from mine. Barefoot, in a pair of boardshorts, he looks like he's getting ready for a swim. I'd think that's what he was actually doing if not for the fact he has his cell phone stuck to his ear and I can hear him talking—not the words, but the tone of them carrying across the water.

He's agitated. Scared.

When Teddy hears the quiet rumble of my boat engine, he looks up. Seeing me heading toward him, his face loses every ounce of color and he mumbles something into the phone before ending the call and dropping the cell into his pocket, shoulders turned like he has every intention of making a fast getaway.

"Hey, Teddy," I call out before he can make a move, down-shifting the boat before cutting the engine entirely.

After a second's worth of tense hesitation, his shoulders slump. "Hey, Ms. Fell," he says, watching as the boat drifts closer. "My dad's not here." He shoots a quick look over his shoulder at the house behind him—a giant box made of glass and steel, it's lines too harsh and modern to fit the island's Victorian flavor—probably giving himself time to recover before turning back to shoot me a friendly, apologetic grin. "He's at the town council meeting," he tells me, a gentle reminder I should be at the meeting too, and not here, sneaking up on him.

"That's okay." Ignoring his reminder, I reach for the rope tied to the rail of the boat and toss it to him, giving him little choice but to catch it as the side of the boat slowly runs parallel with the end of the dock he's standing on. "I'm not here to see your dad. I'm here to see you."

"Me?" He says it before looking at the rope in his hands like he's contemplating throwing it back in my face.

I gesture toward the dock. "You and I are going to have a little chat, so, I'd appreciate you taking that rope and tying me off."

"Look, I don't really have time for a *chat*." He sounds puzzled, like he has no idea what kind of business I'd have with him. "I'm supposed to meet some buddies at the club, so—"

"No, you *look*," I bite back, barely able to contain my impatience because Rachel and Jenna are dead and Julie is missing and even though everything I know is telling me it's totally unrelated, my gut is telling me everything I know is wrong. "I know all about your little side hustle, running drugs for the Reapers, so unless you *do* want me to go to that council meeting and *chat* with your dad, I suggest you drop the act and start talking."

THIRTY-EIGHT

LINCOLN

I've been sitting in an interview room for a while now, waiting for Bradford or someone to come in here and tell me what the hell is going on. My back is aching. My throat is dry. My stomach is in knots. I want to get up and pace. Crack open the bottle of water Levi threw at me almost as an afterthought after he shoved me in here. Flip off the two-way mirror that separates the room I'm in from the observation deck where I'm sure some lop-eared bastard in a uniform has been assigned to watch me. Bang on the door and start screaming about my civil rights. Ask what the hell is going on. Where my kid is.

Even though I want to do all of those things, I won't.

I won't touch the water. I won't start pacing and screaming. I won't flip the deputy behind the mirror the bird because there are cameras in here and I'm being recorded. Any hostile or agitated behavior will be used against me somehow.

Jenna is dead and they brought me here because they think I did it.

I think about Savanna, wonder if she knows. Wonder if they told her I killed her mother. If they've already started the job of turning her against me.

Arms crossed over my chest, I keep my fists clenched tight. My prints to myself. My DNA too. I'm a felon so they have both on file but they'll need a fresh set if they want to—

The lock on the door turns and it opens. Bradford strolls in, file folder in hand, and takes a seat at the table across from me. "Sorry about the wait," he says, amicably, as he slides the folder onto the table between us. "It's been a busy day."

I bet.

Instead of saying it out loud I just shrug. "It's okay. I took the day off, remember?" I say, because it's something I've already admitted to.

"Right." Bradford gives me a nod like it'd slipped his mind. "What for—if you don't mind my asking?"

"My sitter canceled on me, last minute." I do mind but I answer him anyway because if this is going where I think, he's already working on a search warrant for my house. My phone records. He'll know why soon enough.

"Your sitter is Julie Kates?"

Another question he knows the answer to. "Yes."

"She's a pretty girl," he says, like he's just making conversation.

I sigh. "The operative word being girl—Julie is a *girl*."

"So?" Bradford gives me a grin that's just this side of lewd. "I thought you liked *girls*—young, pretty foster girls."

I feel a muscle in my jaw start to tic. "What happened with Jenna was a mistake—an *isolated* mistake I've never repeated," I tell him, regurgitating the same pat answer I've given to everyone who's ever made the assumption. "What does any of this have to do with my babysitter?"

Bradford makes a noise in the back of his throat. "Did Julie happen to mention why she had to cancel?"

Sighing, I shrug. "She's seventeen and it's the middle of summer—if I had to guess she decided to go to the beach with friends or is running around the boardwalk." It's a lie—the first I've told so far. Julie isn't flighty. She wouldn't bail on me to go to the beach. Whatever her reason is, it's real. "When you talk to her to verify my story, you should ask her."

"Yeah..." Bradford grins. "We've been looking for her. Problem is, no one knows where she is. She was fired from her job down at the shaved ice stand Saturday night, and this morning she stole about ten grand in cash and a car from Georgia and then she just... disappeared."

Julie is missing.

I feel my whole body go tense. The fists I have buried in my armpits crank so tight, I feel my knuckles crack. "Yeah? Well, she's a foster kid." I shrug like it doesn't matter to me one way or the other. "They tend to do that kind of shit."

Bradford nods again, this time like I've made a valid point. "You haven't asked about your wife, Lincoln—why is that?"

"Because you've already told me she's dead, *Alex*," I say, dropping his first name, just so I can watch his eye twitch. "And I've done this dance before—you wouldn't have hauled me down here unless you suspected foul play and you wouldn't have walked in here with that smug look on your face and that file in your hand unless it was full of circumstantial evidence that I'm the one who killed her."

"I keep forgetting you have a degree in criminal justice," he says, sliding back in his chair. "What was the plan again? Law school? A stint with the public defender's office? Make your mark before opening your own private practice, getting scumbags like your Reaper buddies off on technicalities."

Actually, I wanted to be a prosecutor. I wanted to put people like King and his partners in prison. Make sure they stayed there. Instead, I somehow ended up turning myself into one of them. "You seem a little lost so, let me help you..." I lean forward and stage whisper the rest: *"This is the part where you ask me if I killed my wife."*

Muffled laughter erupts from behind the two-way and the grin on Bradford's face goes cold. He hates being laughed at. "Did you?" he asks, friendly pretenses suddenly gone.

"No." I look at the file on the table between us—can't help it, because whatever is in it will work to prove otherwise.

Instead of calling me a liar, opening the folder and shoving whatever's in it in my face, he chooses a different route. "Where were you last night?"

Tell them I was with you.

That's the text Will sent me this morning.

I could. I could tell Bradford that Will came over after I put Savanna to bed and we hung out all night, drinking beer. I *should* because even though beers with someone like Will Hudson is a flimsy alibi, he's better than the one I've got. Instead of doing what I should, I don't do anything. Don't say a word.

Taking my silence as some sort of victory, Bradford smiles. "When was the last time you saw your wife?"

"Monday night—after I left the hospital, I went to the Den around eight," I tell him, surprising him with the truth because he already knows when I saw her. Knows where I was. Cops rarely ask questions they don't know the answers to. "She was there. We talked. I left."

"You talked?" Now the grin he gives me is genuine. "You sure that's what you want to call it?"

Again, I don't say anything.

Bradford sits back slowly in his seat. "Because you didn't just *talk*. You fought—*loudly*."

Instead of developing diarrhea of the mouth, trying to defend my position, I give him a bored shrug. "You've arrested Jenna more than once—if anyone knows how much she likes to fight, it's you."

"She was screaming some pretty incriminating things—threatening to *tell everyone the truth about you*." He cocks his head to the side like he's suddenly enjoying himself. "She stalked off across the parking lot, into the trees... and you followed her."

"That's a pretty detailed account of what happened," I tell him, keeping my cool, even though it confirms my suspicions. Someone else was out there that night. Listening. Watching—either me or Jenna. Which one of us is anyone's guess. We both belong to King. Both of us are caught up in this thing. Present problems he knows will need solving, sooner or later. "Were you there too?"

"No." He shakes his head at me and gives me one of his smug smiles. "I was with Georgia." He says her name softly, dangling the bait. "I was with her last night too," he adds, his whispers too low for the cameras to catch.

I see myself lunging across the table. Tackling him out of his chair. Imagine the kind of damage I could inflict in the fifteen to twenty seconds it would take for the clowns behind the two-way to bust their way in here.

The only thing that stops me is the fact that Savanna is stuck in some room somewhere, scared out of her mind and counting on me to keep my head. To get us out of here. Keep us together for as long as I can.

Time to wrap this up.

"You are *precious...*" Instead of killing him, I chuckle and give him a *nice try* head shake. "But I'm getting bored, *fast*, Sheriff." Bradford's jaw tightens at my tone, his glare locked on mine, because he was hoping I'd take a run at him so he could book me on assault charges and hold me indefinitely. "So why don't you just show me what's in the file already."

Before he can say anything there's a curt knock, but neither of us pay it any attention. The door opens and a figure I recognize appears in my peripheral, taking this situation from *moderately concerning but manageable* to *I'm completely screwed* in a heartbeat.

"Sheriff, if you don't mind, I'd like to try to talk some sense into him."

"Of course," Bradford says, his jaw relaxing just enough to let out sound. "Maybe you can get him to understand the gravity of the situation he's in." Standing up, he leaves the file behind and exits the room, shutting the door behind him while the figure in my peripheral slides into the chair he just vacated, bringing himself into view.

"Hello, Lincoln," he says, his tone carrying just the right

amount of sadness. The perfect balance between condemnation and concern. Looking at him, I feel my entire body go loose. Give up on me completely.

Because there's no way out of this. No way to beat him. I've already tried and failed.

I'm going to lose.

Preparing to fight the losing battle that's bearing down on me, I plant my boots, pushing myself up in my seat. Slip a mask of casual indifference over a face that's a mirror image of the one staring back at me and smile. "Hey, *Dick*," I say, giving my father a cocky half-smile. "What are you doing here?"

THIRTY-NINE
GEORGIA

Teddy Nelson is proving to be a tougher nut to crack than I gave him credit for and frankly, I'm running out of patience.

When I told him Julie stole my car and a bunch of cash, he just gave me an insolent, rich-boy shrug and said, *Sounds like you need help—maybe you should call a cop.*

"Not really the kind of *help* I'm looking for, Teddy," I tell him, glad for once I no longer carry a gun. "And considering what I know about you, and how you've been supplementing your allowance as a drug-runner for a biker gang, I'd think long and hard about watching my mouth if I were you." It's a bluff. I don't know anything. Don't have any proof. All I have are a few half-baked theories and that near-constant tugging in my brain, telling me he's involved and that Julie didn't just run away. That she's in trouble and for all his spoiled simpering and sullen shrugs, Teddy knows where she is. "Where is Julie?"

Teddy scoffs. "Why would I know that?"

"Because she's your girlfriend." I say it carefully. Like I actually believe it.

"My *girlfriend?*" Now, he outright laughs. "Is that what she told you?" He gives me a smirk and shakes his head. "Julie's not my girlfriend."

"Then what is she exactly?"

"She's just a *girl*," he replies, like it's a stupid question. "We hooked up a few times—that's it. I don't know where she is and I really don't care."

Tired of his bullshit, I sharpen my gaze into a glare and lean forward, shoving my face within an inch of his. "You take your father's boat into Canadian waters and use it to mule drugs back to the United States—that's called *international drug smuggling*," I tell him, having the pleasure of watching my words wipe the smug look off his face. "That's not something your rich daddy can just disappear with a game of golf and a few well-placed handshakes. You'll do time, Teddy—*real time*." When he doesn't so much as flinch at the mention of prison, I take a chance. Change direction. "So will Julie, and it'll be so much worse for her than it will be for you because she doesn't come from a wealthy family who can afford an army of lawyers. They'll find a way to pin all of this on her." I give him a grim smile and nod. "Forget what I just said... your lawyers play it right, and I'm sure they will, you might *actually* walk. Worst case, you'll end up serving a few bullshit years in some club-Fed facility with tennis courts and internet access and be back in the world in time to backpack around Europe for your twenty-first birthday while the *just a girl* you hooked up with a few times takes the real fall." Sitting back, I force the corner of my mouth to quirk in a half-smile like I have it all figured out. "Is that why you started taking her with you on your drug runs in the first place? So you'd have someone to hang it on if it all went sideways?"

"No." He jerks back, eyes wide, like I just spit on him. "*No*—that's not—"

Whether he realizes it or not, he's just exposed his soft underbelly. Julie isn't just *some girl*. He's in love with her. Thinks by hiding her, he's protecting her somehow. And because he thinks he's protecting her, he's not going to tell me where she is. So instead of asking the same question over and over, I ask something else. "How'd you end up running your boat up on the Rock?"

"I—" His mouth snaps shut and he shakes his head, trying to buy himself some time to figure out how telling me the truth will be a mistake. "We go to the lighthouse on the backside of the island sometimes, to be alone," he tells me carefully, because even though he hasn't denied the fact that he runs drugs for the Reapers, he's still smart enough not to admit it. "I got... distracted. Wasn't watching where I was going. There's a pretty gnarly outcrop on the eastern curve of the Rock—I got too close to the shoreline and got caught." He gives me a helpless shrug. "That's it," he tells me, his tone laced with anxiety. "That's what happened. Can I go now?"

"No." I shake my head. "How'd the cops get involved?" Because that's the part I can't figure out. The part that's making him nervous. "If it was just a stupid accident, then how'd Julie end up in jail?"

"I'm supposed to go to Thailand with some friends for a few months, before I leave for college," he tells me. "If my dad found out I was dicking around on his boat with some eastern chick, he wouldn't pay for the trip, so I asked her to lie. Say she stole the boat while I hid in the lighthouse."

"So you talked Julie into eating a felony, and pretty much ruined her chance at a decent future, just so you can go to Thailand with your buddies?" I repeat it back, making sure I understand what he's telling me. When he gives me a reluctant head nod, I scoff. "No, you didn't."

"What?"

"I don't believe you." I say it slow, watching his expression waffle between anger and anxiety. "You love Julie. She's not *just a girl*. She matters to you," I tell him, laughing a little at the way he's looking at me. "Trust me, kid—I'm just as shocked as you are."

Teddy's shoulders go stiff. "Whatever. You asked me what happened and I told you—can I go now?"

Instead of answering him, I hold out my hand. "Give me your phone." When he hesitates, thinks about refusing, I cock my head slightly to the side and stab him with another sharp glare. "*Give. Me. Your. Phone.*"

It's fumbled out of his pocket and in my hand before I can count to three.

Swiping the screen, I ask for his passcode and he reluctantly gives it to me. "You're wasting your time," he tells me. "There's noth—"

"*Shhh.*" I wag a finger at him while I bring up his call log. It's completely empty—not even a missed call from his mother. "You got Julie into something bad and you know it." Switching to his text log, I find the same thing. Nothing. Going into his settings menu, I scroll through his apps until I find it—a scrubber app, used to automatically erase calls and texts, seconds after they're read or received. I've seen them used before. Backing out of the menu, I jump over to his contact list. "She's in trouble—you both are—and the load of bullshit you just tried to feed me is your sad and misguided attempt at protecting her." His contact list doesn't yield better results. Phone numbers—probably all attached to revolving burner cells—but no names. Just another dead end. Regardless, I keep scrolling and wouldn't you know it, there's a number I recognize.

The same number that texted me Friday night, claiming to be Jenna.

"Who's this?" I ask, showing him the number.

Looking at the screen, he shrugs. "A friend," he mumbles back. "Teammate. From school. We're on the sailing team togeth—"

Tapping the screen, I call it, lifting the phone to my ear. When I do, Teddy goes from *entitled little prick* to *terrified little boy* in a heartbeat. Face completely bloodless, mouth hanging open, he looks like he can't decide if he wants to start screaming or pass out.

"*Shhh*—I'm on the phone," I say before he can decide and his mouth snaps shut, just as the call is answered.

"Are you really *this* fucking dumb?" The voice on the other end of the line growls at me. I recognize it instantly. "I told you I'd call *you*—"

I hang up.

"That's weird," I say, in a conversational tone that sends the color rushing back into his face. "I didn't know Will Hudson was on the high school sailing team."

"Jesus, lady..." Still staring at me, he lets out a long, slow breath. "You have no idea who you're messing with."

"You're right—I don't," I say, agreeing with him. "But I'm *super* excited to find out."

"You're nuts." He shakes his head at me, completely flummoxed. "You know that, right? Like, *completely* out of your goddamned mind."

"I'm aware." I give him a smile. "You're dismissed."

Teddy stands but doesn't jump over the side of the boat like I expect him to. "Can I have my phone back?"

"No." Still smiling, I slip it into the snug pocket of my yoga pants. "Now, get the hell off my boat."

Giving me another bewildered look, he does what I say. On the dock again, he unties the boat and tosses the line over its side while I start the engine. "You know," he says, still staring down at me, "if you really cared about Julie, you'd just let her disappear."

Because I don't have an answer for that, I don't say anything. I just ease the boat away from the dock, leaving him standing there while I motor away.

FORTY

LINCOLN

So, handsome—exactly like your father.

People used to stop us in the street to comment on how much I look like him. When I used to hear it, growing up, it made me feel good. Not because they thought I was good-looking but because they thought I looked like him. Because it meant I *was* like him.

That we were the same.

When I was young, knowing that meant everything to me. Looking in the mirror made me proud. Now, it makes me want to break every mirror I see.

"Don't you have some place to be?" I ask him in a conversational tone. "It's the last Wednesday of the month—town council meeting?"

He frowns at me like I'm being ridiculous. "You're being accused of murdering your wife, Lincoln—I think that's more important, don't you?"

"Am I?" I shoot a quick look at the two-way behind him. I'd bet my left arm the room behind it is empty. That the cameras are shut off. No one is watching. Whatever's about to happen isn't being recorded. This is just between us. What my father would call a *family matter*. "The sheriff and I hadn't gotten that far."

He flushes, his neck and face turning ruddy under his perfect sailor's tan. "This is serious, son," he says, his tone full of concern. "I think we—"

"Don't call me that," I tell him, a sudden rush of anger hardening the casual, friendly tone of my voice. "I'm not your son."

"You *are* my son." He sighs. Shakes his head like he doesn't understand the person I've become. "You're my son and Savanna is my—"

"They turned off the cameras in here. No one is watching," I tell him, my tone flattening into something dangerous. "So, if you say her name again, I'll kill you before anyone can stop me."

His mouth snaps shut and he sits back in his seat, moving away from me as far as he can get without actually getting up. "What happened to you, Lincoln?" He says it like he has no idea how I got this way. Like it's all a big mystery, and I laugh. Can't help it.

"I spent seven years in prison for attempted murder, for starters." Still laughing, I rub at my eyes. "Why are you here?"

"The sheriff was kind enough to call to tell me about poor Jenna and to let me know you'd been brought in for questioning." He says it carefully, like I might not understand what that means. Like maybe I'm crazy. "When he explained the situation to me, showed me the evidence against you, I—"

"Show me."

He frowns at me. "Excuse me?"

"The evidence—show me," I tell him, jerking my chin at the folder Bradford left behind. "I want to see it."

He stares at me for a moment before flipping the folder open to pull out a crime scene photo of a large, black handgun laying on what looks like white bathroom tile, a bright yellow placard, marking it as evidence, next to it. "They found a gun at the scene —an M9."

There are guns in my truck.

That's what Georgia told me when she dropped her truck off at my shop on Saturday afternoon.

... an M9 in the glovebox and one stashed under my seat. A Benelli pump-action behind it.

"... serial number. It's registered to Georgia. They've spoken with her and confirmed there were two such guns in her truck on the day of her accident, even though only one was recovered at the scene. You were there. First on the scene, weren't you?" He says it like it's something that'd slipped his mind until just now.

"Fuck. You," I growl at him, barely able to push the words past the clench of my jaw.

Ignoring my outburst, he sets the photo aside and reaches back into the stack. The next picture he shows me sends my stomach bouncing into my throat. "They'll run ballistics on it against the bullets they dug out of Jenna's brain to do a comparison." The photo is of Jenna in a blood-splattered bathtub, her thin frame, desiccated by drugs, twisted into an almost unrecognizable shape. Arms and legs askew. The holes punched into the back of her head almost perfectly aligned, burned black around their edges. Her face almost completely gone, blown away by the force of the bullets that ripped through it. "I know what you're thinking—it's hard to tell who that is, given the damage to her face, but I assure you, it's Jenna. Deputy Tate made a positive ID at the scene."

He sets the photo aside and shows me another. This one a close-up of Jenna's hand, encased in a plastic evidence bag and secured with a zip-tie. "They found tissue samples under the fingernails of her right hand," he tells me, unable to keep the gloat out of his tone as he looks at the still-healing wounds on my face. They look bad. Ugly and red. Scabbed over. Like I attacked a woman and she fought back. "They'll be running them against samples they have in their database and are confident they'll find a match."

Jenna was killed with a gun missing from the scene of Georgia's accident.

One I had access to.

My skin is under Jenna's fingernails and there are clear defensive wounds on my face.

I have no alibi. No one beside a fellow convicted felon who is able or willing to vouch for my whereabouts.

"Is that it?" I ask, even though it's enough. More than enough to put me back in prison, especially with a previous conviction for a violent crime hanging around my neck.

"The sheriff is in the process of obtaining a search warrant for your house." Closing the file, he pushes it toward me like he's giving me a gift. "Once executed, they're confident they'll find additional evidence tying you to the murder."

Swallowing another curse, I force myself to relax.

"What do you want?" I ask, because he wants *something*. He wouldn't be here if he didn't.

"I want you to confess," he says, like it should be obvious. "I want you to confess to all of it."

"All of it?" My heart takes a flying leap again, this time getting stuck in my throat where it throbs so hard and fast, I can't breathe. Can feel my vision begin to swim and gray. "I don't understand."

"Yes, you do, Lincoln." He gives me an encouraging nod like I'm much smarter than I give myself credit for. "I want you to confess to what you did to those poor girls—Rachel and Jenna... and Julie."

Julie.

I forgot about Julie.

We've been looking for her. Problem is, no one knows where she is. "What did you do?" My words bounce back to me, muffled and flat against my own ears.

"I didn't do anything—you did," he tells me. "You raped poor Jenna until you got her pregnant and then forced her to marry you so you could *keep* abusing her, but when she no longer satisfied you, you turned your lustful depravities on Rachel."

"No..." I shake my head, no longer sure of who I'm trying to convince. "That's not what happened."

"It *is* what happened, Lincoln. I caught you in the act, remember? The night you tried to kill me—I walked in on you attacking Rachel and when I pulled you off of her, you became enraged and nearly beat me to death. Unfortunately, she ran away in shame and fear before you could pay for what you did to her."

"I didn't hurt them." Still shaking my head, I look over his shoulder, finding my own face in the two-way mirror behind him. "You're the only person I hurt."

"Rachel came back to the island to find her best friend destroyed by what you'd done to them both, and you raising a young girl you could easily prey on... she was determined to stop you. To make you pay for what you did. She was Julie's case manager, wasn't she? Did Julie tell Rachel you were hurting her? That you'd done the same sick things to her that you did to all the others?"

"I should've killed you." Taking another punishing swipe at my face, I smother the laughter bubbling in my throat. "That night—I should've snapped your fucking neck."

"Rachel confronted you, didn't she?" he asks, ignoring me completely. "Friday night—at that dreadful bar you and your criminal friends frequent. She found you. Confronted you about the abuse you inflicted on her and all those poor, helpless girls. Threatened to tell. Take Savanna away. So you killed her and, realizing how fragile and unstable Jenna has become over the years and that you no longer controlled her enough to keep your secrets, you killed her too."

"Rachel died of a drug overdose," I say, telling him the same lie that's been fed to me for days. "The ME—"

"Lied." He gives me an apologetic smile. "At the request of the sheriff—he's been investigating you and your friends for quite some time. Gathering evidence. Building a case against you. He knows all about your drug-smuggling operation—"

"*My* operation?" I can barely get the words out. Almost choke on them.

"Yes—*yours* and this King character you've partnered with. When Rachel was found dead, Sheriff Bradford was afraid a murder investigation would spook you, so he asked the ME to write up a false autopsy report and place it in her file—a necessary misdirection—as part of his investigation." He gives me a small smile. "But the real report, filed with the state of Michigan, marks manual strangulation as her cause of death."

I force my gaze to his face. Force myself to look him in the eye. "Where is Julie?"

"You tell me, Lincoln—the sheriff has been looking for her but so far..." He gives me a puzzled shrug. "I'm starting to worry she might've suffered the same fate as the other young girls you've taken an interest in. My only comfort in all of this is I'll be able to save Savanna from you before it's too late."

Like her name is a trigger, I shoot up from my seat and he sits back in his, hands raised in defense. "Lincoln, there's no way out of this. You won't get away with it."

I force myself to relax. To think.

I came here voluntarily.

No one read me my rights.

That means I'm free to go if I want.

Turning away from him, I head for the door. Taking the knob in my hand, I give it a twist and the door swings open onto a short, narrow hallway. At the end of it is an exit that leads directly to the station's parking lot. Directly across from me is another closed door, the sound of some mid-afternoon game show leaking out from under it. I open it and there she is, sitting on a worn couch, staring blankly at a small, flatscreen television mounted in the corner of the room.

"Van." Rusty and thin, her name barely makes it out of my mouth, but she hears me anyway, the sound of it yanking her vacant gaze away from the screen in front of her. Fills it with fear and trepidation, and for one terrifying moment, I think it's me she's afraid of. That they told her things. Poisoned her against me. "Van..." This time when I say it, the trepidation bleeds away and she jumps up at the sound of my voice.

"Dad." Running, she flings herself at me and even though she's too big, I lift her in my arms. "I thought they—"

"It's going to be okay," I lie to her. "Let's get out of here."

"Where are we going?" She sounds scared. Small. Sure someone will come and rip her away from me at any moment, just like last time.

"I don't know." Another lie. Turning away from the room, I carry her down the hall toward the exit at the end of it, intent on leaving and taking my daughter with me before someone tries to stop me.

FORTY-ONE
GEORGIA

On my way home, I use Teddy's phone to call Archie.

"Where are you?" he demands, his tone telling me he already knows I'm about to lie to him. "Whose phone is this?"

"Borrowed it." I tell him the truth. "I'm on the lake—I took the boat out."

"Jesus, George," he gripes at me like an old woman. "Why can't you just do what you're told for once in your life?"

"Because I'm terrible at it." Killing the engine, I glide through the water, the bow of the boat aimed at the manor's dock. "What's going on?" When my question is met with stony silence, I sigh. "Come on, Arch—we both know you're going to tell me eventually so—"

"Lincoln walked out of his interview with the sheriff."

"Savanna?" I spent one afternoon with her and I'm already attached. Already care too much to be considered prudent.

"Linc took her," Archie tells me, like Lincoln performed some sort of magic trick. "He was in the interview room and then he just... *wasn't*—he walked out of the station and disappeared. No one's seen him since."

I'm not surprised. Lincoln is a violent offender who just happens to have a degree in criminal justice. He knows his rights.

My guess is, he stuck around just long enough to find out what sort of evidence Alex had on him before he stood his ass up and walked out, because he's smart.

It's what I would've done.

I let the boat drift until it bumps into the dock. "And you guys just *let* him?"

"He wasn't under arrest, George. He was brought in for questioning—that's it," he reminds me defensively. "All we have is circumstantial evidence."

"Alex could've detained him," I say, unwilling to accept his excuse. "He had seventy-two hours. He could've—"

"Well, he didn't." I can feel the frustration rolling off of him in waves. "I'm sure he wished he had—especially after what Richard McNamara had to say."

"Lincoln's dad was there?"

"Yeah. Sheriff called him in hoping he'd be able to talk some sense into him... he said some things," Archie tells me quietly. "Made some accusations. Said Linc did stuff. To Jenna and Rachel for sure, but he thought maybe..." He trails off, either unwilling or maybe unable to put the rest of it into words.

This was a mistake. It won't happen again.

"Lincoln never hurt me." I don't know what it is. Why I still feel this need to protect him. Stand up for him. All I know is what I'm telling Archie is the truth. "And believe me, he had plenty of opportunity."

Archie clears his throat, obviously uncomfortable. "Well, Mr. McNamara seems to think otherwise—he sat down with the sheriff and gave an official statement but the gist of it is Lincoln is coming after you and you're in danger—I'm sitting in my patrol car outside your gates right now."

"What?" From where I am, I can see the back of the manor. Everything looks fine. Undisturbed. "No—you're supposed to be looking for my car. I don't need you or anyone else babysitting me. I need you to find Julie."

"Yeah." Archie blows out a harsh, loud breath. "About that..."

"What?" I'm instantly on guard. "What happened? Did you find her? Did you—"

"I did—well, sort of."

"What does that mean?"

"It means I found your car parked in the ferry lot. But when I got there, Tandy Shepard was already on the scene. She—"

"*On the scene?*" I'm suddenly confused. "I asked you to *quietly* find my car, Arch—not launch a full-scale investigation."

"I didn't *launch* anything," he tells me, suddenly defensive. "I don't know how she knew but she did. Said your car had been reported stolen and Julie jumped bail. I figured you came to your senses. Called the sheriff and told him what was going on and he—"

I brought Tandy Shepard and Don Levitt in too, just in case you're keeping track.

"Tandy?" I say her name carefully. "Tandy Shepard found my car?"

"Yeah..." He sounds about as apprehensive as I feel. "You did call the sheriff, didn't you?"

"*Ummm...*" I didn't call Alex, but he's a cop and not just some lazy island cop who'd rather sit at his desk and eat apple fritters and read romance novels. He's a real cop—or at least he used to be —and he's been investigating the Reapers on his own for a while now. Building a case against them. Up until a few days ago, I was suspected to be a part of it. He wasn't sure he could trust me.

Am I under surveillance?

That's what I asked Alex at the hospital and while he didn't confirm my suspicions, he didn't deny them either.

"What's going on, George?"

"Yeah—" I can't tell Archie anything without breaking my promise to Alex and inadvertently jeopardizing his investigation, so I lie. "I remember now—I did call Alex. This morning before I called you. Maybe I mentioned it. I took a pain pill last night and things are fuzzy..." I let myself trail off. Sound confused. "Where's the car now?" My head hurts. My chest. The gentle pitch of the boat against the dock is making me dizzy. Nauseous. I should go inside. Take another pain pill and let the cops do their job. Let *them* find Julie. Save my strength for the fight Alex and I are going to have when he finally comes home because I'm pretty sure he tapped the manor's landline and that's how he knows Julie is missing.

"Tandy had it hauled off to the impound lot."

If they thought Julie would be back for the car, they would've left it. Keep it under surveillance and wait—but they didn't.

That means they think she's off island and won't be back.

Or they want to make it look that way—and if they're going through that kind of trouble, that means Alex believes me—he thinks Julie knows more about what's going on than she's pretending—and he's taking her disappearance seriously.

"I don't need you to sit on my gate, Arch," I tell him, gaze aimed across the water, toward the Rock. "Lincoln isn't going to bother with me. If he killed Jenna then he's got bigger things to worry about."

"I have orders," he tells me, making it clear he has no intention of moving. "I'm supposed to sit here until end of shift and then Levi'll come and relieve me."

Alex couldn't have chosen better watch dogs. Archie is, for all intents and purposes, my brother—he'd kill without question to protect me; and Levi hates Lincoln so much this is probably a dream come true for him. He's been waiting for a reason to kill Lincoln and he'll take it without hesitation. If Lincoln is stupid enough to show, he might even make one up.

"Okay," I tell him, backing off. "You're right—you have orders and it's your job to follow them. I'm just feeling extra stupid right now—everyone warned me not to help Julie but I did it anyway."

"They'll find her," Archie reassures me. "They've got both Haughton and Marquette counties involved in the search. She can't get far. Just get off the damn boat, go inside and take it easy."

"Yes, Mother," I say, teasing him because it's what I'm supposed to do. What he expects of me.

"You don't need a mother," he teases back. "You need a prison warden."

Before I can think of a clever comeback, a text comes through on Teddy's phone.

"You're right."

"What?" He sounds confused. Like he doesn't understand a word I just said.

Another text comes through.

"I said *you're right*—I know, I can't believe it either," I tell him, careful to keep my tone playful. "But you are—so, I'm going to go inside. Get off my feet and take some meds. Maybe even a nap."

"A nap." Relief laced with apprehension. He doesn't really believe I'm going inside to take anything. "You're going to take a *nap?*"

"Don't believe me—come up here and check on me." He won't. His orders are to stay on the gate and he's not going to budge.

"Okay," he says, giving up. "If you need something or if—"

"I'll call," I promise, before hanging up the phone. Swiping my thumb over the screen, I pull up the unread text messages. Unsurprisingly, they're from an unsaved number.

Someone's outside, are you here?

I thought you were going to wait until it was dark to come.

Julie.

It has to be.

I can't ask her where *here* is because this is Teddy's phone and he obviously already knows where she is. She's smart. If I ask, she'll know something is wrong.

Before I can figure out what to say, another stream of texts comes through.

Shit.

It's King.

He's here. I can hear him talking.

He's right outside the lighthouse.

He's not alone.

FORTY-TWO

Aside from the lighthouse on its northernmost tip, Devil's Rock is completely feral. Sugar maple and hemlock. Yellow birch and basswood—their trunks and branches laced so tight together the island feels like a fist, clenched and angry, trying to keep me out.

I blame the concussion on why it took me so long to figure out where Julie is hiding. Why I had to literally have it spelled out before it dawned on me. Either way, it makes perfect sense. The lighthouse is their refuge. Where Teddy and Julie go to be alone. They feel safe there.

Right now, Julie is anything but safe.

Hide.

That's the one-word text I sent back before I pulled up the anchor and restarted the boat, pointing its bow toward Devil's Rock. It took ten minutes to cross the water and another five to avoid the outcrop that damaged Teddy's boat.

There are three docks on the Rock. I tie off on the southeastern curve of the island, furthest away from the lighthouse. Getting out of the boat took another five because adrenaline blasted away the last of the pain meds I took this morning and climbing onto the dock has me sucking wind. Even though pain meds and the nap I told Archie I'd take sound like the way to go right now, I push myself past the thick line of trees guarding the shoreline and aim myself toward the back of the island and the lighthouse the Fells planted on it nearly a century ago.

The sun all but disappears, its light and heat struggling to penetrate the thick green canopy that towers above me. I go slow. Take my time. Push my deck shoes into the thick underbrush carefully, clearing away dead leaves and fallen branches before I put my weight into each footstep, moving as quietly as possible because even if I could run right now, it would be the wrong thing to do. I'm alone, injured and unarmed. King is here and he is none of those things. Julie said she could hear him talking to someone. If I had to guess, I'd say it's Lincoln. He knows Alex is close to arresting him for Jenna's murder. Getting off Angel Bay will be his number-one goal and if he's as smart as I think he is, he'll know the bridge and ferry will be under surveillance.

That means he'll try to leave the island by boat.

Unsure of how far I've gone, I stop walking to try and ease the ache in my ribs and chest, impatient and angry with my pace, no matter how smart I tell myself I'm being. It's been nearly half an hour since Julie sent that text to Teddy. Chances are, I've missed King and whoever was with him. I can only hope Julie hid like I told her to. That I'm not too late to help her.

Leaning against a pair of sugar maples grown so close to each other their trunks are fused together, I scan the landscape ahead of me. Spotting the back of the lighthouse through the dense spread of branches, I sigh. I'm closer than I thought. So close I can see a door, partially hidden by some close-hugging branches, secured shut by a rusty old padlock.

Julie said King was right outside the lighthouse. That she could hear—

"What the hell took you so long?"

Holding my breath and leaning against the tree, I shift my weight to peer carefully around its trunk.

It's King, standing with his back to me, less than ten feet away, in the narrow easement between the back of the lighthouse and the wilderness behind it. Will is even closer. Off to the side and behind

King, he's leaning against the trunk of the tree directly to my left, arms crossed over his chest.

The man King is talking to is someone I've never seen before. Even though my view is obscured, I catch a glimpse of a navy button-down under loose white linen. Preppy haircut and sunglasses. That's it, but it's enough to tell me whoever it is, it isn't Lincoln. Easing myself further out of view, I lean against the tree to keep myself steady and listen.

"You're lucky I showed at all," the man tells King. "I'm here as a favor to McNamara. Where is he? Where's the girl?" Whoever he is, he expected Lincoln to be here. *The girl* is almost certainly Julie. Suddenly, Teddy's refusal to cooperate and his reaction to my calling Will on his phone doesn't seem so dramatic.

"He's not coming," King says, carefully, like this guy isn't someone he wants to piss off. "Neither of them are."

"Not coming?" The guy says it like he doesn't understand. When neither of them answers, he makes an ugly sound in the back of his throat. "What the hell is that supposed to mean?"

"It means *he's not coming*," Will says evasively. My guess is telling this guy Lincoln got hauled in for questioning for his wife's murder would be a wrong move.

"You're new here, so let me explain something—I take McNamara's little problems and make them disappear as a *favor*." The guy says it slow, like he's talking to a child. "A professional courtesy —one you should all appreciate and be thankful for, because I'm guessing the used-up scraps he throws me could cause big problems for him and your little business if left unattended, free to run their mouths about the nasty shit McNamara does to them."

"*Scraps?*" King's tone loses its deference, its edges sharpened by temper. "We *give* you quality product—young, pretty white girls who know their place and won't be missed, and all it costs you is a day trip on your fancy-ass boat, so you can take that *professional courtesy* shit and shove it straight up your ass."

They're not just trafficking drugs.

They're trafficking girls.

Not just *girls*.

They're getting rid of Lincoln's victims.

Oh, my God.

The realization twists inside my guts and I have to take deep, slow breaths in an effort to stave off the waves of sickness that wash over me.

They're trafficking girls.

"Whatever." The guy makes another sound, this one like it's trying to pass itself off as laughter. "You can tell McNamara there isn't going to be a second trip—I'm not coming back. He wants this girl disappeared, he'll—"

"I'll bring her to you," Will breaks in. When his offer is met with silence, he laughs. "I'll even gift-wrap her. Tie a pretty bow around her neck and drop her on your doorstep, how's that?"

"When?" The guy is all business now. *Scraps* or not, he knows King is right. The arrangement he's complaining about is just as beneficial to him as it is to Lincoln.

I have to look again. Get a better look at the man they're with and try to commit his face to memory because this might be the only chance I have. Careful not to move my feet, I shift my weight slightly, just enough to angle the top of my head around the tree trunk, gaze aimed in their direction.

Will is looking right at me.

As soon as our eyes meet, he turns away. Less than a split second of connection but I know.

He saw me.

Before my brain can register the threat, Will shifts his stance, placing his shoulder in my line of sight. "When I'm ready," Will tells him, using the same insolent tone I've heard from him a million times before. "I'll be in touch."

"*You'll be in touch*... You sure you're the one in charge here?" the man says to King with a genuine chuckle. "Whatever—just tell McNamara he owes me one." With that, he leaves, his retreat punctuated by the careless scuffle and crunch of his feet against the dense forest floor.

I move out of sight again. Hold my breath while I wish for a gun. A knife—hell, I'd settle for my taser right now, because Will is going to give me up. He hasn't yet because Lincoln was a no-show to their meeting and the girl they promised their buyer is in the wind. Admitting they got found out, even by accident, is just too much incompetence to swallow for one day. But the buyer is gone and Will is a climber. Loyal to no one—not even his own brother— and giving me up will earn him favor with his boss.

"What the hell was that?" King growls at him, the sound of it followed by a short skirmish. I imagine King has Will by the throat and shaking him silly. "I bring you on one meet and all of a sudden you're making deals? Think you're running shit?"

"No." I can hear the fear and panic in Will's voice. He overstepped. He's in trouble and he knows it. "That's not—we need this guy, right? I'm stalling him—buying you some time. That's it." Something pushes past the fear and panic in Will's tone. Something flat and intentional that sounds like it's aimed directly at me.

I'm stalling him—buying you some time.

Will isn't going to give me up.

He's provoking King. Trying to give me time to get away because simply waiting them out isn't an option. My boat is docked on the southeastern tip of the island. To get back to the Den, they'll have to pass right by it. There's no way King won't see it and once he does, he'll know someone else was on the island during his botched meeting with *Mr. Fancy-ass Boat*—someone he'll look for.

And the first place he'll look is in the lighthouse.

Holding my breath, I ease myself away from the tree. Take a slow, careful step, followed by another.

"So you promise to deliver a girl we can't even find?" The question is punctuated by the rough sound of flesh connecting with flesh, the crisp snap marking it as a heavy, open-handed slap, meant to humiliate as much as hurt. "I got a feeling you're tryin' to make me look stupid."

"No. No way." The pain is back, squeezed tight around Will's throat. "I told you I got a line on her. Nelson kid is dumber than shit. He thinks I'm gonna help 'em off the island. I just have to—"

"You better." Another slap, this one hard enough to knock the words out of Will's mouth. "You don't find that girl—*you make a fool of me*—I'm gonna make you all kinds of sorry, you hear me, Prospect?"

Will's response is too faint and garbled to understand but whatever he says, it earns him another slap, quickly followed by the thick, meaty sound of a fist connecting with soft tissue.

Shut up, Will.

Just stop talking.

Shoulders stiff, I keep moving. Keep putting one foot in front of the other, moving away from the sounds. I shouldn't care. Will just offered to deliver Julie to a man who intends to sell her. All but admitted he traffics girls for Lincoln. The sound of him getting smacked around should be music to my ears but it isn't. Knowing he provoked King into giving him a beating to give me time to get to my boat makes me sick to my stomach.

As soon as the sounds fade completely, I pick up the pace. Ignoring the painful stitch my urgency tattoos against my ribs, I bob and weave my way through dense underbrush, branches and bushes snapping and whipping against my face and arms. Thorns and barbs scratch and snag at my clothes and skin, the sting of it making my eyes water. The pain in my chest is building with every step. Catching a glimpse of sky and lake, I swallow the swell of relief rising in my chest. Giving a final push, I stumble a bit as the Rock unceremoniously spits me out onto the beach.

No time.

I run for the dock, my soft-soled shoes slipping against coarse sand and rock. Somehow managing to keep my feet, I reach the dock—the slap of my footsteps against the weathered wood echoing across the water like gunshots. Skidding to a stop, I unwind the rope securing the boat to its mooring and toss it in. Behind me, I hear the start of a boat motor, muffled and broken as it pushes its way around the island.

King is coming.

Not bothering with the ladder, I jump down, locking my jaw against the fresh jolt to my abused ribs. Fighting the urge to pass out, I wrestle the key from my pocket and jam it into the ignition. The boat roars to life. I open the throttle and it takes off like a shot, speeding across the water like an arrow, aimed at the stretch of soft sand almost directly across the lake from the southeastern tip of the Rock. I don't have time to try for the manor's dock. I have a few minutes, five at the most, before King rounds the back of the Rock on his way back to the Den. If he sees me on the water...

The manor's beach looms ahead, a strip of brown and green rushing up to meet me. Easing back on the throttle, I let the boat's momentum carry me the rest of the way, bracing for impact because I'm suddenly sure I overshot the beach and am going to end up launching myself into the trees behind it. As soon as I think it, I'm thrown into the steering wheel, the boat's momentum grinding to a sudden halt as it slides onto the shore. Within seconds I'm over the side of the boat and scrambling across the beach toward the tree line, not daring to turn until I'm swallowed by it.

Hopefully hidden from view, I clutch a hand to my ribs and scan the lake for King's boat. Finding it, I feel a wave of apprehension because he's not heading for the Den like I hoped.

He's headed straight for me.

FORTY-THREE

Turning away from the beach, I push myself deeper into the trees, rushing blindly away from the boat, my only goal to put as much distance between me and it as possible. My foot snags on something and I stumble into the trunk of a sugar maple. Somehow managing to keep my feet, I move around the curve of it, using its girth and the shadows that surround it as camouflage. Heart galloping in my chest, I watch the shoreline intently while reminding myself sometimes retreat is necessary. Sometimes evading your enemy is your smartest course of action—especially when you're injured and unarmed and he's roughly the size of a compact car. Regardless of what I objectively know is smart and necessary, I feel like a coward for running.

Be smart.

Think of Julie.

The nose of King's boat appears, breaking around the top of the manor's inlet and I hold my breath as he passes slowly, hugging the shoreline so tight I can hear Will, his voice muffled and flat against the sound of my stampeding heart. "She ain't in there," he says, drawing my attention away from his boss. His face is a mess—busted, bloody mouth. An eye that's already swollen shut. "I already told you—"

"And I told *you* to shut the fuck up," King snarls back while he scans the tree line. "You aren't running things, Hudson. Maybe you need to lose a couple more teeth before you get the picture, that it?"

"No, sir." Will shoots a dirty look at the back of King's head before leaning over the side of the boat to spit out a mouthful of blood. "Just tryin' to help, is all."

King laughs. "The fuck makes you think I need your help?"

He thinks Julie's disappearance is a ruse. That I'm hiding her in the manor. If I can foster that suspicion, maybe I can keep him off the Rock long enough to help her. Rushing forward, I charge across the sand until I'm less than a foot from the water. "Can I help you boys?" I call out, drawing King's attention away from Will.

Hearing me, King sets his boat to idle and stops his progress along the shoreline before answering. "Ms. Fell," he says, shooting a quick, calculating look at the manor, beyond the trees behind me. "What're you doing out here?"

"Hanging birdhouses," I lie to him, ignoring the *what the hell are you doing* look Will is shooting me behind his back while pointing up at the worn wooden box above my head for effect. They're all over the place down here. Someone, I suspect Savanna, spent a lot of time and effort on them and right now, I'm so thankful I could kiss her.

"Weren't you just in a car accident?" King asks, shooting a quick, over-the-shoulder look at Will before turning his grin on me. "Shouldn't you be doped-up on painkillers and watching Netflix?"

"I don't have Netflix." I once completed a thirty-mile ruck with a fifty-pound pack and shin splints. While cracked ribs are no joke, I could turn cartwheels down this beach if I had to. "I heard about Jenna." Ignoring his attempt at baiting me, I cast my own line. "I'm sorry."

"Shit happens." Still smirking, King shows me his palms. Dropping his hands, he gives me an appraising look, slowly raking his gaze from my face to my feet. "First that nosy friend of hers, then Jenna herself... and now I hear you went and lost that cute little eastern girl you were dumb enough to bail out of jail." He shakes his head, making a sad clucking noise in the back of his throat. "Dangerous time to be a woman on this island—makes me wonder how you're still alive."

"Well, I'd say it was dumb luck..." I give him an answering smirk of my own. "But to be honest, I'd probably chalk it up to lack of knowledge and gross incompetence." I cut Will a quick look before refocusing on King. "Whoever messed with my brakes should've taken an extra five minutes to tamper with my seatbelt because without it, I'd be dead." Grinning, I give him an exaggerated shrug that rubs my cracked ribs together. "A for effort, but execution earns you a C minus at best."

"Trust me, Ms. Fell..." The look on his face tightens, his gaze sharpening into a glare, slashing at me from across the water. "If I wanted you dead, you'd know it."

"Because I'd be dead, right?" I keep grinning, hands on my hips while I give him a head shake. "You, and I mean this sincerely, are cuter than a baby duck in a raincoat, but on the off-chance you're serious, I feel compelled to tell you..." I lean forward a bit and cup my hand around the side of my mouth for effect. "I will *completely* fuck you up if you even think about coming for me or anyone else I care about."

King gives me an amused chuckle of his own. "Is that right?"

"It is." I drop my hand and give him a solemn nod. "And the absolute best part is when it's all over and you're on a liquid diet and shitting in a bag for the rest of your life, everyone'll know you got your guts rearranged for you by a woman." I look at Will. He's as white as a sheet, busted mouth hanging open. One good eye yanked wide in disbelief. "Alrighty—well, this was fun," I say, sliding my gaze from Will's face to King's. Lifting a hand off my hip, I aim a thumb over my shoulder. "But I'm sure you boys are *super* busy, so I'm going to go back to hanging my birdhouses now."

"You got a smart mouth, bitch," King snarls at me in response. "One of these days, someone's gonna come along and teach you how to keep it closed."

"Maybe..." I tilt my head and roll my eyes. "Okay—probably." Giving him an agreeable nod, I start to back my way off the beach. "But I can guaran-*damn*-tee whoever that *someone* is, it won't be an adorable baby duck like you." I give him a wink. "Thanks for stopping by." Adding insult to injury, I turn my back on him completely. "You two take care now," I toss over my shoulder, raising my hand in a wave just before I disappear back into the trees.

I expect him to come after me. If I'm honest, I want him to. I want to make him bleed, even if it earns me a return trip to the hospital.

But he doesn't.

Instead of coming after me, all King does is restart his boat. "See you soon, Ms. Fell," he calls out over the soft rumble before opening the throttle. Hearing it, I stop walking and turn to watch him leave, Will now at the back of the boat and staring at the place where I disappeared into the trees, a strange mixture of anger and worry pulling his features together in a tight scowl.

As soon as they're gone, I feel my shoulders sag and I let out a breath.

So much for being smart.

Turning again, I start to weave my way through the trees. Retracing my steps, I come to the place where I stumbled—to find the leg of my extension ladder peeking out from under an overgrown bush. Hands on my hips again, I tilt my head back and aim my gaze into the treetops.

Directly above my head is one of Savanna's birdhouses.

I drag out the ladder and open it halfway before leaning it against the tree to retrieve the birdhouse. On the ground again, I give it a shake and am rewarded by a metallic jangle.

Julie was right—I never would've found them.

Tucking the birdhouse under my arm, I make my way through the trees to begin the hike back to the manor. There's about an acre and a half of rolling green lawn between me and the back porch and I have to push myself to take every step.

I check the time on Teddy's phone. It's close to three in the afternoon. Sunset won't come for another four to five hours and going back to the Rock for Julie before full-blown dark would be flat-out stupid. That means I have roughly six hours of sitting on my hands to contend with. Knowing it'll go faster if I formulate a plan of attack, I climb the long set of steps that lead to the back porch while forcing myself to think my way through the obstacles between me and my objective.

There are a lot of them.

Probably too many for me to tackle on my own.

Instead of accepting it, I shove that uncomfortable truth into the corner with the rest of them and concentrate on working the problem.

Unless I want to stuff steak knives into my yoga pants, I don't have a weapon.

Coming to the top of the steps, I sigh with relief as I make my way across the porch. Leaning my shoulder against the back door, I palm the knob and give it a turn.

The weapon is an easy fix. I gave Evie an M9 of her own for her birthday a few months ago and I know for a fact she hasn't even taken it out of the box. I'll just—

Pushing my way through the door, I'm three steps over the threshold before I see her.

Savanna.

Eyes round and frantic, aimed in my direction and set in a face so much like her father's I'm not prepared for the sight of her. Something moves in my peripheral and I drag my gaze away from the little girl sitting at my table to find Lincoln standing just a few feet away.

FORTY-FOUR

LINCOLN

"Why are you carrying a birdhouse?"

It's the wrong thing to say to someone when they come home to find you squatting in their kitchen, but considering we've been here for nearly an hour now and I just watched her emerge from the trees down by the lake carrying a birdhouse, of all things, it's a valid question.

Georgia cocks her head at a dangerous angle before taking a half-step in my direction, her intention obvious. She's not going to answer me. She's probably going to *show* me by trying to shove her birdhouse up my—

"You found them."

She stops and we both turn toward the table where Savanna has a front-row seat to what is shaping up to be a pretty spectacular assault. "Excuse me?"

Savanna looks at the birdhouse, a scowl dug into her face. "I said, you found them."

"Yeah." Georgia's gaze narrows slightly for a moment before she slams the birdhouse on the counter between us, what sounds like a bunch of silverware jangling inside its belly. "I found them."

The scowl on Savanna's face softens into something wounded. Worried. "Are you mad?"

"Yes." Georgia bites the word in half and spits it at me.

"Okay, but don't be mad at Julie," Savanna pleads, dividing that wounded look between us. "It was my idea to hide your keys in the birdhouse; she just—"

"She's not mad at either of you, Van." Looking at Georgia, I sigh. "She's mad at me."

"Oh. Because we broke into her house?" Savanna jogs a nervous look between us before settling it on Georgia. "That was my fault, too," she says in a rush. "Dad wanted to wait on the back porch, but the door was open and I didn't think you'd—"

"Van." When she looks at me, I shake my head. "I need you to go do the thing we talked about."

"Really?" She looks panicked. "Now?"

"Yes." I nod at her. "Now."

She slides out of her seat slowly to stand beside it. Staring at Georgia, she gives her head a fast shake. "He didn't kill my mom. He wouldn't—"

"Right now, Savanna." I put weight in my tone. Use it to push her toward the door. We already said our goodbyes—letting her stall will only make things harder for the both of us.

"You didn't do it," she says, like she's trying to convince me while she swipes the walkie-talkie off the table and shoulders her backpack. Before I can give her another verbal push, she turns away from us and runs out of the room.

"Where is she going?"

"I don't know." I shake my head, reaching into my back pocket. "This house is almost fifty thousand square feet." Pulling out another walkie-talkie, I set it on the counter next to the birdhouse. "I told her to find a place to hide and not to come out until either you or I tell her to."

Georgia's glare zeros in on my cheek. "What happened to your face?"

Again, I resist the urge to reach up and finger the furrows Jenna raked down the side of my face. "Jenna. She—"

"Tried to claw your eyes out right before you murdered her?" Her mouth curves into a cold, hard smile. "Good."

"I didn't kill Jenna." Saying it feels like a lie. "I'd never—"

"Why would you come here?" Georgia makes a noise in the back of her throat that sounds like it's caught somewhere between a scoff and a growl. She doesn't believe me. "Of all places—why would you come *here*?"

Because this is the only home Savanna really knows.

Because you're the only person I trust on this god-forsaken island.

Because I love you and if this goes as bad as I think it will, I wanted to see you one last time.

Before I can say any of those things, she pushes herself away from the counter to pace the kitchen. "I mean *seriously*, how stupid are you?" She turns on me and throws her hands up, her face flushed with temper. "You come *here*, looking for sanctuary from *me* like the goddamned Hunchback—"

"Not for me." I shake my head, lifting a hand between us. "For Savanna. I know I can't stay here. I know you—"

"I hate you." She snarls it, her rage pushing her forward, closing the gap between us.

"I know." Dropping my hand, I let her come, even though I'm sure I'll end up regretting it. "I know you do and you're right to. I never—"

"I know what you did to them." She stops herself short, her face inches from mine. "Your father told me everything." She whispers it. Looks sick to her stomach. "You raped them. First Jenna and then Rachel. He caught you in the act—that's what happened the night you tried to kill him. He walked in on you assaulting Rachel and when he tried to stop you—"

You raped poor Jenna until you got her pregnant and then forced her to marry you so you could keep abusing her but when she no longer satisfied you, you turned your lustful depravities on Rachel.

"No." Even though I knew this was coming, I'm still not ready. Hearing Georgia say it out loud still takes me by surprise. Still makes me want to throw up. "*No*—that's not what happened. I never hurt anyone. I *never*—" I take a sidestep away from her and lift my hand again. "You know me, Georgia. How many times were we alone, growing up? How many times did we go sailing or sit on the dock together and—" The look that passes over her face, anger and hurt mixed with confusion and shame, stops me from saying more because she's remembering the same thing I am. The night she kissed me. That for a handful of seconds I kissed her back. Let myself slip, and the memory of it makes her sick. I shake my head at her, suddenly desperate to make her understand. "I never hurt you and I never hurt them."

"I swear to God..." She leans into the space I put between us and laughs in my face, the sound of it unhinged and dangerous. "If you tell me they *wanted it*, I'll kill you."

I believe her.

"I never hurt anyone." I say it again, dropping my hand because if she's going to come at me, a hand isn't going to stop her. "I never *touched* anyone."

"Really?" She laughs again at my obvious lie. "Well, there's a kid who calls you dad, hiding somewhere in my house, whose existence serves to prove otherwise."

"That's the lie."

Her pale green gaze narrows dangerously. "Excuse me?"

"That's it. That's the lie—the only lie I ever told you. Savanna... she's not—" Lifting a hand, I take a rough swipe at my face, trying to loosen my jaw. Force the words out of my mouth. "She isn't my daughter."

It all rushes back to me. Standing on the dock with Jenna that night, half asleep because she knocked on my door and I opened it, thinking it was Georgia. I shouldn't have. Even as I was doing it, I knew it was wrong. That if I opened my door to find Georgia standing on the other side of it, I wouldn't be able to stay away from her. That I'd do the wrong thing. Something I'd end up regretting, but it wasn't Georgia. It was Jenna and she was crying, almost uncontrollably. When she tried to push her way into my room, I stopped her. Took her by the arm and led her to the dock and asked her what was wrong.

I'm pregnant.

I wasn't surprised. Jenna was barely sixteen but her behavior had always been what could be categorized as hyper-sexualized. She'd come on to me more than once. Made it clear if I wanted sex from her, all I had to do was ask. It always made me feel sorry for her. Uncomfortable around her. Wonder what happened to her before she came to live with my parents.

So, no. When Jenna told me she was pregnant, I wasn't surprised. It was what she said next that shocked the hell out of me.

"Bullshit." Georgia hisses it at me, her face screwed up in disgust. "She looks just like you."

"Yeah, she does." I nod because it's true. Looking at Savanna is like looking in a mirror and when I do, I can't deny the truth of where she came from, even though I still have a hard time accepting it. After all these years. After everything I've seen and everything I know, I still can't make myself believe it. Have to push the rest of it out on a hard expel of breath that carries no more sound than a whisper. "That's because she's my sister."

FORTY-FIVE

GEORGIA

He's lying.

He has to be.

Lincoln is lying to save his own skin. To manipulate me. To loosen the noose that's rapidly tightening around his neck. I know that. Everything coming out of his mouth is a lie, meant to infect me. Make me feel sorry for him.

Believe him.

Even though I know all of that, I let him talk. Let him lie to me. Tell me his version of events that led to the night he tried to kill his father.

"She told me the baby she was carrying was my father's and if I didn't assume responsibility for it, she was going to ruin him." He rakes a hand through his hair before dropping it against his thigh. "I didn't believe her—she was lying. She had to be. After you... left, I went to my dad," he says, skimming over the conversation I heard on the dock and what happened between us afterward. "I told him what Jenna said—that she was claiming they'd had... *an affair*." He says it like the idea of a sixteen-year-old girl having a consensual affair with a man old enough to be her father is ridiculous. Maybe a little disturbing. "That she was threatening to tell everyone—ruin him—unless I took responsibility. I expected him to tell me she was lying. That it'd be okay. He'd take care of it."

"And?" I ask him in spite of myself. I want to tell him Jenna would never do something like that, but I can't because she would. Even at sixteen, Jenna was opportunistic. Conniving. *Warped. Desperate. Damaged.*

"He told me that of course she was lying but even a false allegation of impropriety would be enough to tarnish the family name. That it would devastate my mother. They'd lose their foster care license. All the good, decent things they'd done for *their girls* would be questioned. His character would become suspect. There would be investigations—not just into him but into me too, and that would ruin my chances at law school... and wouldn't it be easier and quieter if I just gave her what she wanted?" The last of it comes out on a *I can't believe I fell for it* kind of laugh. "I'd post-pone law school. Move back to the island and marry Jenna. She was sixteen by then, the age of consent, and I was only twenty-two —enough of an age gap to raise some eyebrows but not criminal. We'd stay married for a year and then I'd file for divorce. Ask for a paternity test and when it came out the baby wasn't mine, it would be enough to call into question every allegation that might follow. We'd give her a sizable settlement. Send her and her baby off into the sunset and I'd get to go back to my life like none of it ever happened."

"But it didn't go as smoothly as it was supposed to," I say, remembering the story his father told me. "Jenna stuck around just long enough to have Savanna and get you hooked on drugs—"

"No." He shakes his head. "There were never any drugs. Not for me," he says, firmly. "I never touched them. I'm sure this all would've gone easier for him if I had, though." He laughs again, a rough, ugly sound that tells me exactly what he thinks of his father. "But, yeah—Jenna left when Savanna was only a few months old."

"Why?" I ask, challenging him because his claim reminds me this is all a lie. "She got what she wanted. She got *Lincoln McNamara* to put a ring on her finger—her ticket to the big time—why would she just leave?"

Clearing his throat, Lincoln looks away. "*Why* she left doesn't really matter—what matters is she did, and I suddenly found myself playing single father to a kid that wasn't mine and I was stuck because—"

"Because you loved Savanna."

"From the first moment I saw her." He nods, looks a little relieved I seemed to understand. "It was weird. I was just a kid—lying to save my father's reputation—but as soon as the nurse put her in my arms, it didn't matter where she came from. None of it was Savanna's fault. Things were okay for a while. With Jenna gone, I focused on raising Van. I was just a dumb kid, trying to keep my head above water. Be a good dad. A good son. Solve everyone's problems but my own. Before I knew it, a year had gone by and I'd decided I didn't want a paternity test. I'd still divorce Jenna, according to plan, but I wanted custody of Savanna, even if it meant giving up on law school altogether. That's what I'd decided," he tells me, his expression clouding over. "I'd keep Savanna. Raise her. Be her dad, even though I wasn't—but then... I took her down to the boardwalk." His mouth twists into a grimace and he shakes his head. "It was right before her first birthday. It was too cold for the beach but she loved to feed the gulls so I bought some popcorn at one of the stands and as the lady working the booth filled the bag, she looked at Savanna on my hip and she said, *she looks just like you.*" He looks at me, that helpless expression mixed with anger and something that looks like nausea. "I laughed because it was obviously a lie—just something people say to parents because it's expected—I mean, how could she look like me? She wasn't my kid. Not really, but then I looked down at her and I realized it wasn't something she just *said.* She was right—Savanna looked just like me."

"Because she's your *sister.*" I say it carefully because I want him to hear how ridiculous it sounds. How stupid I would have to be to believe anything he's telling me. "Because your dad had an affair with one of his girls and fathered a child, and then somehow talked you into sacrificing your entire future to safeguard the family reputation."

Even as I say it, I can hear the strange, twisted logic in all of it. Jenna had made sure she was too far along for an abortion before she announced her condition, even though she had to have known a man like Richard McNamara would never admit to having had sex with one of his fosters because, regardless of the age of consent in the state of Michigan, it would have been seen exactly for what it was: predatory, and a gross abuse of his position.

But it would have sounded outlandish for just that reason. She'd know that if she aimed for Richard, she'd miss. But Lincoln—he was a target she could reach. He'd been the dutiful son. Willing to do whatever was asked of him. Fulfill every one of his father's expectations, even if it meant shaming himself and sacrificing everything he'd ever wanted.

"He didn't have an *affair* with Jenna—" He barks it at me, scrubbing a hard hand over his mouth. "She was messed up, even before she came to live with us. She might've thought that's what it was, that it was consensual, but it wasn't. He—"

"Tell me about Rachel." I take a step forward, closing the space between us. "Tell me what happened that night." When all he does is stare at me, I start the story for him. "You broke into your parents' house to steal your mother's jewelry. It was something you did all the time to feed your drug habit. When you got there, you found Rachel awake and lured her to the boathouse so you could—"

"*No.*" He growls it at me, his face contorted into a snarl. "I *never* did drugs. I *never* stole anything and I *never* hurt Rachel. I —" He must realize I'm trying to bait him because his face relaxes and he sighs. "I was there to break into the boathouse, not the main house. What I was after didn't have any value for anyone but me."

"What were you looking for?"

Instead of answering my question, he just shakes his head. "I hadn't spoken to my dad since before that day on the boardwalk—mostly because I knew if I tried to confront him with what I knew, he'd just find a way to twist it. Make me doubt myself—he's good at that." He makes a sound in the back of his throat that sounds like it wants to be a laugh. "I decided I was going to take Savanna and leave the island. Start over somewhere I wasn't *Lincoln McNamara*. I had some money saved—not a lot, but when you're a kid, you don't really think about stuff like that. I just wanted to get away—but there were things in the boathouse I needed first. When I got close, I could hear... things happening." He looks sick again. "Crying. Other sounds—and then I heard him say, *I like it when you cry.*" The words sound strangled when he says them. Dry and brittle, crumbling to dust the moment they're exposed to light and air. "I tried the door but it was locked so I kicked it in." He says it like he's reading it from the pages of a book. Like it's something someone else did. "He had Rachel on the bed and he was..." He swallows hard, like there's something stuck in his throat. "He was raping her."

"Then what happened?" For a moment, I forget it's all a lie. Just a story he's making up to deflect blame because it's so close to what his father told me only a few days ago that it sounds like the truth. "What did you do?"

"I don't know." He gives me a small, fast headshake, face contorted in confusion. "I don't remember."

"You tried to kill your father," I say like it's total news to him. "You almost beat him to death with your bare hands. He was in a coma for three days."

He laughs at the admonishment in my tone. "Am I supposed to be sorry about that?" he nearly shouts at me. "*He was raping Rachel.*"

"No..." I shake my head at him. "*You* were raping Rachel and your father tried to stop you."

"No." His face falls, like I've disappointed him somehow. "That's not what happened."

"Then why didn't you tell someone? The police?" I ask him, using logic to dismantle his claim. "If what you're saying is true, then—"

"Because Rachel was gone." He takes another swipe at his face, this one rough and impatient. "She was *gone* and there was no one left beside me who knew the truth. I knew what would happen if I accused him of raping her. He'd already managed to convince everyone I was an addict. That he caught me in the middle of a home invasion. If I told the truth, no one would listen to me and now... he *owns* the police. Not all of them, but enough to make it impossible to know who to trust."

It's almost exactly what Alex told me yesterday. That he suspects he inherited a dirty department when he came to Angel Bay. That he doesn't know who he can trust. "What about Savanna? If what you're saying is true, it can all be proved with a simple DNA test. Maybe not that your father is a rapist but—"

"No. I won't do that to her. I won't use her like that. I won't hand her over to my father or back to the state, just to vindicate myself. Rachel understood that. When she came home, she told me she knew I wasn't Savanna's biological father, but she still—"

"*Enough.*" My tone is sharp enough to shut him up. "What Rachel *knew* was that you never stopped. That you were still hurting girls so she threatened to expose you. Stop you." The theory is loose. Full of holes but I give it a voice anyway. "She was a case manager. She found out about the other girls. What you and your partner are doing with them—"

"*What other girls?*"

"The girls, Lincoln." I say it quietly. "The girls you rape. You sell them. You and King use your connections to get them off the island."

He jerks back like I took a swing at him. "What?"

"You heard me just fine." Smelling blood in the water, I follow him, hemming him in against the kitchen counter. "I know all about the drug operation you're running with King and I know about the—"

"King isn't *my* partner." He gives me another head shake. "Yes. Okay—yes. I build traps inside cars and let them pack their drugs in my shop before they smuggle them off the island," he says, jaw clenched tight against his admission. "But I don't have a choice and I don't know about any girls. I'd never—"

"Ohhh... King isn't *your* partner." I catch the inflection in his tone. What it's supposed to mean. "So your *father,* Angel Bay's answer to Mother Teresa, is the serial rapist, murderer, human trafficker and drug kingpin—not *you,* the violent felon, and known sexual predator?"

"I don't—" He looks sick again, shakes his head like he's having a hard time understanding what I'm saying to him. "I didn't know... it's the truth. I thought it was just about the drugs. They threatened to take Savanna if I didn't—"

"No." I shake my head at him. "The truth is *you* killed Rachel —you strangled her when she threatened to expose *you. You* killed Jenna because she was a loose end. Knew too much and my guess is after she saw what happened to Rachel, she started to unravel. She was going to talk, so you took my gun from the scene of my accident and used it to kill her."

"Sounds like you have it all figured out," Lincoln says, softly. Pushing himself away from the counter, he advances on me, giving me no choice but to retreat. "So explain this—Rachel was Savanna's case manager. She's the one who recommended family reunification. Brought her to visit me my last six months in prison. I'm Henry's godfather. He's named after me, for fuck's sake—Henry *Lincoln* Alcott. If I'd done and am all the things you think, would Rachel have helped me get my daughter back? Would she have honored me that way?" His words push me back until I'm the one pinned against the counter and he's standing over me, so close I can see the flecks of gold and black in his eyes. "And while we're at it, given everything you *think* you know about me, shouldn't I be hurting *you* right about now? You know everything, don't you? Got it all figured out—that makes you a loose end, just like Jenna. Shouldn't I be shutting you up instead of trying to convince you that I'm innocent?" His mouth flattens into a grim parody of a smile. "I mean, I *am* a violent felon, and serial rapist, right? Hurting women is kinda my thing." I feel my mouth open but before I can formulate an answer, Lincoln's hand shoots up between us, his fingers slipping around the curve of my neck to wrap around the back of it. "I'm dangerous. A despicable monster." The rough pad of his thumb skims along the line of my throat. "According to you and my father, I killed my wife a few hours ago and that isn't even the worse thing I've done this week..." He lifts his other hand and it joins its partner around my neck. Tightening his grip, Lincoln squeezes just enough to remind me I just accused him of strangling my foster sister to death. "And here I am, standing in your kitchen, with my hands wrapped around your throat. Shouldn't you be scared right now?" He leans in close, his gaze dipping to my mouth for a moment before bouncing back up to find mine, his own mouth twisted into a nasty smirk. "Maybe kicking my ass?"

"I'm not afraid of you, Lincoln." Finally finding my voice, I use it to push the words up my throat, past the gentle pressure of the hands he has wrapped around it. "I've never been afraid of you."

"That's because you know me better than anyone." The smirk melts away, leaving behind a puzzling mixture of relief and regret. "You always have." Before I can answer him, Lincoln drops his hands and moves away from me completely. The sudden loss of pressure leaves me with a strange, buoyant feeling. Like I'm floating. Lost. "There's an envelope with your name on it in Savanna's backpack."

"Where are you going?" Fifteen minutes ago I was angry he'd had the nerve to break into my house, and now the thought of him leaving is enough to send me into a tailspin. I tell myself it's because I know what he's done, what he's likely to do if I let him leave. That he's a monster and it's my responsibility to do what I can to keep him caged. That Julie is still out there and if Lincoln and King find her, she's as good as dead.

Or worse.

Much worse.

I tell myself that's what it is, but I'm a liar.

I feel this way because I want to believe him.

Trust him.

Even if I can't allow myself to do either of those things, I want to, and that wanting makes me stupid and soft. A lovesick teenage girl, willing to accept anything Lincoln McNamara tells her, as long as it means they can be together.

Like he can read my mind, Lincoln smiles again, that same flat, grim smile that makes him look like a stranger. "I'm going to go finish what I started." Closing the distance between us again, he leans in to press his mouth against mine and there must be something seriously wrong with me. More serious than a concussion because I let him. I let him kiss me—a soft, almost chaste press of lips that inexplicably leaves me breathless. Pulling back, his mouth twists into another smile, this one almost wistful. "Try to give me a couple hours' head start before you call your boyfriend."

FORTY-SIX

LINCOLN

I expected Georgia to try and stop me.

Chase me down.

Kick my ass and call Bradford.

Maybe call my father.

She doesn't do any of those things.

When I move to leave, Georgia just stands there and watches me go, a strange, helpless look on her face that I recognize. Understand. It's the same look I must've worn the night she left the island. Left me behind.

The night this whole nightmare started.

At least for me.

If I had to guess, my father's been in the business of making nightmares for most of his life.

The girls, Lincoln.

The girls you rape.

You and King use your connections to get them off the island.

Somehow, I'd missed it.

Managed to convince myself what my father did to Rachel and Jenna were isolated incidents. It makes understanding how he's managed to fool everyone for so long seem so easy. Because even with everything I know about him and after everything he's done to me, I still have a hard time believing it. I don't *want* to believe it, because believing it means I've been willfully ignorant all these years.

When I was eligible for parole, I almost didn't bother putting in my request to have my case reviewed by the board. My father is one of the most powerful attorneys in the state. Rubs elbows with congressmen and senators. He's played golf with more than one sitting vice president. Keeping me in prison would be easy for him. I figured I didn't stand a chance, but then Elizabeth Fell showed up at the prison one day and asked me point-blank if I was Savanna's father. For some reason, I told her the truth—not just about Savanna but about everything. I told her all of it and she believed me.

Six weeks later, I was granted parole.

I focused on keeping my head down. Getting Savanna back. Building her a home. Making us a family. I didn't see anything else. Nothing else mattered. When Elizabeth died, everything changed. She was the only thing on this island that my father was afraid of and I was no longer under her protection.

She left me a small inheritance—just enough to open my shop and put a down payment on a place for Savanna and me. King strolled in the day I opened the doors, a grim-looking Will not far behind him, and told me how it was going to be—*You're gonna help me and my partner run drugs off the island or I'll kill your daughter.*

He never said who his partner was but I knew.

Just like I know that for all his delusions of grandeur, King isn't my father's partner.

He's his henchman, his underling—just like everyone else on this island.

Because I can't change any of it, I put it away. Focus on what I need to do now.

Jogging down the back-porch steps, I round the side of the manor but instead of heading toward the front of the house I keep heading west, following a path that runs parallel with the lakeshore. Feeling exposed, despite the fact the Fell property is nearly a hundred acres and the most secluded on the island, I don't breathe again until the path I'm on is swallowed by trees. At the end of it is a gate, hidden by overgrown bushes and vines. The gate opens into a narrow easement between the Fell property and the Tates', so narrow I have to turn my shoulders to the side to squeeze myself down its length to the street.

Back in my car and feeling like a sitting duck, I dig a phone out of my back pocket and power it on. It's not my phone. It's a burner cell I bought a while ago and stashed in the trunk of an old car at the shop, along with the walkie-talkies and Savanna's backpack. At the time I told myself I was being ridiculous. Paranoid. Right about now, I feel like a clairvoyant genius.

As soon as the burner's powered on, I send a text.

Meet me. You know where.

It takes less than a minute for Will to answer me.

On my way.

FORTY-SEVEN

GEORGIA

Using Teddy's phone, I dial one of the few numbers I have memorized.

"Hello?"

"Hey." I shift myself in front of the kitchen window just in time to watch Lincoln disappear into the trees. "It's me."

Evie sighs when she recognizes my voice. "I heard about Julie. Is everything okay?"

No.

Everything is definitely not okay.

"I need you to come here," I say, instead of getting into it. "I need help. I—"

"Thirty minutes," she assures me. "I'll be there in thirty minutes. We'll figure it out, okay?"

"Okay." My throat tightens because whatever I do next, whatever I need her to do, Evie will be here. She'll say yes. She always does, even if she disagrees with me. Even if she thinks I'm being crazy and irrational.

"*Thirty minutes*, George." Something about my tone must tip her off. Tell her I'm already knee-deep in what she considers crazy and irrational. "Don't do anything stupid until I get there—can you manage that?"

I told her to find a place to hide and not to come out until either you or I tell her to.

"Yes." I nod again, thinking about the young girl hiding somewhere in the maze of rooms upstairs. "Just hurry—and bring the thing I gave you for Christmas." Hanging up just long enough to clear the line, I make another phone call.

"Hello?"

"Jill—it's Georgia. Don't hang up, okay?" I say, quickly. "Look, I know I was an asshole the other day but I—"

"No," Jill says, with a quiet sigh. "You weren't—I mean you *were* but so was I... I just really miss her, you know?" Her tone thickens with tears. "I don't know how to do this without her."

"I know." I close my eyes for a moment, allow myself to feel it. The grief I've been holding at bay. "I miss her too." Opening my eyes, I find the top of the lighthouse in the distance, its single, dull white tower glowing orange in the setting sun, barely visible across the dark treetops. "I need to ask you something. It's weird I don't know, considering I'm his godmother but... what is Henry's middle name?" That I don't know isn't just weird. It's almost shameful—indicative of the self-imposed separation between myself and the people I love.

"Lincoln." She says it like it's some terrible secret. "His name is Henry Lincoln Alcott."

I'm Henry's godfather. He's named after me, for fuck's sake.

"Lincoln McNamara is his godfather." This time it's not a question.

"Yes." Sniffling, she sounds almost apologetic. "Unofficially. Rachel wanted to invite him to Henry's christening but she was afraid it would upset you for some reason..." She sighs. "It was really important to her that Lincoln be involved in Henry's life. She never said why, but I always got the feeling Rach felt like she owed him. His daughter was one of the first clients on her caseload when she landed her job at DCFS and she worked really hard to help him get her back."

—if I'd done and am all the things you think, would Rachel have

helped me get my daughter back? Would she have honored me that way?

No. She wouldn't have. If Lincoln was her rapist, Rachel never would've named her son after him and she would've moved heaven and earth to make sure Savanna was safe and as far away from him as she could possibly manage.

That means he told me the truth.

Lincoln didn't rape Jenna or Rachel, and if he told me the truth about that, then that means he told me the truth about everything.

FORTY-EIGHT

LINCOLN

Despite his answer, I didn't expect him to show.

I thought I'd have to hunt him down but when I walk in and scan the sparsely populated bar, I spot Will sitting in one of the back booths almost instantly, a pint of cheap beer on the table in front of him, eye blacked and swollen shut. Mouth busted. Someone put a beating on him.

When he sees me, he shifts in his seat uncomfortably, almost like his lower half is thinking about running. Instead of bolting for the back door, he stays put. Probably because the last time we saw each other, I almost choked the life out of him and he figures he's safer here, in a public place, than in some back alley with me chasing him down.

He's wrong.

His safety doesn't depend on where he is or who's watching.

His safety depends solely on what he tells me in the next ten minutes.

Most locals avoid this side of Angel Bay like the plague, leaving it to the tourists. Looking around, I note the place is pretty much empty and the few people who are here aren't giving me the time of day. They have no idea who I am and what I'm being accused of. That I'm considered to be a walking disease by most of the people who live on this island. Sliding into the booth opposite Will, I watch him shift in his seat again, that lower half of his getting restless.

"How did you know?" I ask. When all he does is sit there and look confused, I elaborate. "That the cops were about to knock on my door. How did you know?"

Will swallows hard and looks away. "I tell you, you can't get mad, alright?"

"Alright," I agree mildly, even though we both know if I don't like his answer, there's a pretty good chance I'm gonna come across this table at him.

"You know the lady who lives across the street—Mrs. Somner?" When I give him a nod, Will sighs. "I sorta... pay her to watch your place. She saw Bradford and Levi roll up on your house, so she called me."

"You pay my neighbor to spy on me?" I remember the old woman across the street watching the show from her porch this morning. I have no idea what her name is but she'd been on the phone, talking a mile a minute to whoever was on the other end of it. "Why?"

"Because we swore a long time ago to watch each other's backs." Now he flushes, either from anger or embarrassment, it's hard to tell. "I take that shit seriously—even if you don't."

"Were you watching my back when you killed Jenna?" I ask him in a low tone that barely reaches across the table.

"That wasn't me." He stares at me for a second, his faded blue eyes narrowed slightly. "Jenna was Savanna's *mother*." He says it like it matters. Like it made her worth something in his eyes. "I'd never do that to her. Never."

"Not even if King told you to?"

Will shakes his head at me, his swollen jaw locked tight.

"Is that what happened to your face?" I ask carefully, because I'm suddenly convinced he's telling me the truth. "He tell you to kill her and you refused?"

"No." Will lifts a hand, pointing a finger at his split lip and crooked nose. "*This* is what happened after I caught Georgie poking around the Rock earlier today."

"Georgia?" I barely breathe her name but it's enough to shut him up. "*She* did this to you?"

"No." Will makes a weird half-scoff, half-laugh, in the back of his throat, even though he knows as well as I do that rearranging his face is well within Georgia's wheelhouse. "But I caught her, sneaking around by the lighthouse."

What was Georgia doing on the Rock? Instead of asking him to speculate, I lean my shoulders back against my seat and try really hard to look like I don't give a shit. "It's technically her island," I remind him. "Sounds like you were the one *sneaking around.*"

"I wasn't *sneaking* anywhere," he gripes at me. "King needed muscle for a meet-up with some guy, so I volunteered."

"What guy?"

"I don't know. Never seen him before." He does that shifting thing again. This time I think he's going to rabbit for sure but he doesn't. "Linen suit. No socks. Preppy haircut. Crazy white teeth. Flashy watch. Looked like *Miami Vice* and Tom Cruise had a baby. Had a hundred-foot yacht anchored about a mile offshore. He asked for your dad by name."

The description doesn't sound like anyone I've dealt with while laboring under King's thumb. "He asked for my dad?" My father doesn't involve himself in the dirty business he's built here on the island. That's what King is for. He's the front man. My father is much more comfortable pulling strings from behind the curtain while he smiles and plays the part of Angel Bay's version of JFK. "You're sure?"

"Yeah." Will nods. "Seemed to expect him to be there. Was pretty pissed he wasn't."

The girls, Lincoln.

The girls you rape.

You and King use your connections to get them off the island.

"They were talking about girls." Before I can even ask, Will confirms my suspicions. "From what I could gather, he was expecting to pick one up—Julie." His lip curls slightly like he got a whiff of something bad. "King didn't say it outright but I think he and your dad are tryin' to get rid of her."

I don't have to ask why—I know.

"Problem is, no one can find her. She's gone. Disappeared," he tells me, his mouth flattening into a thin, grim line. "King thinks Georgia's hiding her in the manor."

We've been looking for her. Problem is, no one knows where she is.

That's what Bradford said to me. That Julie quit her job, stole ten grand and a car from Georgia, and took off... but maybe she didn't.

Maybe King is right.

"Maybe she is," I say, quietly. "Maybe not at the manor, but the stolen car and missing money could be misdirection. Maybe Georgia has her stashed somewhere."

"She doesn't," he tells me, his tone firm and sure. "Georgie isn't the one who's hiding Julie."

For some reason, his tone stiffens my spine. Sits me up a little straighter. "How do you know?"

Will gives me one of his sullen shrugs and looks away. "Because I am."

FORTY-NINE
GEORGIA

When Evie shows up I tell her everything I know.

That Lincoln is most likely not Savanna's biological father—that he's actually her half-brother.

That Richard McNamara is a serial rapist and drug trafficker who preys on the young girls he and his wife take into their home under the guise of altruism.

That he traffics them when they age out of the system to ensure their silence.

That he most likely killed Rachel and Jenna because they were loose ends.

That everything I thought I knew is completely wrong.

While I rant Evie, is quiet. Watches me pace around the kitchen like a crazy person. "It's insane, right?" I say, making what must be my fiftieth trip to the kitchen window, only to turn around again. "It's completely crazy. I mean—I lived in that house. Rachel was my roommate. How could I not realize what was happening? How could I—" I have a sudden flash of standing in front of my dresser drawer, packing my bag while Lincoln loomed over me in the doorway, begging me to slow down. To listen to him. Give him a chance to explain.

It's not like that, Georgia. Please... please just wait a min—

I snapped at him, so loud he was instantly afraid I'd wake his parents. That he'd have to explain why he was standing in my bedroom doorway at 2 a.m., watching helplessly while I angrily shoved clothes into the bag his mother gave me when I was thirteen. His caution was contagious and I looked at Rachel's bed, expecting to find her wide awake and watching us.

But Rachel wasn't awake.

She wasn't watching us.

She was gone.

Perfect little George—Saint Georgia—*too good for what the rest of us got...*

Stopping in my tracks, I feel the weight of a wrecking ball swing into my chest. "I was there, Evie." I whisper it, turning to look at her. She's sitting at the kitchen table, her dark gaze soft and wounded as she watches me and listens. "I was there and I let it happen... and then I just *left*. I left her there—"

"No." She gets up from her seat and crosses the room to stand in front of me. "Don't you *dare* do that to yourself—I won't allow it," she tells me, gripping my shoulders firmly. "You were just a kid, fighting to keep your head above water, same as the rest of us."

That's a lie.

One she tells because she loves me but she knows the truth as well as I do.

I was never like the rest of them.

I never really struggled.

Because I was always treated differently.

Better.

"I have to go get Julie," I tell her, reaching up to push her hands away but they don't budge.

"No." She glares at me, tightening her grip like she's thinking about shaking some sense into me. "I released you from the hospital *yesterday*. It's barely been twenty-four hours, for Christ's sake. You can't just—"

"Yes, I can."

"Alright." Her fingers dig into my shoulders, trying to make me listen to reason. "Maybe you *can*, but that doesn't mean you should or that I'm going to just let you."

"I have to help her." Pushing against her hands, I finally manage to dislodge them. "I can't just leave her out there on her own."

"Okay." Dropping her hands, she sighs. "Then I'll go with you."

"No, you won't." I shake my head and try not to laugh because as dire as this situation is, the thought of Evie traipsing around the Rock in her hospital scrubs and bright yellow Crocs is just this side of ridiculous. "I need you to stay here with Savanna." As if to prove it, I swipe the walkie-talkie off the counter and turn it on. Depressing the button, I speak into it. "Savanna—it's Georgia. I need you to come to the kitchen."

Soft static is my only answer for what feels like an eternity before she finally answers. "My dad didn't kill my mom."

Chancing a quick look at Evie, I sigh. "I know."

"He asked her for a divorce—she was *so* mad. Started screaming about you and how you ruin everything..." Static hisses again for a brief moment while she tries to collect her thoughts. "Why would he do that if he was just going to kill her?"

"He wouldn't," I agree with her. "I believe you. Please, Savanna—just come down. We'll figure it out, okay?"

More static.

"Promise?"

"Yeah." I nod even though I'm not in the position to promise her anything. "I promise."

"Okay."

Clicking off the walkie-talkie, I set it back on the counter before risking another look at Evie. "I'll go get Julie. It shouldn't take me longer than an hour—"

"I know." She blurts it out, her generous mouth held tight in an effort to keep it from trembling.

"You know *what*?" I ask carefully, my guts suddenly feeling like they're being wrung dry by invisible hands.

"What happened to you. Your medical records. I..." She looks away from me, swallowing hard against the words cluttering her throat. "I requested them from the VA." When I don't answer her, she risks a look at me. "You were in a *really* bad accident and I'm your doctor. I had to know your medical history in order to treat you effectively," she tells me, rationalizing her decision to pry.

"Injuries are common among active service members," I tell her, attempting to explain away what she must've seen. What she might know. "Especially those who were deployed."

"No, Georgia..." She shakes her head at me, brow furrowed. "Not like that. I know—"

"*Stop!*" I shout it. Take a step back, away from her, before I put up a hand between us. "Just—" I suddenly can't breathe. My eyes go hot and dry. Feel like they're on fire because I know what she saw. What she knows. "Stop." Looking at the hand I have raised between us, I realize its fingers are trembling. Closing them into a fist, I drop my arm, letting it swing listlessly to my side. I want to tell her she had no right. That my past is *mine* and whatever reason she fed herself to justify her intrusion into it is complete bullshit. That what happened to me is none of her business. "I'm going after Julie," I say instead. "*Alone.*"

"Don't do this to me, George." Mouth screwed shut, she shakes her head. "Please, just—Call Alex, okay? Call him and explain. He'll go with—"

"Where are you going?"

Evie and I both look over to find Savanna standing in the kitchen doorway, backpack strap slung over her shoulder. Walkie-talkie clutched in her hand like a lifeline.

"I have to go get Julie." I glance at the old-fashioned wall clock hanging above her head. It's nearly eight o'clock. "Dr. Jones is going to stay with you."

Savanna looks past me. When her gaze settles on Evie, her expression softens a little. "You're the clinic doctor that hands out the lollipops. The rest of them give out smiley-face stickers."

In answer, Evie reaches into the pocket of her scrub top and pulls out a grape-flavored Tootsie Pop. "Those stickers are lame," she says, offering the sucker to Savanna. She hesitates for a few seconds before she takes the bait, coming forward to snatch the candy out of Evie's grasp with a grin on her face. As soon as the grin makes an appearance, it disappears. Her mother is dead and her father—the only father she knows—is accused of killing her. Things like smiling and Tootsie Pops must feel like a betrayal.

"Your dad said you had something for me in your backpack," I say, trying to offer her a bit of normal. Pull her back from wherever she went.

"Yeah." Giving me a jerky nod, she lets the strap of it slip off her shoulder until it lands on the table. Unzipping one of its pockets, Savanna fishes around until she finds what she's looking for. A large Manila envelope, my name stretched across it in careful block lettering, its flap shamelessly ripped open. "I opened it," she announces without an ounce of regret before holding it out to me.

I know I should admonish her for being nosy. Tell her she's just a kid and what's in this envelope isn't any of her business, but I don't. I can't because if I did, I'd be lying. Savanna isn't just a kid. She's never been *just* a kid—her upbringing saw to that—and what's in this envelope is probably more her business than it is mine.

Lifting the torn flap, I see another, smaller envelope and a thick packet of papers held together with a paperclip. Since I have the feeling what's in the second envelope might be personal and not something I want to deal with right now, I ignore it and pull out the packet of papers instead. Giving them a quick scan, I feel my heart heave against my ribcage like it's trying to squeeze itself between the cracks.

Guardianship papers.

Lincoln is giving me custody of Savanna.

"Where's your father?" I say it to the papers clenched in my hands, the neatly typed words a blurry jumble, jumping around in my field of vision. When she doesn't answer me, I drop the papers to find her, tight-lipped and staring at me. "Where's your father, Savanna? Where did he go?"

I'm going to finish what I started.

Try to give me a couple hours' head start before you call your boyfriend.

A hand appears over my shoulder, reaching for the papers, and I let Evie take them. I know when she realizes what she's looking at because I hear the sharp intake of breath that comes with it. "Savanna…" I say her name again in what I hope is a calm, reasonable tone. "I need you to—"

"He didn't tell me." She shakes her head at me stubbornly. "He didn't say."

"Where did you go after you left the police station?" I ask, hoping there'll be a clue in her answer. "Did you go home? Maybe to see Will Hudson or—"

"We went to the shop…" She says it slowly like she's sure telling me is a mistake but she can't figure out how. "He parked around back and told me to stay in the car while he got out." She bounces a wary look between Evie and me. "He opened the trunk on a really old car… he has a gun. I saw it." Her hazel eyes go wide and round with worry. "And I heard him on the phone. He was talking to someone. He said, *'I'll do it. I'll do what you want. I'll confess to all of it but we're going to meet first.'*" Her eyes flood with tears, mouth trembling. "Then we got into some old car and drove here."

I'm going to finish what I started.

Holy shit.

Lincoln is going to kill his father.

FIFTY

LINCOLN

It takes me a few seconds to process what Will just said.

That Georgia isn't the one who's hiding Julie from my father.

He is.

"You?" The word comes out flat. Lifeless. "You're the one who stashed—"

"*Jesus*—keep your voice down." Will wheels a paranoid glare around the near-empty bar before leaning into me across the table. "Yeah." He gives me a single nod before sitting back in his seat again. "Me."

"Why?"

"I dunno." Will gives me one of his insolent shrugs in return. "Maybe because it's the right thing to do."

"*The right thing?*" Despite everything I've seen and learned over the last forty-eight hours, I feel laughter bubbling in my throat. "Come on, man..."

Something flashes across his face. Something that looks a lot like hurt, but he looks away before I can get a good look at it. "You know what I did to get myself tossed into juvie my first time?" Before I can guess he answers his own question. "I stole a pair of those stupid light-up sneakers for Archie from a Payless when I was eleven. We were both in the system by then but we were still together. Fucking foster mom wouldn't pay the extra five bucks to get him the shoes he wanted—so, I stole 'em." He looks at me, his jaw tight. "She found out and called the cops—they took me to juvie and shipped Arch here. We lost each other after that." The way he's looking at me tells me it doesn't matter how we met. Right now I'm not the guy he shared a cell with in prison. I'm not his best friend. Right now, I'm one of *them*. My last name makes me one of the do-gooder assholes who stood between him and his brother. "Julie's a good kid. She doesn't deserve to get mixed up in this shit."

"Why does my father want to get rid of her?" I ask, even though I have a pretty good idea.

Like Jenna and Rachel, she was one of his girls. A loose end.

"I don't know." Will shakes his head at me, his lank, greasy hair flopping into his face. "All I know is that Nelson kid called me last night, frantic because Georgie was going to send Julie to go stay with your dad and he said that can't happen. If it did, she was as good as dead and if I didn't help her, he was going to run his mouth about the product we got flowing through your shop." He says it low, mouth barely moving. "So I told him to take her to the light-house to lay low until I could figure out how to get her off the island without someone seeing her."

He's not lying about the island. Getting on and off unseen, especially during the summer months, is practically impossible. Between Bradford running his sobriety checkpoints at the bridge and King and my father using the ferry to ship their drugs off island, there's no way off unnoticed unless you're an Olympic swimmer.

"Yeah—but why you? Why didn't Julie come to *me* if she needed help?" As soon as I ask it, Will gives me that look again. That *you're one of them* look that says that no matter who I am now, I'll never belong. Never be fully trusted.

"I don't know that either." Another lie but instead of pushing him on it, I let it go. Why Will is protecting Julie and why she'd trust him to do it isn't important right now.

What's important is that he *is*.

"So when King said he was going to the Rock for a meet-up

with one of his connects, you offered to tag along so you could make sure they didn't find Julie." When all he does is stare at me, I nod. "And if they'd decided to go *inside* the lighthouse—?"

More staring but it's all the answer I need. It's enough to tell me if that'd happened, King and whoever he met on that island would still be there—probably face down in the dirt with a couple of bullet holes in the back of their heads.

The realization shouldn't make me feel better, but it does.

Looking at the mess King made of his face, I begin to put the pieces together. "Georgia was there, probably looking for Julie, and when you spotted her, you... what?" I tip my chin at his messed-up face. "Pushed him into giving you a beating?"

"King's already convinced Georgie is the one who's hiding Julie. If he spotted her on the Rock, the first place he'd look for Julie is the lighthouse." Will looks away, the tip of his tongue sneaking out to run itself along the jagged split gashed into his lower lip. "So it was either distract him long enough to give her time to get away or shoot him in the face, and Georgie isn't going to be willing to help the likes of *me* bury a body."

"But you were still willing to take a beating for her." No matter what he says, what happened on that island was as much about keeping Georgia safe as it was about Julie. The revelation surprises me. Will has always harbored a deep well of resentment where she's concerned. "Why would you do that?"

"Arch'd be pissed if I let something happen to her." He looks at me and grins, blood pebbling along the split in his lip. "Besides, it wasn't hard—you know me. I have a knack for pissing people off." The grin slowly disappears. "But I didn't know King was meeting someone *about* Julie, I didn't know your father was supposed to be there and I didn't know about the other girls—what they've been doing to them, or why." He shakes his head at me, expression grim. "I swear on my brother's life, I didn't know."

Maybe it's a mistake, but I believe him.

"You said King thinks Georgia is hiding Julie at the manor." Suddenly the safest place on the island isn't so safe. I remind myself Bradford has Archie sitting on the gate and Savanna knows the manor like the back of her hand. She has a backpack full of protein bars and dried fruit. She can stay hidden for weeks if she has to, moving from room to room, no matter who's looking for her.

"Yeah—but your dad's got him on a pretty short leash. I heard them arguing—he's not going to let him go after her until all their other options are played out. It's got King pretty worked up, considering the sand Georgie kicked at him earlier today."

He tells me that instead of lying low, Georgia confronted King when he cruised his boat past her dock. She did more than *kick sand* by the sounds of it. She all but yanked his pants down and laughed in his face. I know why she did it—because she knows Julie is on the Rock. She plans on going after her and was doing everything in her power to make sure King is looking in the wrong direction when she does.

Sometimes, with Georgia, brave and stupid are the same thing.

FIFTY-ONE

GEORGIA

Lincoln is going to kill his father.

When the realization hits me, I expect to feel... something. Alarm. Apprehension. Maybe a measure of responsibility.

The Lincoln I knew could never kill someone. He believed in justice, not vengeance.

But that Lincoln is long gone. He died the night he caught his father raping Rachel—and even if he'd survived that night, seven years in prison for what he did afterward surely put him in the ground.

"What are you gonna do?"

Savanna's voice reaches out to me, small and unsure, from where she's sitting at the kitchen table. She regrets telling me her father's plan. She's afraid I'm going to call Alex. Tell him where Lincoln is going. What he's going to do.

That he has a gun.

I probably should.

It's what the cop in me is telling me to do. She's reminding me it's my responsibility to uphold the law. That if something happens to Richard McNamara as a result of my silence or inaction, I'm just as culpable as Lincoln. I may as well be the one to pull the trigger.

But then I think about Rachel.

How her bed was empty the night I left the island. What she must've endured before Lincoln put a stop to it.

I think about Jenna.

How damaged and destructive she was. How much she hated me for things I never knew about. The filth that never seemed to touch me.

I think about Julie.

The way she averts her gaze whenever she feels like you might see too much and wakes up with tearstains on her cheeks.

I think about them, what Richard McNamara did to them, and the cop in me goes quiet.

"Nothing's changed." I answer them quietly, gaze still locked on what lies beyond the window. "I'm going to go get Julie while the two of you hide upstairs."

"Hide?" Evie sounds alarmed. Like it never occurred to her until just now she might actually be in physical danger. "Why? What are we hiding from?"

"I pissed off a huge biker today and there's a pretty good chance he's going to come here, looking to teach me a lesson," I tell her.

"King's coming here?"

It's the tone of Savanna's voice that has me turning away from the window—sheer panic, bordering on blind terror. "Maybe." I tell her the truth because she needs to understand how serious the situation is. Why I can't worry about her father right now. "He's looking for Julie and I tricked him into thinking I might be hiding her in the manor—*before* I knew your dad had plans to stash you here." Looking at Evie, I feel a burst of regret for involving her in this mess. Instead of giving it a voice, I shove it into the corner with the rest of everything I don't want to deal with. "Did you bring what I asked for?"

Already pale, Evie's color slips a few more shades but she nods in response before she turns back to the table where she dropped her bag. After a brief rummage, she pulls out a flat rectangular box and sets it on the table. "There aren't any bullets," she reminds me. "I never even—"

"—took it out of the box." I give her a small smile. "I figured. It's okay. I'm sure I have a few rolling around in my nightstand."

Sure enough, I do.

Twelve of them.

Nearly a full magazine.

Carrying them back into the kitchen along with a large folding knife, I set them down on the table next to the box. I cut the security tape and free the M9 from its fitted foam cushion. Popping the magazine from the bottom of the gun, I feed it full of cartridges, rubbing each of them dry with the hem of my shirt before pressing them home with a crisp, metallic *click*. When I'm done, I slap the magazine home and rack one into the chamber, making sure the barrel of the gun is pointed away from my houseguests. "Okay—" I look up to find both of them staring at me like I'm juggling chainsaws. "Savanna, I need you to take Evie upstairs," I say, dividing a *don't argue with me* look between the two of them. Fitting the gun back into its box, I close the lid and push it across the table toward Evie. "I'll be back in forty-five minutes. Hour, tops."

"Nope." Evie pushes the box back across the table and scowls at me. "No way—this is for you. You're the one who's leaving to go traipse around that stupid island in the dark on a rescue mission."

"And you're the one who's staying behind to potentially face down a vicious biker gang, with a pocket full of lollipops and a *kid*. Sorry—" I shove the box back at her, firm and final—"You lose."

Evie doesn't say anything back, just casts a long, worried look in Savanna's direction because she knows what I'm saying— protecting her is our first priority. That nothing else can matter. Not even each other. "What about you?" She shakes her head, the fast movement sending her corkscrew curls bouncing. "You can't go out there unarmed."

I pick up the knife I used to open the box and fold it closed before slipping it into the wide, secure waistband of my yoga pants, reminding me why I bought them in the first place. It's no Ka-Bar but with its sharp, six-inch blade it's not exactly a Swiss Army knife either. "I'll be fine." Giving her a wry smile, I pick up the walkie-talkie, turning it on before looking at Savanna. "Channel five," I tell her, while I hold it out to Evie. "In case you guys get separated."

Like with the gun, Evie hesitates. Knows without it, I'm essentially cut off from them. "George—"

"Take it," I tell her, all but shoving it into her hand before I look at Savanna. "You stay with Evie. And you listen to her —got it?"

Savanna gives me a solemn nod, her face a mirror image of Lincoln's, wavering somewhere between panic and resolve. "Got it."

"It's going to be okay." We both know it's a lie. Even if everything else goes right tonight, she's likely seen her father for the last time. "Now take Evie upstairs and pick out a good hiding spot," I say, as I move across the kitchen, toward the back door.

Instead of following Savanna, Evie trails me onto the porch.

"Archie's on the gate so if they come, it won't be from the front," I tell her while I head for the steps that will take me to the dock. "It'll be from the water." Stopping my retreat, I gesture toward the soft slope of grass that tumbles into the trees. "They'll come up from—"

"Call Alex."

When I don't answer her, she tries again.

"You can't save that girl with a goddamned pocketknife, George," she hisses while coming at me, because she's terrified and feeling pretty salty about it. "You need *help*—even you need help sometimes."

"Okay."

She wasn't prepared for that. For me to relent, so my answer stops her short at the top of the steps. "Did you say *okay*?"

"I did." I give her a curt nod. "I'll call Alex on the way. Ask him to meet me and help me bring her in."

"Are you just lying to get me to shut up and go hide?"

"No." I shake my head. "You're right. I can't do this on my own."

And if I call Alex and keep him busy off island, maybe it'll give Lincoln a chance to finish what he started.

FIFTY-TWO

An hour ago, I had a plan.

Kill my father.

Turn myself in.

Plead guilty and go back to prison.

That was it.

The totality of my plan.

Shitty plan, but it was all I had.

When Rachel came home to the island, she apologized for running away. For not sticking around and speaking up about what my father did to her. I told her I understood, and I did. I *did* understand. She was an eastern girl. Just a kid, and my father is a titan. There was no fighting him—there still isn't. He's too beloved. Too powerful. He's Richard McNamara and I'm the wayward son—the alleged drug addict. The convicted felon. The disgraced man who has a predilection for troubled young girls.

I can't fight him and expect to win.

But I can kill him.

For Rachel and Jenna.

For Julie and Savanna.

I can do that.

I *am* going to do that and not lose one night's sleep over it.

I'm not worried about Savanna. What will happen to her.

Georgia might hate me but she'd never turn her back on an innocent kid—especially one who needs her help. She'll move heaven
and earth to make sure Savanna is safe. Taken care of. It's not what
I want but it's the best I can hope for.

"What are you gonna do?"

I look up to find Will watching me with that worried look
of his.

"I don't know." I shake my head at him. It's a lie. I know what
I'm going to do. We both do.

I'm going to kill my father.

My mind is made up. Has been made up since I sat across from
him in that interview room and listened to him tell me it's only a
matter of time before I'm arrested for Jenna's murder. That he'll
find a way to pin Rachel's murder on me too. That he'll find a way
to get his hands on Savanna.

"Linc—"

"I need you to do something for me." I cut him off because I
know what he's going to say and it's not going to matter. "I need
you to go to the manor and—"

"The manor." He says it like I'm crazy for even suggesting it. I
probably am. *"Fell manor*—where your girlfriend lives. Where
about a dozen Disciples and a very pissed-off King are just waiting
to—"

"Savanna is there."

As soon as I say it, Will's mouth snaps shut like a spring-loaded
trap.

"It's her home," I tell him, trying to explain why I took Savanna
there. Why I trusted Georgia with my daughter. "It's where she
belongs. Where she can be happy and—"

"And Georgie'll take care of her." Will nods his head. "I get it,
but she ain't gonna just let me waltz in and post up in her kitchen
while we wait for the big bad wolf to blow her house down."

No, she won't.

But if I know Georgia, she's not at the manor. She's on her way
to the Rock right now, trying to save Julie. She wouldn't leave

Savanna alone. She'd call someone to come stay with her—probably Evie. I like her well enough but I don't trust her to kill for my daughter if it comes to that. There's only two people I trust to do that and one of them is sitting in front of me right now.

"I know, but—"

"Okay." He nods again. "I'll do it."

"Thanks." It's a dumb thing to say to someone who's agreed to risk their life, simply because you asked them to, but it's all I have to offer him.

"You sure you trust me to do this, man?" Will's face crumples a little bit, like maybe he thinks I'm a bit crazy for even suggesting it. "I mean, it's *me* we're talking about here."

"If it was me or if this was about Georgia, I'd tell you no." I answer him honestly. "But this is about Savanna and I know you'd never hurt her, so yes—" I move to stand up from the booth we're huddled in—"I trust you." Digging my hand into the front pocket of my jeans, I pull out a few crumpled bills and toss them on the table. "I'll try to call you after..." *After what?* After I kill my father? I laugh a little because it's another dumb thing to say.

Deciding to leave it alone, I just turn away from him and make my way across the bar and out into the parking lot. On my way to my car, I send my father a text.

Boathouse. Thirty minutes.

He texts me back almost immediately.

I'll be there.

He seems just as eager to get this over with as I am—which tells me he knows exactly what I'm coming to do and he has a—

"Linc."

Looking up from my phone, I watch as Will jogs toward me across the parking lot. Suddenly anxious to get this whole thing over with, I contemplate just getting into my car and driving away because I'm sure whatever Will is following me to say is something I don't want to hear. Something I can't consider. Not if I want this whole nightmare to finally be over.

Instead, I shove my phone back into my pocket and wait for Will to get close enough to talk without being overheard.

As soon as he's a few feet away, he stops short. "King just called," he tells me, slightly out of breath. "They know. I don't know how but they—"

"They?" My heart knocks against my chest, the pound of it heavy and uneven when he says it because it's not just Julie they're going to find. If I know her as well as I think I do then Georgia is there too, trying to rescue her, and that means she's in a hell of a mess. "Who? How many?"

"King for sure. I don't know who else—but he knows," he tells me, his tone grim. "He knows Julie is on the Rock and he knows Georgie's there with her."

FIFTY-THREE

GEORGIA

It took me about ten seconds to realize there was no way I was going to get the cruiser back into the water by myself. Remembering the johnboat, bobbing along the side of the dock, I send up a quick prayer its more seaworthy than it looks and climb in. Despite the fact it's obviously being used as a home for spiders and there's what feels like a bird's nest under the seat, the motor fires up on the first try.

This time, I head straight for the lighthouse.

There's a moon, bright and full enough to show me the shoreline, and I use it as a guide so I don't have to turn on my running lights.

Piloting the boat around the eastern curve of the island toward its back, I rely on the trolling motor rather than the more powerful outboard in an attempt to mask my approach. It's much slower going but what I lose in time, I make up for in stealth. Taking out my stolen phone, I wake it up. The little battery symbol in the corner of the screen is red and blinking. After a moment's debate, I give in. Keeping my promise to Evie, I call Alex.

"This is Bradford," he barks into the phone when he answers—a reminder I'm still using Teddy's phone.

"It's me," I say, lifting my voice just above the whine of the trolling motor and the sounds of lake water lapping against the side of the johnboat. "I—"

"George?" Alex's tone is laced with apprehension because I'm not calling from the manor's landline. "Where are you? Who's phone—"

"I need you to meet me at the lighthouse."

"The light—" Confusion smooths away the sharp edges of his tone. "What's going on? *Where are you?*"

"On my way to the Rock. Julie is there and—"

"Julie?" He says it carefully because he isn't supposed to know she's missing.

"I know you know, Alex," I tell him, setting aside the surge of self-righteous indignation I feel for later. "I know you know she's missing. I know tapped the manor's landline. Probably my cell phone too. That you've been monitoring my calls as a part of your investigation into Lincoln."

"George, I—"

"Don't worry, we're gonna fight about it later," I tell him as I round the last eastern bump of the island. "But I don't have time for it right now. I need your help. She's alone and she's scared and I don't have a gun and I don't think I can get her off the island without your help."

"Jesus Christ, George." The apprehension in his tone bleeds into something heavier. Something that sounds a hell of a lot like resignation. "Why can't you just stay put and do what I ask you to?"

"Because that's not me." It's similar enough to what Archie asked me earlier to set my teeth on edge. Make me angry. "Staying put and following directions isn't who I am and it's never going to be—especially when there's someone out there who needs my help, so if that's what you're looking for in a woman we can add it to the list of shit we're going to fight about later, but right now, if my boyfriend won't help me, I'll settle for the sheriff—is *he* available to help me save a helpless teenage girl from getting killed by the henchman of an international drug smuggler?" Rounding the backside of the Rock, the lighthouse comes into view—a tall white spire breaking through the dense wilderness that surrounds it. "I'm asking for help. I need *your* help, Alex." It burns my throat to say it out loud but Evie is right. There's no way I can do this by myself.

"Okay." It comes out quiet, almost like he's talking to himself. "Okay." More forceful this time. More sure. "I'll be there as soon as I can—just stay inside the lighthouse and keep Julie close until I get there."

"I love you." I don't know if it's true but I say it anyway because I suddenly *want* it to be. I want Alex to be the man I love and right now, that's enough.

"I love you too, George." He clears his throat like there's something stuck in it. "Stay out of sight and wait for me—got it?"

"Got it," I tell him, before I end the call and shove the phone into the pocket of my yoga pants.

The dock directly in front of the lighthouse is empty and I tie the johnboat to the end of it before using the rickety rope ladder to pull myself out.

The lighthouse glows eerily in the moonlight, its face shrouded in bramble. Saplings and bushes encroach onto the beach, their roots holding onto the sandy soil with loose, shallow fingers—blocking what should be the lighthouse keeper's entrance from view. Its windows are shuttered tightly from the inside and out, as if it's trying to hide from the world and all it has to do to remain invisible is close its eyes.

Rather than waste precious time trying to find the front door, I skirt around the back, heading for the door I spotted earlier. It's secured with a padlock but it looked pretty old. If I can find a rock or—

The phone in my back pocket buzzes, signaling a text. I expect it to be Julie, texting Teddy because she hears me creeping around out here and she's getting spooked. In a hurry, I dig the cell from my pocket and check its messages, ready to shoot back an *it's okay, just me* text to placate her until I can find a way inside.

The text isn't from Julie.

It's from the number I identified as Will Hudson's earlier. The same number that texted me Friday night, pretending to be Jenna.

They know where she is. They're coming for her.

Shit.

Scrounging around in the brush, I find what I'm looking for.

A rock.

It's barely bigger than my fist but I don't have time to look for something bigger. Hoping it and a hefty swing will be enough to break the padlock, I carry it to the back of the lighthouse. Pushing my way past the low-hanging branch I used as a marker this afternoon, I see it.

The door is there, right where I remember it.

It's open, its hasp swung away from the staple. The padlock is gone.

Instead of dropping my useless rock, I tighten my grip on it as I reach out and test the old cast iron doorknob.

It turns easily in my hand.

Pushing the door open, I stand in the doorway for a moment. Peer into the dark and give my instincts a chance to do their job. Satisfied that I'm alone, I shut the door quietly, blood rushing in my ears, fingers clenched around my rock like a lifeline. Fishing out my borrowed phone again, I find the flashlight function and use it to look around what would probably be considered a workshop or above-ground cellar. Directly in front of me is a set of concrete stairs, caged in by a rickety-looking banister. To my left, about fifteen feet from the foot of the stairs, are sandbags, more than a few of them split open from age and dry rot, their guts spilled out across the rough concrete floor, mixed with what looks like rat droppings and other evidence of vermin. A dusty workbench shoved against the wall under the stairs with a few rusty tools—screwdrivers and different types of pliers and wrenches—scattered across its top. A cold fireplace that hasn't seen a spark in fifty years or better directly to my right.

I switch off the phone's flashlight to conserve what little battery is left and shove it back into my pocket. There's light leaking out from under another closed door, this one at the top of the stairs. Using it as a guide, I shuffle-step my way forward until the toes of my deck shoes hit the bottom step. I can hear voices.

Julie's—slight and frightened. Gaining strength and speed with every word. A man's deeper, agitated tone weaving through her words, its urgency so heavy and thick it can barely squeeze itself between them.

"We can't stay here, Jules. We can't—"

"I can't just leave. I can't just—"

"I'm asking you to leave with me. It's what we've been planning all along—it's why we got mixed up in this shit in the first place. So we could leave—we're just doing it sooner than we thought. I love you, Jules. I love you and I can't just sit here and wait for him to—"

"I love you too but he killed her. I watched him kill her—I can't run away. I thought I could. I thought I could but I—"

"Rachel is dead, Jules. She's dead. Sticking around isn't going to change that. I didn't know her that well but I can tell you she wouldn't want you to get yourself killed just—"

Somehow, I've made it to the top of the stairs without even realizing it, their hushed voices growing louder and louder until I'm standing inches from the door they're fighting behind. Reaching out, I palm the knob and this one turns as easily as its predecessor. Pushing the door open on a large circular room, I stand in the doorway and stare at its inhabitants.

Teddy, pacing like a caged animal in the middle of the room.

Julie, sitting on the edge of what looks like an inflatable mattress, held off the ground by a platform made out of plastic milk crates and plywood. A small wooden table shoved against the wall, a low burning lantern and a backpack on its top. A pair of ladder-back chairs crowded around it. When he sees me, Teddy stops digging a trench with his feet, his expression going from mildly panicked to *holy shit, we're screwed* in the blink of an eye.

Because he knows I heard what Julie just admitted.

That she knows who killed Rachel.
That she watched it happen.

FIFTY-FOUR

When she sees me, Julie comes up off the bed, her gaze going directly to the floral duffle bag sitting at the foot of it and I almost laugh. It's open. I can see the money she stole from me, loose bills sitting on top of her worn foster kid hand-me-downs.

"Really?" The word and the anger I use to push it out of my mouth pushes *me*. Through the doorway and into the room. "You think I give a good goddamn about the money right now?"

"I—" Something flutters in her throat—an excuse. An apology. I don't know and to be honest, I don't care. Not right now. Eyes wide, she looks at Teddy just as I catch movement in my peripheral and I turn to find him a few steps closer than before, fists clenched like he's thinking about using them on me.

"I know what you're thinkin', junior." I say it casually. Like he isn't twice my size and scared enough to see me as a threat. "And while it probably wouldn't be the dumbest thing you've ever done, I can promise you if you take one more step, it'll be your *last* dumb thing in a spectacularly bad run."

He doesn't fold as easily as he did this afternoon—probably because it's not just him at risk anymore. Because Julie is here and he loves her, really loves her, and he's willing to make things a hell of a lot worse by trying to get her out of here—*through me,* if it comes to that.

"Teddy." Julie's voice sounds off somewhere to my left, almost shrill with urgency because she sees the same trapped animal I see and she's suddenly afraid of him. "Stop. Please, just—"

"How many people have you killed, junior?" My tone is still casual. Friendly even, like I'm asking what he's going to major in when he heads off to college in the fall. "People who tell you they don't keep count are liars. They keep count. We all do. I've killed eleven—two of them with my bare hands." I raise them. Show him the rock I have secured in my grip. The other one clenched into a fist because I've faced down trapped animals before and they don't respond to reason, soft voices and soothing words, like they do in the movies.

They respond to threats.

The absolute knowledge that lashing out will be the end of them.

"I'm betting that's about eleven more than you, so..." I slowly lower my hands, slightly blading my body in anticipation. "We're either gonna get on with it and see what's what or you're gonna get out of my face and sit your ass down."

"Teddy, please..."

Neither of us look at Julie but we can both hear it. She's near the breaking point, and it's the sound of her cracking that finally backs Teddy down, not the threat of getting beat to death with a rock by a woman with cracked ribs and a concussion.

Jaw clenched, he moves toward the bed and sits, pulling Julie down to sit beside him. "How did you find us?" he asks, fingers laced tight between Julie's like his hold on them is the only thing keeping him sane.

"Come on, junior—we're way past the stupid question portion of the program." Pulling his phone out of my pocket, I waggle it at him a few times before shoving it back in. "I'm guessing you knew it was only a matter of time before I got here—but you had to wait for dark to come back, same as me." Looking at Julie, I ask a question of my own. "Did he rape you?" I don't have time to be delicate, build trust. A relationship. "Richard McNamara—did he rape you?"

As soon as I ask it, the blood drains out of her face and her mouth goes slack. Eyes wide with denial. I look down at their hands. Expect Teddy's grip to go slack as soon as he processes what I just asked his girlfriend. Realizes she's a rape victim.

It doesn't.

He already knew or it doesn't matter to him.

Either way, it doesn't change the way he feels about her.

Against my better judgment, I'm starting to like this kid.

Unable to wait for her answer, I keep up with my questioning.

"He killed her, didn't he?" I take a step forward and crouch down in front of Julie while ignoring the scowling young man sitting next to her. "You and Teddy went to the Den to pick up the payment for the drug run, like every other Friday night, and while he was inside, you stayed on the boat. You saw them fighting— arguing about something. What was it?"

"She told him she knew." She whispers it, gaze turned down. Centered on the place where she and Teddy are joined. "That they were selling girls." Her color slips even further when she says it. Has to lift her head and look away from us completely to keep herself from throwing up. "She told him she was going to go to the cops and he laughed at her. He laughed and—"

"He killed her," I prompt her. She's spiraling fast. Seconds away from shutting down completely and we haven't even scratched the surface. Haven't even come close to putting the puzzle of that night together but right now, that's the only piece I need. I need to hear her say she saw Richard McNamara kill Rachel. The rest of it can wait. "She said she had proof he's been trafficking girls off the island and he killed her. You watched him strang—"

"They're gonna kill *her*," Teddy growls at me, his long, blunt-tipped fingers digging into the back of Julie's hand. "I'm sorry about Rachel—I know she was your friend or your sister or what-ever but as soon as they find out where she is, and they will find out because these guys aren't half as stupid as you think, they're coming here to kill her."

I don't tell him it's already too late.

That they're already coming.

Might even already be here.

Instead, I make a decision.

Looking at Teddy, I sigh. "I'm assuming you have a gun somewhere?"

"A what?" He stares at me like he's never heard the word before.

"*A gun.*" When all he does is keep staring at me, I stand up and give him another sigh. "At least I hope you do—I mean, it would take a special kind of stupid to run drugs through international waters for one of the most vicious biker gangs in the country *without* one."

His gaze narrows slightly. "Yeah—I have a gun."

"Fantastic." I toss my rock onto the bed beside Julie. "Give it to me."

FIFTY-FIVE

You can tell a lot about a person by the way they handle a gun.

When Teddy pulls a holstered VP9 out of his backpack and hands it over without protest, I know with absolute certainty that, while proficient in its handling, he's never so much as aimed it at another living thing, much less squeezed the trigger.

"What are you going to do with it?" he asks, as soon as the gun passes from his hand to mine, like it just occurred to him that giving it to me might not have been the smartest thing he's ever done.

"Well, junior..." Removing the VP9 from its holster, I pop the magazine from its grip and give it a quick inspection. It's full—thirteen rounds. "Those super-smart bikers you're so worried about—they know Julie's here and they're coming for her. Could even already be here." Pushing the magazine back into the grip with a firm hand, I rack the slide back to chamber a round. "So, I'm probably going to have to shoot some people with it." I'm being flippant on purpose because as soon as I said that King and his goons were on their way, Julie started to cry and Teddy suddenly looked like he swallowed a bucket full of worms. We're in some deep shit and one of us has to at least *pretend* to think we're going to make it out of this thing alive.

"Here?" Teddy looks around like they might be hiding under the bed or behind the door. "Now? They're—"

I give him a solemn nod. "Yes, here. Yes, now."

"We need to go." He looks at Julie, a convoluted mixture of anger and panic swirling across his features. "I told you"—he looks at me again—"we need to get out of here. I have a small aluminum boat pulled up and hidden—"

"It's too late." I give him a firm head shake. "Our best bet is to hunker down here. The door I just came through—is that the only way in or out?"

He gives me a stiff-jawed nod. "Yeah."

"Good. Where's the padlock?" Holding out my empty hand, I wait a few seconds before I wiggle my fingers. "The padlock, Teddy. For the door downstairs—where is it?"

"I—ah..." He looks around again before reaching into his pocket. Fishing it out, he all but shoves the padlock at me. It's open, its key shoved into its bottom.

"Hopefully the next time the opportunity to run drugs for a biker gang presents itself, you'll remember this moment and politely decline." Just like I hoped, Teddy stops freaking out and starts getting mad. "Is she your girlfriend?" I ask, without preamble.

His mouth snaps shut and he looks at Julie, sitting on the bed, sobbing quietly. "Yeah." He turns his gaze on me and nods. "Yeah, she's my girlfriend."

"Do you love her?"

He nods again. "Yes—I love her."

"Good." I hook the open arm of the padlock into my waistband so I can reach into my pocket. Pulling out my folding knife, I slap it against his chest. "Then you're going to take this *and* her and you're going to go hide and if anyone who isn't me finds you, you're going to kill them with it—can you do that?"

"Yes." He reaches up and wraps a hand around the knife, pulling it out of my hand. "I can do that."

Even though I have grave reservations about his ability to follow through, I don't have a choice but to leave them here.

Retracing my steps, I make my way toward the door I came through a few minutes ago. When I turn back around to reiterate my instructions to go hide, they're already gone.

Stepping onto the landing, I shut the door behind me, plunging myself back into full-blown dark. Free hand gripped around the banister, the other gripped around the gun, I make my way down the stairs carefully. At the bottom, I dig the phone out of my pocket and text Alex.

Where are you?

He texts back almost immediately.

I'm here. Close. Moving toward the lighthouse. Get Julie. Meet me outside.

Relief rushes through me and I almost do it. I almost double back. Find Julie and Teddy. Drag them from their hiding spot and tell them we've got a new plan. Between Alex and me, we can protect them. Get them off the island—but then the phone vibrates again, signaling another text.

It's Will.

They're there.

Shit.

Thumbs flying, racing the red, blinking battery icon in the corner of the screen, I text back.

How many?

The screen goes dark before I can hit send.

Staring at the place where the screen was only a second ago I hear something outside—the snap of branches. Brush and bramble being pushed aside. Scraping against the side of the lighthouse.

I shove the useless cell back into my pocket, just as the doorknob starts to turn, barely giving me enough time to raise the gun in my hand and take aim.

Please be Alex.

Please be Alex.

Please be—

A huge silhouette materializes in the doorway, perfectly outlined by the full moon.

Not Alex.

King.

"Man, I was *really* hoping I'd find you here," he says, right before he shuts the door, plunging us both back into the dark.

FIFTY-SIX

LINCOLN

They know.

That's all it took for me to change course.

Abandon my plan and move in the opposite direction.

Julie is in trouble and so is Georgia.

"What do you want me to do?" Will asks, looking at me with that same *Ol' Yeller* look he's been giving me for days now. "I can call Arch. Tell him what's happening. If he thinks Georgie's in trouble, he'll—"

"No." I don't have to elaborate. Will gets what I'm saying and even though he doesn't like it, he knows his little brother's badge puts him on the wrong side of things. That means we're on our own.

"Okay..." That look of his intensifies. "So, I guess I'm going to the manor and you're—"

"Don't worry about me," I tell him, giving him a firm head shake. And he *is* worried because no matter what I do now, no matter what choice I make, no matter which situation I charge into, the chances of this ending well for me are between slim and none. "Just get to the manor." Opening the car door, I reach down into the map pocket to retrieve a third walkie-talkie I kept for myself. "She'll be on channel five and Evie Jones will be with her, so it might take some convincing for her to tell you where she is."

"So... what?" The look slips into a *holy shit he's gone crazy again* expression I've seen more than once. "I'm just supposed to Butch and Sundance this shit with a moody pre-teen and an uppity doctor?"

"Pretty much." I slide into the driver's seat and turn my key in the ignition. The car's engine roars to life.

He laughs but there's no humor in the sound. "And they all think *I'm* the crazy one."

"Look..." I slam the car door closed. "I know it's a lot so if you're not up for it, if you don't think you can get there, then—"

"*Getting there* has never been my problem." I can almost hear the *click* of it, like one of those old-fashioned viewfinders, flipping from one image to the next. Away from Will. Into something else. Something hard and flat. Something that snuffs the light out in his eyes and turns him into a stranger. Seeing it now fills me with a nauseating mixture of relief and gut-grinding terror. "I can *get there* just fine."

Yeah, I might be the *crazy one* but Will is something else entirely.

According to the psychiatrist at Marquette, among a myriad disorders, he's a diagnosed sociopath. I don't know if they're right. I don't know what Will really is, what's wrong with him. All I know is there's a piece missing. Something inside him that makes killing as easy as breathing. Turns him into a black hole, completely void of anything that even vaguely resembles a human being.

And God help me, that's who I need right now.

I don't need Will.

I don't need my best friend.

I need the black hole.

I need the monster.

"I'm counting on you." Palming the gearshift, I slip the car into reverse. "I'm trusting you with my daughter," I remind him, because he's plan B through Z. The end of the line and we both know it.

"I know." He steps away from my car; his mouth stretches into a wide grin but there's nothing there. No light. No sound. "Go do what you gotta do, man, and leave the rest to me—I got this." He's the monster now. The black hole. For Will, it's as simple as turning out the lights. As easy as breathing.

Always has been.

For him, the hard part is finding his way back.

FIFTY-SEVEN

GEORGIA

As soon as he appears, King disappears again.

There and gone too quickly for my concussion-dulled reflexes to react.

"That a gun, I saw?" he mocks me from the dark, my body turning instinctively toward the sound of his voice. He's by the door he just passed through, putting him at a seven o'clock position to my high noon. "You aren't supposed to have that."

Like his taunt carries weight, my arms start to shake, the tremor forcing me to drop them and the gun. I ease my finger off the trigger, the sudden movement stitching pain into my ribs. I have to hold my breath against the groan that threatens to give away my position, swallow it down along with a healthy dose of pain.

Put it away.

It's nothing.

Less than nothing.

You're a soldier—now fucking act like it.

"Too bad you're too slow to use it," he says, trying to bait me into giving away my position. "Probably just as well though... you start taking potshots at me in the dark, my boys outside'll hear and come running and we can't have that, now, can we?"

He's right.

I don't know how many of them are out there. I don't know

where they are. What I do know is I'm the only real thing standing between him and Julie, the only thing I trust, and if I use the gun not only will I give up my position and risk having it stripped and used on both me and her, I'll bring King's lackeys running like I just rang a dinner bell. I'll bring them right to Julie. If that happened, I might be able to handle one or two but not much more than that. Not in my condition. Not on my own.

Where are you, Alex?

"No, ma'am, we can't have that..." He's moving. Closer to where he saw me standing. "We're keeping this party private, aren't we?" Even closer. Inching past eight, into the nine o'clock position. Moving slow. Playing with me. "Just you and me, Ms. Fell. We're gonna have a *real* good time, just the two of us."

Calling up my mental snapshot of the room, I map it out. A pile of sandbags behind me. The stairs at my four o'clock. The fireplace and workbench at my five and six. Lifting my foot, I take a lunging sidestep toward the stairs, careful to put my foot down as softly as possible before I lift the other to complete the move. Both feet planted, I run my thumb along the grip of the gun, stopping when I find the magazine's release lever.

"What's the matter, Ms. Fell?" He's at nine o'clock now. Moving faster, my silence irritating him. "Baby duck got your tongue?"

Using his taunt as cover noise, I press the release lever, ejecting the magazine from the grip of the gun because I can't use it. Not here. Not now.

But he can.

And if he manages to strip it from me, he will.

"I got boys at your house too." Nine o'clock and holding. Waiting for me to make a move. Make a noise that will tell him where I am. "Disciples—imagine how disappointed they're gonna be when they find out you aren't there."

Reaching under my shirt, I tuck the magazine into the high waistband of my yoga pants before taking another deep, clockwise step toward the stairs, wincing slightly when the toe of my deck shoe scrapes against the bottom step.

"Maybe not *too* disappointed—" Ten o'clock. He heard me and is on the move again, the sound drawing him closer. "After all, they'll have that pretty doctor friend of yours and sweet little Savanna to play with."

He knows Evie and Savanna are at the manor.

Doesn't matter.

Not right now.

Keep your head in the game.

"Do me a favor," I say, finally answering him because he's irritated but not nearly as reckless as I need him to be. "Make sure they wipe their boots before they go inside—I have a feeling that Persian in the front hall is a bitch to clean."

"There it is—that smart little mouth of yours." Eleven o'clock. "You don't have to worry. I'm not going to kill you. I'm gonna keep you as a pet." Twelve o'clock. "I'm gonna teach you all kinds of tricks—starting with what a woman's mouth is *really* for."

"*Huh...* am I supposed to be scared?" I lift my foot and set it down, the sole of my shoe sounding like sandpaper, sliding across the bottom step. "I am, aren't I?" I take another step, claiming the first step completely before moving up to the second. Reaching behind me, I tuck the gun into the waistband of my yoga pants, against the small of my back. It's heavy, bulkier than the Ka-Bar, and I have no real hope it'll stay put but I need my hands free for what comes next. "I'm *really* going to have to start writing this stuff down."

He laughs, the sound of it like a shovel hitting hot asphalt. "Don't worry—I'll help you remember."

One o'clock.

Directly in front of me.

Less than ten feet away.

Push him.

"Help me? How are *you* gonna help *me* when you're nothing more than Richard McNamara's *step-and-fetchit*?" I sneer into the dark, wrapping my now empty hands around the banister before easing myself onto the third step. "He's the real monster—not you. You're just a sniveling little bitch who licks his shoes and takes out his trash."

King growls softly. I finally hit a nerve. "Careful."

I loosen my knees, getting myself ready. "That's why you're here, isn't it? To do his dirty work. Get rid of Julie because she saw him murder Rachel—McNamara snaps his fingers and you come running like a dumb little puppy dog, ready to play fetch."

"You got it all wrong, Ms. Fell..." He snarls it, inching closer. Enraged now but managing to keep himself in check. "I'm not here for him—I'm here for you."

Not enough.

Push harder.

"Right... all those tricks you're gonna *teach me.* Well, I've got a secret for you, baby duck—" I mount the fourth step, my hands sliding along the banister for support— "you better get used to disappointment because even if you do manage to beat me, you're *never* gonna break me because harder men than you have tried and I'm still here. You could keep me until the day I die and the only *trick* you'd ever teach me to use my mouth for is to spit in your stupid, worthless—"

He charges me with a roar, sand and dirt crunching beneath the soles of his heavy motorcycle boots, so loud it sounds like machine-gun spray.

Not yet.

I tighten my grip on the banister, my arms and shoulders tense with anticipation, forcing myself to wait until I hear it. Bracing myself for what's to come.

Not yet.

He's close.

Close enough to lunge at me, close the gap in an instant, breath so hot and ragged I can feel the whisper of it on my face, tearing through his chest like a hurricane so loud I almost miss it—the telltale scrape of the toe of his boot hitting the bottom step, same as mine less than a minute ago.

Now.

Bending my knees, I launch myself upward, using my grip on the banister to swing myself over it. One moment, I'm in the path of a bullet train, the next I'm sailing through the air. I'm in flight for the space of a heartbeat before I crash-land, ankle twisting painfully beneath me as I go down, my knee smashing against the concrete floor. I barely have time to lift my arm to protect my head before I'm rolling across it to land in an agonizing heap, just feet from the door. I can see faint, gray shadows—moonlight slipping under the crack to play across the floor. Rolling myself onto my hands and knees, I feel something inside me shift, sending splinters of white-hot pain shooting through my ribs.

Not cracked anymore.

Broken.

It's nothing.

Less than nothing.

Now get up and MOVE.

I give myself a breath.

One shallow, wheezing breath before I force myself to my feet. Stagger the few yards to the door before I fall against it, struggling against my own weight to pull it open when I turn the knob.

"*Bitch!*"

The curse comes from above. King's rage and momentum carried him nearly to the top of the stairs before he realized his mistake. That I'm not where I'm supposed to be. That I'm about to escape. Alex is out there somewhere. If I can just find him, lead King away from here, maybe somehow manage to circle back and slip the padlock in place...

The door at the top of the stairs suddenly opens, letting in the soft glow from the lantern Julie and Teddy left burning on the table in their haste to find a secure hiding place. The dull, yellow light slices through the dark, pinches into my eyes, nearly as bright as the sun, forcing me to close them.

"But she's in *here*, isn't she?" King mocks me from the top of the stairs. Stopping me in my tracks. "Pretty little Julie's in here and if you run, you'll be leaving her alone. *With me.*"

No. Not alone. Teddy is here and he has my knife. He'll do everything in his limited power to protect Julie. But it won't matter. Won't be enough.

King will kill him.

What he'll do to Julie will be infinitely worse.

"I won't chase you." He says it like he's reading my mind. Knows exactly what I'm thinking. What I'd been hoping. Eyes still closed, I lean heavily on the door, trying to figure out my next move. Formulate a plan. It comes quick—half-formed and so reckless it borders on stupid, but I'm all out of moves. It's the only one I have left.

"You run, I won't chase you," he says. "I'll stay right here and—"

"Quit your quacking, baby duck..." My hand drops away from the knob and I turn away from it. Look up at King, the dull, yellow lantern light perfectly framing him in the doorway, the halo of it barely wide enough to reach me, revealing the gun in his hand and the fact that it's aimed directly at my face. "I'm not going anywhere."

FIFTY-EIGHT

LINCOLN

I stole Mark Tate's boat.

Considering I'm a confirmed drug smuggler, convicted felon, and suspected wife murderer, it bothers me a hell of a lot more than it should.

Telling myself I'll offer him free lifetime oil changes if I make it out of this shit alive, I push it away from his dock—a little fifteen-foot pleasure cruiser—and jump in, letting it glide through the water and away from the shoreline rather than risk starting the engine and drawing attention to my theft.

I'm barely more than a few yards from the dock when my phone rings.

Pulling it from my pocket, I swipe the screen to answer it.

"Where are you?"

It's my father.

"Sorry, Dick..." I look back over my shoulder at the dock I just shoved away from. The house behind it is dark. It's edging toward ten o'clock on a Wednesday night—Mark's either working late or he's already asleep. Even though I'm in the clear, I don't start the boat. "Something came up—rain check?"

"I don't think so," he says, trying for dismissive but I can hear tension in the undercurrent of his tone—he's nervous because I'm supposed to be there and I'm not. And if I'm not there, that means

I'm an unknown entity. An unmitigated risk. "I've given you ample opportunity to take responsibility for the things you've done. I'm—"

"Who's there with you?"

"I'm sorry?" He says it carefully. Like my question confuses him.

"I mean—I was planning on killing you." I reach behind me to touch the grip of the gun I have jammed into the waistband of my jeans at the small of my back. It's nothing special. A Glock 17. I bought it off some guy in a parking lot in Marquette months ago for three hundred bucks. Just being in possession of it is enough to send me back to prison. What I planned on doing with it would've sent me back to prison forever. "So I can only assume your plan was to kill *me*—there's no other reason you'd agree to meet with me alone, but we both know you don't have the stones to do it yourself, so..." I turn further east, aiming my gaze at the trees guarding Georgia's shoreline, catching glimpses of the moon-washed manor between their branches. It looks quiet. Dark windows. Closed doors. Savanna's inside and there are men in there with her. Looking for her. The only thing that keeps me moving forward is knowing Will is inside too and he's looking for *them*. "... who's there with you? Is it Levi? I bet it's Levi."

"No one is here with me, Lincoln." He sighs like I'm being ridiculous. Like talking to me is a chore. "You reached out to *me*, remember? You agreed to confess your crimes and turn yourself in if *I* agreed to meet with you. I was willing to do that if it meant putting an end to all of this but I'm afraid you've given me no choice but to—"

"You'll never get your hands on Savanna," I tell him, turning away from the manor. "No matter what happens next—no matter what happens to me—she's out of your reach. I've made sure of it."

"I see..." He makes a sad sort of clucking noise in the back of his throat—it's his *you've disappointed me, Lincoln* sound. I grew up hearing it. Every time he aimed it in my direction, my stomach would start to churn. My mind would start to race, trying to find a way to fix it. Make him proud. Make him love me. "You've involved Georgia, haven't you? Infected her with your lies." He says it like the realization makes him sad. "That's too bad, Lincoln. I hoped you would've thought better of doing something so foolish."

"*You* involved Georgia when you killed Rachel." I wonder if he even understands what he did. How sorely he's underestimated her. "As soon as you learned Georgia was the one who found her body, you knew she wouldn't just let it go because she saw what you did to her. She *saw*, so you couldn't let her live, but she's not just some ex-junkie like Rachel was, is she, Dick? She's not some eastern girl you can just strangle to death and leave in a parking lot or force into a bathtub and shoot in the head. She's the Angel Bay Baby—she means something to the people who live on this island and they wouldn't let you just sweep her under the rug like the rest of them, so you had to make her death look like an accident."

"I didn't kill Rachel and I didn't kill Jenna." He says it carefully, enunciating every word. "You did, and I'm confident once the sheriff serves his search warrants on your home and business, looking for evidence connecting you to their murders, he's going to find your tools were used to tamper with Georgia's brakes."

"She knows the truth about you." It's a stretch—I told Georgia the truth but that doesn't mean she believed me. Doesn't mean she trusts me. "She knows what you did—what you've *been* doing. That you've been raping *your girls* for years. That you've been trafficking your victims off the island. Selling them." Now it's my turn to laugh, the sound of it ringing harsh and hollow in my ears. "I think you forgot who she is. I don't know—maybe you never really understood her, but Rachel and Jenna were her *family*. The only family she's ever known and you killed them, so it doesn't matter what you do to me because now that she knows what you really are, she's going to run you down like a dog and she's not going to stop until you're dead and buried."

"That's... regrettable." His tone is tight. Clipped. Its edges rubbed thin, exposing the ugly thing that lives inside him. "No matter—my associates will take care of her and circumstances, as they've been directed, will take care of you."

"That sounded awfully close to a confession, Dick. I'd be careful if I were you—your slip is showing." Ending the call, I jam my phone back into my pocket and start the boat. Pointing its bow northeast, I head for the Rock.

The dock is occupied.

I recognize the boat. A black Four Winns F190.

King is here.

Feeling like I have a million eyes crawling over me, I throw a rope onto the dock and clamber up. Executing a quick bowline, I secure my stolen boat and hurry across the beach. My phone vibrates in my pocket, right before I step into the trees.

Thinking it's my father again, I reach back to retrieve it with the intention of switching it off completely. It's not my dad. It's Will. Gut suddenly churning, I answer it because there's only one reason Will would call me right now.

Trouble.

"Archie's gone," Will tells me without preamble. "His squad's here but—"

"I thought we agreed to keep him out of this," I remind him, keeping my tone low and tight in an effort to combat the relief that's coursing through me. Relief because Will didn't call me to tell me Savanna is hurt or worse. "He's a *cop*. We can't—"

"I don't give a shit what he *is*," Will bites back, his tone just as low and tight as mine. "He's my *brother*."

"Okay." I sigh. "You're right... okay." Staring off into the trees, I watch for movement in the shadows; some sort of clue I'm not alone here. I'm not. I know I'm not but so far, all I can hear are the far-off shouts and laughter of kids partying on Seraphim. The chug and zip of their boats racing between the island and the beach club. All I can see in front of me is darkness. Shades of black layered on top of each other, tangled and twisting together like snakes. "Where do you think he is?"

"I don't know..." His voice sounds far away, like he's calling up to me from the bottom of a well. "He loves her, you know? She was there for him. Kept him safe when I couldn't—but he's different now. Got different when Georgie left. Sometimes when I look at him, I don't see him. I see someone else—"

"Arch's okay." It might be a lie. Archie is a cop and Will's right —he's not the same. The Archie I remember was lighter, somehow. He pretends he's still that guy—goofy, affable Archie, but that's not who he is. Most times he can pull it off but sometimes I catch a glimpse of it: a hardness in him that was never supposed to be there. A darkness that took root in Georgia's absence. Maybe even because of it. Whatever it is, whatever the reason, Will's right.

He got different.

So, he might not be okay—he might be something else. Something neither of us want to consider. Will knows but he doesn't argue with me when I say it because he doesn't care. It doesn't matter to him. Whatever Archie is now, he's his little brother first. That's all that matters to him. "We'll find him."

"Pretty sure I killed Baltimore." Will's tone goes hard. Flat. "I killed Eddie for sure. Killed him in Georgie's kitchen. Broke one of her fancy teacups. She's gonna be pissed at me."

"That's okay, too." I feel a sudden surge of urgency. The push of it telling me I have no business standing here. I'm wasting time. "We'll find Archie after this is over. Right now I need to find *her* and you need to find Savanna."

"Alright." I can practically hear him nod. "I keep texting Teddy but he's not answering me."

Teddy.

Julie's boyfriend.

"He's probably partying on Seraphim with the rest of the rich kids," I say with enough disdain to convince myself I was never one of them.

"No—he's there. He loves Julie." Will sounds sure. Like he knows things I don't. "Something's wrong. Better find him too."

The line goes dead.

Curbing the urge to call him back, I switch my phone off and jam it back into my pocket before stepping into the trees.

FIFTY-NINE

GEORGIA

There's a fine line between brave and stupid. You want to live—you better find that shit and learn how to double-Dutch.

It's something my drill sergeant used to bellow at us during live-fire exercises.

It means it's always better to live smart than to die brave—but sometimes living smart isn't an option and if you don't want to die brave, you have to find the line between brave and stupid and start double-Dutching while praying to God you don't land on the wrong side of the wire when shit blows up.

King's standing at the top of the stairs, still looking down at me. Gun still aimed at my face. I'm not surprised to see it.

When he sees my gaze sweep over it, King smiles. "You afraid yet, Ms. Fell?"

The door behind him is still open.

I have no idea where Julie and Teddy are. They spend a lot of time here. Reason tells me they know more about this place than I do. That they've found a good place to hide and are as safe as they can possibly be. It also tells me that pissing this guy off even more and testing that theory are on opposite sides of brave and stupid.

"Meh." I lift my shoulder in a half-hearted shrug. "Let's call it *mildly concerned.*"

My answer tightens his jaw. "You still got that gun?"

I nod my head. By some miracle, it stayed put when I jumped the banister, for all the good it's done me. Even if I could use it without drawing the attention of every Reaper skulking around outside, I'd never get to it and manage to load it in time.

"Show me"—he gestures with his own—"*slowly*."

Left hand held away from my body, palm flat and aimed in his direction, I bend my right and reach behind me. Carefully lifting my shirt, I find the grip of the gun wedged into my waistband. Giving it a three-finger pull I hold it out, showing him it's missing its magazine. Now he grins at me. "Whatdya go and do that for?"

I give him a small shrug. "Double-Dutch."

My cryptic answer wipes the grin off his face. "Where is it?"

Using my raised left hand, I aim my finger at the pile of sand-bags at my nine o'clock. "Tossed it back there," I tell him, indicating the narrow space between the wall and the pile. He frowns, trying to decide if I'm lying or not. I don't move, don't even breathe, waiting for him to either buy it or give up the high ground and come frisk me.

"Then I guess you're going to toss the rest of it over there," he tells me, jerking his head in the opposite direction, toward the fireplace. "*Now*."

I fling the gun in the direction of the fireplace. It hits the cement with a clatter, skittering across it on a spinning slide that carries it across the floor and under the workbench next to the fireplace.

Shit.

"Come up here."

"Let me guess..." Raising my gaze from the place where the gun disappeared, I force a smartass grin onto my face. "Class is in session?"

"Gold star for you." The corner of King's mouth kicks up, raising his pock-marked cheek in a lewd expression that makes my skin crawl. When I hesitate, the look on his face falls flat. "*Move*."

I do what he says, taking a short, shuffling step toward the stairs, hand pressed to my stomach like I'm trying to hold myself together. I take another step, breath hissing softly when my abused ankle wobbles like bearing my weight is something it really doesn't want to do. The next step brings me to the center of the room and, hand still pressed to my stomach, I look up at King standing almost directly above me. "Tell me something, baby duck," I say, stalling. Trying to steel myself for what comes next. "How did a low-level scumbag like you get hooked up with a high-functioning sociopath like Richard McNamara?"

"Oh, Ms. Fell... you haven't figured it out yet?" King laughs—a real laugh that turns my stomach because it tells me whatever he's about to say next, it's going to hurt like hell. "That's the best part. You're gonna—"

Gunshots outside.

Three of them in a tight cluster.

Alex.

The ugly bark of them was muffled by the thick cement walls of the lighthouse but they were close. Close enough to jerk King's attention away from me.

Now.

Heart jammed in my throat, I dive right, the hard landing stealing my breath when I hit the floor, sending it rattling and wheezing through my chest, away from my lungs in a sizzling hot rush that grays my vision. Fries it at its edges and turns it white.

It's nothing.

Less than nothing.

Now MOVE.

Pushing myself across the floor, arm outstretched, I reach into the dark place that swallowed Teddy's gun while the other digs itself into the waistband of my pants to retrieve the magazine. I slam into the workbench before I can get my fingers around it and pull it loose, sending dust and rusty tools jittering across its surface. King roars a curse above me. A second later the gun in his hand clatters down the stairs and he's stealing my play, vaulting over the banister to practically land on top of me, even as I find the one I tossed. My fingers brush against its barrel, sending it spinning like a drunken carousel. I grit my teeth and stretch, a scream humming against my ribs, a split second before I feel King's hand roughly grab my hair, pulling my head back to slam it into the side of the workbench—once, twice—breaking its leg and toppling it over. The hand still fisted in my hair flips me over, pulling the staples holding my scalp together loose before it and its partner close themselves around my throat.

"Well, that was rude," King jeers down at me, straddling my chest. Laughing when I start to slap uselessly at his hands, legs kicking, the slick soles of my deck shoes useless against the sandy concrete floor. "Guess I'm gonna have to add *manners* to my lesson plan."

"*Fuck you*—" I push it out with the force of a scream but it comes out on a wheezing croak that instantly sets my throat on fire.

"Don't worry, Ms. Fell..." King starts to squeeze, those rough, dirty fingers digging into the tender flesh of my throat, the web between his thumbs and fingers pushing against my hyoid bone. Grinding it against my larynx. Choking the life out of me while my hands drop away from his—stop slapping and start scrambling across the cement floor. "We'll get there." He squeezes harder, hard enough to push a gurgling wheeze past the pressure of his hands, bulging my eyeballs from their sockets. Hands still scrambling and pushing through the sand and debris on the floor around me, searching for something. Anything...

More gunshots.

Another tight cluster.

Three. Maybe four.

"Music to my ears." King uses his grip to lift my head from the floor, giving me a short, vicious shake that rattles my brain inside my skull, waking up my concussion, instantly setting off a dizzying churn of nausea and pain. He leans into his grip, elbows locked, the added weight ratcheting the pressure of his hands tighter around my neck. "That was the sound of your boyfriend getting smoked..." He laughs, just as my vision starts to go gray again. "Your hero, come to rescue you, is dead, and pretty soon you're gonna start wishing you were too." I can feel his feral gaze burn into me, his face mere inches from mine, swimming in and out of focus, just as my oxygen-starved fingers tremble over something hard and thin. I don't know what it is. I don't care.

Digging deep, I close my fingers around it, gripping it tight.

"No one's coming for you. No one's gonna save you."

I quietly slip my arm into the exposed space between his extended bicep and the side of his chest.

"No one cares—just like no one cared when I killed—"

Leaning into the noose of his hands around my throat, I stare up at him. Watch as his vicious grin is washed away by a flood of pain and confusion, his eyes going wide as I use my final reserve of strength to drive my mystery shiv into his armpit with an upward thrust that tightens the grip of his hands around my neck for just an instant.

"*You—*"

I twist, accessing and opening the axillary artery. A worm of dark blood squirms warm and sluggish down my arm. Something thick and wet gurgles in his throat and his arms go slack as his chest cavity fills with blood. I reach up with bloody, shaking hands and shove, dislodging his loosened grip from around my neck. He topples over while I drag in deep, wheezing pulls of air that set my chest and throat on fire, flooding my tear ducts with what feels like acid.

It's nothing.
Less than nothing.
Now MOVE.

Kicking out from under the lower half of King's body on a surge of adrenaline, I flip myself over onto my hands and knees, head hanging down. I watch as fat, wet drops of my own blood splatter against the concrete before clotting in the sand that covers it.

It's nothing.
Less than nothing.
Now MOVE.

"Holy shit."

I raise my head with considerable effort to find Teddy standing at the top of the stairs, staring at me over the banister, my knife open and clenched tight in his hand. Sighing, I swing my gaze to my right to find King lying crumpled on his side, staring at me with dark, flat eyes, blood bubbling on his lips. Chest rising and falling in short, arrhythmic bursts that remind me of a fish trying to breathe air. Lifting a hand, I reach over with an arm that feels like over-cooked spaghetti and yank my shiv out of his armpit.

It's a rusty screwdriver.

"Is he dead?"

"Not yet." It comes out choppy. Like I fed the words through a meat grinder before spitting them out of my mouth. Dropping the screwdriver on the ground, I reach out again, this time shoving King onto his back. "Give it about thirty seconds."

I reach under the pile of splintered wood that used to be a workbench and pull Teddy's gun from beneath the rubble. Relying on the adrenaline surging through me, I lock my elbow and push, wobbling myself onto my knees. "Where's Julie?" I ask, while I finally manage to dig the gun's loaded magazine from the waistband of my pants.

"She's still hiding." I look up to watch him gesture with the knife over his shoulder. "I heard the gunshots and thought maybe you needed—" He looks past me, at the man who is either dead or very close to it on the floor behind me.

Help.

He came out here to help me.

Damn it, I *really* didn't want to like this kid.

"I don't." I shake my head, force-feeding the magazine back into the grip of the gun with shaky fingers. "Go back. Don't come out until I come get you. No one but me and only if I'm alone—do you understand?"

Gritting my teeth, I groan softly, pain humming along every nerve as I push myself onto my feet, swaying under the pull of my own weight. I look up again to find Teddy still staring at the man behind me. I swing my gaze in the same direction.

He's dead.

I expect to feel something.

Relief.

Remorse.

I don't.

I don't feel anything.

Not right now.

I can't.

But I will.

I know I will.

Looking back up at Teddy, I sigh. "*Do you hear me, junior?*"

My tone yanks his gaze away from the dead man behind me and he nods. "Yeah." He keeps nodding. "Yes, but—"

"Back inside. Hide." Taking a wobbly spin, I aim myself at the door and stumble forward. "Because this isn't over."

SIXTY

LINCOLN

The lighthouse is about a hundred yards northeast of the dock where I tied off. Leaving the sound of distant laughter from Seraphim behind me, I push myself deeper into the trees, the tangle of them so dense and thick the sounds of teenage partying disappear almost completely once their bramble closes around me.

Will will find Savanna.

He'll do everything in his power to protect her.

Knowing he's left a trail of dead Disciples littered around Georgia's house like discarded trash is more comforting than it should be.

Keeping the top of the lighthouse in front of me, I keep walking. It doesn't take me long to doubt everything.

Because there's no one here.

No Reapers.

No King.

No one pushing themselves through the brush. No snapping branches. No harsh whispers or glow of cell phone flashlights. Despite what I'm seeing and hearing, I know King is here. The fact that there's no one else just means he played it smart. Came alone. His guys might know they're running drugs but that doesn't mean they know about King's extra-curricular activities.

Drug trafficking is one thing.

Human trafficking is something else entirely.

The lighthouse looms up ahead, a dingy white tower glowing in the dark. It's slow, revolving light skimming the treetops as it splashes light across the water. I stop walking to get my bearings. Try to remember where the back entrance is located. Will said he's been trying to reach Teddy but he—

I catch a glimpse of something moving. Something big. Human-shaped, standing just inside the treeline like it's waiting, not more than ten feet in front of me.

I stop walking, sure whoever it is heard my approach. That I'm going to have a fight on my hands. I lift the gun from my waistband and wait.

As soon as I do, I understand how I got so close to whoever it is without being heard.

He's talking on the phone.

"King's inside looking for them now."

I know that voice.

Hearing it now tightens the skin on the back of my neck. Tightens the grip I have on my gun.

King didn't come alone after all.

"I haven't seen him." He sighs, lifts his empty hand to rub at his temple in frustration. "I've been standing here for—We're not gonna fuck it up. I understand what's at stake... No," he says, his tone hard and tight, "they won't get in the way. You can count on me, Mr. McNamara."

My father.

He's talking to my father.

He lowers his phone, swiping it off while he shoves it into the pocket of his jacket. I don't even know I'm moving toward him. Don't even realize I have my gun raised until I've closed the gap and I'm practically standing on top of him.

"That you, Linc?" He tosses a quick look over his shoulder. When it lands on the gun I have trained on him, he turns around completely, arms falling to his sides, putting his hand within easy reach of the gun on his hip. "That was your dad on the phone. You've got him pretty worried."

I should tell him to put his hands up but I don't because a part of me is hoping he'll go for his gun so I can shoot him without having to feel bad about it.

"Screw my dad." I spit it at him. "How could you do this to her?" I don't have to explain. We both know who I'm talking about.

Georgia.

Like I said her name out loud, he frowns at me. "I didn't have a choice." He shakes his head while he inches his toward the grip of his gun. "By the time she came home, it was already done. I was already in too deep to get out."

"She loves you." Saying it tightens my grip on the gun. I can feel my finger trembling on its trigger. "Trusts you."

"George doesn't love me." His expression tightens, blue eyes narrowing slightly. Hand hovering over the grip of his gun. "She doesn't love—"

From the corner of my eye, I see something—*someone*—moving in the dark behind him. A glint from the moon, bouncing off metal.

A badge.

Maybe.

I don't know.

Whatever it is, it's enough to distract me for a split second.

Long enough to give him time to palm his gun and pull it clear from its holster. Before I know it, he squeezes off three rounds at point-blank range that have me diving for cover behind a snarl of half-felled trees and wild blueberry bushes. The first two slugs sizzle past my face and neck, so close I can feel the heat of them sear my skin. The third one hits its mark, tearing into me and spinning me around with enough force to put my face in the dirt and knock the gun from my hand.

"Shoulda shot me, Linc," he tells me, his tone barely held above a whisper. "Good thing for you Daddy needs a scapegoat."

I see it again. Something—*someone*—moving closer. Slipping

from tree to tree for cover. "Did I say screw my dad?" I say, flipping myself over to find him glaring down at me. "I meant screw *you*."

As soon as he sees my hands are empty, he smiles. "You've always been a smartass—never know when to leave well enough alone." He sighs, gesturing with the barrel of his gun. "Get up— nice and easy."

Gritting my teeth against the pain, I plant my hands in the dirt, getting ready to launch myself at him, when my fingertips brush against something warm and metallic lying on the ground next to me.

My gun.

"Don't get any cute ideas." He grins and shakes his head at me like I'm the dumb kid in class. "By now the Disciples have Savanna and—"

"By now, I'm guessing they're all pretty much dead." Movement again. Another dull glint as the thing in the shadows materializes behind him and shows its face. Raises its gun. "Will loves Savanna—he won't let anything happen to her."

"Will is as incompetent as he is crazy." The man standing over me laughs. "If he's your ace in the hole then—"

More gunshots.

Four of them, aimed at the man standing over me.

I don't stick around to see if they hit their mark.

As soon as the bullets start flying, I grab my gun and run.

SIXTY-ONE

GEORGIA

I stumble through the door and into the small clearing between the lighthouse and the wilderness of the Rock behind it. I close the door behind me and, leaning heavily against it, I sigh.

It's the best I can do.

The padlock is long gone and I don't have the time to try and find it right now.

I'll have to rely on Teddy to do the rest—at least until I can find Alex and figure out a way off this island without getting us killed.

Alex.

Just thinking about him, out here alone, closes my throat and shoves me away from the doorframe. Hand locked around the grip of Teddy's gun, I push myself forward, shoulder dragging along the rough, weathered side of the lighthouse. I can feel blood from my unstapled head wound trickling down the back of my neck. Soaking the back of my shirt. The ACE bandage holding my ribs together are doing the best it can but every wobbly step I take threatens to be my last.

I know the difference between *hurt* and *injured*. I know when you're operating on borrowed time. When you've stopped double-Dutching and firmly landed in stupid.

Right now, I'm hip-deep in stupid.

It's nothing.

Less than nothing.

Now MOVE.

Reaching the end of the lighthouse, I stand in its shadow, leaning against it to catch my breath. Hold it and listen. The Rock is quiet. No branches snapping under heavy boot treads. No thrash of big bodies through the trees. There's supposed to be dozens of them here. Reapers—all here to *keep* me here. Keep me from leaving the Rock with Julie. Kill us if they have to, and they wouldn't have to be quiet about it. Alex and I are woefully outnumbered.

We're the hunted.

They're the hunters.

... you start taking potshots at me in the dark, my boys outside'll hear and come running and we can't have that, now, can we?

My boys.

That's what King said.

But there's no one here.

Only... there has to be, doesn't there?

That was the sound of your boyfriend getting smoked...

Someone came here with King and that *someone* shot at Alex.

The thought jams grief and panic down my throat. Tries to choke me with its bulk but I force it down. Force myself to set emotion aside and think rationally. Triage the situation. Prioritize my objectives. Stay on mission.

Get Julie off the island.

Make sure she's safe.

A new plan tries to form itself in my head but the pieces of it are torn and broken. I can't make them fit together right.

Get Julie off the island.

Make sure she's safe.

I'll need help to do that.

Casting a quick look over my shoulder at the closed door behind me, I push myself clear of the shadows. Exposed, I stagger along the packed dirt trail that leads to the dock in front of the lighthouse. The johnboat is equipped with a two-way radio. Hopefully, Archie is still parked on my gate and within range. I'll call him for help.

But the johnboat I left tied to the dock is gone.

Either sunk or set adrift by King's partner while he and I were trying to kill each other.

Oh, Ms. Fell... you haven't figured it out yet? That's the best part. You're gonna—

Wheeling around on drunken legs, I watch the lighthouse sway in front of me. Force myself to stay focused because between the concussion and the blood loss from my re-opened head wound, I don't have much time left.

King had to have had a cell phone.

Julie still has hers.

I can still call Archie.

He'll come and—

Something moves in my peripheral and I turn toward it, almost weeping with relief when another surge of adrenaline rushes through my system, giving me the strength to raise the gun in my hand because this time I'm going to use it. This time I don't give a shit if the sound of it brings a thousand Reapers. This time I'm going to—

Alex.

Standing in the treeline, not more than fifteen feet away.

Dropping my arm, I rush forward, closing the distance between us. I stumble the last few feet and Alex reaches for me. "Jesus, George." He turns me into the trunk of a nearby tree, leaning me against it to keep me on my feet. "What the hell happened to—"

"King."

When I say his name, Alex's expression goes wary and his gaze shifts to the lighthouse behind me. "Where is he?"

"Dead." I lift my free hand and run it over his chest. His shoulders. Looking for bullet holes. Blood. There isn't any. He's wearing Kevlar under his street clothes. Regardless, I keep searching. "Are you okay? I heard gunshots and I thought—"

"I'm fine." He grabs my searching hand and holds it. "Are you sure he's dead?" When all I do is blink at him, he gives my hand a hard squeeze to keep me focused. Grounded. "George, are you sure King is dead?"

"Yeah..." I give him a nod that sends my brain pinballing around my skull. "I stabbed him with a screwdriver and"—I look at the arm he's holding. It's covered in King's blood—"that's his blood. There was a lot of it. I—"

"Okay." He gives me a grim nod and steps backwards into the trees, pulling me along. "We need to get out of here—*now*."

"No..." I try to tug out of his grip but my arms are noodley again and I can't make them work right. "We can't just leave. Julie is still here."

"We don't have a choice." Alex gives me another firm tug, pulling me further into the trees. "You're bleeding bad. I have to get you to the hospital. King is dead. They'll be okay until I come back for them, but right now I need to get *you* out of here." He drops his chin and pins me with a desperate warning look. "We're not alone here, George. We need to go."

He's doing the exact same thing I did just a few minutes ago.

He's triaging the situation.

Prioritizing his objectives.

Staying on mission.

I'm his mission.

Keeping me safe.

Alive, to the detriment of everything else.

"I can't." I pull on my hand again, harder this time. "I can't leave her. *I keep leaving.* I can't do it. Not again—I can't..."

I catch movement again. This time behind Alex, shifting in the shadows just over his shoulder as a figure materializes from the trees.

Archie.

He has a gun.

It's pointed at Alex.

SIXTY-TWO

"Archie..." I tug on my hand again when I say it, confused, because I have no idea how he got here—*why* he's here. When I say his name, Alex drops my hand and turns to face his deputy, placing his body between me and the man standing in front of us.

"Come here, George," Archie says in that firm, heavy tone I don't recognize as his.

"Archie?" I don't recognize that tone either. It sounds small and confused when it comes out of my mouth. "What are you doing? What—"

"He's here with King," Alex says quietly, shoulders squared. Hand working around the grip of the gun, aimed at the ground and useless.

Archie works with King.

As soon as the thought forms, my brain rejects it.

No.

No, that can't be right.

Not him.

Not Archie.

"I've suspected him for a while. I just didn't know how to tell you. They've been working together for over a year. Hooked up through his brother when he got out of prison. Had a pretty sweet set-up until you decided to come home and—"

"Shut up," Archie barks at him. "Toss the gun." He gives the barrel of his a terse jerk. "Now."

"It's okay." I say it quietly, pressing my empty hand against Alex's shoulder while I brush the gun in my other against the back of his thigh, reminding him I still have it. "Do what he says."

Alex's shoulders slump under my hand a second before he does what Archie says and tosses his service weapon into the brush, raising his hands to shoulder height, palms out.

Moving out from behind Alex, I take a step in Archie's direction.

"Christ..." Alex makes a warning noise in the back of his throat. "What the hell are you doing, George?"

"Double-Dutch." The adrenaline is back, stomping and slamming its way through my veins. Sharpening my vision. Steadying my gait. Chasing away the dizziness. Beating back the nausea. It'll all be back, sooner rather than later and with a vengeance, but right now I do the only thing I know how to do.

I finish the mission.

"Archie, please..." I hold up my empty blood-covered hand and step clear of Alex entirely, putting myself between them. Keeping the gun in my other hand tucked close to my leg, I take another step forward. "Please don't do this. I'm sorry. I'm so sorry I left. I'm sorry... I know this is my fault. I know I left and things got messed up but we'll figure this out, okay? Together." I take another step in his direction. "Please..."

Please don't make me shoot you.

Please don't make me shoot you.

Please don't make me—

It all happens at once.

Alex reaches for me, his hand closing over my elbow in an iron grip to jerk me back, away from Archie, just as someone shouts *"Get down!"* and I drop, reflexes bred into me by two tours in the Middle East, sweeping my legs out from under me and putting me on my belly, just as the bullets start flying, a tight, barking cluster of them that sound like bombs going off inside my head. I watch Alex fly, lifted off his feet by the force of them, to land on his back, several feet away. Turning my head in the direction of the shots, I spot a third figure bleeding back into the trees.

He shot Alex.

Go.

Whoever it is, go after them and kill them.

Scrambling to get my hands and knees under me, I ignore the instinct to follow.

I crawl to Alex.

Blood.

There's blood this time.

A lot of it, spreading fast from under the bottom of his vest.

"*Shit.*" His eyes are wide open and staring up into the trees, hand pressed against the wound in his belly, just below the Kevlar. "George..."

"It's okay... it's going to be okay..." Dropping the gun between my knees, I strip my shirt off. Wadding it up, I push his hands away and jam it under his vest. Tightening the Kevlar's Velcro straps across his chest, I use the vest and my shirt to apply pressure to the wound before I place his hands on top of it. "Hold this—press as hard as you can," I tell him as I reach into his pocket to pull out his phone to call for help.

"No... wait... George..." He lifts a hand off his wound and tries to take his phone from me, words slurred and slow. "Just—"

"George."

I look up to find Archie standing over me, face stark white, gun dangling uselessly from his hand. Reaching between my knees, I grab the gun I dropped there and lift it, aiming it at Archie's face. "*Drop it!*" I shout at him, and he immediately complies, his gun landing in the brush at his feet.

"George—"

"*Back up!*" I yell at him, still fumbling with Alex's phone. "Just back up, Archie. Don't make me—"

"George..." He does what I ask, backs up quietly, hands empty and held up in surrender. "You need to listen to me. Just lis—"

I aim the gun at him again. "*Shut up.*"

The phone in my hand vibrates, signaling a text, and Alex makes another grab for it, his hand slipping, useless and weak on my wrist. "Don't... Let me..."

Pulling myself out of Alex's grip, I swipe my thumb across the screen and the text appears.

You told me your feelings wouldn't get in the way this time.

Everything stops.

Goes quiet and still.

I look down at Alex but he's gone—the sporadic rise and fall of his chest tells me he's unconscious, not dead.

But he's close.

Before I can make sense of what I'm reading, what it means, another text comes through and I suddenly understand perfectly.

That bitch better be dead.

That's the last thing I remember.

SIXTY-THREE

LINCOLN

It's been four days.

She's opened her eyes twice. Both times her gaze has been soft. Unfocused. Confused. A little afraid.

Not Georgia at all.

Every time I see it, it scares the hell out of me, and I know that even though Evie won't admit it, seeing her this way scares her too.

She's going to be okay. She's been through worse.

That's what Evie says every time she comes into the room with her pen light and peels back Georgia's lids to peer into her flat pupils and check her chart, right before she checks the bandages covering the gunshot wound Bradford plugged high into my shoulder. A through and through. I was lucky—luckier than Georgia.

Intercranial hemorrhage.

Punctured lung.

Fractured hyoid bone.

Ruptured esophagus.

It all means the same thing.

I almost lost her.

Whenever I think about what she went through—what happened to her—I can feel myself start to spiral. Spin out of control. The only things holding me together are in this room.

Savanna. Julie. Georgia. The fact they're all safe is the only thing that keeps me from completely losing my shit and—

"Julie... Savanna..."

When I hear her, my head jerks up and my heart does a double-tap because she doesn't sound drunk when she says it. She sounds like Georgia. She looks like Georgia too, beneath the layer of bruises and lacerations. Her gaze is clear and focused on the place where I've been sitting and sleeping for the last four days and seeing it aimed at me pulls me out of my slump.

"They're okay." I nod, practically tripping over my own tongue trying to answer her. "They're here." I shift to the side so she can see Savanna and Julie sleeping on the fold-out couch on the other side of the large private hospital room they assigned to her. Her gaze slides past me to settle on the bed behind me for a moment. When she sees the girls sleeping soundly her entire body relaxes and she sighs.

"Good..." Her eyes slip closed again and she nods. "That's good... Teddy?"

"Him, too." I give her a nod. "He comes by every day to see Julie."

"He loves her. Really loves her..." She opens her eyes and looks at me. "I didn't think he did. I thought he was just using her. Stringing her along..."

"He's a good kid—" I clear my throat, giving her a short nod. "He just got caught up in a bad situation."

She gives me a small smile. "Sounds familiar."

She doesn't say anything else and I think she's slipped away again. I should get up. Find Evie and tell her Georgia woke up. That she was coherent and clear-eyed but I don't because I don't want to leave her. I can't leave her so I lean back in my chair, letting my head fall against the back of it and close my eyes.

"Your dad?" She whispers it like she's afraid someone will hear her. "Did you..."

The question pops my eyes open but I don't lift my head. I don't look at her.

"No." My jaw goes tight and I shake my head. "He's gone." I don't say anything else. I don't elaborate. Just give her time to put it together on her own. What must've happened. Land on the only thing that would've been more important to me than killing my father for the things he did.

"You were there. You came for me," she whispers again. "Alex shot you... and then you shot Alex."

It's not a question. Not really—but I answer her anyway.

"Yes."

I expect to feel something when I admit it.

Guilt.

Regret.

The only guilt I feel is after I did it, I had to leave her there to go make sure Savanna was okay.

The only regret I feel is that I can't shoot him again.

"Is he dead?"

"No."

She saved his life. She was dying in those goddamned woods, nearly killed by a vicious animal set loose on her by Bradford and my father, and she saved his life because she loves him.

"Has he said anything?" She sounds small again. Confused. "Has he..."

"No." This time I lift my head when I answer. Look at her because I'm an asshole. Because I'm in love with her, always have been, and I need to see her face when I say what comes next. "He's refusing to talk to anyone but you."

SIXTY-FOUR

GEORGIA

"I don't like it."

I look up and over to find Evie scowling down at me. I don't have to look at Lincoln, who's behind me, piloting my wheelchair down the hall, to know he's wearing a similar expression. Neither one of them likes any of the decisions I've made over the last forty-eight hours—least of all the one they're currently pestering me about.

Alex has refused to talk to anyone but me.

I'm not talking to anyone except Georgia Fell.

He said it only once, to the FBI field agent who came in to question him about his involvement in the drug smuggling and human trafficking rings he ran for Richard McNamara.

He hasn't said a word since.

He's double-cuffed to a hospital bed with a deputy posted outside his door.

Not one of *his* deputies.

One of mine.

That's one of the decisions Evie and Lincoln have teamed up against me over.

Two days after I regained consciousness, the town council sent Big Ted in with an offer.

We know it's unorthodox but given the circumstances and

everything that transpired, we'd like you to take over as Fell County's interim sheriff until the next election.

I said yes.

"Do you have a better idea on how to get him to talk?"

"I have a few..." Lincoln growls behind me.

"Let me clarify—" I angle my head so I can look up at him. "Any ideas that don't involve abuse of a suspect."

Lincoln sighs.

Evie keeps scowling.

"I didn't think so."

No one says anything else until we get to Alex's room. Levi is parked outside his door. When he sees me, he straightens his frame and squares his shoulders. "Sheriff. Dr. Jones." He splits a nod between Evie and me while ignoring Lincoln altogether.

"Deputy Tate," I say, trying to sound as official and commanding as I can in my hospital gown while I move to get out of the chair.

"Nope," Evie says, planting a firm hand on my shoulder while she motions Levi to open the door. "You're not getting out of that chair, George—don't make me get the duct tape."

So much for professional and commanding.

Instead of arguing, I suffer through the indignity of allowing Lincoln to roll me through the door and into Alex's room.

He's awake.

Sitting up in the bed he's handcuffed to and waiting for me.

I don't say anything while Lincoln wheels me to the foot of it and sets the brake. For a second, I think he's going to refuse to leave. That he's going to launch himself across the bed and beat Alex to death. I know he wants to.

We both do.

Instead of giving in, Lincoln frog-marches himself out the door, stiff-necked. Hands clenched into fists at his side. "I'll be right outside."

As soon as he's gone, Alex looks at me, just as quickly looking away when he sees the full scope of damage done to my face and neck. "George." Shaking his head, he swallows hard. "I can explain every—"

"You have the right to remain silent," I tell him. "Anything you say, can and will—"

"What are you doing?" He looks at me, brows dropped low over his narrowed gaze.

"I'm reading you your rights, Mr. Bradford." Reaching into my lap I lift out the black leather case. Flipping it open, I show him his own sheriff's badge. "Mine is still being engraved."

He looks at the door Lincoln just disappeared through. "I don't understand."

"I think you do," I tell him, dropping the badge back into my lap. "But let's keep pretending you're stupid, shall we?" Moving my hands to the arms of my wheelchair, I nod. "I was sworn in as Fell County Sheriff this morning. You are my prime suspect in the murder of Jenna McNamara and *this*—" I lift a hand and swirl it between us—"is an interrogation."

"You think I killed Jenna?" He laughs but the sound of it is off. Hollow. "Did I kill Rachel, too?"

"No." I shake my head at him. "I'm pretty sure King is the one who killed Rachel," I tell him, pointing at my neck and the obvious signs of strangulation that mark it—the same type of bruises I saw on Rachel's neck the night I found her. "I thought it was Richard but then I realized... men like him don't get their hands dirty—they leave that to men like you."

"Men like me?" He gives me that weird laugh again. "Come on, George—you know me. You love me. You said—"

"I found them." I cut him off. "The taps on my cell and the manor's landline—"

"I told you, George." He says it carefully, like I might be confused. "We talked about this. I had to be sure you weren't a part of it. I was—"

"We found *all of them*. The bugs in my kitchen. My bathroom... my bedroom." Thinking about it makes me sick. "That's how King knew Savanna and Evie were hiding in the manor—you told him."

"Is that what *he* told you?" Alex aims a glare at the door Lincoln just walked through. "If he did, he lied to you. He's the one working with King, remember? Him and Arch—"

"No, *you* lied—you weren't a homicide detective in Detroit. You worked vice—that's how you met King. You were undercover with the Reapers for years and just got sucked in..." When I say it, his face goes still. Loses that *this is all just one, big misunderstanding* expression. "You did tell the truth about one thing, though—Will Hudson *is* the one who suggested you bring your traveling shitshow to Angel Bay." I don't know how they ended up under Richard McNamara's thumb—I might never know. What I know is that Dennis Bleche, the supposed transitional case manager assigned to the majority of the girls in the McNamaras' care, is a ghost—just a name on paper. A shield to keep prying eyes off what was really going on in that house. I don't want to think about what that means —that the corruption on this island is systemic. That I might not ever have a hope of rooting it all out and exposing it to the light. What other sorts of monsters have found a home here in my absence?

"Everything was rainbows and unicorns until Rachel came home and started snooping around, gathering evidence against Richard McNamara she could take to the authorities and have him charged with rape. There's no statute of limitations for the rape of a minor in Michigan. I think Rachel had been pushing Jenna to come forward about what he did to them when we were kids." I sigh. Shake my head. "I don't think Jenna knew what she was doing when she told King. I don't think she understood what would happen to Rachel but when she did, she inadvertently tipped McNamara off. He ordered King to kill her. King used Jenna to lure her to the Den and..." I can't bring myself to say the rest out loud. "When I called you after I found Rachel, you called King, warning him to get out before you got there. Ironically, Will Hudson is the person who texted me that night, pretending to be

Jenna." Even though none of it is even remotely funny, I laugh, the sound of it rusty and torn against my swollen throat. "I should've known it was him—he's the only one who ever calls me *Georgie*, but I digress," I tell him with a small sigh. "King killed Rachel and Julie saw him do it. She was waiting for Teddy on his boat while he went inside to get the money for their weekly drug buy. When King realized there was a witness, he called you to clean it all up..." I give him a grim smile. "You and Tandy intercepted Julie and Teddy on the Rock—probably would've just killed both of them if not for the fact that Deputy Tate happened to be with you at the time. Since you couldn't kill them, you arrested her on some bullshit charge with the intent of holding her until you could traffic her off the island..." I give him a small shrug. "The only thing you didn't account for was me."

He watches me for a few moments, the silence stretching between us, thin and tight, before he finally nods. "You're right, Georgia..." Something in his expression shifts, lets go, a split second before the corner of his mouth lifts in a sad half-smile. "I didn't account for you—in more ways than one."

I want to ask him if it was real. If he ever really loved me or if it was all an act. A way to get close to me, keep tabs on me. But I don't.

"Did you kill Jenna McNamara under the direction of Richard McNamara?" I ask him instead, forcing myself to stay on mission.

"No." He shakes his head. "I killed her on my own. No one told me to do it. She knew too much. She was a liability—King thought he had her on a leash but after what happened to Rachel, it was pretty obvious she was losing it. I knew it was only a matter of time before you got to her and she told you everything. I couldn't let that happen," he tells me in a matter-of-fact tone. "So I tracked her down and put two in the back of her head."

I'm suddenly glad I'm injured. That we're doing this in a hospital and I'm in a wheelchair because if I were able-bodied and we were at the station, I'd have killed him by now. "Who took my gun from the scene of the accident? Tandy?"

"No one." He shakes his head. "I took your gun out of the glovebox that morning. *Before* the accident."

I think about that morning.

As soon as I got into my truck, I checked for my weapons. Under my seat and behind it. The map pocket on the door and the sun visor—but I didn't check the glovebox. Instead, I allowed myself to get distracted by the note left, wrapped around my knife. "But she *is* the one who took the banker's box and the autopsy report from the wreckage." I know she is because she told me so herself not more than a few hours ago. "She gave it to you and you gave it to Richard McNamara."

Alex gives me an evasive shrug.

"What was in it?"

Even though I can't be sure, I imagine it was full of evidence against Lincoln's father. Proof he was a monster—all gone now.

Alex gives me that shrug again.

"Will Hudson is the one who caused the accident." It's not a question. It's the only thing that makes sense, even though it doesn't. Why would he text me the night of Rachel's murder, pretending to be Jenna, only to try to kill me later? Nothing he's done over the past several days makes sense. None of it fits.

Alex must see the confusion on my face because he laughs. "Will Hudson is *complicated*," he tells me, with head shake. "You never know which version of him you're going to get—another loose end King was too full of himself to see, flapping in the wind. He thought Will was just a worker bee. A soldier, like the rest of them. King never saw him sneaking up behind him. Never even bothered to look..."

"What about Archie?" I hate myself for asking. For doubting him. "Is he involved?" It's the only way I can figure out how he knew about what was happening on the Rock. Why he was there that night.

Instead of answering me, Alex laughs. "I dunno, Sheriff... maybe you should ask Deputy Hudson yourself." His laughter dies and he suddenly grows serious. He looks tired. Wrung out. "Any last questions before I invoke my rights to an attorney?"

"Yeah—I have one more," I tell him, leaning forward in my chair. Getting as close to him as I can so I can see his face. "Is King the one who came after me because you didn't have the balls to kill me yourself?" I think about how easily he could have done it. How vulnerable I was with him. How close I came to convincing myself that I could love him.

Like he's reading my mind, Alex gives me another shrug and looks away. "Like I said, we all have our blind spots—don't we, Georgia?"

SIXTY-FIVE

ANGEL BAY ISLAND, MICHIGAN

Four Months Later

"Little to the left."

Sighing, I drop the large metal sign in my hands and turn away from the gate to look at them over my shoulder. "You just said *a little to the right*," I gripe, and Savanna sighs while Julie laughs.

"Yeah—*a little*," Savanna says like she's talking to a slow-witted toddler. "You moved it, like, *a foot*."

"That's it," I say, shaking my head on a laugh while I turn away from the manor's front gate completely. "You two are the experts—you get up here and hang this thing." Leaning the sign against the gate, I back away from it with my hands held up in surrender, trading places with them while they scramble off the hood of the car they're perched on, excited and eager to show me where I've been doing it all wrong.

It's okay. I don't mind. If the last four months have taught me anything, it's that Alex was right—I have a lot of blind spots. I don't always get things right. I don't always see things for the way they really are. Despite my best efforts, I have a tendency to lead with my heart instead of my head.

Alex pled guilty to Jenna's murder. The DA offered him a deal in exchange for his statement that the drug-and human-trafficking operations he and King ran were for Richard McNamara. Not only did he decline, he claimed he and King acted alone—that Lincoln's father was never involved. After nearly four months of digging, I can't find a single shred of hard evidence that ties McNamara to any of it. All I have on him is a single charge of sexual misconduct with a minor. If he ever resurfaces, I'll be lucky if he gets community service.

Archie is gone. He left with Will before I regained consciousness. I found a note on my kitchen counter when I came home from the hospital, held in place by a pile of broken porcelain—what looked like the remnants of one of Elizabeth Fell's ridiculously dainty teacups.

Hey, Georgie ∼

Archie and me are gonna take off for a while.
    Don't worry—I'll take care of him this time.

Will.

p.s. Sorry about your teacup

"You sure about this?"

I look over to find Lincoln leaning against the fender, looking down at me with a strange, convoluted mixture of admiration and apprehension. He has every right to look apprehensive—what I'm doing here is big. Bigger than anything I've ever done.

"It's a little late to back out now, don't you think?" I ask him with a laugh. "Jill and Henry move in tomorrow." It isn't. I could call Mark Tate right now and tell him I changed my mind, that I've come to my senses, and he'd probably weep with relief.

But I won't.

"It's never too late," Lincoln reminds me, giving me the kind of smile that always made me feel soft and loose inside. Like it was okay to let go if I wanted to. We're taking it slow. Dancing around the thing that's always been between us. Trying to figure out how to make it work as versions of ourselves that we were never meant to be. All I know is when he smiles at me, I feel warm. Like I want to let go. Like everything will be okay when I finally do.

Before I can answer him, Savanna and Julie step away from the gate each holding their hands up, framing the sign they just hung like a pair of Vanna White wannabes. "What do you think?"

Reading the sign, I feel something swell in my chest. Something big and powerful. Something that feels good.

Right.

Elizabeth Fell's Home for Girls

"Perfect," I say quietly, re-aiming my gaze at Lincoln's face. "I think it looks perfect."

A LETTER FROM MAEGAN

Dear Reader,

I want to say a huge thank you for choosing to read *The Darkwater Girls*. If you did enjoy it, and want to keep up-to-date with all my latest releases, just sign up at the following link. Your email address will never be shared and you can unsubscribe at any time.

www.bookouture.com/maegan-beaumont

I hope you loved *The Darkwater Girls* and if you did, I would be very grateful if you could write a review. I'd love to hear what you think, and it makes such a difference helping new readers to discover one of my books for the first time.

I love hearing from my readers—you can get in touch on my Facebook page, through Twitter, Goodreads or my website.

Thanks,

Maegan

maeganbeaumont.com

 facebook.com/thrillersandkillers

ACKNOWLEDGMENTS

Thank you, Joe, for being my tireless hype man. My perpetual cheerleader. My crutch and my rock. There's no one else I'd rather lean on. To my kids, Jaime, Julian, Mathew, and Sampson—thank you for being you. I'm not the perfect mom—but I'm yours. Thank you for letting me be *me*.

For my family and friends—thank you for everything. Seriously —*thank you* for every time I forgot to text you back. For every time I canceled plans. For every time I disappeared and took forever to find my way back. Thank you for still loving me. I love you too.

Thank you to Emily Gowers—for so long I shied away from traditional publishing again because there was just no way I could believe that I'd get lucky *twice* in one lifetime on the editor front. I did. You're amazing and patient and so, so encouraging. If it's for you, I'll keep writing forever.

For Shannon, Terri, Matt, Deb, Susana, Holly, Mary, Charlie, Heather, Rebecca, Todd, Roni, and the rest of my wonderful tribe of writer peeps—thank you for the laughter and encouragement. There's just no way I could do this without you weirdos.

Thank you, Rachel, for keeping me organized and for picking up my slack. It's a lot.

And last but never, ever least, thank *you*. Thank you for reading and thank you for believing. You make it all worthwhile.

Made in the USA
Coppell, TX
06 March 2023